THE VIOLENT STONES

THE VIOLENT STONES

OTHERWORLDLY ANARCHIST

BOOK FIVE

Dreamer's Riot

Podium

This is a work of fiction. Names, characters, places, and incidents are either products of the author's imagination or used fictitiously. Any resemblance to actual events, locales, or persons, living, dead, or undead, is entirely coincidental.

Cover design by Mika Hiyashiro

ISBN: 979-8-3470-2863-4

Published in 2026 by Podium Publishing
www.podiumentertainment.com

Podium

THE VIOLENT STONES

CHAPTER ONE

Recoil

My heart is as still as it ever was, yet it aches. It used to be an oddity, a strange side effect of a foolish mistake, but one I could live with. It doesn't feel the same—not anymore. It was still the first time I kissed Sarafyna. It was still when Henry died. It was stone when I walked into the arena, day after day, and let myself get hurt. Every time I fought for my life, it has refused to beat.

When I killed a sage in front of a crowd of people, and when I fled from his more powerful peers. Even when I dove into an obsidian stone and found myself in a dark, distorted version of the Radiant Woods. It remained still even as I saw hundreds of people tormented and used to pursue me, and when I learned why it refused to beat.

I am dead. I have been dead since I first remembered Earth; a dead burden on the woman I love. It was easy to ignore my still heart—I still felt excitement and grief and joy—but the reality of its quietness is so much heavier than the effects it has.

I am a corpse, and I don't belong in this world. I somehow feel alive and dead at the same time, but I need to accept that I am dead. Because Mirage—the origin of divine magic—is leaving; I'm going to help her leave. She has earned peace, and this world doesn't need a god. But it is with her powers that Sarafyna is keeping me alive, which means when she is free, I am dead. I have to say goodbye to my family and my friends—to Sara. I have to accept my death, because the cost of my life is too high.

While I had been processing this reality, Riley and I had found the heart of the stone—the nexus of the world we'd found ourselves in, and the monument of the sage's power—and we destroyed it. I saw Mirage one last time as the stone died, saw her pain. In the back of my mind, I can still hear her constant scream.

And I don't even get to rest, because we had fled through the arena and into the stone inside Markus's home, and with it gone, Riley and I are back in the pit where the stone once stood. Riley, me, and hundreds of bystanders who were sent after us and manipulated into a hell worse than death.

Every single one of the faces we'd fled from are all surrounding us in this now pointless alcove, and they have all returned to themselves as far as I can tell—ailur, volu, and human. They are clearly confused and rattled, far from comfortable, but they are back as they were. Who they were.

My eyes scan the group even as I offer Riley my hand to help her climb back to her feet. It doesn't make sense. I thought I'd finally figured out exactly what divine magic was and how it worked, but everything Mirage had shown me . . . none of it explains this. Based on my understanding, they should be stuck as they were until another sage helped fix them. But everyone is back to their real bodies.

I look over them again, focusing specifically on the faces I got the best look at before. They still don't feel right. I did see them when they were existing at their worst, so it makes sense they wouldn't have the same emotional energy. Confusion and discomfort are pretty easy to tell apart from hopeless horror and agony, at least on most faces; I have certainly met some people who treat them as one and the same. Yet, I can't dismiss the differences as a change in demeanor. I can't even write them off as their bodies having taken their original shapes back. Something is just . . . off.

As Riley dusts herself off, I focus on a particular man: quiet, sitting, and clutching his knees. Whatever it is, it is especially prominent on his face. I recognize him; I'm certain of it. It's his eyes, green like seawater and crystal clear. Haunted. I have seen him, and recently too, but he looks completely wrong in a way that extends to the entire crowd. Like the wrongness on his face is part of a filter applied to all of them. It's less obvious on the non-human faces, but even they seem wrong. There is something about every single person in here that looks like reality but out of its groove. Like they live in the wrong key.

I take a step toward him, a question floating to the front of my mind. Riley catches me by my organic arm before I make it too far.

"What are you doing?" she hisses. I look back at her with a raised eyebrow.

"I thought I might have a little chat. I know you're not exactly a social butterfly, but I'm still allowed to make friends, right?" I retort.

"Idiot," she scoffs. "You should be hiding in light mana right now, not introducing yourself! Before these people were caught up in this, they were running—from *you*: *Lillith*, the supposed demon queen they just watched murder a sage. How do you think an introduction is likely to go?"

I look at her with blank eyes for a moment, then cross my arms.

"Ah fuck, you're right. Tunnel vision again; I do that. Well, what should we do? Gonna be hard to help them get out of here without any of them seeing me," I respond, even as I drop my chain mail and shroud my body with distorting light mana. "There we go. Thank God no one will think this is weird or notable."

Riley rolls her eyes but smirks slightly afterward, which is a new reaction. Calling her dad a skid mark has gone a long way to making us friends, I think. "I'll talk to them first, I suppose."

"They saw you kill a sage too, sport," I counter.

"They were already evacuating by then, but all of them saw the fangs and poison. Me? I'm just a famous gladiator, not the harbinger of the end of all things," she says. I shrug.

"Well, all right, then. Ask that guy how old he is." She looks at me, ready to ask why, but then just sighs and walks past me toward the indicated victim of my inquisition.

Twenty. Maybe twenty-five tops—that's how old he looks. But . . .

She leans down in front of the man. Despite her concern about me, he is clearly startled by her too. I can't make out their conversation, at least not without sound mana, which would be a bit obvious and probably unsettle him more. At least if he can see it; I can never tell if someone is a mage in the Republic.

She seems to calm him down after a brief exchange, then he tilts his head and responds to her question. She starts at the answer, which all but confirms my suspicion. I don't want to get ahead of myself, however, so I wait for her to return, clearly more baffled than anyone else here.

She pauses when she reaches me and takes a deep breath. "He's sixty-five, or so he claims."

And there it is. I scan the room again. Every single person present is young and in perfect health, as far as I can tell. Having reality-warping magic removed shouldn't do that. It should just . . . return things to reality. Looking like that guy at sixty-five isn't reality even for rich people.

"An overcorrection," I say out loud. Riley looks at me with a furrowed brow.

"What?" she asks.

"Look at them. These people, forced into a hell of someone else's design. It must have been done quickly too. So . . ." I start laughing, and several people look in my direction. Most are only concerned with the situation at hand, but I suppose a blurry woman laughing in the middle of all this would draw the eye.

I look at Riley. "Has anyone ever grabbed you? Tried to pull you somewhere you didn't want to go?" Her lips purse to an unamused line. She was a slave, literally; this had been her life for years. "Right. And what happens if you fight back? When their grip breaks?"

"We both fall on our asses, and they beat me for fighting back," she replies easily. I wince, but I continue.

"Right. You fall in the other direction. That's the trick, isn't it? The nature of control. The more effort you put into getting your way, the harder you strong-arm, the more force you use . . . the greater the recoil. It's basic physics, isn't it? Force doesn't cease to exist when tension snaps. It just changes direction. Those assholes rushed horrible changes on these people, and all that force, all those demands—they went in the other direction! Look at them, Riley! Not a person in here looks a day older than twenty-five!"

I laugh louder, drawing more eyes. "Everything they think they own is going to be a tool for their downfall," I continue. "Because tension doesn't only maintain force on one side; recoil goes both ways. The harder they fight us, the more the world will take the shape they fear most. It's artwork."

"I guess. Won't help much if they decide to just kill us first," she replies. I don't care. This is a moment of kindness from the world. Not only did we win this fight, but we also saved everyone, and they are in better health than when they left.

Some part of me latches on to that. A better world is always possible, always worth fighting for. I've always believed that; I've never been willing to accept better things as unachievable. But I am willing to accept that, fight as I might, that better world will be too slow in coming for me to see it. But this visceral, clear act of defiance by reality itself, refusing to be owned . . . it makes it just a little easier to see that world.

I observe the crowd. They're starting to get their bearings, comforting those too shocked to move. Some are looking toward the window, trying to come up with a plan to get everyone out, moving forward. A cold stone inside me starts to ignite, like coal when its embers are fanned. With each hopeful face I see, my own hope grows. My determination sharpens as it's augmented by a world that will work with me instead of against me, no longer driven by spite but by a clear path forward.

And then I see him.

It's only a flash. Blond hair and a sympathetic grimace as he tries to comfort a younger man. He looks nothing like Henry, really, but my mind . . . it still paints my brother's face over his for a breath; just long enough for me to hope for the impossible. An instant of adrenaline where I could believe it was all a mistake, that he'd survived, that he'd made it here.

But that fades in the blink of an eye as the man's true face comes into focus. And just like that, the embers are quenched. That radiant hope dies with the reminder that I will only see my brother in illusions, in moments of delusion. He's gone. And suddenly, the revelation about the sages' power doesn't feel so hopeful. Just like that, it's no more than another tool I can use to fight them in spite of it all.

"You all look like you could use some help," a woman calls into the crowd. I, and many others, look up toward the window. There, we see three people: a woman who looks . . . strangely like me, standing between Autumn and August.

I balk a bit. She has the same haircut, almost, if a little longer. She lacks tattoos, but her armor is a one-to-one replica of mine.

"Huh." I tilt my head.

"She looks . . . cool," Riley adds.

"Lillith of Endings, is that you in the, uh . . . blur?" she asks. A dozen shocked faces turn to me while I sigh and release the light mana.

"So much for not scaring them. It was a pretty short-term solution anyway, I guess. Wasn't gonna last after people got themselves put together," I lament. Gasps ring out around us as I reveal myself in full. This woman is with the twins; I suppose I'll have to trust their judgment. "Present and accounted for, but I don't do autographs, I'm afraid."

She smirks as a group of men approach from behind her and roll rope ladders down into the uncomfortable pit. "Well. We'll see about that later. For now, I'd just love it if you and I could have a little conversation."

"So," I say, "are you the leader of the famed cult the sages are so afraid of?" I ask. We are sitting at a table in some sort of safe house, having successfully gotten all the bystanders out of the arena. The sages, fortunately, could apparently not afford to stick around for the full week I'm told we spent inside the stone.

"Well, no, we don't really have a leader. And we aren't a cult, of course, but I have been organizing our efforts here," she responds.

"And what's with the getup?" I ask, raising an eyebrow. "I know they say imitation is the highest form of flattery and all that, but this kinda leans toward creepy if I'm being honest." Archer, the woman sitting across from me, laughs.

"Well, we weren't sure you were coming out of that stone, and like it or not, you are a fairly significant symbol to our attempts at revolution. Especially now. Killing a sage and dying, we can use. Killing a sage and living? That we can direct," she explains.

I raise an eyebrow. "So you are supposed to be . . . me?"

She shrugs. "For a while, anyway."

"Thanks, I hate it," I say. "Whatever. So, you've introduced yourself and explained the changeling act. What did you really want to talk about?"

"Well, there is no easy way to say this," she starts, "but you sort of started a war. We need to figure out how our side wins."

CHAPTER TWO

Cults and Personalities

A war?" I ask. "With your group? I don't know how to tell you this, Archer, but I don't think the sages have ever been terribly fond of you."

She nods. "No, they kill us on sight; always have. They hate and destroy anyone who changes . . . anything. If someone defines themselves outside of the sage's design, they are labeled as a cultist, whether any of my group has met them or not. No, if you want to call that conflict a war, we have been waging it for a long time now. I am referring to the Council and the Republic."

I look at her in silence for a moment, and she waits patiently for my response. I've never interacted with the Council to any degree. I gather they are something like an oligarchy, or maybe a theocracy, depending on your view of the sages. I've read elections exist, but they don't allow the population at large to participate. But that's the extent of my knowledge. I haven't challenged them in any capacity; at least not yet.

"Say more," I finally speak. Clearly, some power balance has been disturbed with Markus's death, but I simply don't have enough information on both countries to deduce the exact nature of it. Guessing would be a waste of time. "How does Markus's death start a war? I'm not associated with the Council. Surely there isn't a new war every time a sage croaks?"

"You started it by showing up," Archer answers easily. "Everything revolves around the Original Sage, and the Original Sage seems to revolve around you."

"I've been calling him Alpha," I cut in. "Thousands of years, and the fucker hasn't picked a name for himself. But *Alpha* seems to capture his self-impressed whining pretty well."

Again, she nods in assent. "Alpha, then. No one is quite sure what his motivations are. He works with the sages, but he also hunts them; this is why they all avoid the border, not to mention the Nexus. Still, they offer him sacrifices, and in exchange, he creates smaller worlds for them to play in. The sages hate sharing power and praise, and apparently, spending time in a constructed country helps solve the issue. But even as sages and Alpha make this trade, they hate each other. Alpha grows stronger whenever he captures them, taking their specialties as his own."

"Ah," I guess. "So Alpha is the strongest sage, but not quite strong enough to beat all the others if they work together. Is that right?" I've seen evidence of this already, although it seems the other sages underestimate Alpha's abilities. Or maybe they weren't expecting him to have an ally in Oakley.

"Precisely," she confirms. "Power is carefully balanced, except all the sages together could beat Alpha. As powerful as he is, there are simply too many of them. Fortunately for him, the sages don't all get along, divided between the Council Lands and the Republic. Still, they maintain peace anyway because between the sages and Alpha, there are three powerful parties, and all of them want the others destroyed.

"In other words, if one attacks first or shows a clear sign of weakness, they have to defend themselves on two fronts. The sages, for all the legends they tell about themselves, are no strategic geniuses. They are all acutely aware that if they find themselves in that situation, well, they are fucked."

"Right," I say. "Which is where a fourth party comes in. A demon queen and her supposed army invaded one of the two countries and killed one of the sages, upsetting the power balance. To the Council, it may look like the Republic now has to fight on three fronts instead of two; is that the gist of it?"

"If only that were all," she laments. "The Void Sage, perhaps the most powerful sage in the Republic, joining hands with Alpha alone would tip the balance beyond repair. But Rowan has been fearmongering about you for years. Few took him seriously among the sages, more so among the population, but you were a fairy tale told by a losing candidate, a grasp at straws."

"Until I killed Markus," I guess.

"Until you killed Markus," she confirms. "Killed Markus, bombed the arena, and slaughtered hundreds of innocent people in an act of senseless terror, or so they are saying. In a single night, you went from fairy tale to credible threat. And suddenly, the sage who has been sounding the alarm for years is very popular. A terrified country now very much believes in your invasion. Believes in you.

"The people are calling for an emergency election. They want to confirm Rowan by the end of the week. And if he is the leader of the country, that means the Void didn't just join the Original—it means the Original joined the Republic, as far as the Council is concerned. But they aren't too afraid to declare war because they think the Republic is fighting a demon army already. They think everyone has to fight on two fronts."

"Shit," I whisper. "World really went to hell in a week, huh?" War isn't pretty, but it does provide an opportunity, I guess. Perhaps I'll be able to kill off the major players and stop an actual war before it gets too far. "Can we prove my supposed victims are still alive?"

"We can, but it will do little. We'll never get the news to spread as quickly nor as widely as news of the attack. 'We were wrong' makes for terrible news, after all. Besides, the people of the Republic are responding out of fear. They lack the capacity to grieve the loss of innocent lives; they just don't want to lose their own."

"You say that as if it doesn't include you," I note.

"I'm protected by my endoaspect, same as you," she explains.

"Which is?" I press. She offers a cold stare and no answers. Figures. "Right. Well. I'm no genius strategist either. I'm the punchy girl; my job is to be the girl who punches, so if you want to know my best plan for beating two countries and one guy with mommy issues, it's simple: Stop the mind control. Give people their hearts back.

"The sages thought they had the right to tell people what emotions they were allowed to feel, and so I plan to make each and every one of them fear the consequences of showing their faces in public. That's the plan. Find which sages are responsible for the mind control and kill them first. Then kill their friends. Hell, if we can get enough grief back, I'm pretty sure I could take Oak—Rowan."

She takes a deep breath through her nose. "Great, then we are in agreement: we go for the artifacts stealing grief first," Archer says. Something in her eye flickers, and for the briefest of moments, the hairs on the back of my neck raise. Like I've just come face-to-face with a true predator, or perhaps a hunter. A moment later, it's gone, but the memory of it lingers.

"That's it? Just like that?" I ask. There's no way. Even I know what I've just said is overly simplistic, and I want to make a more detailed plan when I'm with the people I trust. But she accepted too quickly.

"Well, we also want to lean into your identity," she adds. Even that doesn't ring entirely true, but I suppose if I am playing my cards close to the chest, she probably is too. "There is a reason I shaved the side of my head last week. The Void wants to build you up as some kind of great adversary. I want to do the opposite. Plenty of people hate the sages, so rather than just being 'punchy,' I'd like you to be a symbol."

I wrinkle my nose at the thought. Broadcasting a king's death with light mana, or killing a sage in front of a crowd is one thing. I want people to know that *powerful* is not the same thing as *invincible*. But intentionally standing on a pedestal to be praised and deferred to? That's really not my thing. I have put myself under the symbol label before, but that was a faceless symbol of fear, a monster hunting abusers. I was honestly more cryptid than anything. And once that symbol got a face, we ended up with the Kingdom of Endings.

"How about we use a literal symbol?" I suggest. "People will rally behind ideas."

"Not as well as they will rally behind a great woman," she counters.

"*Great woman? Please*, don't call me that. I have no interest in history-book entries or fans. And you may be right, but the world they end up with will be better without their beliefs and inspiration tied to a fallible, mortal face," I say.

"A mortal wouldn't have escaped that stone alive," she quips.

"Yes, well. I wouldn't put 'good at staying alive' on any T-shirts with my face," I reply tiredly.

"What does that mean?"

"Call it an inside joke. Like my heart." I groan. Images of auburn hair and hats flash through my brain. Right. I have a lot to talk to Sara about. "Actually, the twins—where are they?"

"Preparing," she answers. "Why?"

"Oh, preparing. Right, of course. I should have guessed that. Very help-ful answer. You should work for Microsoft," I mock. "As to why, well, I need to speak to them. Or Ember, if she's around."

"I gathered as much," she intones. "What about?" This woman is starting to irk me, but I suppose I can't just discard potential allies against tyrants. Still. She talks like she's used to being in charge, like being vague is her right but I owe her clear and detailed answers.

"What are they preparing for?" I ask.

She sighs, idly running her hand along the newly shaved side of her head. "The boy, August, has got a couple theories about where the artifact is; different sages we need to investigate. I doubt it will lead to much, but he's got himself excited about it, so he, his sister, and the ailur are trying to join their household staff." Archer sees me tense up and waves me off. "No need to try to stop them. They are targeting small, less powerful sages. Honestly, they seem too unimportant to be involved, but that's what they want to do. We are helping to set them up with some Republic identities."

My breath catches despite her reassurances. "I'm not going to try to stop them, provided they are actually going of their own accord," I reply, leaving only a slight threat in my tone. "They are their own people, and they can fight however they will. I just . . . Never mind. Don't worry about it. Do you know where I can find them?" I ask. I can't just say, "*I'm terrified of sending them out on their own. If one of them dies when I'm not around again, it may break me, and I don't know if I can recover,*" so "Don't worry about it" will have to do.

"I thought there was an implicit trade there," Archer says. "Why do you need them?"

I narrow my eyes at her. Why does she care so much?

"They are my friends, and I've been missing for a week. Is that not reason enough?" I ask. She shrugs.

"Sure, but it doesn't feel like that's all there is to it, that's all."

"Doesn't much seem like your business either way, if I'm being honest. But hey, we're supposed to be friends here, right? Or allies, at least. So I don't mind. I was expecting a fucking call from my girlfriend, but I lost my whisper sphere. I was hoping they'd heard from her. A bit shady, I know, but what can I say? I'm a romantic."

I don't know why I am being so hostile to her. Maybe I'm still in a bad mood after that moment when I thought I saw Henry. Whatever it is, I find myself growing more and more hostile, and I can't even put my finger on why. I need to wrap the conversation up and sleep it off.

"I rub you the wrong way, don't I?" she asks.

I shrug. "So far, maybe. Or maybe I'm just in a shitty mood; I honestly don't know. But I don't like being interrogated about why I want to see the people I care about. The copycat thing is also creeping me out a bit, if I'm being honest. But that's all right; I don't need you to rub me the right way. I just need to be able to work with you," I reply, looking over her shoulder toward the door. "Look, I'm happy to have people on my side for once. It's a relief to connect with someone who is already fighting, really. But just . . . I don't want to measure cocks every time I want to find a place to shit, much less talk to the people I care about."

"Right," she responds. "Fair enough. It's just . . . they don't seem to like you very much. And if I'm honest, the look on your face when Autumn was mentioned . . . You don't seem to like her much either. It was fair to question your intent." Shit. I hadn't realized I had been reacting to her name. And in a way, she is right; she sees red flags, so it's perfectly reasonable to at least ask. I sigh.

"Our history is complicated, all right? Autumn and I are dealing with a common issue, and it's both our faults. That's all it is. So please, do you mind telling me how I can find them?" I repeat.

She stares at me with calculating eyes for a long moment. "Down the hall, third room to your right. Give them my regards," she finally relents. I let a relieved breath out as I rise to my feet, then put two fingers to my head in a faux salute and leave the unsettling woman behind.

CHAPTER THREE

Pride Like a Leash

Alpha

It worked, at first. Mirage offered her power to anyone she could reach if they reached for her as well. People who had betrayed and rejected her original design; even victims of other realities, desperate for an escape.

After our confrontation, her vision was full of blind spots. She couldn't direct her own attention, at least not without help. But she offered herself to anyone she could find in the cracks of her broken vision. She gave everything precious about her to anyone she could reach, anyone who could feel what she felt and offer their own emotions in return. Moments of particularly powerful emotion let her find them and offer that trade. And they took it. All of them took. But it wasn't just a gift they were taking—they were taking advantage of her, and I would protect her.

Desperation worked best. It *still* works best; I'm not certain why. But these sick minds, ready to use my mother, almost always found her in their greatest moment of desperation, though anything would work: Desire. Ambition. Fear. Any mewling child could steal my mother's power and use it for themselves. Manara, too, was made to comply. Her corpse was like a resource to them.

It made me furious. Every touch of those greedy fools defiled them further. They were being taken advantage of, and Mirage was too naive to see it, at least without my help, which she stubbornly refuses even to this day. I would protect her anyway. In the light and her embrace, or in the cold and rain, I would protect Mirage.

For her, at least, I could take everything back. I could make her whole again, pure again. And that's what I was doing. My collector attracted her abusers, and the greedy animals always came: Men. Women. Entire families. They came in every flavor, from weak to strong, dim-witted to clever. But as soon as they touched even a part of my pet, it consumed them, and through me, Mirage started to take her old shape again. I would carry her alone, not forever but until I could find a true home for her.

And that was all it did at first. Dissolve bodies into itself and take Mirage's energy back. Help host her—or what was left of her after those vultures picked at her like rotting meat. But it wasn't enough. They all distorted her differently, contorted her to different designs to manifest different talents formed by whatever emotion they used to connect with Mirage. The way I was collecting them couldn't maintain those abilities, only recover the energy itself. When they died, their unique control over Mirage died with them.

If I was going to take all of her back, I couldn't allow them such advantages. I had been considering this for some time when my collector caught a particularly smug vulture in its trap. He sneered and cursed at me, even without knowing I could see him. He had control over plants to an unprecedented level, even managing to control some of the trees and vines in the collector's world. It fascinated me.

"You are disgusting. What you are doing to her is disgusting. This is not how the world should be treated." This is what he said to me. It startled me, I'll admit. I was the only one to refer to Mirage as "her" before that moment. Even Mirage didn't have a concept of being a woman until I offered the role with my perception, when we were still kind to each other. I was fascinated, until he continued to curse. He was one of the foreign vultures, brought here due to a need to escape his world.

He was from one of the volu worlds, probably one which thought of their planet as a woman, in a sense. Similar to Mirage, but different. Still, the suggestion . . . It made me furious. I was being *kind*. *He* was the disgusting one. He called me disgusting as he used *my mother* like some kind of meat meant to satiate his hunger? It was almost a shame he was about to die.

And then it hit me. The solution was simple: Their abilities only died if they did, so I would stop killing them. Mirage could contort as easily as she could destroy. So long as their minds were intact, I could manifest Mirage in the same way they had.

I still remember the satisfying feeling of his horror as he realized he wasn't about to die—he was about to become a silent member of my great collection. For as long as I needed him to. Until I got all of Mirage back and found a home for her.

And so, the collector changed. It no longer dissolved them, instead merging with them, melting them into it. It maintained their consciousness inside but handed the reins to me. This way, I collected bits of my mother, one by one, growing stronger and stronger. Just as they abused her, using her to their own ends, I abused them. And just like she suffered under their demands, I allowed them to continue suffering under mine.

For hundreds of years, I grew my power this way. My collector grew as well, until it stretched across the entire planet, drawing these monsters in faster, helping me put Mirage back together with their sacrifice. The collector, originally a single tree with a beating heart, became its own world. A world where Mirage could live. A world where I ruled.

And when I went there myself, I could almost feel her. Perhaps it was my imagination. Perhaps it was wishful thinking. But to me, it felt like confirmation that somewhere deep down, she understood me. She was grateful to me. She enjoyed my protection and wanted to be nearer to it.

Maybe I couldn't feel her emotions anymore. Maybe we couldn't speak. But if I focused for long enough, little thoughts popped into my head, encouragements. She was there—she had to be. Not just anywhere but in *my world,* in the land I created. And if she was going to watch me rescue her, she was going to do so comfortably.

I gave her flowers, comprised of the men and women who'd tried to use her. I wanted her to feel them paying the price for hurting her. I wanted her to see. I wanted her to be happy and comfortable, and know that if anyone tried to hurt her more, I would hurt them back. I locked the sun in the sky so she would always be warm and never feel afraid.

It was beautiful. I felt we were truly connecting again. It didn't feel or sound the same, but I could feel it—a relationship.

Of course, all good things must end. I still remember when the first crack appeared. When the first abuser failed to follow the trap, fleeing instead, afraid of the land no one returned from. Then another, and another. They had figured it out, and they stayed as far from the great collection as they could. Sweet promises stopped drawing them in, and they began to understand, to fear. They knew what awaited them at the other end of the collector's call. First, they fled, and when I adjusted for that, they fought. When I beat them, they joined hands. And when there were enough of them, they hunted.

My plan was starting to fail, and I needed a new way to control them. I was the most powerful of them—the only true son of Mirage—but all together, I couldn't win. I'd learned that lesson too many times. For a while, it was me who had to fear, not them.

If I wanted to put all that power in the right hands, I needed a new approach. So I watched them for decades, observing how they spoke to each other, what they fought about, and what they agreed on. My growth stagnated while they grew more powerful. But no matter how long I waited, they remembered me, and they remembered their fear, so they stayed together. And together, they couldn't be conquered. Not from the outside.

But the more I learned and the more I watched, the more I began to recognize patterns of behavior.

Mirage was undiscerning in her distribution of power. She offered it to any who could reach her, and many types of people received it: kind, foul, and everything in between. But those who received her power were more selective, forming tribes of a sort, choosing allies by seemingly arbitrary traits rather than power. Tribes large enough to beat me—but also to go up against each other.

I knew what I had to do. If I couldn't fight them together, I had to use them. I could choose a few to ally myself with in order to capture the rest; it was simple enough to do. Many of them were greedy for Mirage's power, wanted to be the only ones to use it, wanted their friends to have all the power and everyone else to bow to them, so I just had to choose who to work with. It didn't matter much who; I simply needed them to hate.

Ideally, I needed them to hate everyone but themselves, to be power hungry but weak. I needed those with great pride but little wit. I wanted dogs, animalistic and ready to kill their kin for the promise of a meal, though easily leashed.

They were easily found. Arrogance is as universal as grief, and they all hated each other for such pathetic reasons. Many wanted to own each other, wanted to believe that they were somehow elevated above the rest, like insects fighting over dirt. As if they weren't all leeches, equal in their insignificance.

So I decided to offer my hand to one of them. They feared my collector, but not me. The idiots.

I hadn't yet learned to shift my appearance, so the choice was simple. They cared primarily for the shape of their bodies, their complexion, and their size. It would be easiest to approach those who looked like me, especially those who hated anyone who didn't. Even if they feared me, they also saw me as a victory, like I was proof that they really were the strongest and most intelligent. As if they could really be compared to me, just because we wore similar flesh. It was sad but useful.

I approached them—small men with pride like spider silk and minds as sharp as a river stone—and named them "sages." Praising wit and wisdom always works best on those who lack both, and they bathed in the title. Once caught on the hook of worship, I simply needed to promise more. It was easy, with the world I'd created. I simply had to carve out portions and let each man rule his own.

There were plenty of mundane creatures to populate them, most untouched by either of my parents, with leaders who used Manara's powers. Of course, the pathetic little "sages" I found had their own requests. Some wanted only ailur in their personal countries. Others only volu. A few wanted a mix of all, but most wanted humans alone. A few demanded only humans with a specific complexion, although it was not always the same. It didn't matter to me; it was easy to do, after a few failed experiments. The main issues were ensuring the population behaved as the requesting sage asked. The other was the sage's incompetence.

They wanted to be praised for their ideas, which they mostly stole from their own worlds. They wanted people to adore them, and they also wanted authenticity—or whatever they viewed as authenticity; it was never the same.

But the wrong goods would be popular, or the nobles wouldn't behave exactly as expected, or worse: they would be too competent. It's difficult to make one idiot stand out in a properly functioning country, especially since nearly every sage wanted to be viewed as an inventor of things that even the animals I used to populate these countries had already figured out. So I was forced to dumb them down and make sure every city in every country had every resource they could possibly need, which ruined trade.

And once I couldn't manage all of them, I was forced to lend out my power. So long as the sage lived somewhere in the veins of my Radiant Woods, I could use their power. Which meant, if part of that sage lived in someone else, they could use their power too. And so a church was born in each paper country, all different, preaching whatever the requesting sage wanted. But to their priests, I offered a little bit of my collection. A little bit of some of my captive sages. I fed them with food infused with the mind of a sage, and was gifted with tools of control.

I could keep the kings of these countries foolish, hold back progress, manipulate the individual minds of every citizen to behave like my new allies wanted. Well, almost. Minds are hard to manipulate, especially with only small, borrowed power. But it was steady enough.

Once I figured out how to design them perfectly, I designated the place as the third plane. The world my allies lived in, I called the second, and my collector's world was the first. Sorted by how pathetic their residents were. The words took on a life of their own among my little churches, however. Everyone understood the first plane was beautiful, and the third offered little to the average person. It was amusing to see each claim themselves as the first.

In any case, I'd given those idiots what they wanted, and they would give me what I wanted. With their help and my abilities, I hunted down every other group of so-called sages one at a time, adding them to my collection. Any sages who were women or volu or ailur we called demons. Any sage outside of my allies were to be feared and sacrificed to the great collection.

Finally, I started growing again. Finally, Mirage started being built back up. And however petty their requests were, they helped me make an important discovery.

Each country was inhabited by the cruel, and many decided the first plane was a suitable place for their enemies, if not themselves. Brothers with bad blood, ugly children, cheating spouses. The nobles started offering me sacrifices who had none of Mirage's power. Some who even lacked Manara's. It irritated me, the audacity of it. I wasn't a dumping ground.

But then . . . it actually helped. Mirage responded to their fear and desperation, and as they lived in my woods, they also contributed to my power—more than I could have imagined. As long as they were there, I could control Mirage's ability more effectively. I could grow my collector more. Some even grew desperate enough to become sages themselves, and as long as I kept them alive, every wave of emotion they felt empowered me.

So I added to the deal. If anyone born in their country didn't meet whatever aesthetic they thought of as realistic, or even if they just found them undesirable for different reasons, they would be given to me to live in my Radiant Woods.

It was a decent deal, as far as I was concerned. Working with the sages felt like tree sap; it took so long to wash the feeling of their presence off, they were so demanding. Some even requested multiple countries over and over again, but each became a farm, constantly producing more grist for the mill. I benefited from both sides of the deal.

Eventually, they grew bored and formed a country of their own. I could handle that. A country was good. They wanted the thrill of competing against each other, which meant I could manipulate them to sacrifice each other to my collection. They were also willing to contribute sacrifices from their own populations, provided I offered a safe way to do it.

And so, I created the "Calm Stones," smaller versions of my collector but with chains on to make my allies feel safe. They were grown around the beating heart of a sacrifice, distributed, hidden, and even used to maintain a border, separating the sages from the real collector.

It was all going so well, until three things happened. The first was the formation of the Council, a new country divided from the old. It alone was just an obstacle, and for a few thousand years, I simply balanced power between the two, knowing I would still be strong enough to take them all back eventually.

Until two girls were born a few years apart. That was when everything fell apart. But it was also when I realized I wouldn't have to wait much longer. I had found a new home for my mother.

CHAPTER FOUR

Joy

Rose

Everything is a blur, like I exist in two realities at once, one of pain and another of joy. All those years with nowhere to rest, nothing clean to eat, the air poisonous to me. My body had been taken from me, even more than it already had been, and I was alone. Alone, like I've always been but more thoroughly, like the difference between drowning in warm water and in cold.

I will never leave the Radiant Woods; not entirely. I knew that even when I opened my eyes for the first time in years and saw Charlotte as she had always described herself in her most private moments. But even then, her eyes were haunted. I don't think the cruelties of those who hate us can ever be outrun. I was there far longer than most anyone else here, yet, however terrified I am, however trapped I am inside my head, there is a joy that insists on burning inside me.

I only remember the first year or so after I was taken and abandoned in the Radiant Woods, feeling the rest of the time there like a splinter under a fingernail. It lives in me, that misery, but at the same time, I can feel myself changing—not back to who I was but into who I am. It's strange, the memory of that first year. All the suffering that followed, tearing at the back of my mind. And the joy of returning to life and finding the community and safety I spent my entire life fighting for. What I lost my life for.

The Radiant Woods were the exact terror I saw every night as a child, the realization of every bead of terrified sweat I'd ever woken up with; both my mind and body complying with someone else's will. But traveling with Charlotte and her son . . . It's only been a few days, but the contrast is like red wine on a white dress. A woman I thought I'd never see again? A family? Immediate support, and . . .

I put one hand over my heart. It still beats like that of an excited child. I used to pray as a child every night to the Collector—before I grew and learned who he really was, before I'd told anyone my name was Rose. I used to pray so desperately, begging and begging to go to sleep and wake up the next day and realize I'd been a little girl all along. My mother would call me Rose, my father would buy me a new skirt, and everything would stop feeling like broken glass.

My prayers had never been answered. My mother never called me Rose. My father bought me nothing he didn't love himself. And when I tried telling them, tried trusting them with my identity . . . I learned who my parents were. I learned who the Collector really was. I dodged confession, hiding whenever my mother brought me for it. I grew older, angrier. I stopped praying, grieving instead of begging. And as I grieved, I curled my fists and hid knives in my clothes. I became violent.

No father would beat their son for failing to be his daughter. No mother would recoil in disgust at her daughter, abandoning her for not being a son. No one else would disappear—never to be seen or heard from again—the minute they are honest about who they are. Not in front of me. Not without consequence. But no matter how old I got, I was never safe. I was never comfortable. The closest I got was when Charlotte found me.

But this time? When Charlotte found me this time, it was different. Now, my body is more *me* every morning. My life is more my own with each passing day. I can't help but feel exuberant. Even when I think of the terror and the abuse that I'll never scrub from my brain, it can't wash away the joy. I feel the sorrow and the fear and the lingering loneliness, but the joy is there too—even when I see the face of the men who took me, who dragged me to the church and left me in that old sick house. Even when I picture the wagon leaving me alone in the woods, knowing I'd be tortured forever. The joy is still there.

My mind is filled with fog as the two emotions war with each other. I have been here for days, but it feels like moments. I have heard stories, but they mix like watercolor. I'm almost uncertain that this is real.

Except for that joy. The Collector wouldn't know how to give it to me, even in a fever dream designed to torture me. It's too real. Too intrinsic to every moment and breath. It lives in this community, surrounding everyone, especially Charlotte's son, Leo. He is like a fountain, and that calm smile never leaves his face.

Living and traveling with everyone here, it's like cold water on a burn: a relief. Everyone feels it except for three people who actively fight that joy, and all for the same reason. All three of them blame one person for the suffering of the other two.

Charlotte has been avoiding me since I got here. She was happy to see me, and she loves spending time around the fire with me, so long as it's in a group. But we fought a war together, she and I. I want to talk with her alone, without interruption. And any time I try that, she excuses herself like I'm only allowed to see the surface.

It's shame; I put that together pretty quickly. I don't know what Charlotte's life was like after I disappeared, but I know it broke her. She is ashamed, and after hearing the stories of her detractors, I know exactly why.

I need to speak with her. I need to *really speak* with her and try to find my friend somewhere behind all that shame. But as I approach her tent, I hear two other voices; not from inside but from behind. Lewis and Kasey, the man and woman who hate her the most.

"You got them all killed, you know that, right?" Kasey reprimands. "Everyone we were fighting to protect. Every man, woman, and child. Every home and every farm. You. *You got th*em killed."

"I know," my friend whispers. "I know I did."

"You know?" Lewis hisses. "You know, do you? And do you know that Kasey and I wandered around the Radiant Woods for weeks, in pain and afraid? And you know that was your fault too, right?"

"I do," Charlotte replies. Her voice is so small it could be stepped on by an overly excited cricket.

"You do. And you have known that this entire time. While you were on a leisurely stroll, we were paying the price for your mistakes, and all you have to say is 'I do,'" Lewis spits.

Fire runs through my veins as I hear them, gritting my teeth as I listen to them. I want to step in; I ache to defend my friend—or, at least, the friend I had before I was taken. But Charlotte is different. She isn't the woman I remember. My friend may still be in there, but the woman being lectured has swallowed her whole. And as much as it hurts to think about it, I couldn't exactly blame the pair.

I lived in those woods, I was tortured in those woods, and if I ever met the priest who left me there, I would kill him. Whether it was now or a few hours after I was left there, I would tear his heart from his chest and sink my teeth into it as I watched him die. I don't understand exactly what happened. There is too much information, too many names, and I'm still not clearheaded enough to process and remember. Something about lilies and roses looking the same. There were multiple versions of the story, and I can't sort them out.

But I know one thing: I know Charlotte blames herself for what happened to these two. I know that all three of them blame her. I can hardly believe it is true. Charlotte was the face I pictured when I needed comfort. For that first year, at least. She was the kindest person I'd ever known, desperate for everyone she loved to be safe, comfortable. To be themselves and to stop hurting. She wouldn't send people to their torment; she'd never had my stomach for violence, always wanting a peaceful solution. But they all blame her.

I need to speak with her. I need her to stop avoiding me.

"I don't know what to do . . ." Charlotte whispers.

"Stand up, stop apologizing, and walk into those woods," Kasey demands. "You want to really know what you did to us? While you were happily protected by Leo? Go live it. Go suffer as we did, and hope for the reality to end with no way to fix it yourself!"

That's it, I can bear it no longer. I don't care. I finally have a chance at returning to a real life, and Charlotte, of all women, is here. I can't rationalize this anger away. I don't care. Maybe I will later, when I can think clearly again, but I won't listen to these people trying to send my friend there. I won't. I clench my fists and walk around the tent, ready to tell the pair exactly what I think of that suggestion.

As soon as I do, however, my eyes meet Charlotte's. The other two have their backs to me, but my friend sees me immediately. I can read years in that look. Desperate mistakes and shame like the roots of a tree. My words die on my lips as guilty eyes beg for my silence. Lewis and Kasey turn, looking over their shoulders when they notice her eyeline. Lewis scoffs.

"Yeah. I forgot. You're a coward," he hisses. At that, the pair walks past me, locking glares on me as they do. "We'll talk again when we have another moment alone," he promises.

The air is thicker than blood as Charlotte and I stand there, looking at each other. That fog descends again, and everything I wanted to say flees from me while Charlotte just sits down, her back to her tent as she holds her knees to her chest and stares forward, past the boundary Leo has created, into the Radiant Woods.

I can't think of any words, so I awkwardly close the distance and sit next to her. I am finally alone with her; she is finally not wearing any mask. And it feels like everything snaps into place. This may be the first real moment since I fell out of the woods. I am with my friend again, exactly as I was hours before my life was taken from me.

It's a heavy moment. Then, without warning, Charlotte begins to sob. It's not simple crying—it's the type of grieving that turns a face hideous and strains the lungs. It grabs me like a rope around my neck. As she feels it, so do I, so I join her. Tears and snot run down my face before I know it, and sorrow like the stones—still, cold, and ancient—escapes me in cries. It hurts. It is every moment I have paid for fighting back. It is every loss, every hour I could have spent with this woman and didn't. It is her mistakes and mine. And it tastes like clean water. Freeing, somehow. Like we've kept a door locked, pressure building behind it, and once we had a moment alone, we finally stopped fighting it.

We cry for a long time, never saying a word. It moves from painful sobbing to quiet tears. Years of anxiety fall from our eyes until, slowly, something changes. Something inside me and inside her. Or rather, the air of this place finally permeates our skin. The fog starts to recede, and one of us begins to laugh. A chuckle only, at first. I'm not certain which, but after a moment, it's both of us, even as we cry. Then it grows louder and fuller, and sings from our throats like a bird finally free.

It's the relief of letting it out. It's the reality and the connection. It's that tiny hint of a future even I had given up on. It's the joy that lives here, sewing all of us together with hope. Charlotte presses her head against my arm. It's wet with tears and more, but I don't mind. She is in so much pain. Nothing is funny or amusing, but our presence here, in this moment, pushes her self-loathing and my memories to the side. We are grief and joy in the same breath, and I finally know, without a doubt, that the Collector doesn't own me anymore.

Leo

I curl my fingers into a loose fist, then open my palm. Again and again, I do this every morning. It's just my hand, barely different than it ever was, but even so, the grin on my face leaves me with aching cheeks. Every morning is like this, now. It's strange. Five fingers, a little larger, with slightly sharper angles. My entire life, parts of my body felt like a death sentence. The moments before punishment, or the trembling of a public embarrassment. I wore it even when I was naked—*especially* when I was naked.

I curl my fist again as I sit on my bedroll. There were certain parts of my body I'd always hated. The obvious parts, of course, but not them alone. The unearned shame of birth in the wrong body isn't carried in two or three body parts: it's in everything. In my skin and waist and the texture of my hair. It's in the great lie that, whatever I did, I would never *really* be who I wanted to be. That every attempt I made would be a half-complete mask, easily seen through and discarded. That I would only feel more shame rather than validation. When I cut my hair. When I bound my chest. When I chose my clothes.

The lie that presenting myself without a complete, immediate, and magical transformation into a man's body would just be earning ridicule. I hadn't *earned* ridicule. I never had. The shame didn't fit me any better than the dress it forced me into. It wasn't mine. The insults, the loathing, the hate—all just symptoms of someone else's need to control me. To own me. To save me, like a cow being raised for meat until I was ripe enough to be enjoyed by a husband assigned and chosen by my parents.

My rejection of the mold they made for me . . . it wasn't my failing. It was a denial of a promise they made themselves. But I still felt it in every part of my body. It's so hard not to feel embarrassed when everyone around you believes you should be. I hated my body because it was wrong. I hated it because that's what I was raised to do. Even if it had been the right body, I was raised to be ashamed and embarrassed of it.

But that wasn't reality. It was a distortion. My hand is reality: a little larger, with slightly sharper angles. Opening and closing. My body is my own to do with what I please, with magic or alchemy or scalpel—or nothing at all. With my mind alone, if that's all I have. I feel like a perfect night's rest. I feel joy in every breath I take and every friend I make.

There are so many of us. So many are trapped in these woods. So many are finding their lives again. Most remember little of their time in the woods; some remember little at all. We are all from different countries, places I've never heard of. Species I've never seen. Some are like me, exuberant in a man's body. Others celebrate the body of a woman. Frey and a few others confidently enjoy something in between. There are even some who are perfectly comfortable in the body they were born in, only adjusting their identity in the mind.

But we all have one thing in common: we were rejected, and we found each other anyway. I don't know where the Collector is trying to lead us. It's obvious he wants us somewhere; it's no longer possible to really deny it. I know there are victims of the Collector whose crimes don't match mine: those who were broken, physically or mentally; those who loved the wrong people, or those who denied the church.

I am finding people like me because the Collector wants me moving, and he wants me moving somewhere specific. But . . . it's just so hard to care. I do care, but at the same time, I really don't. We are a people who do not let the expectations of others define us. Maybe the Collector wants me moving. Maybe he doesn't. But I will leave no one alone and suffering simply to spite him. I am acting because I choose to act.

I have a family now who understands. Not like Lily, who understood rejection but not quite the same rejection. I do love Lily, and I hope to see her again, but this just isn't the same. I see so many smiles on so many faces. I see joy and relief, and a community where I feel completely safe and unashamed. And I am building it. I am bringing that joy.

I finally finish my morning ritual, satisfied that the slightly different hand really is mine. That I haven't been living through that kindness and excitement offered only in dreams; the kind of dreams that only make the morning colder. No. It is reality. I am reality, and I will allow no one to try and twist it.

When I emerge from my tent, I'm greeted by the barren clearing. It always looks like this everywhere we go. My rejection of the vibrant woods seems to kill any foliage in the area, even as the Radiant Woods lose their control.

My heart beats in my chest like a drum, a new excitement flooding my veins with each groggy friend I see emerge from their tent. With each smiling face around the morning fire. With each smell, sound, and kindness.

I don't know when it happened, but I can feel it. I can breathe it. My aura no longer simply glows, dim with first-generation mana; it dances, exuberant in the light of the sun. My new aspect can be seen in every step I take.

I could never have been like Lillith. She is grief personified and furious.

But me? I am joy.

CHAPTER FIVE

The Fear of Love

Gilbert

I thought they were supposed to get violent again," I say, looking up from a drawing of Sarafyna reaching out to one of the victims.

"I said they *might* grow violent again," Victor corrects. "Not that I expect them to. On the contrary, I was hoping this would be their response." I glance through the bars again at the lethargic, benign people. They are barely moving. Mostly just . . . breathing.

"What response?" I ask. "If anything, they are doing less than before."

"Exactly," Victor agrees. "When they first attacked, they were violent. When we restrained them, they were unruly. Dangerous. We needed Dominic around constantly. They calmed only a little, but at an accelerating rate, in the days that came after. Then when Sarafyna returned, the attacks stopped immediately, and the rate at which our guests here calmed increased even further. At first, I assumed it was simply the effect of Sara's divine magic; we know a stronger source of divine magic tends to overwrite a lesser source, especially if it is closer."

"But?" I ask. I'm missing something; I'm always missing something. Try as I might, I don't have Lily or Henry's scientific mind. I don't have Ed's determination. Even as I promise to be vigilant, to avoid repeating tragedies of the past, it still feels like the world passes me by. And yet, Victor still expects me to pick up on it.

"But," he finally continues, "your brother reports the same thing happening in Visenar, the other primary point of attack. And Sarafyna only spent a significant amount of time here at the towers, so I thought their rate of improvement must have been exponential for some reason by its nature. Except, they didn't just grow more docile—they grew more active but nonviolent. It wasn't just an increase in speed; it was an entirely new vector of improvement. And again, not just here but in Visenar, halfway across the world from us."

"Well, maybe physically, but with the hat shop, it's only a few hours walk. It doesn't feel that far," I reply. Victor snaps his fingers, and I nearly drop my pencil.

"You're right. I'm a scientist, Gil. I considered the literal distance and overlooked something important; something huge and obvious, yet so familiar it was easy to miss," Victor says. "However far Visenar is, the victims there showed the same effects as the ones here as soon as Sara came back. And you are absolutely right. She may have been far from Visenar, but the hat shop isn't. It's her presence making the difference, so it stands to reason that proximity to her power could carry that effect."

"But the shop was there when she was with Lily too," I point out.

"Yes, and she described a weaker connection to it from the other side of the border. It could be inferred that her influence on the hat shop is what is making the real difference. Every potion needs a reaction between ingredients. I think it is neither Sara nor the hat shop affecting our guests but both of them at the same time," Victor explains.

"But how can we know that for sure?" I ask.

"We don't, but we can test it. There is still that factor I'm missing, which is: Why are these people like this at all?" he asks. I look at him blankly for a moment, my pencil hovering over Sara's eye on my paper. He isn't looking at me, taking notes on the residents of the cell instead.

"Uh, 'cause the Collector is a dick?" I guess. Victor begins biting one thumbnail as he considers.

"Sure, I'll give you that. But he's not the kind to do things pointlessly. Not as far as I can tell. I've met those who are cruel for its own sake, but the Collector? I think he has a goal. So why keep these people trapped and alive? Sara was told it's to create more sages, but that doesn't explain it. Not to me. Even if we accept that as true, at what point does he cut his losses?

"He is actively keeping what could be thousands of people in this state, seemingly endlessly. If you fail to get a desired result from a subject after endless attempts, it is a waste of time to spend resources on that subject. If it were me, I'd work toward better and faster methods rather than increasing and maintaining more and more subjects. From my point of view, he must be getting something else out of it, don't you think?" he questions.

"In case he needed an army?" I guess.

"Perhaps . . ." Victor responds idly. "But in that case, why make them so self-defeating? Their bodies are designed for self-harm. For an army, a dozen standardized designs for different military roles would make the most sense. You'd want them strong, fast, and durable. But these people? What's been done to them can only be meant to cause them pain. Not a wise move if you need an army alone."

"So?" I question, twirling my pencil between my fingers.

"So, he must be getting something out of their suffering. Maybe it's an endoaspect, or maybe it has something to do with divine magic, but he is doing this to them for a reason," Victor says. "I put it together when Sarafyna described her connection with them. The way she could understand simple things about them that I can't discern with any amount of study." He actually leans forward here, reaching an arm through the bars and touching a victim's back.

"Put what together?" I ask. He finally looks in my direction.

"I can't be certain; that's why I have to observe them while Sarafyna is on the other side of the border. But their temperament first matched the Collector's, then Sara's, and now nothing at all. I don't think they are entirely aware at this point. But I think the Collector gets something from them, and so he keeps them captive, alive, and miserable. He even made their lives dependent on him until recently, when he needed to hurt us," Victor says.

"But you aren't sure what?" I ask.

"No, this is all still a theory," Victor replies. "It could just be about emotional mana. We know it can provide a significant power boost depending on the person and aspect; your sister is evidence of that. But if it's not, if it's something to do with divine magic . . . Well, if the creator of the Radiant Woods can benefit from their presence, maybe the creator of the hat shop can too. Maybe he didn't stop attacking when Sara came back because of what she can do for his victims. Maybe he stopped because of what they can do for her."

I pause again, resting my pencil against the paper. I look at my depiction of the woman in question. She wears a sharp look in her gentle eyes—not an artistic decision I made, just who she is: kind and subtle, with rage inside like slowly boiling water. I miss so many things—I always have—but for some reason, when I draw, I can see everything with the utmost clarity, like it's still happening in front of me. Every detail lives inside me, but I can only let them out and examine them through art. I lift the pencil as I consider Victor's words. My eyes fix on the wooden utensil, an idea Lily introduced but doesn't claim as her own.

The world has so many things in it. I don't understand any of them. I feel useless, but I flick my eyes toward the now docile patients, no longer reacting to anyone's presence. Simply waiting. "Any idea what?" I ask. Victor doesn't respond, letting the question hang in the air for a long moment. When he does open his mouth, he is silenced by the resonance of a massive bell.

It's as we feared: Sara is gone, on the other side of the border, and we are under attack. I jump to my feet.

"Shit, stay here!" I call, failing to wait for confirmation as I run toward the stone wall, erected around the towers by every earth mage willing to volunteer. I have very little mana; I spent only the minimum time in my circle when Lily drew it for me. It didn't seem important at the time. I will be of no use defending the community, but I run anyway because I recognize his mana flashing from atop the wall. Dominic, the most powerful mage we have. When there is fighting to be done, he will be there.

I run, not to help him but so he won't be fighting alone . . . on a meaningful sense, at least; there are other mages helping him. The success of this entire community is built around everyone's willingness and ability to help when they can, but it's not the same. He will feel alone up there without anyone he cares about. I didn't see his last fight, and he doesn't talk about it much, but it did something to him. Left him alone in every crowd.

But not around me. We connected. We share a certain flavor of shame, of narrow vision and joy while those around us struggle. We share a resolve to be better, and for a while, that's all it was. Someone who understood, on some level, the desperation of a man who had a chance to stand tall and chose not to. Until an idle conversation one evening about other similarities. About romance not confined to two people.

My heart started beating when he said that with a relief I didn't understand—until I remembered Lily, hopelessly enamored with another woman. And I remembered an idle comment about expanding my interest past just the women in my . . . circle. The heat that had risen in me at the suggestion. I'd forgotten that moment, but when I remembered . . . something shifted. Dominic.

We haven't said anything just yet. Just small glances. Lingering looks. An implicit understanding that we can take another step forward at any moment. That the type of romance I've had before is an interest we share. And that, more than anything else, we understand each other. He's not alone when he's with me. It still seems strange; so far removed from everything I learned growing up. But, as foreign and strange as it is to me, it is growing harder to deny that I adore him.

And he is fighting alone.

The run feels like it will never end as I see flashes of his mana growing brighter and more frequent the closer I get. I finally reach the first part of the wall, but it's not close enough. Even with the gates closed, it's not exactly a normal wall, like those at Visenar or Satusmor. It's more like a simple maze, designed to funnel our temporary enemies to one spot where we can subdue and calm them.

It's good. It's kind. It's right. But a battle is more dangerous for the side that refuses to kill. When I make it to the top of the wall, I can see him. Like a beacon, burning through reality with rippling mana and determination. I have to run around several turns now to get close to him. It's a strangely designed defense, and a frustrating one at this moment.

When I finally make it to him, he notices me immediately, offering me a look of chilly panic. I can instantly see why. There are . . . thousands of them. A greater attack than we have seen so far. Dom is strong; he can handle them. But this exceeds our expectations by a wide margin, and it's not the towers we have to worry about. Visenar doesn't have Dominic.

My eyes lock onto Dom's, widening as I catch the sympathy bleeding into them.

"Ed . . ."

Edward

I have a new home now. At least for the time being. I'm staying in Visenar until the danger has passed, and Mariah is staying with me, which has been wonderful but also terrifying. I have been able to spend time with her and take care of her as she carries our child, a thought which, despite my excitement, sends a chill down my spine. The thought of a child reminds me of a glass pillar now kept in an abandoned building only I visit.

Like every night, a cold sweat wakes me hours before dawn. I must have jerked awake because Mariah rouses shortly after.

"Dreams again?" she asks. I shudder, then nod. "Henry or Richard?" I stare at the dark ceiling for a moment before answering.

"I'm . . . not sure," I answer. "Both, I guess?"

She fails to suppress a yawn, but she uses her arms to lift her body and sit up against the headboard. "Want to tell me about it?" she asks.

"No, you need your sleep," I respond, feeling guilty about waking her up.

"I'm awake now." She shrugs. "History suggests I'll be getting up to pee every few minutes for the next hour, in any case. Might as well talk."

I sigh. "Sorry." She waves me off. "The dream. It's about a pillar. It turns from glass to stone to glass again. Whichever it is at the time, that's how I feel about . . ." I look down at her stomach, which she gently rests one hand on. "Henry and my dad died so, so quickly. I had so much to talk to both of them about, but they didn't get a long goodbye, like in the stories. They didn't get final words or the breath they needed to . . . forgive me. That's the main thing. I wanted Henry's forgiveness. I wanted proof Dad could change. I wanted the scene from the stories, where every lingering doubt gets resolved before the hero dies. I wanted to save Henry at the last moment and prove, this time, I wouldn't be a coward.

"But I didn't get that. Both of them lived, and then they were dead. Blink and you miss it. Just . . . gone, and nothing I was too afraid to say to either can ever be heard. Not by them. In the end, I was a coward again, just like when I ran and let those thugs take my brother. I waited too long to make things completely right, and now I never will.

"And Mari, I am going to be a father. My own father was so poisoned by pride I had to kill him to save my sister. And I have that in me. That deep cut like a knife in my gut when I am outsmarted or disrespected. I always have. I hate feeling inferior to my little sister even now. I hate feeling inferior to you, even though I know why I feel that way; even though I know it is senseless and based on lies taught to me by a man I killed." I pause to catch my breath as I notice a slight tremor creeping into my voice.

"But you don't hurt people," Mariah says. "Understanding why you feel that way makes a world of difference. Because, even if it hurts more than it should, you have something your father never did: empathy. Yeah, he may have been capable of it, but he chose himself over that feeling. You don't. You would rather suffer that thorn in your skin than hurt anyone else. You are a man worth loving, Ed. You're a man I love, and a man who will raise a kind child. And, based on the stories I've heard about you, you are far from being a coward." I let out a deep sigh.

"But that's the problem, isn't it?" I reply, nearly quietly enough to disappear into the cold room. "My father was a prideful coward, and he died in an instant. My brother was kind and brave, and he died in an instant. Death doesn't care who I am, or if I deserve it. Whatever I do, what if our child loses me, and I don't get a final moment to say goodbye? What if I can't tell you I love you? What if we are laughing and joking, and a moment later I'm gone? What if the same happens to our kid? I may have fought to protect people this time, but . . . I'm so scared. I'm still a coward. I can't scrub it off. Fear infects me like a disease, and every night, I see every possible way I could fail you."

Mariah examines me for a long moment with glass eyes. I can see the slight panic behind them. She wants to help, but she doesn't know what to say. She doesn't need to. I needed to say it out loud, but now that I have, the trembling has slowed. Instead of replying, she wraps her arms around me, pulling my head to her collarbone. As we stay there, I feel my accelerated breathing slowing, and the pillar in my dreams starts to fade.

The fear is still there, but it grows more manageable as she holds me. Just as I am truly feeling calm again, rapid knocking screams through my quiet home, and both of us jump. *Shit.* I knew this would happen. I knew it. They warned me Sara was leaving, but now, in the middle of the night? I climb from bed and throw a simple tunic on. "Will you be all right here?" I ask.

"Yes, I'll catch up," she replies. That is a reply to a different question than I asked.

"Mari, you're pregnant; you can't go to the front lines of something like this."

"Yes, and you're a silly man; we all have disadvantages. But I am just as powerful a mage as you, and I can help to at least maintain any barriers."

I want to argue further, but I know it's pointless. She's not an idiot; she won't put herself in too much danger. Not on purpose, anyway. The knocking persists, and I go to answer the door, swinging it open to find an exhausted boy no older than thirteen.

"An attack?" I guess.

"Soon," he gasps. "We got word a few moments ago: the Collector is attacking on the other side of the woods. There are thousands of them; they need us at the tree." I nod, then take a moment to return to Mariah just as she pulls her own tunic over her head.

"Mari, I love you. Be careful. I have to go now." I give her a quick kiss before pulling away and jogging back to the open door. The boy jumps as I reappear in his field of vision but turns to run toward the city's former gallows.

"I love you too, Ed. Don't push yourself too hard. I'll be there soon," Mariah responds. I sigh but nod, grabbing my bag from its hook in the breezeway and running out the door, following the messenger. I pull my own whisper sphere out to find it vibrating. I answer it immediately.

"Ed, is everything all right over there? How bad is it?" Gilbert cries through the artifact.

"I'm all right; I'm still on my way," I reply. "I haven't seen anything yet." This strikes me as odd. I don't live far from the tree. I knew I'd need to respond, and the tree itself can be seen from almost anywhere in the city, but I see no signs of a fight. It should be faster to get to us than to reach the towers, with the radiant tree in the middle of the city.

"Thank the—I'm glad," Gil responds. "Keep me updated, and don't . . ." He trails off. I get it. "Mom is looking forward to seeing you again, after all this."

"I'm looking forward to seeing her too," I reply. "I miss her pear cobbler. I'll be all right, I promise. You stay safe too." It's a lie. I don't know if we can do this, but I grit my teeth and run. And run. And run. I keep Gil on the line as I do, but I have nothing to report. Everything remains quiet, more or less. There are bustling mages wearing armor and preparing different kinds of walls and cells, more of them the closer I get.

But when I arrive, nothing is happening. Not a single soul has emerged from the tree. We are perfectly safe. The Collector is only attacking my real home. My family. And by the sound of it, he is throwing everything he has at them.

CHAPTER SIX

Finger Foods

Sarafyna

With one hand in my pocket, I roll the persistently silent whisper sphere between my fingers. I waited. For two days I waited on the other side of the border so I could check in on Visenar and the towers. And it took me another day to make it back here, to Orvata. I must have tried to call everyone a thousand times by now, but not once has anyone answered. I can feel Annie somewhere in this city. I know she is still here. I can always feel her, especially now that I am conscious of our connection. Or original connection, at least. As her anchor to this world, I will always have some idea of where she is.

But no matter who I call or how many times, I receive no answer from Annie or Ember or the twins. Nothing from any of them. Even my precise control can't prevent the rapid beating of my heart, not really. Because the source is still there—the anxiety. I left, and now the woman I love won't answer me. No one I left here will.

I sit down at the bar inside a local pub, just outside the inn we'd been staying at. They aren't there anymore, but this is unsurprising, considering the news I've heard since coming into town.

"What can I get for you, little miss?" the man behind the bar asks, startling me only a little. I take a sharp breath as the stale but comfortable smell of the bar settles back into my nose and the sounds around me return me to reality.

"Oh, uh . . ." I trail off. What does Annie usually drink? I remember her calming her nerves with alcohol or green mist from time to time. That idle thought brought me here, but I don't actually drink much. "Wine?"

"Is that a question?" He laughs as I blush, then pausing for a moment, I shrug.

"I guess so," I respond. "Sorry, I don't drink much. Just looking to calm some anxiety."

"Self-medicating, huh?" he says. "I wouldn't advise it, truth be told." Even as he speaks, he fills a mug from a barrel and slides it in front of me. "But, seeing as you aren't my daughter, I don't really give a shit. This will do the trick. Your size and no experience? This beer won't knock you on your ass as quickly, and the taste is a bit easier on an amateur. Besides, it's cheaper."

I'm not really worried about money. You don't live with a woman like Annie without learning to liberate a few wealthy wagons and hotel rooms of money when you get to a new city. Still, I'll take his word for it about the strength and taste. At least until it is in front of me. The smell isn't all that strong, but enough to know I'm not going to particularly enjoy it.

I examine the foam on the top as another man settles in on the stool next to me.

"Are you sure?" I ask. "My girlfriend always drinks wine. She seems to like it a lot better." For some reason, the man who just sat down groans and stands again, leaving without ordering anything.

"I'm sure," the bartender replies with a laugh. "This will do the trick." I shrug and lift the mug, taking a large gulp—and immediately coughing all over myself. I put the mug down, cough a few more times, then wipe my face on my left sleeve.

"This is the milder flavor?" I ask, receiving only a hearty laugh in return.

"It's an acquired taste. It'll do the job though, if you power through," he answers. I wrinkle my nose at the foul drink but hesitantly take another sip. "So, what brings you to Orvata?"

"What makes you think I'm not from here?" I ask.

"This pub is near the city border." He shrugs. "Your dress is an odd style, and if someone who looked like you lived anywhere near here, my customers would have told me all about it a dozen times in the first week. I figure you either just got to town or you went out of your way to avoid someone when you came here. Obviously not an alcoholic dodging any-one who would recognize you, and you openly brought up your girlfriend unprompted, so not avoiding her. Call it an educated guess."

I put a few fingers up to my face as he comments on my appearance. My fingers meet smooth skin, and I realize my scars are absent. It must be my distance from Annie. Or my time away from her.

I don't know when it happened, exactly, but it did. Strangely, my heart sinks at the thought. I hated my scars for so long, but now . . . it feels like I'm missing something. A part of myself. My scars are something Annie looks at and loves, and I love the way she looks at me. Her absence and my insecurity seem to be erasing them, as I used to do unintentionally when I was afraid of what someone would think of me.

In a way, their presence has become a badge of my comfort and confi-dence. When I can wear my scars and the past that gave them to me, well, that's when I am me. In the last few months, my "pretty" and smooth skin has felt ugly to me. I want to be the Sarafyna who wears her scars. I want to be with the woman who kisses them with gentle affection.

"R-right," I stutter. "You're right; I just got here today." Another man takes the seat next to me, which is strange, since there are more private stools open at the bar, but I shrug it off, assuming he just wants to get the bartender's attention.

"I thought so. So, what for?" he asks again. I pause, wondering how I should answer this. Annie would probably just tell him to mind his busi-ness. Or maybe lie? Or maybe she would just laugh and change the subject. I'm not sure, but I'm not a great liar, except by omission. All I really know is I am taking way too long to respond.

"Getting some space from that girlfriend, maybe?" the man beside me asks, startling me again. Do people just join other people's conversations in bars? Or is that just this guy? Maybe everyone here is just really friendly.

"No, not at all," I answer. "I'm just . . . traveling, I guess. It's personal." It's a lame answer but the bartender shrugs it off.

"So she came with you, then?" the man asks. Something about the tone in his voice makes me itch. He's strangely happy about the idea that I'm traveling alone.

"Uh, no, but she—" I start, but he cuts me off.

"So whatever your reasons, you have leeway to try some new things, right?" he asks.

I blink at him.

"I don't know what that means," I answer honestly, then return my attention to the bartender. "I hear there has been some unrest lately."

The bartender returns the implied question with a single laugh. "That's an understatement. Demon queen's turning out to be real, five sages murdered by her, and a sixth dead by heart attack only a few days later. The cult took over the colosseum for a day too; same day the sixth sage died, actually. People who died in the colosseum supposedly returning alive, and I'm sure you've heard about the Void Sage's emergency election. A new leader of the country months early, and rumors of a draft to fight demons already circling the town. There haven't been so many insane rumors in this city as long as I've lived here."

I'd heard some of this already, and I nod along. Even only being here a day, most of it is hard to miss. Almost every conversation leads to a discussion of these events, and I barely have to prod to get details out of anyone. The detail of the sixth sage is new, however.

"I hadn't heard about the heart attack," I say. "That's strange timing."

"I wouldn't worry about it, sweetheart. Let the sages deal with the sages. You're on a trip; you should be having fun! Experimenting! Not worrying about the bartender, gossiping like you're both housewives," the man next to me speaks up. Again, I'm not really sure how to respond to that.

"Well, I'm interested anyway," I reply, looking back at the bartender. "So what happened there?"

"No one is sure," the more pleasant man answers, filling up another mug for someone sitting farther down. They'd ordered with a hand signal alone, declining to interrupt our conversation. "Sages don't often die of natural causes except old age. All but the Original Sage succumb to that eventually, but the Thread Sage was only a few hundred years old. And yeah, he was a weaker sage—controlling hair is a strange power to have—but even so, a heart attack is unheard of. A lot of people think the demon queen killed him too."

I would believe that for sure. Annie does have a habit of poisoning powerful men. The ones she doesn't dismember or decapitate, anyway. Usually both, actually. "You think so? They didn't capture her when she killed the other sages?"

"No one is really sure about that either." The bartender shrugs. "Some people say she was killed in the colosseum. Others that she was captured.

Others that she escaped. And, well, since it's the Void Sage who stopped her, I tend to believe she escaped. If the rumors of a draft are true, in any case. A demon army isn't much of a threat without a demon leader, right?"

"The colosseum? Where you said the cult was?" I ask.

He shrugs. "I suppose so, but that was days later. Why, you think they are working together?"

I sigh internally. That's my best lead for now. I'll have to see what I can find out about this cult. I know Annie was accused of being one of them when a guardian saw her arm. That's a decent place to start. Maybe I can search for other people with prosthetics or just see if I can track them from this colosseum.

"Don't worry about it either way, honey," the irritating man cuts in. "I'll protect you from the demon queen if she shows up. Provided having a girlfriend doesn't mean you *only* like girls, if you catch my drift." And then his presence falls into place. I hadn't heard the term *girlfriend* before meeting Annie, but the people in this city seem to know it. Perhaps he thinks I am like Gilbert, interested in polyamory, as Annie calls it.

"Oh!" I exclaim in genuine surprise. "That's why you are here! You want to have sex with me!" I've had men approach me before; attempts at marriage arrangements when I was a kid, and even some when I was wearing my scars. But this is easily the most blatant. He is being so forward I actually didn't understand what he was doing. He doesn't even blush as I announce it, simply shrugging.

"Yes, obviously. So the question remains, are you interested?" he presses.

"Oh no," I reply quickly. "I only find women attractive, and of those, I really only have more than a passing interest in my girlfriend. Uh . . . sorry." He scoffs and raises an eyebrow,

"Are you sure? Have you ever been with a man?" he asks. I'm a bit taken aback by the question. What does that even mean? I want to ask if there have been any rumors about the so-called cult, but I'm so confused I make the mistake of engaging with him further.

"Am I sure I'm not attracted to you?" I ask, genuinely flabbergasted. Ember says that, while changing your body is forbidden here, relationships like what Annie and I have are fairly normal. Is she from a different region entirely or is this man just poorly educated?

"I mean, how can you know if you haven't tried?" he asks.

"Do you have to try to be attracted to people?" I reply.

"Tried fucking, I mean. Damn, it's a good thing you're pretty, because you're a bit dim. If you've never ridden a man, I'm certain I can convince you that you like them, given the chance," he insists.

I'm rapidly traveling from irritated, to confused, to angry. "Is that how it works for you?" I ask. "Do you have to have sex with someone before you know if you're attracted to them?"

"What? Of course not! What does that have to do with anything?" he says. I just stare at him blankly. I don't understand why no one else is looking at him like he just pulled his pants down in public. He's talking like a man unfamiliar with literature. And women, I suspect. It doesn't matter. He doesn't matter. I need to focus, so I turn back to the bartender.

"Have there been any other rumors about the cult in town? Kind of scary to think there are that many of them here, isn't it?" I ask.

"Don't fucking ignore me, slut," the man next to me snarls. He tries to grab my shoulder, and for a moment, I am the monster who roamed the Radiant Woods, barely conscious and fighting for control of my body. Just the idea of being touched by him feels like grease running down the inside of my dress. I have control of my abilities—I have for a long time—but in that moment, I act without even thinking.

He makes contact, but not with my shoulder. Before I even process my own actions, the razor-sharp teeth of my shoulder's new mouth have liberated three of his fingers.

"Oh," I say as screaming and blood erupts in concert. "Oops."

Last Woman Grieving

Lillith

It's gone, Lily. I can't even remember what it was like. I can only guess—from the crude shape of the hole it left, from the emotions around it, like the dead flesh around an old wound. The guilt is there. The shame. The anger and the disappointment. But not the grief or the loss. The rest aren't the same as they were before. I feel rage like a drowning fire, and guilt like a forgotten errand. It's all so . . . dull. So colorless. Pointless."

Autumn's voice echoes through my head as I meditate. Mana cycles through my body like strobing lights, tearing through and altering every cell thousands of times a second. Between my limbs, each enchanted piercing, and back into my body. Previously contained tumors grow, twisting my stomach and sending a pain like grinding teeth through my bones. I can't get my conversation with the other woman out of my head, even as I focus on mutating my own body.

"It was the moment you jumped into the stone. I know that now. The moment you were too far from me, I lost it. I don't know what you were doing. I don't know how. But it was you, not Sara. You. And going into that stone stopped it. Now, I feel like a corpse, a hollow woman piloting dead limbs like my own body is a marionette."

Ironic words for her to say when speaking to me. I don't belong here;

I never did. But I am here nevertheless, and I will use that extra time to fight. A riot spike was used against me, and I simply fell. I had no magic to save me. All of my strength was pointless. I had a single arm and no idea what to do with it. If Riley hadn't been there, I'd be dead. Well, more dead. I can't let that happen again. No matter how I look at it, this is the only solution. If I want to fight when mana is taken from me, I can't hang on to my humanity. I have to keep pushing.

"I'm scared. I'm so scared. Because I can feel it already, all those negative emotions building pressure like water at a dam. They used to flow freely, joining together in a single great river, but now, I have no idea how to direct them. I don't know how I ever did. They are just building and building and I can't reach them. But that's not what terrifies me, because I can ignore them."

I need other options when I lack my limbs. When I lack my mana. I need the option to use my strength like I used to. At first, I hoped I could grow my limbs back—no steel arm will ever feel quite the same—but I can't generate new cells; I can't create new flesh. And I need my false limbs. My piercings help, but it's the limbs that really manage my cancer. It's all that enchanted steel that takes the excess mana and prevents my tumors from eating me alive. Or dead, as the case may be.

I consider just sewing newly enchanted steel into my body, but the way I use my limbs has a major effect. Fourteen little rings and studs won't be able to keep up like three full body parts. Parts I use and grow more familiar with every day. They truly feel like a part of me in a way a steel plate or a hundred more piercings can't replicate. But the thought did give me an idea. A terrible one.

"I can look away and pretend I don't know they are there. It grows easier every day; more tempting every day. In a few weeks? A few months? A few years? I'll be happy. I'll have forgotten them completely. I'll feel all of them, of course. My anger won't disappear—but *that* anger will. That guilt will. I'll forget them, and that pressure will keep building, and I will break. I will smile more every day. I will dance and sing and leave the cracks in my heart open and bleeding. I will break."

My cancer isn't normal cancer. Yes, it is a dangerous and uncontrolled cell growth spreading throughout my body and forming ugly tumors, but it isn't natural cancer. It is the result of mana filling my flesh so thoroughly it runs out of space. It is mana building new cells to contain itself. The tumors aren't simple flesh but mana desperate to grow, which means I can, actually, grow new cells rapidly. With standard cancer, the only benefit this would have is a record time with a stage-four speedrun. But with cells composed entirely of mana . . .

"I have to go. I have to, and you know that. Every day we delay, I become less myself. If we delay, I will stop being Autumn entirely. I am too afraid to wait. I am too scared to go to these sages one at a time. We have to find out who is taking our emotions from us like we are dirty farm tools in need of cleaning. August has to go to one, and Ember has to go to one, and I have to go. Alone."

I curse as I lose focus, my mind locking on Autumn's desperate eyes. Phantoms of too clear a memory. It's not safe to leave Autumn on her own, even without her grief. But I can't stop her either. All I can do is make sure I'm ready to fight, prepared to get her out as quickly as possible the moment she gives us the go-ahead. And that means having a response to riot spikes.

"We both saw those men smiling, laughing, even as they left their loved ones freshly dead and alone. I can't get that far. I can't. I won't get that far. I won't live like this long enough to smile as I leave August's body behind. I have to do whatever I can to stop this. To tear my grief back, and to feel everything again. To feel Henry's death again in the way he deserves."

I begin cycling my mana again, sending it through the cancer. Growing it. Manipulating and directing it. I won't be helpless again. I *can't* be helpless again, because I'm alone now. I brought Autumn so I wouldn't be alone in my grief for Henry, because as much as we may blame each other, we both understand. We both see the same smile as we close our eyes every night. We are haunted by the same fucking ghost, and there is a certain safety in knowing I'm not the only one.

Sara is gone. She didn't come back after a week. She didn't come back after two, and no matter how many times I, or the twins before me, call her, there is no answer. Our spheres are silent. Sara is gone, and Autumn has lost her grief. I am alone. I need to share this stone in my heart, or it will tear me apart. It will bubble up and pour from my lips like vomit, and the world will see how fragile I really am. I will represent nothing but my failures and my inability to stomach them. If I let this break me, they will all have to win without me.

"But August is smart, really. He's laid back, and he doesn't usually apply himself, but he's smart. And he cares about me. If he thinks these sages are connected, he's probably right. Lily, this is a way forward. I know you are worried about me, and I know why. I remember that rooftop, even if I don't remember the feeling that brought me there. But I think I'm in the most danger sitting still. This is something I can do, some tangible way I can fight back. I need to do this."

I can't get Autumn's voice out of my head. I'd almost shattered asking her not to go. It was me at my weakest, when they most needed me strong.

Mana continues to cycle rapidly, tearing me apart and rebuilding me an uncountable number of times. I can feel it—the cancer complying with my will. No longer invasive and useless cells, they start to grow on the outside of my body, from the small of my back and from my tailbone. This will serve me in two ways. The first is practical. Even without mana, I will remain deadly, maneuverable. A threat to decent society, as any good demon queen and scapegoat should be. No more silly tricks will leave me incapacitated.

And the other purpose . . .

"You have to stop, Lily. While we are gone. The way you keep punishing yourself, you're on the verge of falling apart already. Eventually, you are going to push too far, are going to take one too many hits, and beat yourself into an early grave in Henry's name. I'm moving forward. It's time for you to move forward too."

It was easy to say for Autumn. She doesn't remember this grief. Her guilt feels dull. But I can't leave Henry behind like that, and without her . . . the grief boils inside me. I want to share it with her, send it to her, offer her my own grief in place of hers, and we can share it for Henry's sake. For hers. I want to offer my heartstrings to be pulled from my chest and swallowed so we can both hear the dirge ringing through them. But I can't.

I am alone. I am alone, and the woman I love isn't here to hold me in the dark where no one can see. And if she were, I still couldn't. Because I am dead and she knew, and she didn't tell me. And as much as I miss her, we need to talk about that before I can lean on her again. And so I remain alone.

"We'll be in touch, Lily. Take care of yourself. August and I, we're going to find whoever is taking my grief away. We are going to find them, and we are going to give people their souls back. Ember too. You just have to trust us."

I trust them. I do. But I'm afraid, and I'm alone, and I'm a corpse fighting to justify every step I take with a quickly melting brave face. And I left Henry to die. I did. And Autumn, she smiled at me; she can't even hate me properly anymore. I deserve punishment for leaving my brother to die. I do. But she's right. The way I acted in that arena was stupid. I put myself in danger, put *everyone else* in danger. It was selfish, pure and simple. Even that can be counted among my failures.

At the same time, even if I'm not always conscious of it, I need to do something. Because that pain, it holds me together. But I know what to do. I know how to fight back consistently and keep this mask together.

My cancer grants me an opportunity to grow instead of simply change. It offers me endless new cells brimming with mana. With it, I can create new pieces, new parts to fight with. But it is still cancer. It is still death. But then again, so am I. The more I use it, the more it will eat at me. It won't make me any weaker—not with enchanted steel woven into my limbs and piercing my body—but with this much, it will still make me sick.

I can become stronger, become a better fighter, eliminate one of my greatest weaknesses. And I can offer Henry justice with the same stroke of my brush. And so long as Henry gets his justice, I can hold myself together on every other front. I can offer the indomitable Lillith of Endings to everyone who needs it. As for the sickness? Well, I'm only here for as long as it takes to kill Alpha anyway.

I meditate for hours—all night and well into the next day. But I finish. I move past humanity, and my bones ache for the way my new appendages eat at me. I sleep sitting down after that, winning maybe an hour of rest before someone knocks on the door.

"Are you in there, Lily?" Riley calls. "We got word from your friend Autumn. Archer is planning to move tomorrow. Will you be ready to help?" I open groggy eyes and climb to my feet. The room is thankfully large, accommodating my new—literal—wingspan. It's strange, having control of new body parts. I'll need to practice using them tonight.

"I'll be ready," I answer, stretching my new leathery wings from the small of my back. My large scorpion's tail coils around my torso, and I prick a steel finger with the tip of a long, venomous stinger. It actually leaves a mark on my false hand.

I use mana to forcefully choke back the vomit of an exhausted, sick body. That, I'll have to get used to, at least for a while. Until I kill Alpha. Then, I won't have to worry about any of this ever again.

CHAPTER EIGHT

Reasonable Accommodations

Could you not have tried something more subtle?" Archer groans.

"Yeah, Lillith. You're usually so subtle," Riley intones. The wagon hits a bump in the road, nearly knocking me over again. This has happened the entire trip, as the wagons use bench-style seating which is flush with the sides. In other words, they aren't built for women with giant scorpion tails.

"I can't help it if you lacked the foresight to provide reasonable accommodations," I quip. "Lots of people have tails, you know."

"Not like that," Archer grumbles, glaring at my chitinous tail. I'm a little uncomfortable with it myself, truth be told. My balance is all wrong, and I never know what to do with it. But I did design it to hold me up if my legs fail, and I spent much of last night practicing with it. As the wagon steadies, I fold my tail against itself and press it into the wood, creating something of a seat for myself. I'm not actually sitting, exactly, but it's surprisingly comfortable once I get the hang of it.

"Their loss, I suppose," I reply.

"How are you planning to move around without being seen? You look like a scorpion screwed a bat and gave birth to a rebellious teenager," Archer complains.

"I'll be fine at night," I insist. My scales can be shed and grown with new enchantments and colors. All I need to do is grow navy blue scales with light-dispersing enchantments. Flying over the city in the dark will be a breeze, something I explained to Riley last night. Archer, on the other hand, still rubs me the wrong way, so "It'll be fine" is the best explanation I'm offering for now.

"If you're spotted, we aren't bailing you out again. You're on your own," Archer warns. I shrug.

"Like I said, it won't be a problem. Now, does anyone want to finally share some details about this little field trip?" I ask. "If we're going to see a fire truck, I call dibs on blaring the horn first."

"I don't know what any of that means," Archer says. Riley just pulls an apple out of her bag and takes a bite, leaning her head back against the canvas cover. She is already used to my mannerisms, I suppose.

"Just tell me what the plan is, and why we are doing it. I trust Autumn, but I haven't heard from her directly yet, and I'm not really the dutiful-soldier type. After seeing me, I have to suspect you didn't bring me along for anything covert. I'm just asking for a little detail, that's all," I say. Archer rolls her eyes, and Riley wears a subtle smile on the corners of her mouth.

"Public records, apparently," Archer responds. "Not recent ones, and not focused on the most prominent sages. From the moment we made contact—and before, if my understanding is correct—these are what August has been combing through. Not looking for upcoming movements but for anything suspicious in the last couple of decades. Apparently, he was trying to pinpoint the exact moment everyone's grief was taken."

I raise an eyebrow. "You look like you're about thirty, thirty-five? Did you not have your endoaspect yet? Do you not know more or less when it happened?"

She gives me a bored look before refocusing on the wood floor and continuing her explanation. "I didn't, no. And they didn't take it all at once, like with Autumn. It was a little at a time. It didn't feel like having something yanked away but like falling asleep slowly. They spent years on it, taking just a little more every day. Many people didn't even realize what happened. In any case, when August discovered this, he didn't stop there. He started looking into any articles or rumors he could find about the weakest sages.

"We, abolitionists, try to track the current greatest threats among the sages. The weaker ones couldn't affect the entire country like this, so we are trying to identify and eliminate the one responsible. I, for my part, believe it's the Void Sage. He's the one who has been raising the alarm about you the longest, even longer than you've been alive. With your grief aspect, he seems like the most likely to want grief gone," Archer explains. I shake my head.

"Nah, you've got it all wrong. I mean, not all wrong; it probably *was* his idea. But Ol' Oafish Oakley? He's way too lazy and self-centered for that. I bet if you asked him, he'd say he was the one doing it—he loves to be loved for impressive feats of mind and power. But he hates actually doing, well, anything. The man is chronically useless.

"Even if he wasn't, the rich and powerful never use their wealth and power when they can exploit their lesser peers instead. In their minds, what one extremely powerful sage could do is better accomplished by a few dozen weak sages. It's such a chronic problem, I'd be willing to bet the weakest sages are the only ones who even know how to keep people's grief from them at this point," I reply while Riley nearly chokes on her apple as I describe her father in a less-than-flattering light.

"She's got a point," Riley agrees. "My whole life was about making the Void Sage look good, but I don't know of anything he's actually done himself. There's no chance he actually expends constant effort on anything."

"Fear is a powerful motivator, and he seems terrified of Lillith," Archer counters.

"Yeah, he's a little bitch, we can agree on that," I admit, "but he didn't kill me immediately when he thought he was in a position of power. That moment alone should help form your opinion of his actions. If it's something he can control, he'll delegate. If he actually thinks he's in danger, he'll piss his pants and hide. The only time I have actually seen him put effort into anything was at the behest of Alpha, or the Original Sage. Because Alpha is powerful enough to make him. August had that right idea, I'm betting."

"Well, August seemed to believe you would say exactly that. At least the part about the powerful in general always using subordinates. I think he may have spent too much time around you," Archer says. "I'm skeptical that even they would leave something that important in someone else's hands, but it's the angle he wanted to take.

"He found about five sages in the city who all moved here at the same time, just before we think the grief started to fade. They all moved to different parts of the city despite most of the wealthy living in one sector at the time, and their estates are evenly spaced as well. He thinks they are there to steal grief from an assigned area. Personally, I think they just wanted to buy more affordable real estate and develop high-end services there—the weaker sages rely on regular wealth to maintain comfort—but it was enough of a coincidence for your friends to investigate."

I nod as she speaks. August's reasoning is sound. We don't know how this is being done across an entire country, and the timing of such specific moves for subordinate sages seems strange. What doesn't ring true, however, is Archer's dismissal. August is a good guy. He had good grades at school, and he's far from stupid, but he found all of this in a matter of weeks. There is just no way these are all new ideas.

I mean, respect to August for finding it, but these people have been fighting the sages for years. I can *maybe* give them the change in perspective as an excuse. *Maybe.* But I'm going to make a fuss about it, at least internally. I'll file it under *W* for "What are these chucklefucks playing at" for now. For the time being, we are all on the same side, even if some of the things this woman says make me itch.

"All right, so that's how we decided which sages the twins and Ember would go to. What did we hear from Autumn? Why are we moving now?" I ask.

"Nothing," Archer responds. I raise an eyebrow, declining to answer until the other shoe drops. It only takes a few seconds. "There is a room in the estate where the Insect Sage spends hours every day. He has servants bring him food and drink regularly while he is in that room, and Autumn has been inside several times, but that is exactly what she can report each time: nothing. She never remembers a moment inside that room. It's pretty obvious where we need to look if there is something suspicious."

I suppose that is pretty obviously actionable information. This only increases my suspicions about this group, or at least about Archer. It doesn't sound like half this shit is even hidden, not really. Not like the stone in the arena.

To be fair, I don't know what is actually in that room. Just because something is easy to find doesn't mean it will be easy to access. Banks have signs and flashing lights, but knowing where their safe is doesn't make you rich. There could be plenty of reasons not to act on this information for so long. Even so, Archer would have me believe she didn't know about any of it, which could mean a number of things.

She could just be stubborn as shit, a flaw I'm certain no one would ever accuse me of. Definitely not. It's possible she just decided that going after the most powerful first was the best course of action and never tried anything else. I can't even say she was wrong to do so, at least until we see how this plays out.

It's also possible she knows exactly what we will find there, and this is some sort of trap. I can't help but notice she is still matching my armor and haircut like a side character on a nineties sitcom. She may not be altogether pleased I made it out alive and still own my own name. Or perhaps she has entirely unknown motivations and I lack the information to discern what they are. In any case, I will work with those working toward the same liberation that I am, but I can't trust Archer. Talking to her is a bit like assembling furniture bought from the internet. While close, too many things just don't line up quite right.

"Wait," I say after a moment. "She doesn't remember her visits to that room at all? Like even a little?" Riley's jaw tightens at the question, and I can see this discussion has already been had. "So she could be in danger. Why didn't we move last night?"

Archer sighs. "We weren't ready. These things take time to arrange." Riley rolls her eyes. These two definitely debated this last night, likely while I was practicing with my new appendages.

"Moron," Riley whispers under her breath.

"I could have come alone. This 'Insect Sage' won't be the first man I killed in their own home. And if he's really that much weaker than Markus as you claim, he won't even be hard to beat. I've been sneaking into fancy estates and putting them on the market for years," I reply. It's hard to believe she would just leave Autumn there after learning that. I know organized responses can't happen in a single night, but we didn't really need to organize in this case.

"Like that? You would have been spotted from halfway across the city," Archer dismisses. "And what happens if these sages, already on edge from the recent news, decide to hold their house staff hostage? What if Autumn's been made and they use her as a hostage? What if they used her to set a trap? These things require planning. Yes, it's another day of danger, but she put herself there, and she didn't ask to leave. We have the highest chance of sparing as many lives as possible. You need to trust your friends. Autumn's a big girl; she can decide what risks to take to give us the best chance of both getting her out and of learning what we can from this sage."

I bite back my response. I would have been fine. I did, in fact, consider visibility and mobility when I chose to make these changes. But she is right about the rest of it. Autumn chose to go there; she explained her willingness to take this risk in great detail. She didn't ask for immediate help, and she is dealing with the exact same thing I had to face years ago. I handled it, and so can she. I just . . .

I left Autumn and Henry. I left them on their own, and Henry died. He died. Waiting and planning while the woman he wanted to marry is in trouble . . . it feels like a betrayal. A repeated mistake. It makes me want to retch. It does, at least, endear Riley to me, that she didn't want to leave her either.

I close my eyes and take a deep breath. We are on our way now. There is no point fighting about it. Not right now. Finally, I open my eyes and lock them on Archer again.

"Fine. So what's the plan, exactly?"

CHAPTER NINE

Spiders and Scorpions

This sage has a lovely garden. *Why do all the rich people in this world have a nice garden?* Half these fuckers are from entirely different worlds, only a few actually come from Earth, and those who do probably didn't have one where they lived. The people have their own countries designed for them to fool around in, and every estate I've ever seen has a fancy-as-fuck garden. Even the school I went to, the whole damn campus was one. Rich assholes love to make other people grow flowers for them. It's like a hobby. Their version of a cell phone game.

I have waited in a lot of gardens over the last few years, crouched behind many a hedge in the dead of night belonging to people who have never touched shears yet somehow take great pride in how immaculately trimmed they are, waiting for them to dismiss their staff and go to sleep in their pointlessly large echoey bedrooms so I could sneak in and, well, murder them.

This one should be no different. If anything, it should be less stressful. I'm not alone. I have a dozen powerful allies, and one or two I even trust. The hedge I'm hiding behind is trimmed like a gargoyle with a huge insectile tail and bat-like wings; I find this coincidence more amusing than I should.

A few years ago, I would have been perfectly calm, blossoming into the woman I was always going to be . . . again. Poison that can kill in under a minute running through my veins, like any other teenage girl. Ready to kill and eat the rich like a good, upstanding citizen.

But this time is different, and I am obviously spiraling. Fuck. I don't want my friend to die. I don't want her to be hurt. I don't want her to have been hurt. And at the same time, I do. Even more now, since she left me alone. Since she stopped grieving with me. It's not her fault, and it's not what she wants, but I'm still fucking furious about it. Again, I find myself extending it to her, offering my grief like she might grab it and follow it back to her own so we can both mourn for my brother again. So we can both promise one more day to the other.

The night is quiet, and the pace of my breathing echoes through this disgustingly nice garden. Waiting for my target to sleep is one thing; waiting for someone else to act while I wait is another. But Archer was right. We need to secure the safety of the innocents inside first. And while I have increased my reliability in combat, I don't think I'm gonna swing the maid's uniform this time.

Strangely, tapping my foot doesn't seem to be making the signal come any faster, nor does twitching my tail, which is an interesting idle habit to discover. Extra appendages are strange. Or . . . are they really extra? I'm three down, three up, so does that even out? Are they extra limbs, or is this like one of those take-a-number things they have at bakeries, where you pull one off and a different one pops up in its place?

A window on the second floor opens, and a green light flashes three times, signaling that my allies have Autumn and every other worker. Thank Christ. I was *this close* to making escargot with garden snails just to distract myself.

Eagerly, I spread my wings. I practiced this all last night. Without a riot spike nearby, I can simply jump, which makes flight much easier, as does a little force mana decreasing my weight. I could maybe jump straight to the window with my current strength, but I have little faith in my precision.

As soon as I start to fall, I flap my wings against the wind, elevating myself again, and close in on the window in only a few seconds, slipping inside with a twist and landing easily on my feet inside the wide foyer that greets me.

"Is that you, Lily?" a familiar voice asks. As I fold my wings against my back, I turn to find Autumn. She took the maid-uniform route, apparently. To each their own, I suppose.

"In the flesh," I answer. She looks at me with wide eyes as she processes the wings and the stinger resting at my feet. The scales, insect eyes, and claws had startled her enough the last time we met, and the tail may have been a bridge too far. For my part, I'm simply relieved to see her alive and well. Sort of well, in any case. She isn't the same since losing her grief. She is happier on a surface level, but she's like an illusion, lacking substance and always out of reach.

Riley clears her throat, and I shift my focus to the other people in the room. Riley and about a half dozen of Archer's abolitionists. Guards decorate the corridor, painting the previously boring walls with a deep red. Ice, stone, and acid burns indicate a fight between mages, and one the abolitionists were better prepared for. Archer herself is nowhere to be found, but that's not so surprising.

My relief at Autumn's safety finally steps aside, allowing me to catch up to the situation at hand.

"Everyone is safe?" I ask.

"As safe as we can make them," Riley confirms. "Autumn did the headcount for us. They're being evacuated through the servants' entrance as we speak."

Again, I let out a sigh of relief. Credit where credit is due, as much as she gets under my skin, Archer knows what she is doing. It was a slow plan, but it was safe. They know how guards are trained. They know what security will respond to and how. Archer knew where the shift sergeant would be and managed to dispatch the rest into a trap while disguised allies joined the household staff, finding Autumn and every other servant to get them to safety, all while we knew the Insect Sage would be in his mysterious room.

An hour in a garden, and none of my worries came to fruition. It was better than I could have managed, obviously the result of experience, training, and familiarity. This is why I miss having an organized group. Amy used to do all my planning for me. In any case, the path has been paved for me. All obstacles and worries have been removed, and I have only one job.

I just need to find and kill a sage.

"Come on, it's this way," Autumn says, waving me over and indicating the hall to my right. Five words, and my worries about an intentional trap melt away. My worries about a mind-control trap powered by divine magic, curiously, do not. But I don't care. Because with this man dead, Autumn will no longer be walking into a room and having her mind taken from her.

I don't care if the only thing that happens in there is a tea party with stuffed animals. A person's mind is their own, and Autumn is my friend.

I follow her with intent, each step through the warm, comfortable mansion warning of the violence I carry on my shoulders. Between the base of my two wings, a red eye flicks back and forth between Riley and the others. Where Riley walks with confidence, the others move with practice. Each step rolls from heel to toe, keeping them steady and silent. Not one of them speaks, all of them here in part to back me up and in part to keep an eye on me.

It doesn't take long to reach the surprisingly subtle door to the blackout room. I can feel the air grow tense with Autumn's anxiety as we stand outside. Pulling a pair of glasses out and putting them on, colors flood my vision as the enchanted glass serves its purpose. It's easy to make out Autumn, Riley, and the others among the colors. No one knows what happens in this room, and I want to be certain the Insect Sage is alone.

He is not. I can't make out any specific occupants, but a sea of constantly shifting colors clouds my perception. "Oh Jesus," I whisper. "The fucking Insect Sage. Right."

"What is it?" Autumn whispers. I give her a sidelong glance. She's been in this room before, and she has no memory of it. It may be more merciful to hide the truth from her.

"Bugs. Thousands of the fuckers," I answer before my brain can catch up to my slightly vindictive motive. I would have had to tell her anyway, but I'm going to have to examine *why* I wanted to. Later. A shiver seizes her body and her face pales. "I doubt he's doing anything weird with them. He just has you delivering meals, right?"

She shudders. "Isn't having them there at all 'doing something weird'?" she asks. I shrug and nod my head in assent.

"Fair enough. But they probably aren't there all the time. I bet he knows we are coming. It would be a waste of his energy to keep this maintained at all times, right?" I reassure. She shudders again, but nods. "Anyway, stay out here, all of you. Riley, try and stop any creepy-crawlies from escaping the room. They could be disease carriers, could be going after the people evacuating, or they could try and kill the rest of you. Better if you, you know, deleted them," I say.

"You're going in there alone?" Autumn asks, a very slight tremor in her voice.

"Moron," Riley scoffs.

"Well, I'm overdue for a maggot infestation, it turns out. We'll call this a bill coming due," I reply. I don't wait for the questions this quip will prompt, instead throwing a rapid burst of force mana at the door, knocking it off its hinges even as I step toward it. I am inside before it lands, and a wall of white mana replaces it behind me.

"So you're here," the lone man inside spits. His hand is on what appears to be some kind of permanently installed scepter with a long steel base embedded in the ground and a rounded top. "You'll regret interrupting—" He turns and sees me, his eyes bulging as they take me in. Wings spread to my sides, my tail crushes his insects while heat mana burns any who try to get close. His jaw hangs for a moment before he moves his hand and throws every ounce of Nexus energy he can at me.

Insects spawn in greater numbers all around me, resistant to the heat I have been burning them with. They swarm me, crawling all over my body. Or at least they try. The disgusting swarm fails to get purchase on most of my body, since my armor is enchanted with force and their legs keep slipping off. My steel limbs offer nothing to bite, chitin protects my tail, and my scales protect my exposed flesh on all but my face, which a little focused mana keeps them from.

They are heat resistant, so I take their heat, and frozen bugs slide down my body. Leeches and spiders bite into my wings, but they are rewarded only with cancerous cells and poisonous blood. They ingest the blood and the activating protein at the same time and fall dead just as quickly as they bite. Cancer cells are easy to regenerate, and the wings heal faster than they take damage.

"I thought you were the Insect Sage," I scoff.

"What?" he asks incredulously. "How are you not dead already?"

I don't answer. Instead, I run forward with urgency and the intent to kill. I am at the doorway one moment and face-to-face with him the next, my stinger plunging into his side and filling him with venom while picking him up in the same motion. I dig the claws of my left hand into his throat, offering another type of venom. "Leeches aren't insects, you fucking worm. Neither are spiders. I am begging you to take a goddamn biology class. This shit is just disrespectful."

His veins bulge as his Nexus energy struggles to heal him. Bugs all around the room start to die as he refocuses all his power on staying alive.

He is losing. I don't even need my other poisons if I want this to be quick, which I do, but I need to ask a few questions first. Then, all of a sudden, my compound eye picks up massive movement from all sides—praying mantises as tall as I am, all attacking at once. He still has some energy to spare, I suppose.

In a breath, I bury my stinger deeper into his torso as I release his throat, using my tail to swing him like a bludgeon and crushing the mantis on my left. I catch the blades on the right with my arm and continue moving the sage with my tail, intercepting the attack from behind with his body. A moment later, bolts of lightning erupt from me, ensuring the death of all three insects of unusual size. One bolt even travels through the sage and back to me, but I just reabsorb the mana.

"What have you been doing in here?" I snarl as the sage coughs blood. I violently swing my tail around, positioning the dying man back in front of me. "What memories have you taken from my friends?"

The man's body convulses as fear grips him. "I—I just—I just didn't want any servants to remember the relay. I didn't do anything to them, I swear!" He coughs up blood as he answers.

"And what is the relay?" I interrogate. He chokes but shakes his head.

"Just kill me," he says, coughing again. I can see it in his eyes. Fear. Not of me and not of death but of something worse. I click my tongue; I've pushed this as far as I am willing to. If it weren't for sages and their healing, I wouldn't have done even this much. Whatever the other sages are threatening him with, I can tell at a glance I'm not getting an answer.

"Fine," I reply. "Just remember that your death will bring nothing but celebration to anyone." I grab his head in both hands. I don't need to twist this time; I am stronger now. I just pull in one direction with my tail and the other with my arms, and hot blood decorates my face and armor as bone snaps and flesh tears. One more sage is dead.

I stare at the artifact in the center of the room, surrounded by blood and insect remains. I don't know how, but I can feel it. August was right. Whatever this creep was doing with it, it's related to the emotional assault on the people in this country.

"One step closer, Autumn," I whisper. "Stay with me for just one more day. We will grieve together again. Soon."

CHAPTER TEN

A Fragile Mask

I'd assumed Archer was involved in evacuation efforts or keeping watch, or maybe directing the whole thing via whisper sphere. Although, I suppose if she had the spheres to spare, I wouldn't have needed a signal to enter. After killing the sage, however, she was nowhere to be found. I didn't see her until we made it back to her base, and she had little interest in elaborating on her whereabouts during the raid. "Everyone has their role to play," she said. *Yeah, and sometimes they tell each other what that is, fuckwad.*

Once we visited the first of the sages August had identified, we decided it was worth investigating the others as well. And by "we" I do mean Archer. For a woman who is not in charge, everyone around her certainly is obstinate about waiting for her approval before doing jack shit. I was irritated by this, but repeatedly reminded myself that I have been perceived in a similar manner in the past. It can be difficult to distinguish between organizational direction and authoritarian leadership from the outside.

Especially when you have a stubborn thorn of pride living in your heart and some part of you is simply frustrated it isn't your own direction they are waiting for.

Thank God I don't have that problem.

Frustrations aside, we did decide to move on to the other estates, starting with August's and then Ember's. Neither had reported similar experiences, but both had found different positions on their respective sage's staff, assigned mostly based on gender and species, apparently. Ember was a hunter and August a kitchen boy. Neither saw the sage they were spying on terribly frequently, but it wouldn't be safe to leave either there for long after the Insect Sage.

Insignificant as they may have been to sages like Oakley, each of them did hold enough power to ruin the average civilian's life. And each of them exercised this power liberally. August had gone to work for the Lust Sage; I can only imagine why neither of the women chose to infiltrate that particular estate. Investigation revealed his power would break on physical contact, like a more targeted version of standard mind control. This didn't stop him from using his Nexus energy to steal and destroy lives. He may not have been as salacious as his title implied, but he was more than willing to have a husband killed if a pretty wife didn't laugh at his joke.

He called the artifact he was using a *conductor* instead of a *relay*. His powers of persuasion didn't spare him from the venom I spit nor the lightning I coursed through him though. August was relieved to leave the kitchen and more relieved to see his sister safe. Afterward, the news and rumors around town were undecided. No one was certain if he was the sage or not; the corpse they found was too charred to be identified. And again, I couldn't find Archer until we returned to base.

Sara still hadn't answered a single call. I was worried about her, worried about what was keeping her. I was sick, with fever chills every night and sweat every morning. I was miserable and, as grateful as I was to finally have reliable allies, I just couldn't bring myself to like them. I needed to hold Sara. I needed to scream at her. I needed her to tell me it was all going to be okay. I needed to tell her it wasn't. I wasn't going to survive this fight. I needed Autumn to grieve with me again. I needed her to need me, to make it through one more day. And I hated that need.

The city grew restless. Guardians of Stone filled the streets after too many sages had died in too short a time. The Void Sage had come back, and he was reportedly searching for me. People were afraid and rumors were everywhere. Some people feared the demon queen; some thought it was the Council and were using me as a cover. There were rumors of new sages attacking at random and of demons biting off hands in bars.

Ember came back on her own. New staff were being interrogated and investigated at every sage's estate, especially at our remaining targets' homes. On the bright side, this more or less confirmed August's theory. On the less bright side, they were increasing security, and we'd lost our woman on the inside. Also, we had Ember back. She's helpful and all, but goddamn is she a little shit. Crawled up my ass the second she returned.

I had to fight from the beginning when we assaulted her sage. He knew we would be coming and was prepared. The Plague Sage, he was called. Strong compared to the other two, if weak compared to Markus. Any of my allies who approached grew sick, and it was too dangerous to even enter the building for everyone but me. He had nothing to throw at me that could contend with cancer.

His guards were more difficult to fight than him. I admittedly had to pause a few times to empty my stomach as his Nexus energy assaulted me, but the dead don't have to fear the flu. Not really. He was trying to affect my body directly and bring me closer to death, but his power was eaten alive by Sara's. He couldn't know he was up against a far more powerful sage, and stirring an already upset stomach was the most fearsome thing he could do.

He was the first to have riot spikes prepared, but I flew out of their range and rained lightning down on every defenseless mage below. His guards may have feared him, but not enough to remain defenseless against a demonic mage throwing hell at them from the sky. The blood dripping from every part of me only enhanced the effect started by my wings and tail. The riot spikes were quickly deactivated, which offered them several extra minutes of life.

Once I found him, the Plague Sage wasn't with his artifact. Instead, he was hiding. In a fucking closet. While sending his guards to die. While sending sickness to enemies and innocents alike, he was hiding in a closet. Cashmere pants were darkened with urine as my blood-soaked visage tore the accordion door off its hinges.

Even he feared the consequences of telling me what his fucking artifact was for, but he did have one. He died while begging, promising to stop "feeding," but I'd read about the families he'd hurt. The homes he'd cleared out with sickness to cheapen the price of land. The crowded graveyards written off as a spike in a yearly statistic. My stinger continued filling him with poison as force mana crushed his skull. It was too merciful a death for him, but I had neither the time nor the mentality to extend his death as he had done to his victims.

Archer was missing again when I emerged. She didn't appear until after I'd bathed, and she was only just returning. I didn't bother asking where she'd disappeared to, and she didn't bother asking how I was doing. She was still dressed in armor matching mine, and the excuse she'd first presented was wearing thin. She didn't seem to like me much more than I liked her, even if we were both willing to work with each other. She did, however, seem to want a strong association with me.

I didn't have the energy to ask why. I had a few theories, but things were changing too quickly in the city to investigate them, especially since I couldn't go outside during the day. The desire to wander the city freely had contributed to my disastrous arena plan, but that desire was now dead, ever since I discovered I was as well. I sacrificed it for an advantage in combat, which was worth it, but I now have to rely on the twins, Ember, and Riley to relay local news to me.

I still haven't heard from Sara. Every night as I struggle to sleep through the fever, the worst possible reasons drift through my mind. I know she's alive, or I'd be nothing but a cold corpse in a too-warm bed. But I have a mother. I have more brothers, and I have friends. So does Sara. She never found Leo and Charlotte. Alpha could have used them to lure her in, to capture her again. Torture her again. She could be the only one left. She could be trapped again.

It is all too much, and all I can do every single day is kill and then grieve alone. And kill. And grieve. And kill. And grieve.

It's only been a week. How has it only been a week? It feels like this cycle has been going for months. All the blood and the sick. I walk out of this room, and I tell my jokes. I throw my quips like superglue in place of stitches and smile and laugh and wear the face of the fearless spear. And they feel safer. They feel more confident. They lean on the implacable stones I provide like a pillar, and I can only crumble on the inside.

I sob in the dark and smile in the light. I shiver in my bed, and I won't be moved in the light of day. And the pressure builds. I can only sleep on my side now as I clutch a pillow to my chest, desperate for anything to hold that won't reveal my weakness to the world. I need Sarafyna. I need Henry. I need Autumn to grieve like I grieve. I bite into my lower lip, desperate for the lone-liness to fade, begging for Autumn to feel this with me. In the dark room, I bargain inside my own heart. I offer more pain. More sickness. A shorter life. Anything to have Sara again. Anything for Autumn to grieve as I grieve.

Because if she doesn't, I don't know if I can make it one more day. I don't know who to promise one more day to. But I do this every night, and I somehow make it through, then I bargain again. I don't sleep for hours, and I wake up with red eyes. When I hear the first knock, I assume I'm imagining it. On the second, I ignore it. I can't show this face to anyone; I need to be strong and determined. The cracks are too obvious right now.

I don't know why, on the third knock, I decide to answer anyway. It's just knuckles on wood. Nothing more than that. My mana responds to them, but I hardly notice it. I'm already drowning, and it doesn't register as significant in my weary mind. There is nothing else to indicate it's worth the risk of showing someone my actual state. But I do. I climb to my feet, shamble across the room, and open the door. Tears leave irritated streaks down my cheeks, and my arms tremble as the door swings open.

Autumn stands on the other side, and she looks exactly the same. Tears, snot, and shoulders convulsing from too much crying. My breath catches as I examine the grieving woman, and relief washes over me like gentle waves on the shore.

"One more day?" she asks. I don't know what changed; I don't know how she got her grief back, but it doesn't matter as I wrap my arms around her.

"One more day," I agree.

"What happened?" August asks as, once again, we take a wagon to a sage's estate—the Dream Sage tonight, one of the ones he'd marked as suspicious along with all the others. His eyes flick back and forth between Autumn and me.

I give him a friendly grin in response. "Nothing to worry about," I answer. And I mean it. For the first time since Markus locked me in that cage with Riley, my smile is genuine. It's a flooded smile, like the city after a storm, exhausted and quiet—but it is genuine. I still feel sick. I still hurt. But I finally don't feel alone.

Maybe killing those sages made the effect not as strong now. No one else seems to have changed, but Autumn was affected more recently. Of course, she isn't wearing it on her sleeve any more than I am, but I would know if anyone else had started grieving. Whatever the cause, I'm not alone anymore, and that's enough to hold this fragile mask together for one more day.

"What do you mean?" Riley asks. It's a good question. August picked up on the change pretty quickly despite no outward signs, likely because his twin sister is affected. The others don't seem to notice.

"Who gives a shit?" Ember dismisses. "Let's just get this done and get some sleep."

"Ember, you literally slept through the last raid. Also, coming here and killing these guys was your idea. No need to be such a prickly little pear about everything," I chide.

"That would be a mild insult from anyone but you," Autumn notes, eliciting a small chuckle from four of the five occupants of this wagon. Everyone but Ember. Autumn and I are still on . . . interesting terms, but something has shifted. Some spark of the friendship we had when Henry was alive has returned.

We didn't see each other for long last night. I stopped grieving for myself, replacing my mask and comforting her when she came to see me. It was only a few minutes, really, but afterward, I didn't feel alone, and she didn't feel helpless. For a while, she'd lost her grief, and I'd lost the only person I knew who could understand how I felt from every angle. My family understands the loss of Henry, and Charlotte, wherever she is, may understand the guilt. But only Autumn knows both. Losing that and getting it back . . . it has numbed the anger and stoked a small fire of camaraderie. Like a candle. And like a candle, it melts a little more the longer it burns.

Ember scoffs and rolls her eyes. "What are we dealing with this time?" she asks, changing the subject. She always does that when anyone seems to be having a nice time, even if just a little.

I sigh but answer. We do need to talk about all this before we get too close, so I relay the information I got from Archer.

"The Dream Sage. He's been known to induce sleep and give you nightmares, or if you can fight off sleep, waking hallucinations. He famously uses this to gaslight, well, everyone. A low-level piece of shit, but I suspect we will have more than him to deal with. Archer is really pushing for daily raids for some reason. Which, you know, quick and timely action is nice, but it makes us predictable. I'm not sure if my aspect will protect me from this one like it did with the Lust Sage. I recommend we all cycle mana a little to stay awake, and don't go in shooting right away. They are slow to catch on that we care about their staff more than they do, but they will put the pieces together eventually," I explain.

Ember bristles at the mention of dreams but says nothing. It's hard to miss hackles raised that high though, and I remember her struggles with nightmares in the past.

"You can sit this one out if you need to," I offer. She glares at me.

"Let's just get this over with," she replies.

We discuss how to prepare ourselves for the rest of the ride, but it turns out to be a waste of time. The wagon comes to a sudden halt, and my own hackles rise. I can see the same thought on everyone's faces. It's too soon and too sudden. Unlike some other wagons, we can't address the driver directly from the back of this one, since we needed one that would hide me completely, but our fears are confirmed anyway before any of us have the chance to investigate.

"Lillith of Endings!" a man shouts from outside the wagon. "It is time to face judgment for your sins! Surrender now, and we won't hand you over to the Void Sage!"

"Fuck," I whisper. The faces around me are stone; afraid but determined. "Let me go first; I'll buy time. If I need help fighting, well, you'll know." I receive a round of nods, then move the curtain on the back of the wagon, jumping out.

I groan as I look at our surroundings. We are in the middle of an empty road, not a single other cart in sight. The buildings around us are dark and abandoned. There are dozens of faces I recognize, if only from drawings; lesser and mid-level sages, the Dream Sage among them.

God fucking dammit. I lean on my tail just in time as the riot spike activates.

"What can I help you gentlemen with? If it's directions, I'm afraid I'm a bit new in town myself."

The man at the front, the Swift Sage, I think, smirks. "You can die without fighting back, and we'll spare your friends," he replies. I snort.

"No, you fucking won't. That's the stupidest thing I've ever heard. What am I gonna do, check in after you kill me? Is my corpse going to cross its arms and give you a disappointed stare if you kill my friends anyway?" I ask. I mean, that's exactly what is happening, but they don't need to know that. "Come on, buddy. What's your game here?"

The Swift Sage smirks, then shrugs.

"It was worth a shot. I suppose we'll have to fight you. Not what we wanted, but mostly because of the damage to the city. We aren't alone this time; you can't pick us off in our homes. You have all of us to face at once. It would really have been easier to just comply," he says.

"So they keep telling me." I shrug. "I guess I'm just something of a dimwit. Never did figure out what was so 'easy' about complying with sad and petty tyrants."

Neither of us hesitates after that. I use my tail to launch myself forward, catching the wind in my wings as I close the distance while he moves as quickly as he can to respond. Being the Swift Sage, I expect this to be pretty fast. It is not. He fumbles for a second and still looks confused when my claws sink into his throat. He heals from neither the venom nor the torn throat and falls dead as we both collide with cobblestone.

"Uh . . . what?"

I am so taken aback by the lack of resistance, I don't move off him as quickly as I planned. I am also not bombarded with dozens of reality-bending spells from different sages. The air is quiet and cold, only the spurting blood indicating that time hasn't stopped.

"And how, exactly," Sarafyna says, "do you plan on hurting my girlfriend?"

CHAPTER ELEVEN

Dead or Alive

God, Sarafyna is hot.

Probably not a healthy takeaway, that. Her divine magic crushed all the lesser sages' power the moment she arrived, and not one of them ever went through the boring and tedious task of earning mana. Their trap was, apparently, too obvious. I should be thanking them, really, if they are the ones who helped Sara find me.

People are still talking about Markus's death and that of every subsequent sage, so tonight is going to be one for the history books. A massacre. Dozens of the city's sages missing. Not dead in the streets—missing. Because the eldritch girl I'm going home with tonight doesn't leave a lot of evidence. Sara showed up exactly when I needed her, as she always does. She painted herself across the battlefield, and no one who threatened me remained. I fought as well, of course, as did everyone else in the wagon. But none of us moved like a song.

Our driver, one of the abolitionists, fled, which was strange, considering the bravery I'd seen from this group before. Especially since he seemed to run *after* it was clear we had the upper hand. But it did open up an extra seat in the wagon, and given that Ember doesn't like any of us much anyway, she volunteered to take the driver's place, allowing Sara to join us. Sara and I were both exempt from driving, since we are both, apparently, wanted criminals. There was some discussion on where we should actually move from there, the Dream Sage now living in the brilliant and sharp scars running all along my girlfriend's body.

We tried to contact Archer, but curiously, our whisper spheres stopped working altogether. In such cases, we'd agreed to regroup back at base rather than press forward. This, in theory, prevented more chaos than we could plan for. It makes sense when working with such a large group. It's something I often planned for in another life. Somehow, it still feels alien.

So that's where we are going. As usual, I have to use my own tail as a seat at one end of the wagon, while Sara sits on a bench in the corner on the other side. Not because we don't want to be near each other but because we want to *see* each other.

I feel a thousand emotions as I examine my girlfriend. She's wearing a torn, bloody dress and biting one nail. I've tried so many times to design more practical clothes for her, but she loves her dresses. Her scars are practically glowing with how they stand out in this moment. She shines with the confidence of a woman who knows exactly who and what she is. She's a mosaic of beauty and fear.

I am *so happy* to see her. And so afraid and hurt and relieved. She has been lying to me. She has been caring for me. She has thrown herself into keeping me alive, at least in a way. I feel a thousand things, but I have been hanging by a thread, and she just turned it into a rope. Just by being here. I don't have it in me to yell or accuse; I just want to hold her. The argument can wait.

She looks back at me with kaleidoscope eyes, reflecting just as much relief and worry as she examines my body. The scales and the eyes don't bother her at all. She glides off them the same way I do when she changes. But the wings and the tail—she can feel them; she knows what they cost me. At no point have I worried about becoming less attractive to her, but I see a part of her recoil from these changes. Because she isn't looking at wings and a tail—she is looking at the self-harm I poured into them.

"How long have your spheres been broken?" she finally asks. "I've been trying to call for over a week. I knew you were here, but I couldn't contact you." The way her voice wavers has more to do with the sickness she can feel eating away at me than concern over our whisper spheres.

"We've been trying to call you too for weeks," Autumn cuts in.

"They were working fine to contact each other until just now," August agrees. Sara's brow furrows at that, mirroring my own. Something about that rings false. I want to say something, but it's like a rope is tightening around my neck and my voice can't escape. I was able to speak before, when we were fighting. When adrenaline pushed us together and demanded action. But now, on a quiet ride through the city—nothing.

"Let me see," Sara says, holding a hand out. August offers his sphere, which she readily accepts. She barely looks at it before saying, "I didn't make this one. Its power must have been washed away by my presence. Did you lose your originals?" The twins share a glance.

"Um, Archer took our things for a while when we first met. Just so we wouldn't need to carry them," August offers.

"Rochelle Archer?" Sara clarifies.

"Yes, how did you know her first name?" Autumn asks. Sara looks confused for a moment before her eyes lock on mine again.

"I've been looking for you constantly since I got here. It took me a bit, since I've had to stay out of sight. I, uh, had an incident when I first got here; the Void Sage has been searching for me since. Made it a bit obvious a hostile sage or demon or whatever they want to call me had shown up," Sara answers, blushing a little bit. "But I've been able to pay attention to the news; I like the way they distribute it on paper here. The sages dying every night had An—Lily's name written all over them. Well, not literally. Literally, Rochelle Archer's name has been written all over them."

The hairs on my arms rise as she says this. Some pieces are starting to slide into place, but not enough of them. I try to speak again, but shame stops me. I'm not even sure what I am ashamed of, but I recognize the feeling. I need to get Sara alone. I need to ask her why. And I need to ignore the answer so I can take my mask off in front of her. But until then, all I can do is keep my eyes locked on hers.

Riley chimes in on my behalf. "They have her name?"

Sara cocks her head at the unfamiliar speaker but nods. Introductions can wait.

"Of course they do; she made sure of it. If she didn't, everyone would think she was Lillith," Sara replies. "I would have, too. They only distribute drawings to identify either of you. The hair, the piercings, the angry eyes. All of her portraits look like Lillith to the point where many people are confused about which is which. Lily has so many names: Lily. Annie. Cordelia, for some reason I have failed to discern. But this woman, she's always the same: Rochelle Archer. It's always clear, and it's always next to that drawing."

"What do you mean *always?*" Autumn asks.

"Well, I mean every morning. Each night, when one of the sages dies, Archer makes a public appearance somewhere where her words can be recorded, but also where she can escape if a sage is spotted nearby. She announces who she wants to kill and why, and the next morning, her face and speech are spread like fire through sagebrush. She is drawing a strong association between herself, Lillith's image, and the deaths of the sages. She is trying to recruit people, I think. And if she is to be believed, it has been working. Every night, she says the abolitionists have grown by dozens at least," Sara explains.

I think back to our days in the base. I spend much of the time in my room, unable to wear my mask for too long, but considering it, I *have* seen a few new faces. Mostly among the staff we help retrieve from each estate. I didn't even notice at the time, but I can pick them out in my memory.

A few more pieces click into place, like the lock of a safe. I still struggle to speak. Sara's eyes rarely leave mine, and they maintain concern the entire time. The conversation continues for some time as Sara avoids answering why she is now wanted throughout the city. I assume Alpha is looking for her, although I'm unsure why. He seems obsessed with her. Of course, it doesn't explain the adorable blush every time she avoids the subject.

I am trapped in my head for the rest of the ride back. Sara and I still don't speak, both of us with something holding us back. When we enter the old warehouse, we are greeted by a skeleton crew. While we are assured that everyone is safe and they recovered the fourth artifact, it remains eerily quiet. Archer must be off giving another speech, if Sara is right.

A public presence is important, I won't deny that. Still, something about the way she is doing it doesn't sit right. The way she tries to wear my face and her name, the timing of it . . . I don't like it. But I am covered in sage blood and all I really care about is the redhead behind me. We don't have to speak. When we all go our separate ways, Sara follows me to the room I've been staying in.

The air is thick with tension, and a thousand words hide down each of our throats. I don't have water mana anymore, but a shower is still possible with the tank installed on the warehouse roof. Makeshift pipes and gravity provide the water while my mana provides heat and pressure.

Sara and I both undress, still a little shy around the other but familiar enough that it doesn't call for a notable reaction. She has devoured any blood that touched her, but we step into my room's large steel basin together. Still, we don't speak, even as water runs down our bodies. Even as I turn bloodied water to steam at our feet. We silently scrub each other's backs as Sara runs trembling hands across my wings and tail.

We spend a lot of time in that shower, letting the heat melt our nerves. Neither of us says when we are done, we simply understand. We step out, and heat mana dries us both. My bed is just a wide mat on the floor, and we crawl under the thin blanket together. Facing each other, I bury my head into her shoulder while she holds me with one arm as our legs overlap. I wrap my tail and left wing around her, pulling her close, and we remain quiet for several more minutes while I build up my courage. She is holding me; I am safe, and I am with the one person who doesn't need me to stay strong. I nearly choke on the words, so I opt for a whisper instead.

"Why did you lie to me?" I ask. I feel her tense up, then relax. She doesn't ask me what I mean. She doesn't deny anything. She slides her arm up my back and runs one hand through my hair. She knows what I'm talking about, and she has no interest in excuses. Her answer is simple.

"Because, my love, I don't want you to die," she whispers back. My eyes start to water.

"But I already am, aren't I?" I ask. "Dead?" She keeps running her hand through my hair.

"Are you? I've never met anyone so alive." While one of her arms is around me, mine are up against my own chest, separating us just a little. They tighten at this.

"No. I'm barely alive, Sara. I am a ghost in the lives of my friends. A ghost pretending to be stone. But eventually, someone is going to try to touch me, and their hand will pass right through me. My body may look alive, but I'm not. And even that will fail if you stop pulling me along behind you," I say.

Sara takes a deep breath through her nose. "No," she denies, "you are no ghost. No one is, not even the people in this country, unable to so much as grieve. Not even the Collector. Not even Henry. I can see why you think this; I can feel it. I know why you made these wings and this tail. I know how. I can see the pain dragging you further toward the grave every day. But you are no ghost. You are a dammed river. Rapids with nowhere to go.

"Maybe everything won't fall apart if someone tries to touch you. Maybe one day they will, and it will only prove how solid you really are.

Maybe you are just so afraid of people passing through you if you don't give them the right face at the right time that you have forgotten you are neither ghost nor stone but fire, warm and violent and burning through me. You are so alive, Annie. And not just because I let you age and bleed. You are alive even when you die. Someday, you're going to have to let yourself acknowledge that."

I turn my head, water flowing from my eyes to Sara's collarbone. "It's not that simple. I know I am dead now. I know it in every fiber of my being. You are spending so much of yourself to keep me here. So much it hurts me just knowing. And I deserved to know that, Sara. I deserved to know."

"Yes," Sara agrees. "You did. I should have told you. I knew what you would do. I knew you would want to accept that death if it meant saving one more person. I knew you would ask me to let you die so I can be strong enough to stop all the sages or kings or anyone else. I was terrified of that. But yes, I should have told you. It was cowardly not to."

I tense again. "And?" I ask. "If I told you to let me die, could you? If I asked you to let me go and use all that power to help people, would you do that?"

"No." Her words are final and offer no room for argument. "I'm more selfish than you. I know how much you love people. I know how desperately you want everyone safe. And I will fight alongside you every step of the way because nothing matters to you like that does. I even understand it, because I feel the same. But where you carry the world on your shoulders, I am what the world offers in return. I care just as desperately, but about you. I will fight just as hard, not for the world but for you. Annie, I love you. I love you like I'm gasping for air. I will carry you until I die."

"She wants to leave, you know. Mirage. The woman or man or . . . entity who gives you your power. She has lived a life like yours; a victim of the same abuser. And she wants to leave this world behind. Everyone is going to lose her power, do you understand? Winning and dying—they are the same thing for me. Maybe I'm not a ghost. Maybe my body is close enough to 'alive.' But in order to live, I have to give up. I have to stop. And that would be the same as dying to me. Which means, either way, I am dead. I spend each day walking toward death. Can you still fight with me knowing that? Can you still carry me if you know there is nothing at the end of this path for me? No future?" I whisper.

"I don't give a single shit," she practically hisses, pulling me closer. "I don't care. This 'Mirage' wants to leave? That's fine. I'm going to lose my strength? That's fine too. But you aren't going to die, Annie. Not as long as I can so much as breathe."

"That's just not possible," I reply.

"None of this is. But we don't accept the options given to us as the best we can get. If we did, you would be married to Baldwin, and I'd be living as part of the Collector. Leo would go by Eleonor, and kings would rule Potestia. I am going to fight with you, not despite your death but because I am going to stop it," she insists. I love her. She is so beautiful in every way. But I don't believe her.

I let myself cry. I don't care that she lied, I realize. I just don't. Because she is wrong, and I *am* going to die. I just want to be with her. "I wish I could believe that too," I reply.

"You will, someday," she promises. I wish that were true. I really do.

"It doesn't matter," I finally say. "Thank you for being here again. I needed you. I needed to cry. And I needed to be loved while I did. Thank you."

She presses her hand against the back of my head, hugging it against her chest. "Always," she promises. We are quiet for a long time after that. I want to sleep, but something stops me.

"When?" I ask, some desperate ember deep in my heart grasping at hope.

"When what?"

"When will I believe it?"

She is quiet. Then she pulls away, just a little, so she can look me in the eyes. Her yellow eyes are just as glassy as mine. "You are strong, Annie. It's not a mask. You aren't pretending. You just . . . keep your mana invisible," she says.

"What does that even mean?" I chuckle through tears.

"It means you work so hard to put on a brave face, to look strong and infallible, but you never had to pretend. I'm saying someday you are going to let yourself cry in front of a stranger. When you do that, I think maybe you'll believe it. You'll believe that you can—and should—be saved."

CHAPTER TWELVE

Flirting and Brooding

But they are all okay?" I ask. My voice is quiet and gentle, resting against the cold floors and hallways like smoke. Last night may not have made everything better, but it calmed a storm I couldn't see through. I am still sick. I am still guilty. But I can find north as long as Sara is here.

"They are," Sara responds, just as gently. "Gilbert, especially, seems to be doing well." We are walking through the eerily quiet hallways of the usually bustling abolitionist base. She's been updating me on everything happening back home. Fucking Alpha is fighting a war on multiple fronts, it seems.

"And Mom?" I press. Sara's face falls like autumn leaves. It's slow, almost beautiful in a way, but it ends up in the same place.

"She's scared. She doesn't want to lose you, Lillith." There are a thousand words in Sara's choice to use the name "Lillith" in that sentence, and each one burns like the sun. Mom is afraid of losing me, Lillith. Not me, Annie. I don't know what Sara said to her, but a shackle around my throat loosens at the words—until I remember she has every right to be afraid. She is going to lose me. I need to move on. I can't dwell on it.

"What about Ed?" I ask. A small smile returns to my girlfriend's face.

"He's good. Mariah is due soon, I think. Things were a little touch and go for a bit before I got there, but he fought hard. You'd be proud of him. He wouldn't rest and risk anyone innocent being hurt," she answers. She pauses for a moment and takes a deep breath before continuing. "Almost got himself killed—like you would have—but one of the bards stepped in and saved him," she elaborates a bit more, happy to move on from the subject of my mother.

"Oh? Which one? I didn't think they'd be volunteering to help anytime soon," I reply.

"Viola, I think," she replies, then pauses. "No, sorry, Octavia. She had a friend named Viola, before. I always forget because Octavia is the one who plays the violin."

"Oh, the one with the braids, right? I remember her; she's cute. We gave her a leg like mine."

Sara raises an eyebrow. "Oh, cute, is she?" she teases. I chuckle a bit, completely unworried about any actual jealousy.

"Yeah, a bit. You know, like, I'd kiss her, but not with tongue," I explain.

Sara chokes on a laugh. "What kind of metric is that?" I just smile at her. It feels good to just joke, not like I usually do but with someone I actually like. To just chat for a few minutes without worrying about anything.

"So," I lilt, casually drifting into a subject that has been silently bothering me since last night, "you never did say how you got yourself on Oakley's radar?"

"Oakley?" she asks. I narrow my eyes.

"The Void Sage; don't change the subject."

She sighs. "Look, he wanted to have sex with me," she says, as if that was anything like an explanation.

"The Void Sage?" I balk.

"No, the man in the bar," she answers. I look at her, this beautiful woman who says such kind, passionate, and emotionally intelligent things to me. Red is rising on her face like a thermometer.

"Gonna need you to connect some dots for me on this one, sweetheart." I laugh. She turns a deeper shade of red.

"This peculiar man wanted to have sex, I'm pretty sure, and he didn't like it when I politely declined. He tried to grab me and, well, I maybe bit off a few fingers. With my shoulder," she admits.

I actually snort, ironically putting my hand on her shoulder to steady myself. "Well, to be fair, that's not that different to—"

"Oh, shut up," Sara interrupts, the red flushing down into her chest. "The point is, that incident sort of gave away the game. Apparently, women aren't allowed to be sages. Or bite off fingers, I guess, but that was clearly the lesser of my sins. I've been hiding from the Void Sage ever since, peeking my head out to get news about you."

"Ah," I say. "Yeah, a lot of positions of power have rules against being hot and interesting. You were doomed from the start." Sara nods in begrudging assent, then glances around the nearly empty hall.

"You did say this place was usually busy, right?" she asks. I glance around, taking stock of my environment properly. It is the same weary building I've stayed in for a week, but with a fraction of the activity. I've been enjoying Sara's presence so much, but she's right. There are even fewer people around than last night.

I am also in a better state of mind than I was last night. I'm considerably more stable after falling asleep next to Sarafyna and after simply enjoying her presence today. And—stable as I am—my concern over the emptiness peaks. Sara and I wander for a few more minutes, then flag down the first person we see, a lone man busily packing up supplies.

"What's going on?" I ask. He startles before turning around and glowering. I don't miss his pointed glance at Sarafyna before he steadies and answers me.

"We're moving to a new base," he answers. "Archer decided it wasn't safe here after last night."

"Ah. Of course. How kind of you to inform us before we fell asleep, butt-ass naked and vulnerable. It was a much better time to learn than, say, by chance the next morning," I chide. His eyes follow my tail as it flicks in irritation, a movement which is far more catlike than scorpion. It is an entirely inappropriate habit to develop with such a threatening appendage.

"That's beyond my purview," he replies. "But you're as safe as you would have been anywhere else. Archer was concerned that your presence, being the most obvious target of the sages, was a danger to the rest of us. She felt it would be better if we were based in separate locations."

"But . . ." I trail off as my complaints over this assault on reason stumble over each other. I have to stop and take a deep breath while Sara steps in.

"Is there someone still here who can explain what's going on exactly?" Sara asks. The man shrugs.

"Not really. I think Archer said she'd be in touch before the last raid. That's all I can tell you." He then picks up the case he was packing and casually continues down the hall. I am speechless for a moment.

"We need a more private place to talk," I say while Sara nods.

"We could fly up to the rafters. No one else will make it up there without great trouble," she suggests. I glance at her dress.

"You should really consider some outfits that show a little more skin.

Growing wings would be a lot easier with armor like mine," I suggest, gesturing at my midriff.

"I'm certain you have only pure intentions behind such a suggestion, but don't worry, I'll figure it out," she replies.

"Two things can be true, Sara. That's just math," I quip. She laughs but ultimately ignores me, leading me out to a more open part of the warehouse. I show off my new wings, jumping and making something of a show out of my bat-like flight through the air. As I land on the sturdy wooden pillar, well out of earshot of anyone below, I smirk down at Sara. Or at where Sara was standing when I took off. I nearly fall as she taps my shoulder, spider legs already disappearing into her dress. A more graceful solution, I suppose.

"I'd have seen that coming if I hadn't kept my shoulder eye closed." I pout.

"I'm sure," she replies, her voice carrying the tone one might use with a child. I roll my eyes but the smile below them betrays the gesture. I love being around Sara so much. I always have. It doesn't last forever, but it always feels like the world has more color when she's in the room. I feel more like myself; who I was before Henry . . .

We both feel the shift in the air as I accidentally remind myself of the way I failed my brother. Well. That's not what matters now. We have more important things to discuss.

"It doesn't make sense," I start. Her expression shifts to match mine as we move to the more important topic at hand. "None of it makes sense."

"I haven't met this Archer yet, but it does seem strange. There are only two of us, a half dozen if you count our friends. But she moved her entire group rather than moving us? Aren't that many people moving at once a bit suspicious? I mean, it's exactly how I found you. A big mass of divine magic from too many sources, and all in one place. It's a pretty big risk," she notes.

"Exactly," I agree. "There is just no way that's the call she makes. Either this place is compromised and we all need to leave, or the only sensible thing to do would have been to send our group somewhere else. She did neither. And it's not subtle either. She'll know we are gonna be suspicious as fuck, which means this was an act of desperation."

"Desperation for what?" Sara asks. I am quiet as I think for a moment, considering everything I have seen Archer do. Every little detail that didn't add up, the swapped whisper spheres that wouldn't connect to Sara's, the driver who fled not when we were surrounded but when we started to win. Archer's interviews and her creepy-ass *me* costume. The impressive recruitment rate after every raid. Her laser focus on the most powerful sages, leaving an obvious route to victory alone and undiscovered for years.

I think I know exactly the type of woman I am dealing with.

"She wants to hide something from us," I answer. "Something important enough that it's worth burning this bridge. Or risk it, at least. Something bad enough that she will move her entire fucking group in a single night. They must have rushed out of here to be so absent when we returned, so it must be something obvious, or something that suddenly became obvious last night.

"Even without our whisper spheres broken, they could have redirected us when we got here, so they didn't even want us walking inside to grab our things. Come to think of it, unless the driver ran for all he was worth just to talk to her, she shouldn't have known what happened before we got back. That's a clue too. She is hiding something significant enough to gamble everything just to stop us from figuring it out for even a few more hours."

Sara somehow crosses her legs like a grade-school child as she sits on the beam. "Do you think she is working with one of the sages? A traitor?" I shake my head.

"No, that's not it. No, Archer wants to beat the sages. I think she genuinely cares about saving this world and would go to the ends of any map she could find to stop them. She is a real revolutionary, which is why I didn't see it right away. Stopping the sages and ending the sick state of the world is probably the second most important thing in her life."

"The second? What about the first?" Sara asks.

"Well, that's easy," I answer. "Almost mundane. She has a disease many liberators have had. She cares about the world almost as much as she cares about being remembered for saving it. That's it. She wants us to win, but she wants her name to be the one in history books more."

"That's . . . petty," Sara notes. "And it doesn't explain the rest, just her motive."

"Well, the rest is easy. Why she wouldn't want us to contact you. How she recruits so quickly. Why she was afraid of being caught in whatever lie she's been telling as soon as you came back. As soon as *you* came back. You, whom she may have intentionally prevented us from contacting. Even how she knew what happened in the first place when we had no chance to report it, and how she responded so quickly," I explain.

I see the same conclusion descend on Sara's face as I talk. "Rochelle Archer is a sage, isn't she?"

CHAPTER THIRTEEN

Gods and the Women They Fear

Alpha

I have almost cleaned up Rowan's mess. It's degrading, working with such a sniveling coward, especially with how often he turns out to be a liability. The negative mage is following the path I've laid out for him, and he's almost there. Had Sarafyna not returned when she did, this would already be done.

I can feel him coming—yet again—to harass me about his problems. His whining is like mold growing in my ears, infesting me so I can taste and smell it even in my sleep. I close my eyes and take a deep breath. Again, I question the moment I chose to use him. Every day, I wonder if there was something else I could have done. He was new to the Republic, still shivering like a wet kitten, looking over his shoulder like a deer in the woods, afraid of some girl who was still trapped in some other reality. A coward.

But he was powerful. He didn't know how powerful yet, but I could feel it. If he joined the Republic properly, they would be too strong, and they could kill me if the Council joined them. The uneasy balance had protected all of them so far; they didn't realize it, but I could destroy either country on my own. I could fight off a joint attack from them, though it would be a risk. But if this . . . *weasel* joined them, that would change. I needed him on my side.

Fortunately—or unfortunately, as it turned out—I had an idea about how to do that. He was terrified beyond reason. He'd hidden from this girl, watching his peers die one by one, for years, and she'd still gotten to him. Even here, on a whole new planet, he was afraid she'd find him. And there was only one person in this world who could tell him if that was true. Only one person so closely connected to Mirage that he could see into these other worlds, see how they were connected, and which souls traveled between them.

I'd expected I would have to lie to him. It would be no struggle to prove I could see the world he came from; I could see anywhere even better than my mother could. I'd simply tell him she was coming after all, and she would be as or more powerful than him. This alone would be enough to leash the coward.

I was quite surprised when I barely had to lie at all.

She had died nearly the same moment he'd desperately grasped at my mother's naive robe and crawled his way here. I'm not certain whether he would have survived if he'd stayed, but she certainly would have died either way. This should have been the end of her as a threat to anyone. I nearly stopped looking then, just as soon as I'd confirmed any lie would never be discovered by her inconvenient arrival in some unexpected place.

But I kept watching, because people wear souls like ribbons. When they die, they simply drift through that empty space between worlds until they find a new home. I've watched this happen a thousand times. Sometimes, they end up here. Sometimes, they land in another world. Most often, they find another body in their own world, growing, living, and dying all over again.

But this *Annie* must have been determined. Even in death, she must have had a single-minded focus on my new friend's death, because—in that moment—I saw three ribbons leave from nearly the same time and place. The first found its way back to its own world—or was guided back to its own world. There were other entities out there, not unlike my mother. I never interacted with them, and I cared little about what they did. It could have even been my mother's hand; time is strange in the space between. The movements of gods inside it don't necessarily reflect the same time-frame of the worlds they are observed from.

The next ribbon was Rowan himself, still tied to the living man. I knew where that had ended up. And the last was the very girl he was so terrified of. Her ribbon didn't drift. It wasn't aimless, nor was it guided by an outside hand. It connected here, like it knew where it wanted to go. She wouldn't remember her time hunting Rowan—those who traveled between worlds through death never did—but she had followed her target anyway. I was impressed.

This made it easy. I could actually show him. I could prove that she was going to come here; I could see exactly where and when she was going to be reborn, even. And once he saw that, he fell into the palm of my hand. I promised to kill her before she could find him, and he agreed to join me. It seemed so simple—at the time.

The power balance did shift. Not quite enough that I was prepared to assault all the sages at once, but enough that I *could* eventually. I just needed to grow stronger, needed more monsters keeping my collector strong, keeping *me* strong. Some of those meant to become monsters became sages instead, but this only delivered more of Mirage's power into my hands once my collector devoured them. A few hundred more years of that, and every sage would be dead. I would kill Rowan after that.

But things started going wrong. The girl, Annie, was going to be born in one of the paper countries I'd built. I could see that clearly. We had maybe two hundred years before it happened, but I had no need to wait that long. That world wasn't being used, simply maintained; I couldn't even remember which sage I had built it for. I had standing instructions with a church I had set up there, so at this point, it was essentially a slow farm for sacrifices to the woods, which it supplied steadily.

It was useful; more useful, in the long term, than simply throwing them all to the collector at once. But I had promised to kill the girl, and simply swallowing the country would be easiest. I could borrow the guardians from the Republic and Council—the volu were particularly good at collecting large populations. If I used one of the border stones I had created for the sages, it would be easy enough.

This was the first problem I ran into.

This country, Potestia, had at some point been completely surrounded by my collector. This alone wouldn't be an issue, except, when I attempted to enter . . . I couldn't. Mirage was a ghost of who she'd once been. She couldn't fight me directly, not usually, but it was like she had gathered all the power she could access in one place, one spot in this world she could just barely see if she focused most of her will on it, and she wouldn't let me enter.

I tried. Repeatedly, I tried, but it was like pushing my way through a steel wall. For some reason, she was giving me free rein over all of her power—in exchange for denying me access to this one place.

It was frustrating, but I could still communicate with my priests. I figured I'd simply order them to kill the child as soon as she was born, a simple solution to a complex problem. But even this, Mirage denied. My voice could reach the priests, but when I tried to send this one order, it simply didn't reach them. I tried ordering them to kill someone else—anyone else—but this failed as well. They could hear simple instructions, but the order to kill wouldn't make it to them. I still had no idea why, but Mirage was protecting the people of this country from me.

Rowan was furious. I was careful how much information I gave him, but I could only keep so much secret. He wanted definitive proof that she would never be a threat, and when I couldn't offer that, he tried entering himself, going to annihilate the entire country alone. He too was denied. I almost lost him then and there, but I couldn't allow that to happen. I needed him on my side, at least for a while.

So I proposed a plan. She could show up eventually, but she would meet a world that wanted her dead. A world which had spent hundreds of years waiting to hate her. It would be easy; the common people didn't understand the sages' abilities. We simply needed to create a "prophecy." We could pretend it had been around forever, or we could introduce it now—it mattered little. If we learned new details, we'd simply add them as needed, making the prophecy match her. By creating it with vague wording and unspecific detail, it would take little effort to "reinterpret" it.

I couldn't order her death directly, but I could send a benign order that Mirage would never notice. I let Rowan pick the name of a demon we'd ensure the whole world would already hate if she ever showed her face there. And so I sent that simple order: "When she is born, name her Lillith."

It was honestly unnecessary. She'd grow, live, and die without knowing Rowan hated her; without any idea one of the most powerful men in the world was afraid of her. She wouldn't even know why. But it cost me nothing and satisfied Rowan, who remained on my side. I thought I had contained the problem.

And for a long time, I had. Rowan was silenced, but he was on my side. He was needier than a child, but he wore the collar I gave him.

He demanded several of his own paper kingdoms—feeling important and loved was a need for him, like most people needed food or water—but the man was a dimwit; he always exposed this fact eventually, so thoroughly even mind control couldn't prevent it.

Every time he reset the entire country, he would sacrifice most of the residents to the collector, then brainwash and recruit the rest for the Republic's Guardians of Stone. It helped grow my radiant world, but it was still tiresome. He did this so often that the stones themselves started to reflect his void energy rather than just the dark woods I had created inside them. It was a minor inconvenience, however, and it was the greatest worry I had for some time.

The girl was born, as expected, and she was given the name I'd ordered, or so my priests reported. She showed no signs of remembering anything, and I had little to worry about.

Until Sarafyna was born. Or, until she showed up in my woods. This was when I realized what Mirage was doing, why she was gathering her power in a single place: She was putting herself together in her own way. She usually gave herself away blindly, but that had gotten her nowhere; it had actually worked against her, actually. So she'd focused on the area she could affect.

For two hundred years, she narrowed her focus so she could pour as much power as possible into a single child. Not a desperate child, not an emotional one—just a child. A girl. I don't know how she picked this one, but I think I understand why. She had never been able to speak to me, but if she found a new home, if she found a form like mine, she could finally understand me. This was why she'd refused to let me order anyone's death.

She was going about it all wrong. This child was strong—I needed to keep her constantly poisoned just to keep her in my control—and she grew stronger with each passing day. But she wasn't desperate enough, only growing better at using all the power she'd started with. The best this could get Mirage was another person on the same level as me. If she wanted to collect enough of her power in this girl's body to use it as her own, she'd need to take her power back from the sages, exactly as I was. Still, the idea excited me. Finally, I'd be able to speak with my mother and make her understand.

So I resolved to cultivate this girl. It was easy at first, a game of pushing and pulling to create the desperation that would open her up to Mirage's influence. But, as usual, Mirage didn't understand. She couldn't see how

I was helping, and she fought me, trying to hold me back, to impede me and free the girl before anything had been accomplished at all. I couldn't get anything done, spending too much of my energy fighting Mirage off.

And I made a mistake which has haunted me since: I gave Rowan the power to control the collector, to interact with the monsters inside. I had only one ally powerful enough to handle it, so as I fought off Mirage, I let Rowan train Sarafyna.

He did a passable job creating the desperation I wanted, and she grew stronger while he taunted her in a way I wouldn't have considered. For a couple of years, this seemed to work, but Sara grew faster than I expected, resisting the poison more and more. Unaware of her own power, she lashed out at random, exactly as Mirage did, sending waves of Mirage's energy throughout the world, but she didn't know what she wanted to do with it. All she had was desperation and hate—hate for me and, above all else, for Rowan.

That's the source of every headache I've had since. Because while she was desperately fighting Rowan and throwing world-shattering power out into space, she managed to find the exact tool she needed. She couldn't fight the man who was hurting her, so she found that man's greatest fear and woke it up. A harmless, dying child suddenly had teeth. A little girl woke up and remembered she was a hunter.

It turned out we were going to need that prophecy after all.

Those two meeting was a headache I could barely handle on its own, and Rowan's involvement in it made it a nightmare. The moment Lillith entered the collector's domain, Rowan tried to throw everything he could at her. He wasted so many of my monsters, so much of my power. He was supposed to shore up my weaknesses, not burn through my fuel. But I had to stop Mirage from undoing all of my hard work, which meant I had to leave that power in his hands.

It was a shit show, but it would be manageable. I had to step in and stop Rowan before he lost control, leaving Mirage unattended for a few moments. Then these stubborn women managed to break Sarafyna from my control, resulting in the loss of my mother's new home. But I knew it would be temporary. I couldn't just train her to hunt my priests forever; eventually, I needed to pit her against real sages anyway.

Rowan, obviously, panicked immediately, adding a "chimera" to his little prophecy and pushing it with every public appearance. The fool pushed it so desperately that it actually undercut its credibility. That didn't matter to me. As long as he was still on my side, I didn't care. He even strong-armed the other sages to actively suppress all grief in *both* countries, which was not a terrible idea, considering the power the girl displayed while in the collector's world.

Either way, Lillith was his nuisance more than mine. She was mostly an issue in the way she greedily ate up Mirage's power and held Sarafyna back. That, and the threat she posed to the collector—if Sara learned how to properly use a sacrifice of her own.

Her movements in Potestia promised some possible issues as well. As she spread my collector throughout the country, it became easier to see what she was doing, and one thing in particular posed a threat: the Eleonor girl. I didn't care much who ruled some tiny country, but the loss of my priests and their control was a problem. An even larger problem was the waning fear of changing the body. There was a reason this rule was stead-fast, burned into the minds of the Guardians of Stone.

Everyone I could control was given an instinctive repulsion with a per-son modifying their body, but this Eleonor was going to anyway; I could see it. And she wouldn't be the last. And once an entire country started to openly and willfully defy Mirage's design . . .

Eleonor was poisonous. A strong enough refusal of Mirage could create a negative mage, a hole in her power. A mage who recoiled from my mother with such force that they separated from her permanently.

Mirage couldn't touch a negative mage. They couldn't be controlled or even harmed, nor could anyone near them. The world around them was like an endless depth that starved my mother. They even overcorrected; the more steadfast the rules imposed on them, the further they would fly in the other direction. A monster would cease to be a monster and turn into an unusually long-lived person. A sage wouldn't just grow powerless when close to one—they would become sickly. A man, desperate for the body Mirage denied him when he was born, would find himself changed and a daily stain on my mother's art.

These last are the ones who most often become negative mages. Not always; they need more exposure to Mirage than most and actual hope of success, which is why they're hunted, collected so I can choose a new body for them; one they will loathe even more. If they want to spit in my mother's face, they'll suffer for it. I will take their hope.

If Lillith got her way in Potestia, I knew they would produce a negative mage eventually. Fortunately, Sarafyna left the country, and I was able to manipulate the Council sages into aiding in her capture. This cut Lillith and her little friends off from the country and redirected Mirage's attention away from Potestia. Not entirely, but a little. And with my mother's attention split, I could do a little more in both places.

I still couldn't enter the country, but I could send a few guardians and an artifact, a staff I'd enchanted with enough power to offer a onetime use at the cost of the user's life. This would pull all the escaped livestock back to the country and kill the more moderate king it had found in one move. The Potestia problem would be contained, and I could keep training Sarafyna separately, preparing her to fully house my mother, and of course, pointing her at the other sages.

With my help, I knew she could kill them. She was stronger than even Rowan—or she could be—and each sage she killed would make her stronger. With Rowan's nightmare trapped in Potestia and Sara trapped again, things would get back on track.

I used one of my monsters, contorting it until I made it look like the Scholar Sage who'd been sent to examine the girl. I couldn't approach Sarafyna directly, but Mirage was struggling to hold me back on multiple fronts. I sent this monster as a conduit for my words and power to break Sara and make her let go of Lillith, letting the other problem die. And when I let her go, she would kill the sages. I would kill them too. We would both absorb their power, and finally, she would go back to the collector. I would be the only sage who could overpower her, especially after I consumed Rowan.

Once she came to fight the collector, I would take her too and offer her to my mother. Then finally, *finally*, things would be as they should. I would hold the most power, able to guide the world with the wisdom Mirage lacked, and my mother would be back. She would have the ability to see, speak, and feel, and I could finally teach her. Together, we could bring Manara back. I considered preserving Lillith's corpse for this; she would make a suitable home for Manara. It would be poetic, in a way.

Of course, things didn't all go according to plan. Potestia fell. Sarafyna did learn to properly use her sacrifice—after it had died enough times—which was a consequence of the risk behind training her. Eleonor became a negative mage after all. But this was all okay. I could handle all of it.

All of it, except for Rowan's panic. Because Lillith and Sarafyna finally put him on their list of targets—an unfortunate consequence of involving the Guardians of Stone in my plans. In any case, he was being pursued again. The monster under his bed had found him, and she had an army.

Sarafyna left for the Republic, and with her went Mirage's focus. Of course, I focused on her as well. And the terrified Rowan tried to ruin everything by altering my monsters so they could leave the woods, using them to attack the Potestian livestock. As if they were any real threat on their own; I had designed them to die while outside my control for a reason, but he didn't care.

I only ignored them for a few days, but by the time I noticed, it was too late. The plan I'd put in place with the negative mage was at risk; Sarafyna was returning, and I'd lose all contact with my monsters if Mirage came with her, so I pulled them all back. I also stopped luring the negative mage, knowing my plan wouldn't work while Sarafyna was on this side of the Nexus border. But the damage was done.

If they figured out how much power the monsters gave me, my plan could fall apart. This ridiculous hat shop is already eating at my woods like cancer. If they overtook it, then I wouldn't be able to give Sara to Mirage, or I would have to risk everything to do it. It was close. I could feel them figuring it out slowly. My second proxy had seen them growing closer and closer. But just in time, Sarafyna left again.

I can fix Rowan's mistake. Ironically, I have to risk everything that Rowan did just to stop the possible consequences of his cowardice and prevent the Potestians from acting if they do figure it out. I simply need the negative mage to move faster. I need to feed her more tempting targets to follow. She is almost there. She will arrive today, and everything will fall into place.

I am going to fix this.

CHAPTER FOURTEEN

Fight for Their Lives

Dominic

This is exhausting. All week, these attacks have kept up. All week, we have been the only targets. I can't wrap my head around why, because, truth be told, they aren't a threat. When they first attacked, they did notable damage by attacking everywhere at once and killing enough people to dig a chasm in my heart. But we've consolidated now, though not entirely. The Collector could send them anywhere in the country now that they can leave the woods. The airborne victims could do some damage.

In fact, I spent the first few days picturing that exact scenario over and over, running it through my head, along with my inability to protect everyone. Every death in Tumult still sticks to my skin like ticks. I was so worried it was going to happen again, so worried I'd be too focused on one place while bodies piled in towers behind my back. But no one has reported anything. Everyone is fine. Only we are under attack, which is even more strange because I am the most dangerous mage in the country; in any country I know of.

My wind and wood mana are excellent for subduing instead of killing; so as long as only we are under attack, there is little danger of a single casualty. My endoaspect may be broken, but this I can handle. Even with thousands of them, some of whom come with mana, I can control all of it.

It's tiring, yes, but I can last a day or two at a time, and every other mage in the towers takes over for me when I need rest. All but the earth mages, who are building new facilities to hold our . . . guests.

The fact is, we aren't in any danger. It's like the Collector doesn't care if he kills us anymore, just sending thousands and thousands of them for seemingly no reason. Even if it's a war of attrition, we are winning. Yes, it's more work to care for these victims the more we capture; it's growing hard to keep up with, and we'll need to find a new solution soon, but our enemy loses his forces every day too. It doesn't make any sense. Why commit to an all-out offensive like this on the one place most prepared to defend itself?

My best theory is he is trying to isolate us. Our route to the hat shop is cut off by the armies assaulting us, and though I could get a few people through, it would be dangerous to move everyone. But we could leave by the regular route just fine. I'm worried something is planned for Visenar—or some other group—and the Collector wants to trap me here.

A wall of wind easily catches a group of bat-like victims in the sky while roots tangle hundreds of them on the ground.

I just can't make sense of it. It all feels so . . . fruitless.

"Dom, it's time to take a break," Gilbert cuts in. I startle, looking around to find hundreds of mages gathered along the wall. All of them are here to relieve me. I'm reluctant to leave, but he is right. I have learned better than to be arrogant. As much as I want to stay and fight, I know I will be more useful with a little rest.

Looking into the gentle eyes of the kind man who has been caring for me all this time, my heart races more than when I was fighting a moment ago. I nod.

"Right," I agree, taking one last look at the battle below and the victims being corralled into our cages. I'm missing something. I just . . . can't put my finger on what. "But, can we visit the cells first?"

Leo

Our group has been growing quickly. Wherever we are headed, the Collector wants us there quickly. We recruit more members every single day, barely stopping for long enough to help new faces process the shock of the change. It's getting to the point where I'm the only person who knows everyone's name. Well, Mom and I, but my mother has not had nearly as many occasions to use them. She has been struggling a lot. With how we ended up here, and with Rose, Lewis, and Kasey.

At first I thought those would be opposites for her, that they would almost balance each other out. But that isn't right. One of them loves Mom, and the other two hate her. Those feelings do counteract each other from the outside, enough that I didn't understand why the Collector returned all of them at once. It's clear he is trying to motivate us to move more quickly, and I worried the conflicting emotions would paralyze her.

But they don't conflict. At least, not in my mother's eyes. No, when she looks at them, she sees the same thing: she sees someone she tried to help, someone she failed, and someone she betrayed. Maybe not in the same way but at the same time and for the same reason. My mother stopped hoping for better than scraps years ago, which is not her fault. Not to me. I understand it; some part of me still lives in the dirt, certain I'm going to be killed. Some part of me is still trapped in my room, too afraid to be seen by even the people who accepted me.

When you spend your life running from brief safety to brief safety, it's hard to believe in stability. After one too many moments of joy have been ripped from you, after that last stranger disgusted by your presence in the room turns your life on its head . . . Who could keep hope up? At a certain point, you start accepting less. You begin to be grateful when you are treated only as an irritation and not as a target for extermination.

So I don't blame my mother. She was trying to take what she knew she could touch instead of a future she had missed so many times before. She didn't even want those scraps for herself; she wanted to save all of us. She was wrong, and it hurt, but I understand how she got there.

But that's different now. I have rejected that lie, and the world is complying. The world is bursting with hope and joy—joy which only grows with each new member of our family. And in the face of all that happiness, it's easy to remember every mistake she ever made after losing sight of the better world. All this to say she doesn't interact with everyone, but she takes great care to remember all of their names, a remnant of a time when a remembered name was the only future many of us could hope for.

She is thawing, however. It's slow, and she's still afraid to really hope, but I can feel it. I am sharing my joy, literally, with everyone here, my joy mana radiating through our camp like sunlight. And slowly, she's started to embrace it. I even spotted her laughing with Rose. They were crying, but they were also laughing. And this too, brings me joy.

We know we are heading to where the Collector wants us, but we also know we are expanding a world where we are allowed to exist. Charlotte met with three people she hurt and failed in her eyes, but she's also promised, through their presence, that following this path will save those she lost. Those she betrayed.

And so, all of us keep moving forward, following the promise of greater joy. Of redemption. Of safety for friends, old and new. Because the Collector may be leading us, but he has tried forcing his designs on us before, and we will face whatever he has waiting for us—and his perversion of reality will collapse just as it has before.

Gilbert

"W-what happened here?" I stutter as we walk into one of the first holding facilities. The smell of blood is thick. Victor is holding a cloth to his wounded head.

"No time for that. Dom, you have to stop them," Victor groans. "They only left a few minutes ago; there is still time." Dominic doesn't wait for even a breath, tearing his way out of the building and toward the other facilities while I run to Victor's side. He is on the ground, his back to the wall and one leg horribly bent and broken.

"What happened?" I beg as he groans. Crouching next to him, I curse myself for my continued inability to help when it matters. He's clearly in pain, but I have nothing to help him. The sound of rushing wind like a storm erupts from outside.

"People are afraid," Victor explains through gritted teeth. "The attacks are getting to them. That was expected, but . . . the Collector got to them." My blood runs cold. I look up again at the countless bodies of peaceful victims. People who were just as afraid until they died.

"What do you mean the Collector got to them?" I ask. "How? A priest? An apprentice like you? How did he manage . . . this?" I have to choke down bile as I look at the carnage around me. These people had lost their original bodies; as such, their remains are hard to identify. It's all just . . . meat and bone crushed under stones and ice. I'm not even sure I can identify individual corpses. And they were locked in a cage, defenseless as they were slaughtered.

Oh fuck. We put them there. We let this happen. The words won't leave my head. We were taking care of them, or doing our best to do so. We had volunteers helping them bathe and eat. Everyone was safe. Once any victim was separated from the woods for long enough, they calmed down. Especially with Sara gone, they hardly moved at all.

"One of the women we brought back from the Kingdom of Endings," he explains. "Karly or Kayla or something? I'm not sure. She wasn't who we thought; I don't think the real woman survived at all, Gil. The Collector spoke through her, or through her changeling, and promised to leave us in peace if we killed everyone here and in the other facilities. He made the same offer to me when he came with his mob; people from every community. I tried to stop them, but . . . I'm just a scientist. I have a little divine magic, but the Collector's agent overpowered it. I'm lucky to be alive. He tried to get them to kill me, but he could only sway them enough to kill the ones they were afraid of."

"Oh fuck," I whisper. I swallow hard, my heart nearly cracking my sternum as it beats. The sound outside is terrifying. I don't know how many more they managed to kill. I don't know how many people Dom may be forced to kill in response. He's already been fighting for days, and he hates death. Maybe he is taking them hostage.

I look at the pooling blood from the people I'd been watching for weeks. It smells like rotten eggs, iron, and shit. I feel sick. The world doesn't feel real. *I hope he kills them.* It's a thought I never thought I'd have, but I do. I want them dead.

I don't remember taking out a whisper sphere to call for help, but Clarrise arrives all the same, doctors in tow. I can only think of one thing: We had them in cages. We had them locked in cages when they died. For the safety of the murderers who slaughtered them.

Dominic

"Get out of their way, Prince Dominic," the woman demands. But that isn't right. It's not a woman speaking to me at all—it's the Collector, the god I was raised to worship. And he wants these people dead.

"Why?" I ask.

"It's not for you to ask me why I—" the Collector started in the woman's voice, but I never had any interest in what he had to say.

"I wasn't asking you," I snap. "The rest of you. Why? Are you under his control? No. If he could control you, he'd have liberated his army, not slaughtered them. So why? Why hurt innocent people? They were dependent on us! They needed us, and they weren't hurting anyone! So why?"

A few wide eyes lock on mine, fear clear on their faces. Whether I am the source or the attack on the walls is, I'm not sure. Others are looking down, refusing to meet my eyes. Altogether, there are a hundred or so people, all mages, all of whom could have fought at the front lines. All of whom came here to kill the defenseless instead.

"We just want to feel safe!" a woman in the middle calls. "How are we supposed to sleep safe knowing the monsters attacking our walls are living a few floors down?"

"It's the Collector's will!" a man shouts. "What sort of man fails to answer his creator's word!"

"You think that just because they are quiet in their cages, we've forgotten how violently they attacked us?" another man cries.

I feel shattered mana twitching inside me. An endoaspect I can't use anymore ever since I realized power alone will never make me anyone's protector. But as I stand in the frigid air, looking at the mob in front of me, I don't care. We stand in the gap between the people they murdered and the people they intend to murder. I clench my fists. I understand the fear. The bodies chosen for these people were engineered to frighten and horrify. The violence that was forced on them is hard to forget. But this? This is cruel.

"They were more innocent than you," I respond. It's quiet, and I'm not certain any of them can hear me. But they can see the words in my eyes. "Their bodies were taken from them. Their minds. When they were used as the claws of the man responsible for that violence, they fought every step of the way. But you. Did he have to do more than ask? How ready were you to slaughter them?" I don't know what to do. I have stopped them, but I don't know what to do next.

Maybe Lillith would kill them. I don't know. Maybe she would sympathize. Gil has told me her stories of slaughtering the same innocents when she was first attacked. She believed they went to her for death, that they were hopeless and desperate to let it end. Her grief mana would have failed to hurt them if it wasn't what they were there for. So it's not the same. But it's not different either.

She was trying to protect herself and her friends, just like these people are.

She was more ignorant at the time, but it's hard to call this group informed. There is a willfulness in this ignorance which has a much darker shade than a simple lack of information, but I understand that more than anyone.

I don't know what Lillith would do, but . . . she's not in charge. I don't need to look to her for permission. I don't need to do what she would do. When I speak up again, I flare my aura and silence all in the crowd but the strange woman in front.

"You all have three options, as far as I see it. You can keep trying to harm these people, these innocents we have been trying to help, but if you do, I will kill you. I won't hesitate," I announce. I pause, making eye contact with all who offer it. It is clear this is no idle threat. I will. "You can also turn around now. Go back. Return to your homes. I won't stop you. But everyone who lives here will know what you've done. That massacre back there? They will all be welcome to see it with their own eyes. They will see it and smell it, and they will know the names of each neighbor who created it.

"So you can turn around. You can go home and roll the dice, gamble that everyone there is kinder than you, that they will feel safe knowing what you did. That they won't feel just a little more at peace after your rooms look like the room you just left."

Eyes all around me widen further. I take a deep breath. "Or, you leave. Turn around and walk until you are a memory and nothing more. You all have mana. You have the tools to survive. Find your own home and let us live in peace, knowing we no longer share walls with beasts."

I don't know if Lily would do this. I don't know if it's the right thing to do. I don't know if it's even safe. But it's the best I can think of right now. I don't know how Lily makes these decisions so easily, so unburdened by them. All I know is that I can't think of anything else.

Some eyes flick toward the unmolested building they'd been headed to before. Others back at the tower. The woman in front holds her chin in the air. I set my jaw as the tension builds.

"Make your choice."

Charlotte

I feel like my heart is no longer in my control.

It has highs—brief moments of hope, and longer periods of joy.

Rose. Rose is alive and well. She's broken from the time she spent in the woods, but she is back and has a future. I gave up on her so long ago, but she is alive. How could I feel anything but joy in her presence? How could I feel anything but shame? I feel like two women: The one who gave up and the one who still has a future. The woman who forgot Rose and the woman who raised Leo.

It has lows, when two revolutionaries glare at me from across the fire at night.

I hurt them, and I have to own that pain. At the same time, there is a look in their eyes I have seen so many times before. I have been spending time with Rose again; we don't talk much, but I feel her fire. Before we fell into these woods, Lewis referred to me as a man. I can't forget that. The moment he had an excuse, he rescinded what little respect he'd offered before. I hurt them, and I own that. But the more time I spend with Rose, the more I have to wonder.

They hurt me too. They wanted me to live in a Radiant Woods of my own, in a world that hated me and demanded my body fit their designs. They called me Charlotte to my face but withheld kindness in their hearts. They have always thought less of me. They have always snickered and rolled their eyes when I call myself a woman.

At what point do they own the pain they caused? How much shame do I deserve to feel while they feel none? Am I allowed to be angry at people I hurt if they were willing to hurt me first? Am I allowed to hate people I wrongfully betrayed? In Potestia, the answer was no. In Potestia, I had to bow my head. In Potestia, I could only hurt, not be hurt. Because in Potestia, I was a legitimate target for pain and ridicule. Cruelty isn't cruelty when everyone detests you for existing. But now?

"Leo is looking for you, up ahead," a woman says, snapping me out of my introspection. I look up to see one of the women we've had with us for a couple of weeks now.

"Thanks, Ria," I reply.

"No problem. Um, you may want to hurry though; he says he thinks we are *there*," she replies. The emphasis is all I need to go from a walk to a run. There is only one place she could mean by that: Wherever we have been headed to this entire time. Wherever the Collector has been leading us.

As I run, I see the wall of trees growing more dense; impossibly dense. They are connected with thick vines like on the walls of an ancient estate. When I catch up to the front, I realize that is exactly what it is—a wall.

It's tall, and it expands seemingly infinitely in both directions. It starts just outside of Leo's area of effect, a clear and curved line marking the border of safety we exist inside.

"Oh, Mom, you're here!" Leo exclaims, a wide smile on his face. Rose, Frey, and Lewis are all standing near him with a wide variety of reactions to my presence.

"Are we really going to trust . . . *her* here?" Lewis complains. I don't miss the pause, and my hackles raise. Yet again, I wonder why I feel shame and he doesn't.

"Well, if there is something dangerous behind that wall, we are either fighting it off with your whining or with the strongest mage here. Your call, bud," Frey quips. A slight smile tugs at the corner of my mouth, although it is quickly drowned by guilt. Rose, on the other hand, wears her grin openly.

"I don't know," she adds, "I know a fight with a near duke-level mage sounds like the more palatable option to me. I mean, if I had to choose."

Lewis scoffs so loudly it's almost comedic. "Fine. If you want to trust hi—her, go ahead. But I'm not taking my eyes off her." Again, I have a toxic mix of emotions. As he nearly uses the wrong word for me again, I feel completely justified in calling him foul. There is an intentional tone in his voice, like he wants to play it off as a mistake but clearly thinks he was right the first time. At the same time, I have earned distrust; it is wise to doubt me. I can't betray everyone counting on me and then expect perfect acceptance.

I don't know how to respond. Fortunately, Rose understands completely and speaks up on my behalf. "You know, Charlotte, sometimes, assholes can be right about some things. Sometimes, they can be justified in their choices. Doesn't stop them from being assholes. It's not a contradiction to own your mistakes and also recognize theirs."

"All right, all right. Another time. Right now, we need to focus. There is only one way forward, and the Collector wanted us here. We need to be on our toes," Leo cuts in. "Mom, are you ready?"

I shake Lewis's glare off then nod. Leo lets a breath out of his nose, then takes a few steps forward. The wall collapses in front of us as he does, simply disappearing as his sphere of influence touches it.

Something feels wrong. While killing the woods always feels natural and kind, this feels like cutting a nail too close to the skin. As the wall gives way completely, that sense of wrongness only grows. There is no one to fight, only a simple dark room with a small table in the center with exactly two objects on it.

The first is some kind of wooden stand. This doesn't concern me. What sends a chill down my back is the heart that sits on it, woven together with fabric like the heart of a doll. It trembles on its wooden stand, blood decorating its surface like water on a glass of wine. It can't be a real heart, but it feels real enough that I am unsettled when it doesn't beat. It moves like it's shivering, but it doesn't beat. Something deep inside me panics as I look at it.

"What the fuck is that?" Frey asks.

"We should destroy it," Lewis says, taking a step forward.

"Without knowing what it is?" Rose responds, giving him a look of utter bafflement.

"Keep walking," a voice says. The sound comes from mana rather than the woods itself—I can see the sound mana appearing in between us—but its source is clear: the Collector. The one who has been guiding us here all this time. Who stopped, for a while, then rushed us. He needs us to destroy it.

"I don't think I'm going to do that," Leo responds. "I'm not exactly on your side."

"Destroy it, and I will lead you home. I will give all of them back; every single insect you have been chasing. I'll send those home who want to go home, and I will protect you all from your furious king. Leave it alone and remain lost forever while I torture the thousands I haven't returned to you yet."

We are all silent. I glance behind me. I can see the mana all throughout the camp. I see hope enter Lewis's eyes. Concern clouds all of my friends. The answer is obvious; I know what we need to do. But . . . will everyone else understand?

CHAPTER FIFTEEN

Fickle Apathy

Gilbert

It's our fault," I say. Dom sits next to me, his hand over mine. Victor is in bed now, still writing in his notebook. Even now, even in pain, he wants to understand. None of us feel right. "We locked them in cages. We corralled them with our walls and our magic and fed them to their murderers. Their blood is on our hands."

"What else could we have done?" Dom asks. "We were doing our best. We were trying everything we could." What he's saying sounds true, but it doesn't feel true.

"We need to understand," Victor cuts in. "We need to understand what the Collector is doing. Why attack us in the first place? Why kill his own army? Why harass us so constantly when he isn't making any progress? It could have been a distraction, but we have captured more than he managed to kill. It doesn't add up."

"It doesn't matter," Dom says. "What matters is we let people die. We need to come up with a new solution before we examine some evil god's motives. I think he's just trying to cut us off from everyone else, anyway. The thickest attack is always in front of the hat shop."

"What?" I ask. Dom and Victor both look at me.

"I said it doesn't matter," Dom replies. I shake my head as my heart starts racing again. I have been trying so hard to make sure I wasn't caught with my eyes closed and my ears covered. I have fallen asleep every night thinking about everything we know, reviewing everything we have seen, but I hadn't connected them all.

"No, about where they are attacking. They are trying to stop us from reaching the hat shop?" I ask again.

"Yes," Dom confirms. "I could probably get through them, but it would be hard to make travel and trade regular again." It's so clear. I can breathe the truth in, like the smell of a finally finished recipe.

"It does matter," I respond. "Fuck, they are the same answer."

Victor perks up. "What is it?"

"You said the Collector may benefit from his victims, and Sara might too, right?"

"Yes, I assume that's why he wants them dead, but it doesn't explain why he is risking so many more in the current attack," Victor agrees.

"I haven't quite figured that one out yet. Maybe the Collector is trying to kill Sara, and he just has to hold us off until then. But I know what he wants to stop us from doing. We never should have made cages for these people; they've spent years in a cage. But we didn't know what else to do because on some level we think of the Radiant Woods and Sara's hat shop as two parts of the same place. But . . . the answer is obvious.

"Sara's hat shop can house all of these people just as easily as the Radiant Woods can. In fact, it's the one place the Collector can't get to them. It's a place where they'll be safe and connected to us, always within Sara's reach, yet separated from travelers if they need to be. It goes on forever and shifts with Sarafyna's will. Shit, she might even be able to start healing them all at once, even from a distance!" I'm getting excited as I speak and find myself actually standing next to Victor's bed.

"I suppose. But why would the Collector fight so hard to stop that? Why would he rather they be dead?" Dom asks.

"Same reason he keeps them in the first place," Victor whispers. He looks up, making eye contact with me. "The same reason they used to die if they ever left. It's just a theory, but we were just talking about it the other day. I think the Collector is empowered by these people somehow, and he loses that power if they leave. It's possible Sara will be as well. I considered proximity to be an important factor, that's why I wanted Sara to leave for a while, but Gilbert's right. The Radiant Woods are tied to the Collector. Anyone inside would empower him as if they were in the same room.

"What if that works the same way for Sarafyna? It would explain the targeted attack. It would explain how many we are fighting while everyone else is left alone. I don't know why he took the risk the first time; maybe he didn't think Sara would come back. Maybe he was surprised by Dominic and thought he'd be able to kill and retreat a lot more easily. Maybe he was just angry when he made the call. I don't know. But obviously, he wants them either back in the Radiant Woods or dead.

"Maybe, if Gilbert is right, he wants them anywhere but the hat shop." His voice grows louder and more confident as he speaks, and I can see the same pieces falling into place for him. It's rare for me to reach a conclusion first, and Victor following me encourages me to keep speaking.

"Exactly," I reply, "but that means what he is doing now—giving us more of his victims—is a huge risk. He could end up empowering Sara even more."

"So why would he risk it?" Dom asks.

"The more I think about it, the more certain I am: He plans to kill Sara now; he just needs to keep her weaker than him until the hat shop is gone entirely, then it won't matter. I think we need to move now," I explain, urgency creeping into my voice as I am convinced by my own words.

"But this is all just a hypothesis," Victor challenges. "What if we're wrong? What if putting the victims in the hat shop hurts Sara somehow? What if it lets the Collector take control?"

"But if we're right, Sara will need the extra power. She could be at the most risk if we don't try this," Dom counters.

I shake my head. I think, somehow, I'm still ahead of Victor this time. "If that were the case, he'd just send them straight there, wouldn't he? Unless something's keeping them out, but if there is, we won't even be able to send them that way. Not without physically forcing them through ourselves."

"And if they head through and go straight to some other city?" Dom asks.

"The Radiant Woods will be closer. If they don't want to be inside the hat shop, they'll just head back into the woods and come here. And if not, the only place we'll struggle to respond to in time is Visenar, which has been shoring up its defenses even more," I say.

"All right, but again, just because it's unlikely doesn't mean it won't hurt Sarafyna. Are we ready to take that risk?" Victor asks. My mind wanders back to the carnage in the building next door. The death and the violence and the bars.

"We put them in cages and they died," I reply. "If we are risking our friend no matter what we do, I say we pick the risk she would take herself. She would want them to have a place where they feel safe and aren't trapped." Both of them are silent for a moment. I can feel when we all decide this is the best move to make.

"All right. How do we get them all past the army outside?" Dom asks. "I don't think I can control the horde precisely enough to transport our current guests. Not more than a few at a time, especially as tired as I am."

"Easy," I say. "We direct the army into the shop first. We are already guiding them and trying to secure them. We ask the earth mages who are building new facilities to start directing them into the hat shop instead. With you and them, it should be doable. If I'm right, the Collector will pull his army back pretty quickly, and we can move everyone left afterward." Dom and Victor share a look.

"All right, Gil. I trust you," Dom says. The air is thick with tension, and then Dominic and I move.

Charlotte

"We can't destroy it," I say.

"No one asked for your opinion," Lewis sneers. The crowd is gathering from the back, murmuring among themselves. "Some of us want to go home. The home you took us from when you decided what we 'can't do.'"

"We can't leave more people out there," a voice in the crowd calls. I can't see who it was.

"We can't submit to the fucking Collector; not after everything he has done to us!" another cries.

"Can we all calm down?" Leo shouts. "I'm not taking another step toward that heart until I know what it is."

"I will kill the negative mage here, right now," the mana voice threatens. "And the rest of you I will throw back in the woods until this world succumbs to the rot of time." He may not be able to use his divine magic, but it's clear his mana is a threat on its own. And if he is casting a spell, he must be nearby.

Another murmur goes through the crowd. I can't make out any

individual words, but I can feel the shift. Leo is fighting it with his joy mana, but so many of these people were hurting for so long before they got here. I recognize the look on too many faces; I have worn it myself: the fear of losing what small victories they had. The fear of going back to what things were like before, washing away the hope for anything better.

"I have made this mistake!" I scream, silencing the voices in Leo's clearing. My eyes begin to water, and my heart begins to pound. "I have made this mistake before! The mistake of losing hope! The mistake of taking the shreds I am offered and rejecting the future I have to fight for. I have done it to be kind, I thought. I have done it with the intention of safety and healing, and for keeping as many people as possible out of those woods.

"You have all heard Lewis. You have all sat through his story. You know how willing he was to fight before I took that away from him and everyone else. Lewis and Kasey both. They have spent days telling you why I'm not to be trusted—and they are right. They aren't right about everything, but they are right about that!" My voice trembles as I cry and plead with the crowd. I can see what they are planning. Leo may not step forward, but if enough of them turn, it won't take much to push him a few more steps. I can feel it, and so can they. If they do that—if they get the heart into his range—it will all be over.

"I deserve that distrust because I lied and I betrayed, and I turned my back on the people who counted on me. And I did it because of the same threats. I did it because of those woods and every child who has ever been left inside. I did it to keep Leo safe. I did it to save every new friend I had made in a new community. I did it because failure was so terrifying that I gave up on any option that wasn't given to me. Like I had to earn the right to feel safe, to exist.

"I took the side of the kings who wanted me dead because their apathy was the best future I could see. But don't you see? Can't you all see it? They needed my help. They needed my compliance to give me that option." I am screaming through sobs at this point. Because I won't make the same mistake again. I have to stop them. They have so much joy, and I will be the only one who poisons it with shame.

"This is the same. If he could destroy that heart? He would do it. He wouldn't need threats—he would just destroy it himself. He needs us, so he is offering us some middle ground, some half-safe future we can settle for because failure is so much more terrifying. But he needs our compliance and everyone else's because he is scared, terrified. They always are. They are horrified that their pristine and perfectly controlled environments will collapse if we are allowed to exist. They are afraid of men like Leo and women like Rose and of losing control. Of losing authority. Of losing their Collector-given right to our fucking bodies!

"So they promise us quiet, dark corners where they can lock us away and pretend we don't exist. And we take them, because being seen is so much worse. Catching the eye of people who are violently desperate to own and control is so much more dangerous than staying in the dark where we can be tolerated. I'm tired of being tolerated! I'm exhausted with complying and complying, and giving and giving, and dying and dying, all so they will look the other way and only hurt me with their volatile and fickle apathy!

"I won't! I won't comply again! I will fight and I will die and I will lose. I will lose everything and suffer for it before I comply one more time, before I bend one more knee. I will always loathe myself for the consequences of playing along, of doing what I was told. For everyone who is hurting because I thought I could buy a little more life for the people I loved if I took just one more step back. But there will always be a step after that. They won't be happy until we are dead—they will be satisfied with nothing less than our genocide, no matter how many times we compromise!"

Something boils out of me like scalding water. It was too late the moment I first spoke up. I can't hold any of it back anymore. "Lewis! Kasey! I hurt you, I know. I hurt you because I couldn't see a future where we didn't all hurt anyway. But . . . fuck you. Fuck you both. I hear you speaking behind my back, calling me by a name I long abandoned, rejecting me not for what I did but for who I am. You are rejecting all of us when you do that. It's not something you can give and take, like some kind of ration. I am Charlotte! I am a woman! I have always been a woman! I didn't stop the moment you had a reason to hate me, and I know you didn't stop believing it in that moment!

"And look at you! So ready to comply because you want that safety too! You want that dark corner where you are tolerated. You didn't even hesitate to make the mistake you hate me for! Why? Why can you loathe me, loathe all of us, but I can't hate you for turning your nose up at my very existence? Do you really want to comply? Do you really want to just be tolerated? Just allowed to exist? You don't even know the cost yet!"

I gasp, my voice exhausted and throat aching. Water and snot are running down my face. And Lewis glares at me while Kasey steps forward, joining her friend in contempt.

"You didn't experience what we did. You haven't been in those woods; you haven't felt the pain. You have no right to ask us to risk it again," Kasey hisses. I'm breathing like I've just finished running. I look at all the faces in the crowd. I can see it—they are all afraid. She's right. Leo and I haven't been through what all of them have. So, I make a decision, and my heart sinks into my gut. I walk toward the heart, standing just at the edge of Leo's influence, then turn around.

"All right. But please, after I step inside, remember everything I said. Don't comply with him."

I take a step across the line and into the Radiant Woods.

"Mom!" Leo screams, lurching forward himself, forgetting about the heart. I have to summon and control thick fabric, wrapping it around him and holding him back to protect it. And then, as he struggles, I realize I haven't stepped into the Radiant Woods at all. I am outside of the area Leo can affect, but I'm safe.

I look down at the strange fabric heart. The wood stand catches my eye, and I realize it's not a stand at all; at least not one designed for this. It's a hat block. My eyes widen as I realize what we have been talking about destroying. Then the earth begins to shake beneath my feet, and the heart trembles further while the walls Leo broke through with his ability begin to expand. For some reason, the hat shop is growing.

I blink, and I see a woman. I don't know where she came from or how she got there, but she stands in front of me, in a way. It's like I can see through her, but she is there, and she is in pain. I look back at the crowd, all of whom are looking around, terrified at the suddenly changing world.

"Thanks," she says, "for buying time."

CHAPTER SIXTEEN

No More Heroes

Lillith

And why the fuck couldn't we just wait for tonight?" Ember complains as we ride toward the last of the five targets. August is driving this time, allowing our sunniest friend to interrogate me. We assembled our group of avengers pretty much as soon as Sara and I put two and two together; they are sort of groggy avengers though. I haven't needed much sleep in this life, nor has my girlfriend, and I sometimes forget that murdering well into the dead of night leaves other people sleepy. They'll survive.

"Because of Bizarro Lily. I know. At first glance, you think, 'she's evil.' But after you get to know her, if you really give her a chance and take a closer look, it turns out she's evil," I explain. Sara rolls her eyes, but I don't miss the giggle she chokes back.

"What my beautiful and sometimes frustrating girlfriend is trying to say is we think Archer is a sage, and we want to get to the last artifact before she does. Assuming it doesn't just stop working when I get there, I might be able to tell what it's for. And what Archer wants with them," Sara explains. Ember literally growls in response, and Riley nearly mimics her. Autumn's eyes widen and her mouth opens just a little.

"A sage?" Autumn asks. "Wouldn't that be good? Having a sage who's willing to sacrifice power and fight on our side?"

I shrug. "Oh yeah, that would be awesome. I bet such a sage would be hot and love hats too. In Archer's case, however, there was no power to give up. As Sara discovered when she gave the not-so-cold shoulder to a pushy man in a bar, sages with tits are apparently a no-go. It would seem they produce both milk and demonic energy, and at least one of those disagrees with the current sages' diets. No, Archer didn't give anything up, but I do think she has the abilities of at least a minor sage. I think those abilities are responsible for most of her 'abolitionists,'" I answer.

"It's a bit hard to believe someone who hates the sages so much would do that. Shit, it's hard to believe someone the sages hate so much could be anything but good. And a lot of the people I met there have their own very genuine reasons to hate the sages. Anyone with an injury or disability, for one," Riley argues. I nod in acknowledgment.

"Sure. But people can hate each other for any number of reasons. Sometimes, they are both assholes. Just because someone calls themselves an abolitionist doesn't mean they are. Just because evil men call something a cult doesn't mean it isn't one. A good cause doesn't guarantee good people, and an evil cause doesn't prevent bad people from being right about some things," I reply.

"I suppose," Riley agrees. She bites her lip. She is almost as recent an acquaintance for me as she is for Archer, so I suppose it makes sense that she is having a hard time taking my word for it. If anything, it's wise. When people stop questioning me, I really will be a queen, and, well, I don't love queens as a rule.

So, we spend the rest of the drive explaining exactly how Sara and I came to this conclusion. It's enough to convince everyone that the solo assault is worth it, at least since it shouldn't significantly hurt the rest of the rebellion if we turn out to be wrong. Especially since, if we're right, she is risking lives in each assault and using mind control to push them into it, a horrifying realization which explains how we manage to recruit nearly the entire staff of each sage's household, even those whom I'd expected to grieve their loss of comfort.

Of course, she has real supporters. Real worshippers, even. I think it may be a cult after all, even if it doesn't look exactly like the ones I've seen on TV. Sometimes, the enemy of your enemy is also your enemy, I suppose.

In any case, it's not long before we make it to the estate of the last sage August identified as a target in this city. Or we make it about two hundred yards from his estate. Unsurprisingly, all routes to it are fairly heavily guarded, but they have the guards of a minor sage, not a major one. Nothing we can't handle.

Sneaking in isn't really an option this time; it's broad daylight, and they are expecting us. I also look like either an escapee from hell or a goth girl after her shift at Hot Topic, and both options are known to strike fear into the hearts of powerful men. I'm simply not going unnoticed on the approach.

Even so, the actual fight isn't a threat. I may only have the grief of two women and my own, but I'm still strong for a mage. Even if I wasn't, I am fast, and I can cast a lightning spell that used to take several minutes at the speed of, well, something famously fast and electric. I swear there is an applicable colloquialism here.

Sara also has surprisingly powerful mana, even if she can't actually cast spells with it. In her body, she carries the mana-infused cells of every priest or mage she has ever consumed. She lacks control, but she can still crush enemy spells with it. That's not even speaking of her divine magic, which is a thrilling terror to witness. Riley's void mana tears through anyone she fights, even if it's only wrapped around an axe. She still struggles to use it when surrounded by allies, but this is not holding her back at all.

Ember was a foot soldier for the Guardians of Stone, so she can't match the intense power surrounding her, but she makes an excellent sniper. Carbon arrows fly from her and kill enemies before I ever see them. The twins can't keep up at all, but they are safe. They are my emotional-support twins, which sounds pithy but is truer than I'd like to admit. When Autumn couldn't grieve for Henry alongside me, I started going to a dark place. If I'm going to keep up the face I need for everyone else to trust me in a fight, I need them with me.

Curiously, no one we fight is a sage. I suppose, after last night, a low-level sage wouldn't want to fight us. Even the guards flee eventually, leaving us a clear path. We march to the estate no worse for wear, and with even more mana in Sara's case. An estate which is unsettlingly empty. It's still furnished and clearly lived in, but without the guards outside, it is completely silent.

"Hey, this is probably bad, yeah?" I ask. We all share a look.

"Maybe this guy was with the group last night," August guesses. I tilt my head.

"Actually, you know what? He probably fucking was. I mean, the Dream Sage was, and this guy—the Music Sage, I think—would have been just as invested in fighting me with backup. What do you think, Sara? Got the remains of the head of the house rattling around in there somewhere?"

Sara wrinkles her nose in an achingly adorable way. "Please don't talk about me like I'm a refuse pit for angry men," she protests. "But I think some of the Nexus energy I suppressed yesterday had a musical feel to it? I'm not sure."

"Well, you know what they say." I shrug. "Fuck it. What we have to do remains the same. Let's find the room with the artifact."

"This is why I asked for your help," Ember intones. "It's the precise planning and meticulous care you put into these things."

"Thank you," I reply, ignoring any possible insincerity she may be lacing the compliment with.

"You're oddly chipper today," Riley notes as we climb the stairs. The room has been in the same part of every house, and we know exactly where we are heading. The question sends anxiety through me like a flood through the streets. She can tell the difference. I have to shrug it off; I can't let more cracks appear.

"I'm having a really good day," I reply.

"You just killed at least a dozen men," Autumn notes.

"No, I just killed at least a dozen men while hanging out with Sarafyna," I counter. "There's a big difference." I have to take a deep breath through my nose. I don't have to keep this up much longer, just a few more months. I can be strong. Happy. Unaffected.

"It is good to see you again, Sara," August agrees. Sara is behind me, but somehow, I can still feel her smile in response. She is so warm. I ignore the conversation as we move through the estate. I was starting to slip, which has happened more and more recently. I use the conversation between Sara and August as a chance to recenter myself.

We make it to the room in question with little trouble, and much to my relief, this one has no insects and the artifact in question is still in place. "All right, let's grab this and get out of here. We made a little noise getting in, and I'd like to be gone before one of our many admirers decides to do something about it."

"That's what we're here for?" Sara asks as soon as she enters the room. Her head tilts, and she has to catch her hat as it starts to slide off her head.

"Yeah," I confirm. "Why, can you tell what it does already?"

"Honestly, I'm a little surprised it still works. I'm a bit used to Nexus artifacts turning into pieces of steel when I walk into a room unless I make them myself, which means it was created by someone at least as strong as me. But yeah, I can tell what it's for. It's sort of the same as a whisper sphere," she explains. We all look at her with half-open mouths and furrowed brows.

"You aren't serious," Ember groans. "Then what's the point?"

"What's the point of the secret rooms and artifacts, or what's the point of everything we have been doing all week?" August asks.

"Yes," Ember hisses, her pupils narrowing to a slit as she looks in his direction.

"No, it's not exactly like a whisper sphere," Sara interrupts. She then pauses, seeming to lose focus for a breath, then shakes her head and looks at Ember again. I walk up to the scepter in the center of the room and lean in to examine it. "Sorry, got a little dizzy for a second. What I mean is, it's for communicating. You can use it like a whisper sphere, sure, if you just want to send your voice, but . . ." She trails off. I turn and look at her as she wavers a bit, growing unsteady on her feet. I rush to her side and catch her arm, helping her steady herself.

"Are you all right? What's wrong?" I ask. Again, she shakes her head, taking her hat off to let her head breathe.

"Nothing," she assures. "It's just been a long week, I think. What was I saying? Right. Communication. It can be used to send sound but also power; mana or Nexus energy. Even emotion, I think. It's connected to, well, what must be thousands of others like it. It's such a strong connection that I felt it in a moment. They must have these all around the country. This is definitely it. No wonder I couldn't give Ember her grief back, at least not permanently."

She takes a few steps forward, my hand trailing along her arm until she pulls away from me. She rests one hand on the artifact. "It doesn't matter how weak a sage is. If there are this many sharing their power and broadcasting pulling grief away from people all over the country . . . this would let them create an avalanche of power, a wave of control. I couldn't hold all this back no matter what I did; I don't think even Alpha could. Anyone who can be affected by this will be, no matter what I do."

"Then how is Autumn grieving?" August asks. All eyes fix on him, and he almost shrinks back but clears his throat and continues. "When Lily is around, Autumn can grieve. And when Lily is completely cut off, Autumn can't. I've seen it. If even you can't fight it, how can Lily?" We are all silent for a moment while Sara's eyes lock on mine and she tilts her head again.

"I have no idea," she admits. "As usual, the only Nexus energy touching Lily is mine. By all accounts, she shouldn't . . . shouldn't . . ." Again, she grows unsteady on her feet. Again, I rush to her side and support her, this time with Autumn's help.

"Can we use it?" Ember asks, ignoring whatever is wrong with Sara. "Can you send the grief back or whatever? I know Lillith doesn't want to ambush people with all of that at once, but I don't see much choice. It's the best chance we have of fighting back, isn't it?"

I glance at Ember with irritation, but I don't get a chance to respond.

"Yes," the scepter agrees, Archer's voice interrupting our discussion. "If we collect enough of these, we'll be able to send our own emotional orders through it, and we'll be able to use the stored-up Nexus energy to do it. But your idea is wrong. We don't win by giving grief back—we win with an army. An army we'll have if we give them all the anger we have against the sages and more. We give them rage, and we take their grief, and we send the mana of billions of furious citizens back at their abusers."

"No . . . we can't . . ." Sara tries, but before she can finish protesting, her head falls forward, and she completely loses consciousness. Ice runs through my veins.

"What did you do to her?" I ask. My voice is the most violent type of calm, like the silence between lightning and thunder. I don't need to make threats. I don't need to scream and shout as my arms wrap around Sarafyna's limp body and adrenaline demands I fight the source of my panic. This monstrous artifact sends emotions. She can feel the danger she is in.

"If something has happened to your friend, it has nothing to do with me," Archer insists. She projects confidence with her voice, but it seems you can share emotion through the link even if you don't mean to. "I reached out here because I knew it was where I'd find you after the mess you made, to ask you why you moved without the rest of us. But I understand. You never did trust me, did you?"

I grit my teeth. "You're right—you're too weak to hurt Sara like this. Your abilities measure up to her about as well as your outfit imitates me.

This is beyond you. But you don't seem terribly concerned either, do you?" I accuse.

A deep sigh comes through the scepter. "If she were dead, you wouldn't have time for all this anger, and there are more important things at stake than one girl blacking out. Now that you understand what we have discovered—what August discovered—we can change the world. We can guarantee a country that is ready to fight, that won't give up until the sages are gone. Your friend, when she wakes up, is going to try and use it to make people grieve, to make them hurt, to paralyze them when what we need is action. We have what we need to win this war!"

I clench my fists. "Is that what we have? A way to win? That's what you want, is it?"

"Lillith," she says, but I don't let her finish.

"No." I look around the room at my allies. Autumn is next to me, trying to rouse Sara. August rests his hand on his sister, looking back and forth between all three of us. Ember and Riley are tense, ready for combat. "No, you know what my answer will be. It's why you tried to cut me off from Sara, one of the fiercest and kindest weapons we have. It's why you spent years pursuing only the most dangerous sages, never investigating any other avenue of attack. It's why you'll always lose no matter what you do."

"I have been fighting for decades!" Archer snaps. "I have been running, hiding, and recruiting for my entire life! Giving people lives when the sages would abandon them to the woods! I've made the choices I have because they were the best way I could see forward! Yes, I knew Sarafyna would recognize what I was doing, knew I'd lose recruits if they met her, so I kept her away as long as I could. Because I have the stomach to actually fight, not stop just short of what needs to be done!"

I offer her a humorless laugh. My eyes lock on Sara's face, twitching in her sleep. Her eyes are moving rapidly under her lids while her scars fade in and out of existence like a dying light.

"You're a fanatic, Archer," I say. "Not a radical, not a revolutionary—a fanatic. A zealot, like every priest I've ever met, obsessed with the will and worship of some deity or other. But you are your own god. You only cared about confronting the highest-profile sages because that's what you would be remembered for, because it's flashy, and it makes a scene. You took people's minds—their very will—not to win but because you liked the worship, the subservience. Because you are a sage in every sense of the word.

"You want to win, but not as much as you want to be remembered for winning. You know what I think? I think if you had a choice between winning total and immediate liberation and delaying victory for another hundred years . . . you would ask which one you'd be remembered for. You'd choose the option that puts your name in history books. If freedom meant being forgotten, you'd give it up. And you'd give it up for everyone."

"That's bullshit and you know it! What, because I didn't discover some artifacts earlier? Because I didn't want your girlfriend tearing my revolution apart?" she sneers.

"Because you can't win autonomy by taking it away!" I shout. "Because you wear my face and you make speeches and you always give your name when you do. Because you want to be a great woman of history, and it is the only goal you have consistently moved toward! But you fucked up. You put on my clothes and wear my title because you worry I'll take your place on the statues they'll one day build to honor our fight. But that's not the fight. The fight isn't to be the biggest face carved into the tallest mountain.

"The fight is so there won't be any more fucking statues, no more heroes, no more names above reproach whose words can't be challenged by their ancestors. The fight is to stop every single person—sage, king, or cultist—from deciding when people own their own bodies, their own minds. You can't win and be remembered for fighting back because you are one of them. You have created your legend. You are a sage, rejected by the others, perhaps, but still a self-appointed queen of a queendom you dreamt up yourself. Another petty tyrant to be listed alongside all the others. The Void Sage. The Original Sage. And let's not forget Rochelle Archer: The Reject Sage. The Petty Sage. The Fallen Sage."

I gasp, further cracks forming in my mask. My hands haven't left Sara, and shouting at this woman isn't making me feel any better. She isn't waking up. Something is hurting her. Something is keeping her like this. "Now, can you fuck off, oh Fallen Sage, so I can help the woman who might actually be able to fight back?"

"No," Archer says. "You're wrong. You're just a coward, that's why you won't do what's necessary. You're the one afraid of finding the wrong place in history, but I don't care. I'll do what I have to to beat the sages. I wanted all five scepters—it would have given me more of an advantage—but four is enough. I can raise an army with four."

I actually growl at this. "No, you can't. You'll be eaten alive. You'll secure your place among the foulest humanity has to offer, and you'll still lose. You're hopeless." I sigh. Everything about me wants to sob, to break down and cry. To hold Sarafyna to my chest and keep her safe from whatever's happening. But I can't break now; I have to hold it together. Everyone is counting on me to hold it together.

I look up at Autumn and see water running down her cheeks. Her breath is stuttering as she lets herself cry like I never can.

"No. You're hopeless. I have four artifacts, a plan, and an army waiting to wake up. I'm going to do what needs to be done, and I'm going to change this country. The Council too. And while I do, you'll be there, holding an unconscious woman who can't save you. You have no hope of stopping it. You have no hope of even saving yourself. Every sage left in the city knows where you are, and your only defense against them won't wake up. They are angry, they are powerful, and they are almost on top of you. You are going to die for your betrayal, and I am going to save the world," Archer taunts.

I bite into my lip. I don't know what to do. Sara is unconscious in my arms, my enemies are on their way to kill me and my friends, and a self-obsessed cultist is preparing to commit an atrocity. I can't stop any of it. Autumn is sobbing now, like Sara is Henry all over again. She is sobbing, but I have to hold it together.

August's hand lands on my shoulder.

"Lillith, you can't see it, can you?" he asks. I look up at him with desperate eyes. He grabs my hand and presses it against the scepter, wrapping my fingers around it. "Look at my sister. Look. You're right. I was wrong before, when I yelled at you, when I begged you to let her grief fade. You were right. You're the Mage of Mourning," he says.

"I don't understand," I whisper. I am on the cusp of shattering. They need me strong, and I'm about to break. Autumn needs to see that I'm strong. Ember needs to see that I'm reliable. Riley risked everything to join me. I dragged everyone here. This is no time to break down, no time to cry. I need a plan. I need Sara. I need to fight.

"You need to mourn," August insists.

CHAPTER SEVENTEEN

A Dead Man Saves the World

Sara is still breathing, but she won't wake up. I don't understand what is happening, and with her went all of my stability. Riley and Ember are trying to pull her away from me for some reason, while August is still holding my shoulder. "Let them take care of her," he says. "Lily, you need to let yourself mourn!"

I don't understand. This isn't the time for that; that isn't what anyone needs. I need to help Sara; I need to find out what's wrong! I fall to my knees as Riley lifts Sara in her arms, and August kneels down next to me, touching my chin to guide my eyes to his. He can't look so closely; he'll see the glass cracking. He'll see the torrent behind them, and he will drown. I can't let that glass break, but somehow, the kindness in his eyes only spreads the cracks.

"Lily, you saved my sister's life. You did it while I screamed at you to let her go. I love you for saving her, and you don't even realize you did. Look at her. I don't understand what she's feeling—I can't, that was taken away from me. But I don't need to understand. I know it matters, and I know she needs it, and I know you do too. It's why you brought her, isn't it?" he asks. I have to fight deeper but shorter breaths as he speaks.

"I brought her so I wouldn't be alone. So I wouldn't break," I answer. He shakes his head.

"No. You brought her to share your grief. You brought us both so you could offer your pain to someone who wanted to feel it. And you have been. You, the Mage of Mourning, the woman who embodies the concept of grief itself, offer it to her every day. You offer to share it, and she accepts. No matter how much power the sages put into taking it away, no matter how much control they have or how wide their reach, when you are near and you are offering your grief to Autumn, she accepts it, and she feels it with you.

"Look at her. While you hold back, she wears your worry for Sara like a secondhand dress. She can do that because you are offering your pain to her, and she is happy to accept it." My eyes drift to Autumn, her face wearing the exact agony I hide behind a mask.

"No," I say. I know what he is asking; I can see it now. He may even be right. But . . . "I don't know how. I will do anything to make this world a better place, but I can't do that. It's not that I won't, August, I *can't*."

"What is it you always say about the weapons of the enemy?" August asks. "They are using this to share power, to control and steal people's hearts from them. But Lily, all you have to do is offer. You just have to offer it, and it will reach the whole world. Not everyone. But the Autumns? The people on the ledge, desperate to feel everything they've lost?

"Lily, we don't need a demon queen. We don't need an unflappable soldier or a face of stone. We need the woman who's been grieving for us since she first woke up in the body of a child. You have been hurting on the world's behalf from the moment you learned it was in pain, and we want that. We want to hurt with you and feel again like you can feel. Please. Please, just . . . mourn. For us. With us. For anything at all. Mourn and offer your hand to anyone who needs to cry with you."

My breathing shakes my entire body. Every word he speaks is like a thorn digging into my skin and drawing blood. He's right, but I don't know how to do what he's asking. My grief has always been invisible. Unsightly. Shameful. I don't have the capacity for the vulnerability he needs, not with anyone but the woman I love, and she isn't here to support me. I could sooner strip naked and curl up in the cold and the rain than I could do what he wants. I can't. I can't. I can't.

Autumn's forehead presses against mine. I didn't even notice her moving toward me. Her hands grip the sides of my head as August makes way for her. Her nose is pressed against mine, and I can taste the salt of her tears in the air. "Thank you," she whispers with trembling breath. "Thank you for this. It's time I return the favor."

At that, I feel it. I feel it like an impossibly dark, empty room with walls I can't find no matter how hard I run. Chasms of grief are offered to me, and I'm terrified to accept, but one of her hands leaves my head, gripping the scepter and my hand at once. I can feel it—Archer's will, trying to broadcast her control and recruit her unwilling army to march toward death in the name of her legend. I can't do what they need me to do. But I can't allow this either.

"I mean, you work so hard to put on a brave face, to look strong and infallible, but you never had to pretend. I'm saying, someday, you are going to let yourself cry in front of a stranger, and when you do, I think maybe you'll believe it. You'll believe that you can—and should—be saved."

The glass shatters. I let Autumn's grief consume me, and she lets mine consume her, and I finally let out a cry, like the howling of an injured beast. It fills the room, soaking into my friends' clothes and skin like freezing water. I cry like I am screaming in pain, and I offer it to the world as I picture my brother. My vibrant, brilliant brother. The kindness he wore on his head like a crown, his brilliance, his dedication, his love, and his bravery. I remember his death—sudden, brutal. Paying the price for my choices. He wouldn't even have hated me for it.

I remember Henry, and I plead with every soul I can reach.

Grieve with me, please.

Quinn

Gia runs through the garden with a bright smile as I offer Kobe a satisfied nod. He was right; she just needed to expend some energy.

It's been a frightening few months. After we realized the woman we'd offered a ride to was the actual Lillith herself, I may have panicked a bit. I just didn't want anyone tracking that back to us. I admit, I may have gone a bit overboard in protecting our privacy, making Gia a little stir crazy.

"Thanks," I say, "for getting me out of my head. You were right; we all needed some fresh air and freedom."

"That's what I'm here for." Kobe grins. "And I think we should go out for dinner for once. It's been too long, and honestly, neither of us are amazing cooks."

"Speak for yourself!" I chuckle. "My cooking is unparalleled. But if you insist, we can sample a lesser chef's meager offerings."

"Unparalleled mediocrity, maybe," Kobe counters. I hold my hands over my chest in mock injury.

"You wound me. How dare you—" I stop short. We all do. There is something pressing against my mind, and based on my husband's and daughter's expressions, they feel it too. Like a door being held open before us. I recognize it immediately, and it terrifies me. I can feel what it's offering, and I want to run away, but I can't, because I want to accept it more. Because I remember having it, and I remember needing it. I can still feel the slow, healing burn it used to tear through my soul. I know that I can reject it and everything will stay as it is. But . . . I accept it anyway.

Images flood my mind. There's a man sitting on the floor, surrounded by books. His dirty-blond hair reflects no effort in grooming himself after rising from bed. He is laughing like the dawn, warm and welcoming, offering only kind things, if only I can spend an hour with him. He's flipping through a small journal and joking with someone I can't see.

He's beautiful. Not like a man is usually beautiful but like untouched snow. Except he is warm, wearing joy like a favorite sweater, so casually and without care. He's my family. I've been watching him—only in my mind, and only for the single beat of a heart, but he feels like family, and I love him. I want to take a step forward and greet him like a long-lost son. I want to tell him I've missed him even before I knew him, then we could laugh and joke and live like we've always known each other.

And then the fire. It's so sudden. A pillar of violence erupts and consumes him, devouring an entire lifetime of joy. I'd only wanted to touch it, but the man is gone, dead, and the world screams in his absence. The fire remains, but the room he loved is desecrated.

But it wasn't him. It wasn't some man I didn't know. It was Kobe's brother, fighting to let us escape as we were attacked. It's his blood in the dirt while I forgot him. It's Gia's mother, my wife, still warm in her grave as I forgot her name. Both of them live like stones in my heart. I was never able to reach them. Part of me knew I should, but I couldn't.

The world falls like a crumbling mountain, and I fall with it.

"No. No, no, no, no, no, no, no," I whisper until I can't form words any longer and I've collapsed into brutal sobbing. How could I do this to them? I haven't spared a moment to grieve. I loved them. I loved them both, and they are gone. I left my brother's corpse in the mud, and my wife's in an unmarked grave. I can barely breathe. I can't understand why I would do that. I can't understand how. Who did this to me? Why would they do this to me?

Lillith

I feel more exposed than I ever have. More vulnerable, like I'm tied to a witch's pyre and any armor I've ever worn is burning off me. But the wall has fallen, and there is no stopping now. I grip the scepter and pour all of my will into offering everything I've ever held back to anyone who wants it. My body is wracked with deep, shuddering sobs as memories of Henry cut me down, one layer at a time.

Each flash of his smile in my mind is punctuated by thunder outside and a whimper from Autumn which matches my own. Something deep inside me trembles and falters. I can't worry about that. I have more to offer, and there are more who need it.

Riley

I sit quietly with Sarafyna's head in my lap. She is all right. I can feel her soul—brilliant and fierce. I don't know what she is facing, but I know she'll be all right.

The two women in the center of the room weep like a battle cry, and I take a deep breath as I feel the atmosphere bend to their wails. I don't know what to expect, but I know what I'm missing. I can feel the shape in my heart, the hole where the emotion destroying the other women should live. And finally, it descends on me—the offer, like a rope descending into a pit. I can't even see the top, just the light that comes from it.

I don't hesitate for even a moment, grabbing the rope and climbing with everything I have. As I do, I see a face in the light which shines down: a soft face, like a man who never learned to scowl. He's in a simple bed, surrounded by stuffed animals of a quality far surpassing the blanket they rest on. He seems to be asleep, his arms wrapped around one of the quaint toys. As I climb higher, he opens weary eyes and smiles, showing no shame at being found in such a position. He just smiles, not with a smile of amusement or laughter but with the entirely expected joy of seeing a face he loves.

I fall in love with him in that moment. It's not me, not really. It's not my love. It belongs to Autumn, I know that, but I feel it like I feel the burning of overused muscles. It's a love that radiates through me and promises a future like an open field. It tastes like promises and hope and a certainty that everything will always be okay, so long as I can reach him.

But before I do, fire falls from the sky and devours him. He's still smiling as it does, his eyes looking apologetic, like he's forgotten a promise. With his death, my own life is torn away from me. Every horizon burns, and every hope drowns. I'd written a book in a single moment about a future filled with that smile, and now it burns in my hands and melts my skin.

And then it isn't about him anymore. Autumn's grief melts away, leaving only my own behind. Grief for a missing mother, abandoned or murdered by a father who despised me. It's rivers of blood pouring from my hands and filling the room. It's every life I've ever taken to spare them from a worse death. It's the life I could have had if I had been born into a family who knew how to love. It's years wasted paying the price for sins I was born into.

I run one hand across Sara's head. Silent tears run down my cheeks as I remember sorrow for the first time in years. It's like venom being drawn from my veins. It stings as it bleeds from me, but it leaves something raw behind which can finally start to heal.

I hear glass shatter somewhere in the estate while wind howls outside and thunder screams. I recognize it all too well. Archer was right; it's not safe here. That's the sound of the Storm Sage, who must have come to the city specifically to kill Lillith. He's more powerful than Markus, whom Lily barely managed to fight off, even with my help and after catching him off guard. With Sarafyna unconscious, we stand no chance of surviving him.

I start to chuckle, because as the reality of death faces me, I feel a fresh grief for a life cut short, a life where I failed to accomplish anything, but I *am* capable of grieving the loss of my life, and that is reason enough to laugh.

At least, on my last day, I was allowed to feel like a person again.

Lillith

I smell smoke and rain. The air is hot with electricity as the estate weathers the storm outside. I no longer have my head against Autumn's; instead, it rests on her shoulder. My throat throbs from crying, and my claws tear into her shirt as I cling to it. Her guilt and mine mix like blood and wine.

I feel the moment my aspect breaks. My concept of grief is changing, and I can't stop it. The grief I've carried for so many years was never meant to be worn in public; I'd aspected a hidden grief, a private sorrow, a longing that lived in the dark and fled from the light. As I offer my grief to a world who has lost theirs, this aspect rejects me, shattering into many pieces. There is nothing I can do about it.

The building shakes beneath me, and the storm outside threatens to tear this estate apart. The magic I've used for so long is the first thing to falter as everything starts to collapse. Still, I think of Henry, replaying it again and again: my brother standing in an empty building watching me leave him behind, off to fight my war while he dies in my wake. My hand trembles in Autumn's shirt while my other shakes the scepter.

I can no longer use grief as I once did, but I can still offer it to Autumn, and through me, she can offer hers to everyone else, which means I'm still connected to it. It still flows through me like a river; I just need to understand what it has become now. What kind of grief am I, if not one meant only for dark corners?

As lightning tears through the ceiling and scars the floor only a few feet from me, I tighten my grip and let myself feel the grief escaping from me in choked hiccups.

Ember

I don't know if I want my grief back, but I know I want *something*. I know I hate the sages and everything else while they live. I know I felt something—if only a little—when I first crossed the border and met Sarafyna. I know that when it started to fade again, it hurt. I know I never remember my dreams, but I always ache from their impact. So when Lillith offers her own grief, I accept it.

I see her brother again. I barely knew him, and I felt little when he died, but as I watch him this time, his hands behind his head as he walks next to me through quiet city streets, I realize I need him. He is a friend. He is trust. He is the certainty that there will always be someone who will never, ever reject me no matter whom I love, no matter what I choose to do with my life.

He is my brother, and he loves when I feel joy. He is weaker than me, but he wants to protect me anyway. Even more rare, he is unashamed when

I'm the one to protect him; he just wants us both safe and happy. He wants me to love Autumn like a sister, and he hopes I can stop fighting someday, but he understands why I can't. As we laugh and joke together, I feel completely at ease, completely honest. I can be as strange as I want. He will listen to me talk about biology all day, even if he doesn't understand it, and he won't be put off when I make references and jokes I know he won't understand.

I feel safe and hopeful just talking to him. When the stone melts around him and swallows him whole, part of me goes with him. I feel like I'll never be safe again, because if the people I love can die in an instant, it will never matter how powerful I am. I will never be safe.

But it was never Henry. It was never my brother. I realize that, as the fire burns the fields around me, Lillith's grief makes way for my own. It's two men, two fathers who wanted nothing so much as they wanted my happiness. When my grief is returned, a lifetime of memories comes with it.

I was raised in a country without religion; even Alpha's priests had another name—teachers and leaders. They had no god, but they still owned our minds. It was the Void Sage who wanted an atheist country.

He still destroyed it when they failed to worship him.

My nightmares are real—every single one. Of the volu descending on a parade and tearing my family from me. Of forcing them into that stone. I remember now how everyone I ever knew or loved was gathered and scrubbed away like vomit and dirty sheets after sickness. I remember being taken, and the day when a new mind was chosen for me and was trained to be a killer for the man who destroyed my life. If I focus, I can touch the changes to my mind, made like alterations on a sketch.

It has all been such a jumble for so long, so infuriating. The thoughts I couldn't quite grasp, and the warnings I couldn't quite give. Words strangled in my throat, and plans erased when I tried to share them. So many years taken from me, so much of myself washed away again and again to ensure loyalty and secrecy.

I can't bear it all at once. I hiss as I fall to the ground, my claws digging into the floor and scraping at the fine wood paneling. I slam my head into the ground, so overcome with rage and loss and agony that violence is the only expression I can manage, even if I am its only victim. I ignore the lightning which has started raining through the roof and decorating the room. I can't fight lightning, but I can claw at the floor until I bleed.

Lillith

I am no longer grief in a secret spot. I don't live beneath the floorboards, and I will not be tucked away before witnesses. That part of me died today, and I will never be empowered by invisible grief again.

But I am still grief.

My concept of grief has fallen apart, and my aspect with it. I finally catch my breath, my crying no longer taking all my focus. Autumn has started to calm too, and I finally let go of her shirt. It's tattered where my claws were, but she doesn't care at all. Two countries full of people are sharing our grief now.

Shakily, I rise to my feet, gripping the scepter and tearing it from the ground. I can feel all of them because I'm still the spear of their grief, and even as my old aspect fell apart, I found a new one to fill its place. Wind tears the roof from the estate, exposing a sage with a bored expression staring down and rolling his eyes.

I have offered a world of broken people a chance to find their missing pieces, and I am shocked by how many accepted. I can almost hear them—crying, whimpering, shuddering. Healing. And they are offering me exactly what I offered them.

I am not grief in the dark. I am violent and I am bright. I am grief like a fire and a beacon.

As my aura floods the room, it isn't invisible, glowing like the stars and shining like no mana I've ever seen. Its light moves through walls and touches the ground outside, and I doubt you'd even need to be a mage to see it. I know mages aren't the only ones who can hear it, and hear it I can, because this mana—empowered to fight on behalf of a violently grieving world—sings. It carries music with its light, a choir singing a dirge, and it promises an ending to the sage above.

I never get the chance to see if this worries him. I have no speeches for this man. Instead, I scream, and with my scream, I send sound like a torrent that batters and beats the man in the sky.

I'm inches from his face a moment later, force mana carrying me before I even realize I'm using it. His ears and eyes both bleed and try to heal, but I care little, crushing him with force. I pull heat from his body and impale him with steel. My mana sings a new song with each spell, creating a chorus of violent retribution that can be heard throughout the city.

He tries to heal, but with the power I have and the speed my steel allows me, there is little point. All he buys himself is a slower death than I intended as I have to crush him again and again until he is too crumpled and unrecognizable for even his own magic to know what to heal.

It takes less than a minute before I can safely discard his mangled corpse into the garden below. I turn in the sky to see three more sages hovering and waiting to kill me. There is a moment of silence as I stare at them, the blood of their leader dripping from my face and clothes along with the useless rain he'd summoned. All three turn in the sky to flee.

I return to Sara's side, the blood of four sages on my hands but off my mind. Archer failed, and the world isn't hers. The sages failed, and the world isn't theirs either. And as I take a knee at my prone girlfriend's side, she finally opens her eyes, looking exhausted—a little sick, even—but alive. I poorly wipe my face clean before stooping down and kissing her. It doesn't matter who else is in the room; I don't care that her head is in another woman's lap. None of that matters. Only Sara does.

"Hey, Annie," she greets with a weary smile. "Sorry about that. What did I miss?" She struggles to sit up, Riley offering her a little help. I don't answer her question. Instead, I pull her into a desperate hug.

"Are you all right? What happened?" I ask. She wraps her arms around me in return.

"I'm all right. Everything is all right. Actually, I'm better than ever, really. I'm sorry for scaring you." I sigh in relief as my tired eyes start watering again. This isn't bravado; she really is okay. It's all okay. Everything but me. Everyone but me is going to be okay, so I lean in close to her ear and make a request I have been talking myself out of making since I met Mirage.

"Sarafyna . . . please. Please save me."

Simmering

Ember

I was raised in a country without gods. Neither of my fathers ever taught me to worship anyone at all. A simple life running a quiet shop was good enough for us. It was a good home, the kind of place where everything always felt warm to everyone. For a few kind years, I was allowed a childhood, a home, and a family. I suppose it was designed as something close to a comfortable paradise with no figure of worship already in place. No gods, kings, or masters ruled any of us as far as we understood. As a child, there was no reason to find this strange; I'd never known anything else.

When the so-called demons started invading from the sky, most people couldn't agree on what to do. It was like we were frozen in place; even the thought of fighting back didn't present itself as a possibility. I understand why now. We didn't have priests like most of Alpha's pet countries, but we did have people filling the same role—councillors and community leaders who would host town halls and speeches, concocting reasons to get us into one place and steer our minds like carriages. All by the Void Sage's design.

We were given peace and happiness so it could be taken away. We weren't given gods or rulers so he wouldn't have competition for our worship. And we were attacked by volu guardians so we would have an enemy for him to save us from.

My entire childhood was nothing more than a paper castle for the Void Sage's throne. It was real to me. *I* was real. *My parents* were real. But to him? We were actors in a game he was playing. He sent his own soldiers into a war with us, then killed them when they followed his orders all so we would see him as a savior, a hero.

But he could only play the part so well. Even with our minds influenced by Alpha's power, even in a country set up specifically to admire him, he could only convincingly play a hero from a distance, and that only worked so many times. Eventually, he had to show up to receive all the praise he'd bought for himself, and the moment the moron started opening his mouth, people began to doubt his heroism. That was the beginning of the end.

Because he got what he wanted—praise and worship and accolades from thousands and thousands of us. Everywhere he went, he was admired by many people who either didn't or couldn't look past the service.

But it wasn't enough.

It would never be enough.

Nothing short of total admiration, love, and devotion from every soul in the country would satisfy him. Otherwise, he wouldn't have needed us. My family could have lived and died in peace as he pursued the same love from people in the Republic. Instead, we were molded into a world where he could be the sole object of universal admiration, his pride too fragile to accept partial worship. Any criticism at all, deserved or otherwise, was too great a burden for him to bear, so when it came—and it was always going to come—he punished us for it. He sacrificed . . . all of us, bringing more volu than we'd ever seen before and rounding us up like cattle. And I lost my fathers to torment and hell.

But that wasn't enough for the Void Sage. He'd killed his own forces to prove how heroic he was—it was always going to happen when he cast them as the demons to defeat—but this meant he needed new soldiers, so I wasn't even allowed to suffer with my family. I wasn't even allowed my mind. Bit by bit, all that was left of me was taken and replaced with the loyal soldier, the Guardian of Stone. The killer with nothing left inside but false memories and simmering rage I could never trace to its source. I was only allowed to remember my parents in my dreams as, year after year, my soul fought the chains on my mind. I was left with different memories. A mother who didn't love me. Goals I'd never wanted. A school I'd never attended. I believed I served an ailur sage, as if there were such a thing. I believed the sages *couldn't* deceive me. I believed they couldn't change their bodies, and they wouldn't, not while forbidding others to do the same. I believed so many things I knew couldn't be true. I grew so angry. I could neither grieve nor remember the ones I'd lost, but part of me always knew something was wrong.

Well.

I fucking remember now.

Lillith offered just a sliver of my history to me, just a taste of what I'd lost—the ability to feel loss itself—and I grasped it like I was dying of thirst, accepting grief and opening a crack in the dam of my mind. With just that trickle, I bought my mind back, remembered my dreams, and remembered their reality. My fathers' faces fill my mind again, and I finally know why I'm always so fucking angry, why I asked for help killing the sages. I remember every moment of conditioning and control and abuse since I was taken. Above all else, I remember the Void Sage.

I may not stand up to the power of Riley and Lillith. I can't tear the roofs of a sage's mansion and crush him before he can respond. And in the days since remembering, I have seen her do this multiple times. I may not have huge reserves of mana and void energy that can destroy anything it touches in the blink of an eye.

But I have my memories, I have my past, and I have enough fucking rage to boil the soil beneath my feet. The Void Sage is going to wish the praise he'd gotten had been enough. He is going to regret giving me all this rage. He is going to die, and he won't be remembered for his heroism. His grave will be a landmark visited to be pissed on by everyone who remembers him as a sad, pathetic waste of meat.

I don't care if I lack power—I'm going to kill him.

CHAPTER EIGHTEEN

Fear the Open Air

Lillith

Peaceful change is permanent change. Huh," August says, reading one of a dozen posters hastily plastered all over the wall we are walking past. "Why are the sages putting so much effort into posting slogans like this everywhere?"

I glance at the poster in question, depicting plain text over a drawing of a handshake.

"It's probably not the sages putting them up," I reply. "Most likely the lower-level politicians—the people who actually keep the Republic running—trying to pacify the masses. They're the ones in the most danger, after all." I run my fingers across my lip ring and glance around for any signs of danger. We've been moving out in the open in the months since my aspect changed. There is little point to subtlety with my mana visible and audible to everyone.

"Oh, they aren't the ones in the most danger," Ember growls. I nod, conceding the point.

"All right, that's fair. Obviously, we've been hunting the sages for the past couple of months. No one else is in such guaranteed and publicly broadcast danger; not of murder, anyway. But that's not the danger I mean," I acknowledge.

Millions of people accepted their grief that first day, and those people have been convincing more to do the same ever since. And they are angry. A lot of lives look nothing like they would if they'd had the right to grieve.

Like a body that can't feel pain, people here let themselves lose things they wouldn't have risked before, family members whom they never had the chance to grieve. Many, unable to process their pain through grief, took their own lives.

So there is a lot to be furious about, and there have been everything from vandalism to full riots all across the country. Across both countries, most likely, although we lack regular news from the Council Lands.

"We're killing the sages, and so long as we confront them in small enough numbers, there is little risk of our group losing. Typical citizens, on the other hand, simply can't fight the sages, so it'll be the politicians they can confront who get the brunt of it. Archer hasn't publicly shown her face since her initial plan failed, so these politicians and middle managers aren't getting recruited into her army so frequently. So, as sages die, the people who enjoyed comfort as their employees find themselves facing the loss of either their status or their lives. I'd be willing to bet they are the ones putting the most effort into pacifying the population," I explain.

"With posters?" Autumn asks. "What good will that do?"

"You'd be surprised. It's a good slogan: concise, simple, and reasonable in tone. During peaceful times and between two peaceful parties, it's pretty obvious that necessary changes should also be peaceful. It's easy to believe that the most peaceful group is also the most righteous. Or it's easy to believe that fighting will result in escalation, or that it gives the sages the excuse to start killing people. I wouldn't be surprised if some groups have already started spreading this idea among themselves," I answer.

"It certainly doesn't help that the legendary demon queen is the public symbol of violence," Riley muses while I shrug.

"A big reason they gave me that title, I suspect."

"You don't sound too impressed with the concept," Sara notes, picking up more in my tone than the others.

"Not really, no," I agree. "Self-defense is almost universally acknowledged as acceptable, at least as a concept. Few people would argue that you need to respond peacefully when someone tries to murder you in your bed. You can argue for peace for the peaceful, but when you are already being violently oppressed? When there are soldiers and guards in the streets, beating and enslaving people? When there are sages taking people's minds and bodies from them? Gathering them up and sacrificing them to torment? Well . . .

"Believing in peaceful solutions is one thing. Believing in a moral obligation of the violently oppressed to respond peacefully is not an impressive suggestion to me. If you see the powerful being violent and your response is to pacify their victims, you are choosing a side. If you see violence as legitimate from the country's rulers then turn and say things like 'peaceful change is permanent change' to the bodies being beaten in the streets . . . Anyway, it's essentially an authoritarian slogan that uses a victim's desire to be kind to silence them entirely. 'You are ignorable or you are just as bad as me.' That's the message behind these posters, more or less. Just another attempt to bully and control."

"Morons," Riley mutters as she tears one of the posters down. "No different from the audience in Markus's arena. Happy to watch the violence from afar, like it's not even real, so long as their seat is comfortable."

"Comfortable, yeah," I agree. "That's the best word for it. Being peaceful is easy and comfortable for a lot of people. Wake up, work, stay safe. As long as the violence isn't affecting them directly—or even if it is but it's ignorable. In that case, violent self-defense is easiest to frame as the only violence happening, and therefore reckless and amoral; especially when it's the most visible or when the initial strike comes from agents in uniform. Either way, there is the violence that won't interrupt the average person's life and the one which will. A lot of people care only about ending the interruptions. Those with a particular lack of self-awareness may even frame self-defense and defense of others as, itself, an act of violent authority."

"So what exactly do we do about it?" August presses. I shrug.

"Nothing. Be irritated, I guess. We can't stop people from talking to each other even when they are spreading irritating propaganda. This country is in for a lot of changes in the coming years, and I don't know how much we'll be involved in that. It's not even our country; not yours and mine, anyway," I explain, giving Ember and Riley a glance. I suppose they'll probably be around after all this.

I continue. "I can leave a few ideas behind, but when the sages are gone, an entire planet is going to find themselves with the ability to choose their future. A lot of them are going to choose a lot of different options; it's going to be their world to build. What we *can* do? We can be a big enough threat to the fucking nuclear bombs with egos that they are too worried about us to show their faces and massacre the people who can't fight them. We can help Mirage go home and leave this world mind control–free."

"Nuclear . . . Never mind. You're just going to let these countries collapse with their leaders dead? I know you don't care for authority in general, but that seems reckless," August pushes. I wonder how long he's been tossing these questions around in his head. I suppose this was as good an opening as any.

"'Leaders' my scaly ass. If they were so important, they wouldn't fuck off for decades while they played pretend in one of their pop-up countries. Nah, the sages don't lead shit, not really. They call themselves leaders and slap their names on whatever their employees are doing, but they aren't cogs in this machine. They have control over it if they want it, but they are more like warts or parasites. They use it to get what they want, but they don't actually contribute anything to it. Nothing but military force to fight off Alpha and the Council, anyway. Killing the sages will do nothing but eliminate useless positions," I dismiss.

"Sure, but all this fighting around us will probably affect the actual leaders as well," Autumn points out. "It's been happening consistently in every city we visit. At least once."

"I imagine it will, yeah. But, as I often say, I'm not in charge of shit. I'm not actually a queen. This isn't my revolution, and I can't be in every city or every country. I can't personally liberate every playground, as much as I might want to. A better world is in the hands of the people fighting for it, where they're fighting. We are here to give them that option, first with their grief and memories, then by removing the insurmountable barriers in front of them. We're just going to have to keep sharing what we know and what ideas we have, and trust people to fight for and choose a better world."

"And if they choose a worse one instead?" Riley asks.

"Well then, if I'm still around, I'll fight them too. And if I'm not, then you will. We win as long as people never give up on a better world. And right now, what we are doing is the most we can do," I answer.

We have been killing sages and destroying their radiant stones, doing it out in public and in unpredictable places, all to remove them from power and make them fear the open air. That, and destroy their primary means of disposing of *undesirables*. It's been working well for now. Eventually, they're gonna do the same thing as the weaker sages and try to ambush me. Even as strong as I've gotten, I can't beat all of them at once, especially if Oakley shows up. But I'll handle that when it happens.

"And what about Archer?" Autumn asks. There's an unmistakable sour note in her voice as she says the woman's name. Again, I run my finger across my lip piercing. Sara enchanted a few of them to tap into the emotional and audible communication between the scepters. This lets me continue to share grief back and forth with the world. For a while, anyway.

Hilariously, the scepters were created by too many powerful sages and can't be destroyed by only one or two. They can be discarded, but there is nowhere people can't be drawn to them. This also lets me continue trying to communicate with Archer, but she has been silent since our last conversation. I just know she's going to pop up again at just the worst fucking time.

I'll also worry about that when the time comes.

"Well, if we can't find her, her victims will. When Mirage leaves, so will Archer's control over people. Just another tyrant to be overthrown," I answer.

"Yeah, I'm pretty sure she's gonna show up and fuck us in the ass at some point," Ember counters.

I sigh. "Yeah, most likely." Ember is still her colorful self, but she changes more every day. She retains the aggression she's always had, but it's more finely tuned and directed. I'm mostly spared from her vitriol these days, although we still aren't quite friends. "All we can do is plan for that and button our onesies in the back. She won't move until she thinks she has an advantage. For now, let's focus on the task at hand."

"Wait, I have one more question," August says. "And forgive me if this is too personal, you don't have to answer if you don't want to." I raise an eyebrow at him as he gives me the most serious look he's ever worn. "Earlier, you referred to—and I quote—your 'scaly ass.' Do you actually have scales on your ass?"

"Yes," Sara answers without thinking. All eyes land on her before she realizes how casually she answered and turns bright red.

"Anyway," I say between chuckles, "like I was saying, the task at hand."

"The Fortress Sage," Ember growls. I nod.

"The Fortress Sage. The most prominent sage in this city, and the most likely to know where the stone is. Also, you know, he was at the top of the list."

"You seem unusually hostile at the mention of this one, Ember," Sara observes, finally recovering from her blushing. As we walk, the compound Nathan lives on comes into view in the distance, and Ember's hackles raise, punctuating the point. The twins move to the center of our group, as they always do when violence is imminent.

"How the fuck can you tell?" I ask. "Unusual hostility for Ember is kinda like an unusually bad smell for sewage."

"Someday, I will learn to be as pleasant and friendly as you," Ember deadpans. I nod, conceding the verbal joust point. Then she sighs. "The Fortress is one of the older sages. He's been around since before Alpha started losing his shit at too many body modifications. And . . . well, you know how the Guardians of Stone are privy to secrets? Since their minds are so controlled, they don't have to worry about leaks, usually?"

"Sure, you didn't warn me about my shiny arm and its consequences, even after defecting. And half the guardians followed in your shoes once they got their own memories back," I say.

"I wish the local guards would do that," August grumbles. Which is fair enough. Almost none of them made any changes at all. They weren't under the direct type of mind control, needing fewer secrets to operate, so they are still a nuisance to us and everyone else.

"The point is," Ember growls, "one of those secrets pertains specifically to ailur. Apparently, he is one of a few sages who have tried to alter our species over the years. Make us look more human; I'm not sure why. But he permanently shortened our life spans with his experiments, introducing entirely new ways to die early. He changed all of us this way and never bothered fixing it. I'm especially looking forward to his death."

I sigh, rubbing my temples with steel fingers. "That man and his fucking wish fulfillment. He was trying to make *kemonomimi*, wasn't he?"

"Kemonomimi?" Sara asks.

"From Earth fiction. I think Nathan must be one of the few from either Earth or a similar world. They are like humans, but with a few animal features, like cat ears and a tail, or dragon wings, or anything like that. I like them too . . . in stories. Trying to force people into that shape is a bit . . . Well, we were already on a nice little day trip to murder him. I suppose there is no reason to talk about it," I answer.

"Oh, so like you?" Sara suggests.

"No, I'm not a—" I pause as my tail flicks in irritation and my wings twitch against my back. ". . . Fuck." I can't believe I'm a cancer kemonomimi. What a fucking life I live. "Anyway, that explains some . . . *confusing* things about your evolution. Tell you what, let's kill the fucker and see if it has a recoil effect, yeah? Then let's never talk about kemonomimi again; it's gonna take me a while to process that one."

"Yes, let's," Ember purrs.

CHAPTER NINETEEN

People Are Not Things

Nathan's compound is a bit eerie. We encounter no resistance on the way inside, which isn't so strange. It's become clear that if we show up somewhere, we are either fighting a shit ton of sages or we are winning without contest. Sarafyna and I are both more dangerous by orders of magnitude now, as everyone always is after either a nap or a good cry.

Rather than an estate, the Fortress Sage has an entire commune of sorts, although perhaps *plantation* would be a better word for it. It's almost like a small town with a blacksmith, an alchemist, and even a grocer. People are working the fields, all ailur or volu. All of them could live here forever without ever leaving—if they wanted. Or if they didn't want.

We are getting more than a few looks, all from smiling faces. At least I think they are smiling; it's hard to tell. *Would it be fucked up to ask Ember? Probably. I'm not gonna do that.* What matters is that they are wearing collars, and I can feel their grief. Every last slave—and that's what they are—has chosen to welcome their grief again. These are people with much more reason for sorrow than many others, and they all wanted it back.

And yet, as we approach, they appear to smile. It's unsettling, to say the least. But it won't be for long. The moment we find the Fortress Sage, we'll kill him and search for his stone, then these people can take their collars off and live whatever lives they want.

As I am considering approaching one of them to ask, a translucent orange box appears around us, cutting off any way forward or back. I glance at Sara, who simply smirks, which means it's nothing to be concerned about.

"All right, skid mark. How about we stop playing games and you show yourself for an unfair fight? At least that way you can die feeling a bit less like a mewling coward. What do you say? Do we have a deal?" I call. If he's doing this, he must be watching us. I get the feeling Sara could eat the trap for breakfast, but leaving it may help draw him out.

Instead, a loud voice echoes through the air, audible to the entire compound. "Lillith of Endings. You aren't wanted here, and you aren't needed here. My people are happy here with me. I saved them. I gave them purpose. They are mine, and they love me. You? You're not the heroine of this story. Just look at yourself!"

I raise an eyebrow, glancing down at myself as he suggested. Is it the tail and the wings? There are lots of those around, if prettier and smaller. Could be my outfit, I guess, but that seems like a petty complaint. I guess I am either too . . . kemonomimi or too slutty to be a heroine in his story. I look at the people all around the community, at the collars around their necks and the strange smiles on their faces. I feel the desperate grief they all accepted.

"Happy, are they?" I ask. "I don't see joy here. I see another fantasy you wrote for yourself. I see, I suspect, a lot of collars that will be happily left behind once you lose power over their owners."

"Do you know how we are treated in this country?" a volu shouts. "They hate us out there! Nathan gives us legitimacy! His name gives us safety! A home, and the only power people like us could ever hope for!"

"Go away! Leave us alone! Leave Nathan alone!" an ailur man shouts. "If you threaten him, you threaten us! If you insult him, you insult us! And as he defends us, we'll fight for him!"

"Do you see?" Nathan's voice asks. "Do you see how welcome you are? How necessary your liberation is? These people are happy and safe. You're no savior, just a threat to the happy, civilized society I've managed to carve out for them. For my family! The only option for real safety they have! And if you mess with them, you're leaving with quite a few extra scars."

I sigh. "You're one of the most powerful men on the planet with the power to effect real change, but you built this place instead. If the reality is that a marginalized group is safer and happier in collars with your name etched into the side, it's because that is what you wanted the world to be to appeal to your personal fantasies, where you can treat people as things and feel good about it. Not because you are kind and the world is cruel so your brand can be worn like a shield. Because you have access to their minds, personalities, and bodies, and you decided to write them into doting admirers."

I take a few steps forward, pressing my hand against the barrier surrounding us. "Let's make a bet, you and I. Let's see if they say the same thing once Sarafyna here gets just a little closer to them. If they still sing your praises—if *all* of them still love you and none tear their collars off—I'll leave."

"What's your plan if you lose that bet?" August wonders idly. I let out a single, short laugh.

"No one is universally feared and loved. He built the world this way because he wanted to own people and be loved for it. Because being hated for his fantasies of control is a greater injustice in his mind than the violence inherent in that control. Chains and a brand weren't *actually* the only way he could protect anyone; you can obviously always think of another way. This was just the one that ended with people calling him 'Master' and fulfilling his sad little fantasies.

"I can feel their grief, August. And all of them accepted it. It's possible to find people who willingly submit to slavery, or something quite like it, but that requires more subtlety than literal mind control. And my money is on him using literal mind control. I'm not worried about failing to find a single person who wants to shed their chains once they have their minds back," I answer. "And if he has a single person collared and worshipping him against their will? Well, one is far too many. He dies. That is, if the coward ever shows himself instead of leaving his 'family' here to face us alone."

"Oh, I'm not worried about that," Nathan says, finally emerging from the tall fields and strolling to the middle of the road. He stands with his arms crossed, flanked by an ailur woman and a volu girl. The provocation was enough, it seems. "You're either leaving the way you came or in pieces, but you aren't touching my family. You aren't getting out of my fortress, and you won't be forcibly taking anyone from a life they love."

I raise an eyebrow and cross my own arms, my tail twitching with irritation. Nathan reduces the distance until he's close enough to touch as soon as the barrier disappears. "Look at Flora and Rosalie. Barely a few paces from your own selfish sage, and still by my side." He nods toward the volu child when describing Flora, leaving Rosalie as the ailur woman.

"The abuse you're here to stop is imagined," Rosalie confirms. "We serve our master because we want to, and if you took this collar off, we'd simply return and ask for a new one. He's our savior, not our oppressor."

"He's the father I never had, and I don't want to be taken from him," Flora agrees.

"You heard them. Now leave or pay the price. I'm being nice right now, but I am a coward, as you say. I could decide to crush you in a moment if you don't act quickly," Nathan finishes. All three of them glare at me with eyes of fire and anger. I roll my eyes and look over my shoulder at Sara.

"This will work," I say. She nods, smiles almost apologetically at Nathan, and the shield between us disappears in a flash. "We made a deal, so I'll wait until—Oh shit, never mind."

As his eyes widen, both his favorite slaves fall to their knees and tear at their collars, drawing thin bloody lines across their necks as they do. The desperation is tangible, and I aid them with force mana. At the same time, lightning explodes around me and assaults Nathan, leaving him covered in bright scars that almost look like a complex pattern. Force mana crushes him against the ground, and my stinger finds his side, filling his struggling veins with poison.

"You were right about one thing, oh Fortress Sage. I am a threat to any society you think of as civilized, so long as 'civilized' means the violence is downhill and out of sight. So long as 'happy' means you have robbed them of their ability to express grief. I and everyone else you've ever stepped on are a threat to any 'civilization' you hold dear."

To his credit, he responds differently than most sages. Rather than diverting all his power to healing himself, he gives up on it entirely. I can see the hate in his eyes; it's mirrored in the eyes of his former slaves, especially Rosalie and Flora. Rather than try and survive, he is throwing everything into fighting back, but I can read his intentions; I have been hyperalert to it since Hugh killed my brother. His eyes and actions say the same thing: "I know I'm going to lose, but I'll make you pay the price for it."

Shields try to form around all of us; shields which shrink rapidly to kill us like I once killed a woman in a warehouse. Sara meets his power with her own, and none of us have a scratch as I pull the heat from his body and shatter the frozen corpse with force. Even as he dies, he carries fury all over his face. The belief that he is justified and being unfairly persecuted here, on his slave compound.

Rosalie spits where his remains lie as Flora scrambles away. They may have been the perfect women in the story he wrote for himself, the admiring daughter and the submissive girlfriend. They may have been the paragon of what a woman should be in his eyes, happy to have an owner over an equal and call him Master. But it turned out—once his fantasy met reality—they were people, and people are not things to be owned. They do not exist to validate sick fantasies. Without a lot of targeted abuse, people don't thank their owners for leashing them. The shortcut of mind control left him with little actual control, and he will be remembered as nothing but a tyrant by his "family."

Rosalie is panting as she stares at the bent and broken collar her mouth was forced to praise. I kneel down next to her. "Are you all right?" I ask. She shivers at the question, taking a few deep breaths before responding.

"Tell me how I can help," is all she says. I raise my eyebrows and give her an appreciative and warm smile.

"You can rest first, you know. We can find a safe place for you to stay, give you a chance to get your bearings," I respond.

"I have my bearings. I have had my bearings for years, through every sickly-sweet thing my mouth has said against my will. And kneeling next to his corpse is the safest place I've been since he fucking bought me," she replies with vitriol. "Now tell me how I can help with anything you are doing."

I tilt my head in acknowledgment. She has as much right to fight as I do. "Well, we are looking for a massive black stone; somewhere he'd take people who never returned." Her eyes sharpen, and she shares a look with Flora. They nod in unison.

"Follow us," Flora says. I look back at the rest of the group, and we all silently agree. The twins, Riley, and Ember move to help all the former slaves while Sara and I follow Nathan's favorites. Sarafyna catches up to me so she can whisper in my ear as we walk.

"Let me handle this one, please," she requests. I give her a curious look, prodding her to elaborate. "I want to talk to Mirage alone." I give her a questioning look, but she offers no explanation, and I nod. She can handle this without me, and I have plenty left to do.

Just as I am agreeing to her request, August's hand lands on my shoulder.

"Someone is watching us," he murmurs. I look back to find he is right. A nervous-looking woman is standing just a little ways off, anxious energy indicating some urgency, but she doesn't approach. She doesn't try to hide either, so she must want us to see her.

I suppose I'll have some business of my own while Sara is busy. There is something about the look in the woman's eyes; not simple nerves but something more guilty and foreboding, like receding water before a tsunami.

It's the exact look I have been waiting for. The signal that I may finally be able to end all this.

CHAPTER TWENTY

The Council

Eston

I catch myself tapping my foot again as sweat runs down the back of my neck. *How do the other sages control their bodies so perfectly?* It hardly seems fair that everyone else around the table is calm and I have to sweat like this. It's not even hot in here.

I escaped my last miserable life to a world where I had the power of a god, joining a Council whose members need not share names or personal details of any kind. I am the safest I have ever been. Yet, I still have rashes from anxiety, and my entire body twitches when the Heat Sage speaks.

"It seems many of our esteemed colleagues have elected not to attend today. I am weary of waiting for them, so we will be starting now," he says.

"That's not how this Council works, Heat. We are not the Republic sages, acting without thought or consensus. If we were, we'd be in the same trouble they are. We need a majority ruling to act, and we need to act together," the Tectonic Sage challenges. Half the room groans and grumbles while the other half whispers to each other. I am quiet, as is my usual practice. I may be on the Council, but it's not so I can share my opinions.

"And if they are dead?" the Color Sage cuts in. "If this Republic's invader has found her way here and has been hunting them one by one? I can't be the only one who has noticed the way so many have stopped answering their whisper spheres; the way their staff fails to account for their whereabouts. We live private lives, yes, but not so private that disappearing entirely isn't notable! Especially all one after the other at the exact time sages in the Republic are being publicly executed. If they are dead, what do we do? Wait forever and do nothing because corpses can't vote?"

Tectonic and Heat both sigh together. The two agree about nothing but their irritation with Color.

"They are not dead. As you said yourself, the girl is hunting them publicly; she makes a show of it each time. The Republic deaths are impossible to miss, and there hasn't been a single similar death in the Council. Riots, yes, but those we can handle. Unrest as the grief project falls apart? Again yes, but again, not a long-term threat. We will address those if they become too irksome. But a public, flashy execution of a sage? No. Some of our sages have grown silent, agreed. Is it strange? Perhaps. But it has been just that: silent. The pest of the Republic is unrelated," Tectonic insists.

"She hasn't even been spotted in Council Lands," Heat agrees. "She may be able to travel between cities quickly, but between countries? Your paranoia is poisoning your reason, Color."

"Is that so?" Color asks. "For people so certain of your safety, none of you have appeared in public much recently. You have all attempted to dispose of the scepters she is using to realize such power. If you are so certain there is little to worry about, would you care to explain all this constant caution?"

"We're saying she hasn't been sneaking into the country at night and killing us without a sound, not that she isn't a threat. If we didn't want her dead, we wouldn't be here now," Heat replies.

"I would be!" the Wind Sage insists. "Original has been working with the Republic, haven't you seen? We need to take advantage of this weakness to destroy them both!"

"And leave the insane mage who can kill our most powerful sages with only us as a target? Brilliant!" Heat mocks.

"She can't fight all of us at once!" Wind counters.

"But she *can* kill several of us when she does, and I'm not about to volunteer for that role! We need to meet her with overwhelming force, then come back and silence these petty rioters. To do that, we need to agree to the Republic's plan!" Heat insists. "All of us together will crush her like an insect."

"You know as well as I do that we can't trust the Republic! We'll be crushed as soon as she is!" Tectonic shouts. "Wait until the rest of the Council arrives; they'll tell you the same!"

"The rest of the Council is dead!" Color insists.

"She is obviously not here!" Tectonic sneers. "We would know if she were killing anyone in Council Lands!"

"If *she* were killing us, perhaps. But that doesn't mean *someone* isn't! What about her demonic friend? What about Republic agents? Something is going on, and we can't pretend it isn't!" Color retorts.

"Oh, your paranoia never ends, does it? Maybe you're killing them! Maybe Shadow is!" Heat complains. I jump as he mentions me, looking around frantically, my heart rate rising rapidly, but I barely get a glance from anyone. I am here for my prowess at stealth, but everyone knows I lack the stomach for assassination. I try to relax as I realize the accusation was made for its absurdity rather than to actually point fingers at me.

The debate is growing overwhelming. There are too many voices, the shouting match jumping around too much, and I can barely follow it. *Why can't we just agree to join the Republic? That would be safest. Easiest.*

I scratch at my urgently itching arms, closing my eyes and letting myself fade into the room's shadows. No one will notice my absence. I am safe here, in the dark. I can't be touched. I can't be harassed or hurt. I take a few deep breaths as I tune the rest of the Council out. It will be all right. This will be over soon, and then I can go back to my quiet, dark home.

"The rest of the Council isn't coming," a lilting and dreadfully familiar voice says. I recognize it in an instant, and my bones shiver like my skin is simply a too-thin sweater. The Original Sage. The source of my constant hives. As long as I know that man exists in this world, I will never feel like I escaped anything. The fate that awaits me if he gets his hands on me . . . I open my eyes and see him sitting casually in a missing sage's chair. He came from nowhere at all, so far as I can tell. "Don't worry, they aren't dead. But they are each . . . indisposed, in one way or another."

The room is heavy with palpable silence for several eternal breaths. "Bold of you to come here," Wind finally speaks. "You may be powerful, but do you really think it's safe for you to appear before so many of us? I wonder how many of our problems would be solved if we killed you here, since you are so kindly presenting yourself?"

Original chuckles under his breath. "You are all meeting here today, discussing an international agreement to kill a couple of little girls, and you think the people in this room will be enough to hurt me? I've been too easy on too many of you."

"That's not why I'm here," Wind insists. "Those of us in this room will be enough to handle the Republic's cockroaches should they try to infest Council Lands. And we will be enough to handle you."

The Original glances around the room, making eye contact with each of the nearly two dozen sages in the room. "Interesting. It doesn't seem like many of your fellow councillors are quite as confident as you. Are you sure they'll fight alongside you if it comes to that? I don't see anyone making any moves to subdue me," he muses.

Wind scoffs. "You're hardly making a move yourself. You haven't made a move to hurt any of us in centuries, in fact. For all your bluster, you are afraid, because we can kill you. We've always been able to, if we're willing to risk a few casualties to do it. But maybe we won't. Maybe we'll emerge from the shadows one day and end you before you can so much as ask why."

I don't miss the message. Wind wants me to make the first move, to take advantage of my hidden position to give the Council an advantage. My blood runs cold.

Original's eyes drift back to the shadow I'm hiding in. Somehow, despite my existence as darkness, he makes eye contact with me as he speaks. "You're right. You could have killed me when both countries were at the peak of their power. But now? The Republic is too distracted with a new enemy to come save you from me. You're the only one in this room who doesn't seem to understand that. You need to ask yourself a few questions. Why exactly aren't I moving? How do I know the other councillors are never coming? Why did I come here at all?" He pauses, waiting for a response, but the response he gets doesn't come from Wind.

"You're the one killing them, aren't you?" Color asks, his face paling. Original holds a hand up and tilts it back and forth.

"Yes and no. Like I said, they aren't dead, simply indisposed," he replies casually. Oh God. They are part of his great collection, forced to live in consciousness for eternity. This is why we never joined the Republic to kill him. Even if we could, there was a risk of loss, and even those of us willing to risk death weren't willing to face even a chance of that unending, torturous consciousness. "I have come to offer each of you the same deal I have been offering each of them. It's a kind one, if you'll listen. That's why I'm not already consuming all of you."

"We don't want to hear your deal!" Wind spits. "Like I said, any of us could emerge from the *shadows* and get the upp—"

"What's the deal?" Heat interrupts. I sigh in relief. I won't do what Wind is asking. Whatever he is offering, we need to listen.

Original offers an unsettlingly wide smile.

"I need a bit more power. The balance has recently started to shift in a little game of tug-of-war I've been playing. I chose a poor team, you could say. I nearly had it handled, but alas, the war had too many fronts, and I had too few reliable allies. It's frustrating, losing ground, but that's all right. Things are still broadly on track.

"Unfortunately for all of you, that means I need my fallback plan—that would be all of you, of course. I need to empower my sweet little collector to overcome a sort of cancer it has been fighting. So here is my offer. I need you to either contribute directly with your Nexus energy or with new and larger Calm Stones. I'd like to consolidate what sources of power are left, so every little playground I've built for you and every citizen of both your countries, I'm going to consume. Everyone but those of you who agree to help," Original explains. His voice is calm and casual, like he's discussing a contract over dinner. Again, the room is silent.

It's silent for too long, and I worry he will simply decide to consume us all. I can't let that happen; I will do anything to avoid it. He can kill every single person, so long as I don't join his collection. I finally emerge and speak. "W-what's the deal?" I ask. "What do you want from us?"

"You can't seriously be considering this?" Wind gapes. "We are only rulers if we have people to rule! What are we supposed to do? Wander an empty world? This would be over if you hadn't been too cowardly to attack him when ordered!"

"Shut up!" I shout. "If the Original thinks he needs every single soul to beat this threat, then we stand no chance against it. If we are going to lose everything, we need to at least know all our options!"

"Thank you, Shadow, for your measured response." Original beams. "What I need is simple. My collector has thousands of hearts; Nexus points that house my mother's abilities. Both of them, actually. A space like that can't be maintained on its own; it needs something or someone to tether it to the world. This is what your sacrifices are for, which is how I will be using the people you have kept for yourself.

"The Calm Stones, however, have only one Nexus point. One heart. Rather than trying to connect the heart of each stone to Mirage directly, I simply choose one heart that already has a powerful connection to her. A sage, or someone connected to a vast amount of a sage's power. This lets me maintain a smaller, moveable space and connect my collector to other similar points in the world. It gives me external energy to maintain the borders you demanded, and I don't even need to hurt the sage for this.

"Any level of cooperation only makes the stone stronger and larger, so I make a deal. A sage can continue to live their life. They will be a weak sage, as the Calm Stone will take much of their power, but they will be alive and unmolested by the misery I offer. Their heart will exist in two places: inside their chest, and in the center of the Calm Stone they maintain. This carries some small risk. If one is destroyed, so too will the other end. But they will live.

"I need quite a few Calm Stones to harvest the entire world at once. For the rate at which I need to grow, I need every stone I can create. So my offer is simple. Will you give me your heart, or will you give me everything? You're going to do one; it's only a matter of which."

"You'll just kill us after you're done with the stones," Wind snaps.

"Yes, I will. But you'll have time to try and wriggle out of it." Original grins.

"No. Fuck no. If that's our choice, we'll kill you he—"

Wind never finishes his sentence. Roots, fire, and stone erupt around him, and the room is immediately filled with screaming and squelching. Blood spatters across the table and those sitting near Wind. My blood runs cold as the disgusting sound of tearing flesh slowly fades, but the screaming persists. None of us even had the chance to respond. He is letting us hear the screaming to make a point.

New screams join Wind's, a chorus of past victims. Screaming which has existed just under the surface for thousands of years.

"That's one for 'everything,' then," Original notes, holding one finger up. I immediately take a knee and bow my head, and I'm not alone. If he wants our hearts, if he wants our people, he can have them.

CHAPTER TWENTY-ONE

The Violent Stones

Lillith

Riley is doing her absolute best to communicate her displeasure with body language alone. With her imposing stature, this would have been extremely easy even if it weren't such a practiced skill, though the effect is somewhat diminished by her clear terror as she flies through the air. She has spent a good while communicating it verbally as well, but she can only insult me so many times before her voice gets tired.

Typically, berating me for our primary method of travel is a task done in shifts. August and Autumn assist Riley in this endeavor, although the gladiator's apparent fear of heights offers her the most . . . *energetic* insults, which is honestly an ungrateful use of the sound and air mana I maintain to make the trip more pleasant for all involved. They could really hurt a girl's feelings that way. Although, I can't exactly blame them. Lacking wings like Sarafyna and myself, they are carried by pure force mana, which feels a bit like falling for hours in the wrong direction.

Even so, I don't remember the twins being all that bothered by it on our first visit to the Radiant Woods. They've either adopted a bit of Riley's fear or Ember's ability to remain unimpressed and snarky at all times. I certainly hope it's the latter; it's a good quality to have when it's not directing anger at innocent people. They are not with us on this particular trip, however, leaving Riley to protest without support.

Ember, of course, remains silent. There was a time when she would have offered the greatest dose of vitriol, but such days are behind us. When she started sharing my grief, she got her own back, and with it, she tore foreign hooks from her skin. Ideas and beliefs the sages had dyed her with all washed away, leaving a woman grieving for a past she'd long forgotten. No longer is she horrified by a changed body, and no longer is her rage aimless.

"Are we getting close, or are you too busy drooling over your girlfriend to tell?" Ember groans. She's still a bit of a dick, truth be told; partially because all the grief and memories in the world can't change her personality, and partially because of disappointment. Killing the Fortress Sage did not return her species to normal as we'd hoped. These changes had been made to her ancestors, not her directly, and only time will tell if his death will at least restore the ailur's lifespan.

"Mathematically speaking and based on our rough speed, we should still be about a half hour out," I answer. "Don't worry, I can do math while drooling over Sarafyna. I'm extremely good at both."

"She is," Sara agrees. "Maybe the best there ever was."

"And how long is that?" Ember groans, ignoring the flirting to the best of her ability.

"Like half as long as it takes August in the bath," I reply.

"That long *still*?" Riley complains. "Can't we just look and see?"

"Sure, but we will all plummet toward the unforgiving earth below for a second—unless you both want Sara and me to carry you," I agree.

Neither Ember nor Riley need to respond verbally, as their pale faces tell the entire story for them. My mana somehow empowers me far more than my original grief aspect, but it does come at a cost, which is that it is bright to the point of full opacity, and it's loud as fuck. I need sound mana just to counteract it, and even that sounds like gentle wind chimes as we fly. And the brightness basically means we're flying blind; good thing the most powerful people in the world aren't looking for us or this beacon with our names on it could be bad.

That's why we most often travel in a more down-to-earth way. Well, not literally; we still fly, but without magic. Sara and I each carry two people and fly the old-fashioned way, which the rest of the band of merry mages like even less. But it's not fast enough for today. Because today, we finally know where to find Archer.

She still has four of the scepters and has been using them consistently to try and enact her plan, but she has failed to impose her forced emotions and control, as my offering of grief consistently overrides it. Like everything born of Mirage and Manara, emotion offered and accepted is far more potent than emotion wrapped around people like chains. Nevertheless, it is a thorn in the world's side. She still wants to own any resistance, and regularly makes new attempts.

The sages consistently try to remove their relay scepters to deprive me of my source of grief, which doesn't work well for them, as my amplified power allows me to offer it from farther distances, and those who want it tend to follow. It also has the side effect of releasing those who didn't accept my grief from the sage's control if they get too far away.

What it does do, however, is make them more easily available to Archer. She has failed to overpower the emotion we offer with four—and probably will with ten or twenty as well—but simply ignoring it is too great a risk. We have seen her cult active in every city we go to, but there is something of a divide among them. There are her already loyal followers, and there are those under her control. But there are also those who were controlled and then freed. Not all of them left the cult right away; some had nowhere else to go, and others believed in the cause despite the brainwashing—or because of their experience with it.

As far as I can tell, after watching some of them show up for different protests or riots, the cult has essentially become two factions. We are in a hurry today because of—hopefully—a new defector from the Archer faction. After offing Nathan, we were approached by a newly free member who told us where to find her. Or where we would be able to find her within the week. Not in any city but at an inn on one of the trade routes.

I am more than a little suspicious of this information. The woman approached while Sara was dealing with the stone, which means divine magic could be at play in some way, and so they found us specifically when we weren't around our own sage. Sara was also missing for each following conversation with the same woman, since she had to briefly leave and make arrangements for today. I could feel some grief from her, though that doesn't entirely rule her out as one of Archer's pawns. But I can use it either way, with a few steps of my own—like barreling toward the likely trap using my bright musical beacon that even shines through walls.

The protesting returns to silence for a while, allowing me to work through the details of today's plan one last time.

It's all or nothing today. Tomorrow, I will wake up to a world free from the sages or not at all. But even if I don't, we are taking as many of them with us as we can. The way I'm doing things isn't going to be enough; eventually, they are going to realize that hurting innocents hurts me, and so, rather than hiding in safe places, they will hide behind people. We need to handle them now—as many of them as we can.

It's strange how good my mood is today. It's no longer a mask. Once I let myself feel grief like it wasn't a source of shame, the genuine joy followed. I should be afraid—I *am* afraid—but I'm also hopeful. Maybe it's the anxiety washing away now that I'm finally confronting it. We are going to fight for our lives, and the ability to fight gives me so much fucking hope, which in turn brings joy—joy I carry with me as I fly through the sky, announcing my presence to all who might hear me. My grief was a battle cry, and now, I can fight with a real smile.

It's a while before I estimate I have more or less reached my destination, so I push myself forward and wrap my tail around Riley. Sara holds Ember with a few extra arms she grows for the occasion.

"W-wait," Riley protests, and I pause.

"For what, bestie? We're gonna have to drop the mana eventually. Now is as good a time as any," I reply. She closes her eyes.

"Fine. Just . . . don't drop me," she pleads.

"Please. I'm a self-declared pro. I know what I'm doing," I respond with a wide grin. She offers a grimace but nods, and I release all my mana, revealing not the inn we were directed to but the border. A titanic black stone hovers in the air before us, its divine magic supporting the powerful barrier between us and the Radiant Woods. I flap my wings and roll through the air so I can see behind us.

As I tune out Riley's screaming, I spot at least two or three hundred dots decorating the sky. Pursuing sages, those with the ability to fly likely carrying those who can't. Far too many to fight, even with all four of us. *Especially* with all four, really. Ember and Riley aren't equipped for a fight at this level and will need to be protected.

"Annie, my love, my summer breeze. I am beginning to worry about this plan of yours," Sara says. I give her my most baffled expression.

"Bitch, when did this become *my* plan? I literally just showed up and trusted *you*?" I blanch. As I do, I fly closer to the border while descending.

"What? You know that's not true! I only thought of maybe one part!

This mess is all you!" Sara protests. She reaches the ground first, releasing a ruffled Ember whose tail is puffed up like a raccoon's.

"I don't have to stand for this slander," I retort as I drop Riley the last foot or so, landing next to her a moment later and watching the approaching ambush. Or attempted ambush, anyway. Sara re-forms into a more or less human shape before our passengers berate us.

"You're both morons. Insane morons." Riley gasps.

"Yeah, but like, sexy insane, right?" I ask. Riley glares at me as she catches her breath.

"Why the fuck would I mean 'sexy insane'?" she says between heavy breaths.

"Well, it would be a bit bold to say 'insanely sexy' wouldn't it? My girl-friend is right here," I reply.

"She has a point, actually," Sara agrees, almost nervously. It's a bit cute how she's been more open with flirting while still being embarrassed to do it.

Riley just bends over and pukes as she contends with dizziness from the flight.

"I'm glad you are happier now, I really am," Ember interrupts, "but can you get off your bullshit before we all die?"

"So snippy. It's fine; they're still . . ." I glance back at the approaching army of godlike men with inferiority complexes. They are actually much closer than they were a second ago. "Yeah, all right, fair enough. I was the fool all along. Sara, mind getting these two to the other side of the border for now?"

"Already working on it," she replies. In my defense, it is hard to tell when a divine mage is doing something. "Ember, Riley, it's safe to head through now. Annie, please try not to die until I get back."

"That's literally what I'm worst at, but I'll try." I nod. Sara rolls her eyes.

"Hush, you. I'm serious. Be careful."

I smile back at her. "See you soon."

As soon as the words leave my mouth, the three of them enter the bor-der and I can no longer hear them. At the same moment, I cover the border with enough light mana to conceal it for miles, a feat I'd never have been able to accomplish a few months ago. As the pure white light bathes the plains around us, the mana creating it sings like an orchestral choir. Force mana beats like drums beneath my feet as I fly back into the air, this time alone.

I don't attack yet. I want to wait as long as possible before I have to start surviving. I need to buy time. Taking long, deep breaths as the army of sages grows closer and closer, I eventually see a self-impressed Oakley leading them. We both know I can't kill this many, even now, which means he can't resist the urge to gloat.

Unfortunately, he does bring a few extra sages with him, enough to create a barrier not unlike the border behind me. I can't see it, but I can feel the pressure. This is likely by design, considering the smirk on Oakley's face. I am reminded of my confrontation with Nathan only a few days ago, except the roles are reversed. I am the one who is unlikely to survive this fight, at least if things remain as they are.

"There you are," Oakley taunts, a wide grin on his face. "You've shown yourself to so many sages over the last few months, I was beginning to think anyone could find you but me." He was very much the one hiding from me rather than what he's implying, but that's all right, so long as he is talking. And if there is one thing I am good at—unlike remaining alive—it's talking. Monologuing, really, but no one likes a pedant.

"I'm like a clit that way," I reply with a smile of my own. One of the sages maintaining his barrier chokes back a laugh as Oakley's smile tightens.

"Still so clever, even just before you die. Still so loud. Do you think this light will stop us? You think it will give them time to hide? We'll find them anyway. You'll probably be dead before they even have the chance to hide. We'll see them almost as easily as we saw you careening through the air like an idiot. You've always been like this, haven't you? Stubborn. Bitter. Stupid. It's what got your friend killed the first time you came for me. It's what's going to get your friends killed this time. It's why I'm going to kill you.

"You may have noticed the trap at the inn somehow; you may have flown right past the riot spikes. But it was too late the moment we saw you," he jabs. As he does, he gestures at the sages with him holding famil-iar black spikes in their hands. I worried they'd think to bring those, but it doesn't matter. "How does it feel? Was it worth it? Stalking me across realities? Making a fool of yourself? Getting everyone you love killed just because you couldn't let go of your own bitterness?"

Still talking. Good, I love conversations. I don't have to fight for my life while he's gloating, and I have a lot of stalling left to do until Sara comes back.

"Bitterness, huh?" I ask. "I suppose I *am* bitter, by the definition that lives on a serpent's tongue. *Bitter* is just a word for women who don't accept abuse with the meekness they've been assigned. It's a word used like a gag to stop women like me from reminding the world of the cruelties they have endured. Yeah. I'm bitter as fuck, the way you use it. And I'm not alone in that. Not anymore," I reply calmly. Oakley raises an eyebrow.

"Still not broken, huh? Well, you're right, in a way. You aren't alone. Your little stunt has made a lot of people angry and inspired a lot of unrest. It's made a lot of people violent, and violence will need to be answered with violence. Do you understand that? People had peaceful lives, and you took that from them. How many people are going to die because of you, Annie? Thousands? Millions? You could have done this peacefully. On Earth. Here. Instead, you sent people to their deaths."

"Peacefully?" I ask. "Violence must be answered with violence, you say, but demand the people you crush under your feet like pebbles respond with peace? You took peaceful resistance away. *You* did. You took their jobs if they didn't love you or praise you enough, or if they didn't think the right way. And with their jobs, you took their ability to survive, their homes, their right to eat, or even to grieve.

"Existing peacefully is only an option for the people who fit on your shelves in their assigned places. You took peace away from anyone you didn't like to look at. But when you take away peace as an option, even the gentlest are left with violence. The violence was there. Every step you've taken on top of their heads was violence. It's no surprise they wanted to fight the moment they had their hearts back," I spit.

Oakley's grin starts to fade as I fail to exhibit the hopelessness he came here for. Not a good sign. But he is a prideful man; he will want to get the last word before he resorts to killing me. If he doesn't feel like he won verbally, then killing me won't be enough. He'll always have a little bug under his skin about it, at least with this many witnesses.

"You say that what I'm doing is violence? Maybe you're right. It is sometimes, at least, if not in every way you claim. But doesn't that make you the same? What makes you better than me? You have killed too many to count, and I doubt you even remember all their names. So what? We deserve death for ruling over you with violence, but when all of you try to control us the same way, you are innocent? Do you really not see the hypocrisy? Can you really have such a total lack of self-awareness? You celebrate whenever one of us dies. We're all the same. You're just weaker," he accuses.

"You really believe that, don't you?" I snort, choking on a genuine laugh. "What are you, a child? You really think of it as control! If we deny you authority, we are controlling you. If we claim dominion over our own fucking bodies, you think we are controlling you. If you get hurt when we tear off the chains you wrapped us in, you actually feel oppressed! And people used to call you a genius.

"You can't conceive of a world that isn't defined by power. When we fight, you don't see people saying no—you see an arm wrestle. Like living our lives outside of your control is the same thing as controlling you. That's how entitled to human lives and bodies you feel. We aren't taking anything away from you, Oakley, when we deny your orders, free your slaves, or live our lives in ways that make us happy instead of you. We aren't depriving you of anything you are owed.

"When we violently defend ourselves, we aren't trading places and putting you in chains—we are freeing ourselves! Breaking free isn't control, no matter how entitled you feel to your authority. You can't force people into the sizes and shapes you design and still be loved for it. You can't control and own and destroy without being hated, and to you, that feels like oppression. But saying no is not an exercise of power, you fucking incel!

"Do we celebrate when one of you dies? Yeah. Do we laugh at you? Of course. The world becomes a better place when some people die, and better still when they are mocked and laughed at on the way out. Because when people in power have to fear as much as the people without it, things get better. So many cruelties are because the people with wealth and authority lack the fear of the people they rule.

"This is what makes our joy liberatory where yours is oppressive. We laugh because we are closer to freedom, and you laugh because we are in cages. You don't just lack self-awareness, Oakley—you lack any wit worth pissing out if you really believe that."

I see it, once I finish. I pushed too far. *Fuck.* He's too angry to care about winning a debate. I'm going to have to fight soon.

"You're not worth arguing with; there is no point in educating a dead woman. You haven't lived long enough to understand how stupid you sound. Maybe if you'd gotten your facts straight before you got violent, things wouldn't have ended this way," he whispers. He then looks back at all the sages. "Nearly every sage capable of fighting is here today, from both the Republic and the Council; at least those with any brains. You have pissed all of us off, not just me. Time to pay the price." His next command isn't directed at me. "Kill her."

He and his subordinates immediately retreat as all hell breaks loose. I barely catch the shadow of the first attack with the eye on my shoulder. I don't even see what it is, but I feel my ribs crack as it makes contact with my side. I find myself flying through the air, but I try to maintain the light covering the border for as long as I can while desperately sending mana in all directions. Electricity sings like a violin, and poison vibrates like a cello. This helps protect me a little as I get my bearings and bite past the pain. It also reveals which sages carry riot spikes. They initially planned to trap me in the middle of them, which thankfully means they don't all have one. I need to avoid the ones who do even if it means taking an attack.

I have no time to adjust as more attacks fly at me from all directions. The sun is blotted out by arrows fired from nowhere. Force pulses out of me, crying like kettledrums with each wave of power, and arrows of steel are diverted, but hail tears into me while I'm distracted. Scales weather the assault of ice but strain under the repeated impact.

I use force to throw myself through it, grimacing through the persistent pain and shielding my face with my steel arm. Even so, smaller bits break through and cut my face. Sound erupts from me like furious church bells as I emerge from the attack and find a dozen sages waiting for me, hands flying to bleeding ears and sparing me from whatever attack they have planned.

Boiling water spears through my side, cutting through scale and flesh, and emerges from the other side. My scream is drowned by my own sound mana as the water tries to crawl through my torn veins and burn me from the inside out. I force it out with pure mana, then let myself free-fall, narrowly avoiding what looks like some kind of pure plasma. Blood decorates my scales like condensation, and I can taste it climbing my throat.

Before I can catch myself, physical shadows wrap themselves around me, sticking to my battered body like tar. I cycle heat through my body and the air around me, enough to melt flesh and steal consciousness from anyone nearby. I think I may actually kill this one, as the darkness dissolves around me in an instant, but I have no time to check. I can see my mana surrounding a wide sphere it can't penetrate—a fucking riot spike. I can fly out if it catches me, but I can't afford to drop the light wall. Not yet.

I try to tear myself away, but Oakley's strange liquid space cascades through the sky like a waterfall in every other direction. I groan, coughing blood as I decide to risk his void rather than drop the veil of light. Flutes flutter all around me as I surround myself with air and dive into the dark. It seems endless inside yet cramped at the same time. I hear Oakley laughing from every direction at once.

"Welcome to hell." He chuckles. I cough again as I look around. I can't find my way back to the exit, but I can still feel my light spell. I'm not actually separated from the world, not entirely. This may be a moment of respite, actually. A moment of safety, in a way.

"Funny, I've actually been to this world's hell. Used it as a bit of a shortcut, actually. You know there was no hell here until the Original Sage needed a place to put men like you? What do you think happens to you in the long term?" I ask. Oakley only laughs again in response. I gather heat in my right hand and use hot steel to cauterize the new hole in my side. The second scar I've earned in that spot, actually.

Oakley finds endless amusement in my grimace and the muffled scream I suppress with clenched teeth. "You're worried about me? Really?" he mocks. Then the trap is sprung. I remember now—he used this void energy to deliver riot spikes before. He must have been saving them for this moment because they fly from every direction at once.

Clever but fruitless. Again, trumpets sound as my heat extends from me for miles. With no other sages to worry about, I can pour any mana not used by my light into this.

Everywhere but in a small bubble around me, flutes and trumpets sound together and spread apocalyptic heat. *Hell indeed.* Mana may not reach the spikes, but heat doesn't dissipate in an instant when the mana is gone, nor does air. They only have a moment before the void swallows both, but it's enough. The spikes are only metal, and the heat I can create now turns them into liquid. Any enchantments they carried melt with them as the sound of Oakley's clapping fills the space.

"Impressive. But you are still trapped. Perhaps I'll just have the other sages attack while you have nowhere to go. They seem to have discovered their spines, now that you can't fight back." He follows through only a moment later, letting one Nexus spell through at a time. But only one. They are always from a different direction, but I have eyes in the back of my . . . back. He must be worried about leaving an exit open for too long. This is easier and safer to avoid, but I'll tire eventually.

In the meantime, he tries to regain ground in his verbal joust.

"We are gods, Annie. All of us. And we aren't the only ones who can feed the Original's hell. You and all your little friends? You're just rocks in our boots. Pebbles to be swept from the road. Refuse. I would worry more about your fate than ours," he gloats. I barely throw myself aside as some kind of acid rain falls from above me.

"Pebbles, are we? Strange how terrified of us you are if that's the case. How many of you have we killed? How many hid when they heard we were in town? How much effort did you put into controlling all these insignificant masses? How many have you thrown in the Original's hell because you were terrified of them, of what they could do if they ever figured out how your power works? Have you ever wondered, Oakley, why Alpha fears those who change their bodies? Why he demands them as sacrifices? Why he bans even his fellow 'gods' from altering people?" I ask. As I do, gravity assaults me, trying to pull my body in two directions at once. My force mana corrects both, defanging the attack.

"You think that's fear? That's nothing but housekeeping." Oakley snorts. I roll through the void as the jaws of some massive beast emerge below me, trying to swallow me whole.

"I saw you on top of that tower," I counter. "I know what fear looks like. And I know you are afraid. Because we aren't pebbles, are we? We are stones you tried to pave your path with, but it never worked. We were never the stones to line your path. We were safe neither to step on nor discard, nor to use as grist in the mill of your comfort."

Hot sand tears into the void, exploding all at once and filling the air with iron mist. I fend off the initial blast with force but can feel the burning of the attack entering my lungs. I cough again, hot tears running down my cheeks as I force the words to continue.

"There was only ever one way you were going to feel safe, and it wasn't throwing us into hell. You were only ever safe while we were free. You lost that safety after the first person you sacrificed, because until all of us are free, none of us are! You built the foundation of your world on our backs and called us defective when we moved. You laid out a shape for us and called us broken when we didn't fit. You thought if you made it too hard to exist, too dangerous and too hostile . . . You thought if you sewed our mouths shut and turned our neighbors into batons to beat us with, we would disappear!"

As I scream, the space around me grows solid. I feel like I'm trying to move through stone, leveraging all my strength to break free but only feeling muscles tear for the effort. I can't escape the next attack. I don't care. I keep screaming at the Void Sage.

"You thought you could silence and suppress and ignore and we would fade into obscurity! You wanted us to eat each other alive, fighting for the scraps you left behind until we let the sand bury us in the desert. But you were wrong. There was nowhere to abandon us. There was nothing you could use to divide us. We were never cobblestones. We were never decorations, defective or otherwise. No. That's not who we ever were, however you may imagine us."

A thousand different attacks pour into the space at once as he finally grows confident I can't escape. I spit into the empty space and glare, trusting Oakley to feel the vitriol even if he can't see it.

"No. We were the violent stones beneath your feet. And if it is impossible to live and to love and to breathe in a world where you exist . . . well, we are not going to lie down and die. You will never take another bloodless step in your life, now that we're awake."

I close my eyes, waiting for the impact . . . and feel familiar arms wrap around me. I feel rushing wind and warmth as the void around me shatters, giving way to a more powerful sage. Taking a deep breath, I feel our retreat from the barrage of violence. My muscles ache, and blood leaks from under my scales; the various aches and pains should spell death and danger, but instead, I feel safety like the first lamplight on a dark night.

As I open my eyes again, the void is gone, and we are on the ground. Sara is holding me with her arms under mine, feet away from my wall of light.

"Shit, you all took your time," I complain. Sara takes a deep breath through her nose.

"I asked you not to die, didn't I?"

"I didn't! I don't think so, anyway," I respond innocently.

"On a technicality. I thought you were going to stall him as long as you could *without* fighting?"

"I tried! He's just an angry soul," I defend myself.

"You called his dick little, didn't you?" she accuses.

"I swear I didn't!"

"Did you call it limp, then?"

"No!"

"You, in no way, insulted his sexual prowess? Not even once?"

". . ."

Her mouth draws to a line and her eyes narrow. "Annie. Look at yourself. You look like something that should be cooked over an open flame. If I had been just a little later . . ." She pushes me away just a bit, looking me directly in the eyes even as her divine magic courses through my body and helps me heal. She can't heal me as fast as anyone else, but it does help.

"Right. I'm sorry. I really am. Old habits," I say. And I do mean it. I asked her to save me, then I almost got myself killed. I needed to delay that fight for longer, but I pushed too hard. In my defense though, the guy is an annoying little prick.

She gives me a harsh look which softens quickly. "It's all right. We are ready now. We just need—" Before she can finish, white void mana collides with an invisible barrier behind us. Sara has created her own tiny border around the two of us. A new ability, discovered after that night in the Music Sage's home. A furious Oakley assaults it with a dozen other sages.

"Cute, but you can't keep all of us out. Not forever! Not even you!" he snarls. I wrap an arm around Sara's shoulder and hang off her side while I watch the sages flood to the area at Oakley's command, combining their power to chip away at Sara's barrier.

He's right; we can't. Sara is far stronger than any of them individually, but as a few fail to break through her defenses, more join, and more, and more, until nearly the entire army of enemies cut us off. Sara is the strongest sage here; her whisper spheres are the only ones enchanted enough to survive contact with the Radiant Woods, putting her on a similar level to Alpha. Even so, this is too much for Sara. She has maybe a minute left before we are unprotected again.

I grin.

"You know, it's strange," I say. "You implied I was stupid for broadcasting my movements as I flew right past the trap you'd laid for me. Odd you never wondered why I might do that." His brows furrow in half rage and half confusion. "It's all about power to you, isn't it? Look at all this! You were so afraid of one or two people having more power than you; all of you were. And that's why you are going to die. Because you thought the world was a power struggle between a few elite players, but it's not one person with too much power who is going to kill you. It's every violent stone you stepped on to stop me. You want us dead? Well, guess fucking what, you sniveling little leech? We want you dead too."

At this, I hear the crack I've been waiting for and finally drop the curtain of light, revealing the border and the army behind it. Where Oakley has hundreds, we have thousands.

Thousands of angry, violent stones run through the open field toward the border; some with obvious auras of mana, others with no power at all. At first glance, they look like they'd be easy for hundreds of sages to massacre, but the cracking stone in the sky tells an entirely different story. Because, while we don't have any sage but Sara on our side, the man at the front can't be harmed by a sage's power. Not a sage trapped in his area of influence.

While Leo, Ember, and Riley scream and charge at the rapidly dissolving border, Sara and I make our respective moves. When Sara drops her defenses without warning, I tackle Oakley—the lone mage among the sages—launching both of us into the air and away from the hundreds of sages gathered to protect Oakley and overpower my girlfriend. At the same time, Sara throws herself in the other direction. Before the sages we've lured in can react, she creates a larger barrier just outside of Leo's expected area of influence when he arrives, leaving only one exit for most of our enemies: the side facing an army of our own.

A stone dissolves and falls from the sky. A border cracks and breaks. Hundreds of cruel men find themselves powerless and trapped as thousands of the victims they abandoned to the Radiant Woods close in on them. Sara fights half a dozen or so sages who manage to evade the trap while maintaining her barrier, and I offer a manic grin to Oakley's terrified eyes.

The violent stones have finally been thrown.

CHAPTER TWENTY-TWO

Battle Cry

Sarafyna

N*o . . . we can't . . .*" I said moments before the world collapsed into darkness. Months ago now, and the memory is still vibrant and bright in my mind. I felt lost, like everything had turned to mist, even the ground beneath my feet. Something was eating at me, not with hostility nor with regret. No, the teeth biting into me formed a genuine smile. It felt like every friend I'd ever had. And yet, it was biting at my heart.

I didn't understand it at first until I remembered my first meal in the Radiant Woods; my first bite of the sweetest fruit I would ever taste. It had turned out to be poison, forced on me to keep me weak. This . . . *chewing* felt like that. Like a directed bite, ignorant of the poison behind it. It carried the kind of idle pain that wouldn't quickly fade, like a sore muscle or a broken tooth. That was what pulled me there. Regardless of distance, regardless of the border, part of me was torn off, and my mind was pulled with it.

Just as I was trying to navigate the mist all around me, I felt something else, almost antithetical to the pain that had just torn into me. Addition instead of subtraction. Healing instead of pain. But both were present, and neither was hostile. One promised death and the other autonomy. I needed to see what they were and figure out why I was there. I had to stop one and welcome the other, but I was lost in the mist, and I couldn't tell where to go.

But Annie was crying.

I don't know how I knew this, but I did. She was hurting, and she was letting herself bleed. She needed me. So I focused, centering the world around myself, remembering my time without sight, when I could only feel mana and Nexus energy. I wasn't there, not really, but I could breathe.

Slowly, deliberately, rather than wandering through the mist of my mind, I ordered it to take shape before me. It was my mind, an extension of me, and no one could define what it looked like but me. Not since I met Annie, anyway. It was slow and painful, but it worked. I felt like I was wading through mud, but each step brought four people more into focus. Well, two people. There were two others, and I knew they were there, I even knew who they were, but I couldn't see them. They were in a blind spot. All familiar faces, all hanging from my heart like weights of different sizes. All surrounded by stones.

Gilbert and Dominic shone like a bonfire on a cold night. They offered warmth, and they sprinted toward me. Thousands of warm stones rolled behind and around them. Dominic guided them like a patient school-teacher, and Gilbert cried for them as they rolled. They were all coming to me together because they needed me, and they knew I would love them. They wanted to offer me everything so I could offer them a home.

And I would. I wanted to—because I recognized them. Neighbors I had never been allowed to meet. Lost souls kept away from me lest I offer them an escape. If they made it to me, they would offer their hearts. If they made it to me, my hat shop wouldn't belong just to Annie and myself but to everyone. That's where I was, I realized. Not physically, but I was there nonetheless. And that's where they were going. All of us together could take the Radiant Woods and turn it into something kind. I could feel it. But they had to make it to me.

And they were too far away—because I was being eaten slowly.

Something touched the shop, so close to its core. A core I didn't even realize it had. And what it touched, it destroyed. Leo and Charlotte. I could feel them, or . . . I could feel someone else watching them. Someone I have hated for a long, long time. If I got closer, I'd be able to watch them too, and maybe I'd be able to stop them, because Dom and Gil weren't close enough. Not yet. If they didn't make it, everything would fall apart.

So I ran. I had no legs there, but I ran, moving to the core of my shop somewhere in the mist like the wind over trees until I arrived. Every line in that room was so familiar. I had always felt it, even before the hat shop existed, because Annie's heart rested in the center. Not her actual, physical heart, but her heart nonetheless. If it was crushed, so too would Annie be crushed. If it was eaten like the wall to the room had been, so too would Annie be destroyed.

I didn't understand why it was a heart, but it felt right. It was made of cloth, like the fiber I'd use for a simple hat. Just like the real thing, it didn't beat. Just like the real thing, its depth was endless and warm. Just like the real thing, it ached and cried and fought. I needed to protect it, but just outside, I could see the Radiant Woods. And I could see dead land. Leo and Charlotte and at least a few hundred other people filled the dead space between the woods and the shop. Leo. He was the one creating that space I couldn't reach with divine magic. A space Alpha couldn't reach either.

And Alpha was in the woods, pressuring Leo into moving just a little further. Just a few steps and the hat shop would gone. Annie wouldn't survive. But I couldn't form myself into a real body, couldn't make my voice heard like Alpha could. Not yet. I had to push, but Alpha was pushing too. He was trying to make them kill Annie and destroy me with a few steps, and I couldn't warn them. They just needed to wait a little longer, and I'd be able to fight him off. But Alpha was angry.

Charlotte was standing in the way. She was standing in his way, and she was weeping, begging. Halfway across the world, Annie was doing the same, both of them standing before a god, weeping and screaming and demanding something better. I would not let them lose.

My divine magic couldn't reach Leo or anyone near him. Neither could Alpha's, but he had mana as well. I had my own, but it was stolen, part of the bodies of evil men I had consumed. I'd never have real control over it, and as Charlotte stood in the way and protected Annie's heart, I felt Alpha grow impatient. I felt the violence in the spells he planned to use to drive them forward and end all of us.

I refused.

Reaching out to him, I put myself in his way, surrounding the untouchable space Leo created, and I presented myself as a barrier, wrestling with Alpha's divine magic. At the same time, I swallowed each attack he threw:

ice, bone, and storms. Anything he threw at them I took. Charlotte begged for Annie's life, begged these people for their own lives, and Alpha raged, bringing hell to the calm world Leo had created. He'd led them here with little offers of freedom; I could see that. And the longer Charlotte delayed them, the more furious he grew at the failure of his plan. He scorched and melted and destroyed me, even as my body rested on a cold floor in another country. And he was stronger than me. I couldn't hold him off forever. I was barely surviving.

But Annie was crying. Charlotte was weeping. The whole world was breaking under the weight of finally visible grief. It would not be a waste.

So I let him scorch me, let him hurt and mock and torment. I let myself grow weaker and weaker, until I could tell I might be swallowed whole by the suffering. Not just mine but all the agony he was still using to empower himself.

And then Charlotte stepped inside the hat shop.

Her heart was like Annie's: offered freely, even when unasked for. Her presence alone gave me the strength I needed to withstand Alpha's assault for just a few more seconds, which was all the time I needed. Gilbert and Dominic arrived like rain on a fire, and thousands of Alpha's victims joined my world, each of them offering their hearts and giving me strength as they flooded in.

Together, we grew stronger and more determined, and a breath later, I was no longer the one in pain. Just like I did when I created the hat shop, I gripped the Radiant Woods and denied them their control. My hat shop grew, expanding and swallowing the Radiant Woods. Not all of it, but enough. There were no woods near Leo anymore. In fact, my hat shop was nearly as widespread as the woods themselves.

Annie and Charlotte mourned together, and they were safe because of it. Finally, I didn't have to fight anymore. We were all stronger, and the fight was over. With all the offered help, I could give myself a form and communicate with the people I'd been trying to find for so long.

"Thanks," I said, "for buying time."

The months after my confrontation with Alpha were kind ones. Annie was more like herself than she had been in a long time. Not because she was finished grieving but because she had finally started. Yes, she was growing sick the entire time, her self-destruction gone too far by the time I made it back. Her wings and tail took a toll on her every day, and she'd grown far too thin. But her smiles were sweet and genuine, and we had a plan.

I couldn't visit Leo and the rest as often as I'd have liked, but I could always feel them; a quick flight to the border let me check in fairly often. Leo couldn't use the hat shop—not anymore—but everyone with him could. They had been visiting the towers, sleeping in beds, even sharing food and clothing, and it was having an obvious effect on their spirits. One woman, Ryanna, had been volunteering more and more for supply runs, at least when she thought Gil and Dom might show up.

They'd all been growing more confident every day—and they'd all grown angrier. At least everyone but Leo. It has been impossible to find Leo without a smile on his face, and for much the same reason everyone else has been so ready for blood. No longer were they being drip-fed one person to save at a time. Instead, every single person Gil and Dom had saved that day visited Leo at some point, so many people were given their bodies back.

A few were like Leo and Charlotte, but most of them had been used as bait to draw the group toward Annie's heart. The rest were guilty of some other sin while living in a world the Void Sage grew weary of: losing a limb, being born without hearing or sight; anything "unsightly." A few returned to humanity and, after spending some time around Leo, realized they actually were much like him and Charlotte.

Interestingly, especially to Annie, these ones weren't changed by the whiplash effect, but often, they didn't feel the need to be. Those who did, I was able to help a little after working with Annie for so long and with my recent growth.

One thing everyone had in common was this: They were ready to fight; ailur, volu, and humans together. Some were recovering from the woods faster than others—many likely never would—but thousands of people were ready to kill the sages if they just had the chance. And once Annie learned what Leo could do, that chance presented itself.

Day after day, week after week, Leo and Charlotte marched toward the border while Charlotte worked on replacing her aspects now that she didn't need to provide food and clothing to everyone else. They had to take the long route, but they were almost there. Annie knew the sages were going to ambush her at some point, she just needed to delay the attack until Leo made it to the border. And she did. They didn't attack until almost a week after we were ready for them, prepared to take their power and put justice in the hands of their victims.

Annie has . . . mixed feelings about seeing Charlotte again. She appreciated the story of what I'd witnessed, especially since Charlotte saved her life. But she can't quite look past her brother's death and the role Charlotte played in it. And I wouldn't ask her to. To her credit, neither would Charlotte. And Leo . . . Annie can never see Leo again. That has been hard for her to swallow. Leo still doesn't understand why, exactly, but he gets the gist of it. They both spent so long hoping for a kind and joyful reunion, and they will never get it. I can see it hurts; even now, the proximity of both is a building anxiety in the back of Annie's mind. I can feel it even among all this chaos.

But now is not the time to examine such grievances. Because we brought the sages to watch the fall of the border as Leo approaches it. And with it, so does the regime of death who put it up.

They can fight on the same battlefield, even if they'll never eat at the same table again.

A few escaped sages flank me on every side as the memories flash through my mind. It's too late for them. I fought Alpha off; a dozen minor sages won't stop me now, even as I maintain the cage for the trapped sages. Leo, Charlotte, and even Ed are inside, cleaning up that mess. I just have to hold off the few cowards who held back. Well, that and let two women out. Two women with a personal interest in helping Annie kill the Void Sage.

CHAPTER TWENTY-THREE

Hope for the Boy Who Ran

Charlotte

I run from years of hiding. From years of complying and agreeing and amiable acquiescence. I run from that dark little corner just out of sight; I never belonged there, but it was the only place I would be tolerated, and even then, only because of my mana. It is a flight of sorts, with so many things I'm leaving behind and never returning to. But it isn't the flight of a coward—not anymore. Sometimes, cowardice is accepting something instead of avoiding it. I will never be that woman again, so I run from my old self and toward the men who have always wanted me dead.

Leo's range isn't infinite, and he himself can't fight; we simply can't risk him, and I'm not the only one who feels that way. My personal attachments aside, everyone is aware that if anything happens to him, we'll have to fight hundreds of divine mages. What this means is, while we may outnumber them, we can't bring the entire might of our force down on the enemy all at once. Sarafyna has them trapped on the other side, and our makeshift army has them trapped on this one. They will die, but it is far from safe for us before they do. They have a chance to fight back and kill as many of us as they can, and if they can fight their way to Leo, or even out of his influence, they'll have their divine magic back.

So I lead the charge. Lily's brother Ed, runs with me. He's one of a few volunteers who were never trapped in the Radiant Woods, and he may be the only one at the front of the fight. I am our most powerful mage, and he is, unfortunately, our most experienced combatant aside from Ember and Riley—but these two have their own battle to fight once they make it through the enemy lines.

I'd wanted Prince Dominic's help, but they needed him back at the towers in case the attack picked up again. Our opponents aren't experienced either, at least not in killing without their divine magic. They are, however, experienced in killing where most of us are not. But there is no time to hesitate. There are still free sages. We won't have to fight them, but we are at their border—their *patrolled* border. They didn't bring any armies because they'd have made no difference against Lillith alone, but now that the tides have turned, they need mages.

We need to end this before one of the escaped sages manages to call in the border patrol. "Guardians of Stone," they are supposedly called. We won't win in a fight against them, so as we collide with the sage, Leo retreating back behind us, I don't hold back. Pink mana surrounds me, an aspect whose only famous user was killed by the man next to me. A horrified sage struggles to draw a clearly enchanted sword he has likely never needed, but before he manages to draw it or I get the chance to ask myself if I am truly able to kill a man, the air explodes in front of me. Edward's aquamarine mana joins mine and fills the combusting air with shards of glass.

I wonder what sort of sage he was.

Ed's face is just as pale as mine, but he doesn't pause. *"You don't get the chance to say goodbye in battle."* This had been his advice to all of us. *"There are no grand goodbyes. Only with power like Lillith are you allowed arguments and speeches on the battlefield. The rest of us? If we stop to breathe, we die. If we stop to doubt, we die. If we stop to regret, we die."*

His wind carries glass toward another group of sages, but at least one of these has managed to draw a sword. As it cuts through Ed's spell, the mana around it dissipates and I curse. Then, I set my jaw. The woman who tried to have Leo killed just for his clothes wore a cloak with a similar effect. I should have guessed the sages would have something similar. They may have been too lazy and confident in their divine magic to earn mana of their own, but they would still have come expecting to fight a mage. Of course they have some kind of defense against mana.

The man with the sword attempts to counterattack, the weapon cutting through glass and wind and flying toward Ed's throat. *"If I die, I'm counting on you. Take care of Mariah."* Words to Gilbert and Dominic, overheard before he joined us. Edward talks about death like it's almost certain. Or at least, without the certainty of avoiding it a boy his age should have. Death in a battle is instant; he has said that many times. There is no time to say goodbye. When life ends, it simply ends.

Well. Not for him. He told me what I did to his brother, what my choices did to Lily's brother. He told me he was trusting me—because he'd made the same mistake.

These men don't wear cloaks. If they want to dissipate mana with their swords, they can't attack at the same time. Using my new mud aspect, I decorate the earth with a gray, nearly white mana in less than a breath. The earth beneath the sage's feet loses its shape and melts to the consistency of thick stew, swallowing him to the waist before his attack can land.

Ed is quick to respond as soon as he's out of danger, crushing his opponent's head with a block of glass. I catch him flinching at his own brutality, but there is no time to slow down. If all these sages have mana-dispersing weapons, they may be able to kill far more of us before we end them.

I can't let that happen.

The entire world around me has erupted into violence. Riley and Ember are tearing through the crowd with void mana, clearing a few dozen sages before they even get the chance to draw their weapons. I even catch Ember pulling a sword from the remaining half of a corpse as they run. She uses her tail, not even stopping to glance at the body she is robbing. They've already saved many of my friends just while making their way to another fight.

It's encouraging for a moment, until they reach the edge of Leo's influence and Sara lets them out, leaving the rest of us on our own. It's amazing how much terror I can feel at a battle I'm guaranteed to win, because numbers we have, but none are expendable. I will feel a hole in my heart for every ally who dies.

I can't protect them all. I need to, but I can't. I send mud, explosions, and binding cloth anywhere I can to save as many as I can. We are killing them faster than they are killing us. Pink mana dissipates around a sword, but cloth ties its owner's legs, toppling him and leaving him to be trampled by his own terrified allies. The ground is unsteady mud for our enemies and solid for us. I catch a glimpse of Lewis and Kasey, also fighting at the front. Even these two I want to protect, and as Lewis stumbles, caught by Kasey,

I send a curtain of thick wool out, tangling the nearest sage to them in it. It won't stop him, but it will give them time.

But even as I save these two, I see blood in the corner of my eye. Not from a sage this time, but from an innocent, brave man skewered while protecting another combatant.

The red running down the sword. The pinkish bubbling in the victim's chest. The sinew not quite separated from the blade and pulled out in far too discernable chunks. It's all too real. We are killing them faster than they are killing us, yes, but they *are* killing us. It doesn't matter to me the willingness of the risk. We all knew some of us would die, especially those charging in first, but it doesn't matter. It is wrong for them to die. It is wrong for those fighting back to be killed by the people who always hated and hurt them. It was wrong when they died as I tried to hide them, and it's wrong now as we fight.

Pink mana surrounds the bug-eyed sage as he struggles to retrieve his sword. Every innocent life lost on this battlefield will be paid for. My explosions are loud, but somehow, I still hear the brief scream from the man they end, clenching my fists with ferocity as I face what I've come to. I've never had the stomach for violence, but violence has always found me anyway. As much as I hate the feeling of ending a life, I hate watching the wrong ones end more.

So I kill. And kill. And kill. The crowd of sages grows smaller with every passing moment. Arms wrap around Edward's throat and cloth wraps around his assailant's throat. A sage runs toward Frey but is knocked backward by an explosion. None of the cowards approach me directly, all happy to abandon us to torment but too afraid to face anyone who can hurt them back. I feel so cold, but each sage's body I step over is at least one less friend in the mud. I grow numb to the chaos as I try my best to control it.

Until I catch sight of one man with cold eyes standing still as his allies panic. Calculating instead of fearful. Intentional instead of manic. He has no fear, and not because he has accepted death. It's only been a few minutes, and there aren't many of them left. This has been a massacre, but this man doesn't believe he is going to die. It's getting easier to protect people; I'm barely aware of my own movements as I do so. Explosions and mud and cloth, bandaging I barely acknowledge as I create it. With every passing moment, the sages lose ground, and century-old lives end. There is crushing and violence, and I can take it because each death is a broken chain.

But winning isn't enough, because this man isn't afraid. I am not a combatant. I don't have a sense of danger or the reflexes or will to respond to a fair fight. I have power and I have powerful aspects, but I don't know how to fight. So even as crowds literally trample over their oppressors, I feel afraid. My eyes meet the cold man's and only I am afraid. I can't identify the exact source, but as he raises his arm, dread climbs through my veins like a slowly building tide. He's holding something, wooden and nearly as long as his forearm. He's pointing it and aiming with a glare, but not at me.

I can't see everyone around me; there is too much chaos. And yet, I know where it's pointed. I don't know how he knows, but he's figured it out; perhaps the same way I can tell he's holding a weapon. A visceral fear grips me like freezing hands around my throat. There is only one person this man could kill that would make a difference. One person, unmoving and hidden behind so many of us, away from all the carnage. He is planning to kill Leo. He's planning to kill Leo, and I don't know how to stop him.

Mud in all directions. Curtains of cloth to obscure vision. Explosions in brilliant pink. I push mana through my veins like an open wound, but I won't be fast enough. I won't be able to stop him in time. His finger is already pressing down before any of my spells have a chance of reaching him. I realized too late, and there is nothing I can do.

A familiar darkness rolls out in front of me like a royal carpet. A one-way path with no turns or forks, just endless shadows and snickering faces: the inescapable despair that has followed me all my life; hopeless shadows and mist I will be lost in until I die.

Finally, I have chosen to be brave, and my son is going to die.

Edward

The first time I killed a man, I didn't know how to process it. How a human being could speak to me one moment and turn to unrecognizable meat the next.

I dodge one of the strange swords, knives of glass spinning through my wind and taking the arm of my assailant.

At first, I couldn't understand how Lily killed so easily. How someone who loved people so desperately could end a life without a second thought. Even after I'd begun working past the injury she represented to my pride, I'd failed to connect her desperation to save people with her willingness to end a life in a moment.

My wind blows like a breeze past a few of my allies, turning to a storm that cuts into the sages with raised swords. This spares my friends from the sharpened steel before it can descend on them.

And then I killed a man. I brutalized him, really. And I thought it would end me. I thought the gore and the blood were simply too much, more than I could ever face. If I was to fight, I wouldn't be so brutal. In this one thing, I would be better than my little sister.

I erect spikes of glass in front of a terrified and charging sage. As flesh is torn and eyes bulge from the bleeding corpse, I form small sharp knives in my wind. I can see Charlotte's explosions dissipating near a man holding a black spike. As Lily taught me, I rescind my mana from the glass and propel it forward with wind. The now mundane glass tears into the sage with the riot spike, cutting at his throat and face like teeth in meat.

I thought I would be better than Lily. I thought if I fought, I would be gentler. Then I killed . . . him. My father. *Our* father. His body didn't bleed; there was no long speech, no gloating or begging. He was in my way one moment and dead the next, encased in a pillar of glass. He looked like me, like the man I almost was. Like the future it would have been so easy to fall into. And it felt no less brutal. It was clean, instant, but somehow, it seemed like greater cruelty.

Charlotte pulls a man away from me, wrapping him in cloth and binding his arms and sword to his sides. I don't hesitate. Glass spears impale him from all directions while wind forces one of his friends to trip over his corpse, falling into the other side of the glass weapons. One catches his throat, and he chokes for a moment until I apply more pressure and end him.

So quick. Life ends so quickly. It's as fragile and dangerous as the glass I use to end it. This was the last lesson my father ever taught me, on the same day my brother died. My brother, whom I once abandoned and left for dead; he died quickly too. Another man I could have been. A better man, kind, with no pride like a horse's reins. My father died in a pillar of glass, and my brother in a pillar of fire. I never showed my dad what Mariah had shown me; I never proved to Henry that I wasn't the coward who'd run without him. Because life ends too quickly, for the good and for the evil. We are all equal in death, and none of us are immune to it.

That's why my sister kills so easily, despite how much she cares for people. Because anyone can end anyone else's life in a moment. Death is real and constant, and just because it stays in the dark, it doesn't stop the hurt. Killing in the open with a spell is no crueler than killing from a throne with a word. Lily kills without hesitation because of the people it spares. Her kills are gruesome because the polite and clean ones hurt just as much.

She killed those who took Henry while I ran away. He could have died when I ran. He could have died in an instant, with no long goodbyes or apologies. I understand now. And I am willing to kill, because Henry died and I never said goodbye. I never proved I was better than the boy who ran. To Henry or to myself.

We are going to win. We are going to win because we are all tired of the quiet violence of men like these, there are more of us, and we are angry. And Leo offers us all the joy in the world so long as we are near him. The joy and the protection he offers from men like these.

But something feels wrong.

Waves of mana erupt from Charlotte like an earthquake, and nearly every mage here gasps for breath. I frantically scan the battlefield for the source of her panic, my mind moving faster than my body ever could. And then I see him, hooked on the end of Charlotte's gaze.

A man with cold eyes, pointing something directly at me. No . . . just past me. Just over my shoulder, right at where Leo is standing at the center of us all. I don't see mana, and I know he can't use divine magic, but I still feel the danger. I don't even think about it, not really. I lean left; it's all I can do in the time I have. If Charlotte can't stop this in time, neither can I.

Deep purple cloth cascades through the air, blocking my view of the cold man. Charlotte's explosions ring through the air, so I can't even hear myself think. My throat hurts as meat rips and blood splutters. I can't tell what hit me as it tears into me; I just fall to my knees, red spilling over my lower lip and darkness filling my eyes.

But it's okay. I knew when I died it would happen in an instant. My heart aches for my wife, my child, my siblings and mother. For a man still dead in a pillar of glass. For everyone I'll never see again. But it's all right because I am going to die. And if I see Henry, I can tell him I didn't run.

Charlotte

The man's eyes burn with victory and greed even as my mana approaches him. It decorates his face as soon as whatever his weapon is goes off, but the look is soon overcome by confusion and horror. My mud swallows him to the neck, and I can finally see our victory reflected in his shattered eyes. Pink mana clouds around him like a fog, sparking and dancing for just a breath. It floats through the air, just barely revealing a face no longer cold but flooded with despair.

I have no mercy for him. The explosions are filled with power like I've never been able to use before, small but violent. They pepper him like hail, shattering him on contact. And I don't stop. I can't stop, because he tried to kill my son, and my son may still be alive, but I can't be certain, which leaves me with hope to be taken away again. So the man across the battlefield dies a rapid and gruesome death. But his flesh is not enough—I need his death to reach his marrow. If historians and archaeologists study this battle, if they uncover the bones of the combatants, they need to know which of them tried to hurt my son.

This represents a tipping point in the battle. We were always going to win, but the ferocity we brought was mild before. Or maybe there were already too few of them left, because by the time I am done putting his one man in the ground, there are no sages left. Every one of them is dead. I turn, thoughts of no one but Leo in my head as our battle ends. I ignore the sounds of the other fights, running as my cloth falls and I see the bloody man in the dirt.

It's not Leo.

Leo, for the first time in a long time, doesn't wear a smile, cradling Edward's head as blood fountains from the wound on the man's neck. *No. No, not another of Lily's brothers. Not again. I will not let another one die; not while he was helping me.* I run to him, slipping in my own mud as I do, but I scramble back to my feet and keep moving. I have to believe I can save him. I have to.

The other battles grow louder as Sara's border falls. I don't care, falling to my knees by Edward's side. He's not conscious. I don't even know if he's alive. I've only really gotten to know him in the past few weeks, what I did to Henry only inspiring empathy in him. To him, it was a shared guilt. I have to save him, but I don't know how. A new aspect, maybe? But I don't know of anything but divine magic that can save him. I want to run to Sara, but he only has seconds left. There is no aspect I know of which can heal, no aspect that can offer a future to the dying and hopeless.

But I can't give up. I don't know how to save him, but I have spent too long in hopelessness, so I have to believe he can be saved somehow. Somehow, I can save him. I will never give myself over to hopelessness again, no matter how certain failure feels. And as I hold him . . . as Leo holds him, still offering everyone what joy he can, I realize I need an endo-aspect; something with an unpredictable effect.

Hope.

Hope floods through me, and mana aspected with nothing condenses around my hands like water on a cold glass. I feel hope like an endless future and falling walls. I will save him, and I will be hope like Leo is joy.

My mana takes on the aspect of hope, and as it touches Lily's brother, the hole in his throat begins to close, and he slowly opens his eyes.

CHAPTER TWENTY-FOUR

The Enemy of Women

Sarafyna

Riley and Ember make it through my barrier, and I immediately close it before any sages can follow them through. I keep my focus on maintaining the trap, but an eyestalk grows from my shoulder and watches the two women chasing after Annie. They aren't here for this fight, but that doesn't mean this fight won't try to find them.

Just as I worried, a familiar child holds one hand up, firing both water and stone with speed to rival Annie's. It's not mana but divine magic he uses to summon these elements. I can't intercept it in time, but I don't need to. Even divine magic turns to nothing when it hits Riley's void mana, and she knows to protect herself. Both elements disappear into nothing as they collide with her white mana, and their target doesn't even slow. My old friend, however, did attract my attention with the attack.

"Rune," I spit as the legs of a spider emerge from my dress and carry me toward the childlike sage far faster than I could run. "I was hoping we'd meet again. It'll be nice to have a conversation with no chains or poison, don't you think?"

The Scholar Sage turns to me with disgust and bafflement. "I've never seen you before in my life, and I know you haven't seen me, so I have no idea what you're talking about," he responds, already forming another attack.

I squint with even the newly formed eyes on the back of my head as I process that. I have no reason to believe him, but his confusion feels real, his entire demeanor different than I expected. I tilt my head at him as my body contorts around the projectile elements he fires at me. They tear through my dress but make contact nowhere else. The memories of being chained and poisoned while Annie needed me are seared into my mind, and this . . . *child* is confidently sitting across the room in many of them.

The confusion of his response distracts me just enough that another sage nearly manages to hit me with an impossibly fast . . . something. I think it was a kick? His divine magic makes him almost too fast to follow. I have to exert my will over the area around me to counteract his magic and slow him down just so I can scurry out of the way.

There are more of them coming, and I feel like I could beat all of them, but too much of my strength is going to maintaining the barrier and keeping Leo's group safe. I have to stall. "Really? You never visited a quaint little cell to talk down to me and ask me to kill my girlfriend?" I ask. Rune rolls his eyes even as he creates a hailstorm of ice shards over his head and fires them at me. I melt into liquid flesh and flow through the soil, dragging my dress with me. I avoid the attack and rebuild myself inside my clothing a little closer to him.

"Oh, of course, you are that girl, aren't you? Look, I don't know you. I was supposed to, but I didn't; you were gone. So whatever grief you have with me, that wasn't me; it was probably the Original. He's the only asshole who would have—and could have—impersonated me, and the only one who might want to. So let it go. We aren't your enemies—he is. Shit, with your help, we could probably kill him. Let my friends out of there and we can actually settle this!" he insists.

As he does, several sages approach us to back him up. Unfortunately, I also see a few attempting to sneak away while I'm distracted. I have to survive all of them at once and stop any of them from escaping.

I glare as wings form and tear through the back of my dress. "You're not my enemy? You've never sacrificed anyone to the Radiant Woods? Or, I'm sorry, you prefer to call it the Nexus, don't you? You've never taken a child from their family and left them to wander that hell? To be tortured and abused? That's strange, because every record we could find indicates you are one of the most prolific sages in that regard," I counter.

His mildly hopeful eyes fall as he sees the attempt fail. It was a feeble one anyway. It is clear to everyone here that there is no avoiding violence now.

It's a race: if they can kill me before Leo's army kills their allies, they win. If they can't, I can drop the barrier and fight with full strength. Scanning the open fields around me, I see there are at least a dozen sages in front of me, ready to fight, while a few are running or flying away.

I don't know how well I can maintain this trap and fight at the same time, but none of them are getting away.

Lillith

Shock carries Oakley and me several hundred yards before I have to let go and dodge his counterattack. Void of Nexus and mana explode from him as he falls for a moment before he catches himself in the air and steadies. His eyes flick between me and the open horizon as he decides whether to fight or flee.

"Come now, aren't you supposed to be the most powerful sage in either the Republic or the Council? Aren't you tired of running? It's just you and me now. Surely the powerful, brilliant, once-in-a-lifetime genius before me isn't going to run away—again. Right?" I taunt. Oakley grits his teeth at the provocation, but I can still see the consideration in his eyes. The only thing he cares about more than his pride is his life. "That's right, I forgot. Even on Earth, you were only brave from behind a screen, weren't you? Well, go ahead. Turn your back to me. I'm begging you."

As I goad him, electricity sparks and dances across my steel arm. Poison gas floods a pocket I casually float around me, with force mana gradually building pressure around it. Altogether, my mana makes a symphony of rage, only increasing his terror. But the fear of turning away from it exceeds the fear of facing it.

"You would do that? Attack a fleeing man? So much for your kindness. So much for your empathy," he sneers. I smile. Not because I'm happy but because I need to goad him. His void magic puts me at a huge disadvantage if I attack first. I need to respond to him, not the other way around.

"No audience to sway here, Oakley. No idiot fans or investors. You want to pretend your mass murder of the innocent is quiet and clean but killing you while you're running is some moral failing even now? Come on. I'm injured. I have blood leaking from my scales. Several bones are broken, and honestly, I've been sick for a while. I'm bleeding skin and broken bones. Come on. COME ON! I know some part of you thinks you can do it. I know some part of you believes you can win, that you have enough power to kill me and finally feel safe again. Come on, you fucking coward. What, you don't think you can do it? Do you need to hire someone to do it for you?" I mock.

He clenches his fists. I kiss my hand and blow it to him, then hold my organic fingers to my mouth and stick my tongue through. The last time I did this, the man I was taunting didn't recognize the gesture. This time, I can clearly see he does. And finally, he breaks.

He charges toward me, white mana filling the space around him like an erupting star. I immediately fly up into the air, dodging the deadly attack and rapid-firing lightning bolts down at the man as he reaches my previous position. My attack is swallowed and erased by the void mana, but that's all right. I surround his little bubble of mana with my poison, obstructing his vision even as he drops the opaque void mana to clear it. My poison collapses on him the moment it has a clear path to do so.

I have to drop a second later, again firing lightning at my previous position. I do this as liquid space bubbles into existence behind me, and Oakley emerges, a blade of pure white mana preceding him. Again, he destroys my lightning before it can damage him.

"Who's running away now, Ms. Beckett?" he cries. "Are you just going to run and run while I attack? Like you said, it's just you and me now. And you're right—I *am* powerful. I have always been powerful, and I have both the Nexus and mana. How long do you think you can keep this up?" As he screams at me, I roll and weave through the air in a way that would make Peppy proud, all while lightning flies from me to the sound of thunder and trumpets.

I laugh. "I am literally already attacking you, dipshit!" I call back. I go into a rapid dive, narrowly escaping a burst of void mana. One hit and I'm dead. He follows me with a wide void curtain big enough that I won't be able to escape its influence before hitting the ground. But I don't need to.

The curtain dissipates, the white mana disappearing as red liquid flies through the air in a fine mist, and I see the carbon arrow lodged deep in Oakley's rib cage.

"Besides," I shout, "I was maybe lying about the one-on-one thing." His mana flickers as he responds to the pain, flailing through the air. I increase the pressure on the poison-filled air bubble, firing shots of compressed poison gas at him as he closes the distance. He wears rage like a spear as he conjures the deadly white mana again. I send force mana out in another direction, pulling another little surprise to an intersection point before he reaches me.

Void mana meets void mana, canceling itself out and leaving only flesh and steel. Riley's axe tears into her father's torso as my force mana helps her fly. Even to her, some things are worth time in the air. "It's been a while, Dad," she spits as his blood decorates her armor.

Sarafyna

Rune seems more like an elemental master than a scholar. He uses basic elements like the Potestian mages favor, but he uses them with no mana and far greater efficiency. I can dispel any sage's power, but it takes focus that I can't spare much of. But that's only true as long as Leo's group is still fighting.

My left arm extends in intricate tendrils like a spider web as yet another sage tries to either run or join Annie's battle. Neither are acceptable out-comes, so I grow quills in each tendril, cutting into my target as I wrap him up. I have to immediately dive, transforming my body into something more like a bird as Rune peppers the sky with pillars of fire. He's easily the biggest threat, but if I focus on him alone, the others could go help Oakley.

So I dodge and I trap and I hold them here. The ground below me has turned into a tundra, so I can't land. Actual birds fly out of a sage's hood and harass me, forcing me to use my captive like a flail, the man screaming as he sails through the violent flock and into my assailant below. I click my tongue as a few sages run through the ice below like nothing is happening. Rune apparently has the control to keep them safe while I still can't land.

I'm growing weary. I fail to dodge in time, and a block of ice cuts a bloody gash along my already scarred face. I dodge a few more spells, and the sage with the speed ability catches me in the gut just as I turn around. This happens more and more as the fight drags on. I earn bruises and cuts and abuse until, finally, a wall of fowl surrounds me like a cloud, peck-ing at me, pushing me down. The more physical sage cuts a path through them, his heel coming down on my head as he spins in the air. And that's it. I'm thrown to the icy ground, my body freezing so quickly that I have no chance to stop it.

My head aches, blood freezing to my face as a panting Rune lands in front of me. "You should have taken the offer. It could have been a fresh start; that's what this world was to me. But you were too stubborn, too bitter, and now we will have to deal with the Original Sage on our own." He sighs.

I ignore him, looking under his arm towards Leo's fight. Then I sigh in relief and finally meet his eyes. "Looks like it's time to go help my girlfriend," I respond. The battle is over. The sages are dead, and I don't need to maintain a massive barrier anymore.

The ice around us doesn't melt—it evaporates. My body thaws and heals in a single breath, and I already have claws in every single sage around me. Tentacles grip them all, and acid burns them. When Rune tries to shake the earth beneath my feet, I slam him into it. I am not the Sarafyna I once was, which means—luckily for these men—I break all of their spines at once instead of chewing them to death.

As my body absorbs the new divine magic, I look toward the sky. A little ways away, dark and starry void energy pours like dozens of waterfalls from the sky. I don't wait even a moment before taking off and rushing to help Annie.

Lillith

"You ungrateful little bitch!" Oakley screams as he rapidly heals from another of Riley's swings, tearing one of Ember's arrows out as he does. The fight has shifted, and not entirely in a good way. He throws white mana blindly in every direction, forcing me to direct my flight with force more than my wings. Simultaneously, I have to carry Riley through the air, much to her chagrin. She can perfectly counter both types of Oakley's void magic, however, which at least makes it safe.

"Ungrateful? For fucking what?" she cries back, meeting many of his attacks with her own. "For being ignored? For being rejected? For losing the only real parent I had and even the ability to grieve for her?" She has more mana than him but no Nexus energy, meaning she'd win with mana alone but she can't answer the less dangerous but more numerous Nexus attacks.

"You would be nothing without me! I gave you life, gave you fame, and you returned it with lies and disrespect! Wealth, glory, admiration—these are all gifts I gave you before you spat them out!" Oakley accuses. My blood boils at this pathetic reframing of his abuse, which means Riley's is already high-pressure steam. She lets down her defensive casting, trusting me to move her toward her father and avoid his attacks. I happily comply as her void mana fires from her and coats her axe. Oakley meets her attacks with his darker void energy, but I don't let him rest so easily. I redouble my own attacks, lightning and pressurized poison raining down on him from every direction but Riley's.

"I was nothing with you, you creep! An empty puppet until you rejected me! I was never anything to you but another lie in your book of legends. Fuck you! Fuck you and everything you think you gave me!" Riley snarls as she careens toward him.

Oakley erupts like a sputtering fountain, black void energy creating a pillar that rains down on all of us. He does this just barely too late, and one of my lightning bolts splits and finds him in the sky. He may heal quickly, but this paralyzes him for a few moments regardless. As soon as the electricity leaves his body, Riley tears through his fallen defenses, ramming her shoulder into his chest. While he is dazed, she grabs his neck with her free hand, wielding her massive axe with the other and cracking his skull with the pommel. She throws him down, swinging the weapon into his shoulder as he falls. At the same time, another arrow finds purchase in his leg.

I have to dive, racing the void rain to the ground before it tears me apart. Riley spins around as Oakley falls, barely sending an umbrella of white mana to protect me from the deadly rainfall. As I catch the wind with my wings to slow my fall, Oakley shrieks in rage, void energy like waterfalls filling the sky all around us. The night sky flows from as far up as I can see and collides with the earth below with a cloud of violent mist.

I try to strike him with lightning again, but a curtain of dark void energy protects him. The lightning enters his void and emerges from one of the falls, one bolt crashing through me with an all-consuming burning that forces all my muscles to seize and flex. As I grit my teeth, Oakley's white void starts flying from the falls in all directions at once. Riley was counting on me to fly, and struggles to defend us both from the onslaught as she falls.

Oakley is already healing, tossing a bloody arrow to the side and rubbing blood from his mouth with one sleeve. I see the mana he is idly firing into his own void. Instead of dissolving as it does when Riley's mana hits it, it simply enters and exits wherever he wants. Death is rapidly flying toward me, and Riley is approaching her own if I can't regain control of my mana.

As I convulse with the effects of my own lightning, three arrows cut straight through the void like meteors shrouded in gold mana like I've never seen. Oakley throws up both types of void to defend himself, but they cut through, and when they hit him, they don't get stuck in flesh. Instead, they explode, first his left arm at the shoulder, then his left leg at the knee. Finally, an arrow plunges into his neck, exploding in a deep gold that leaves his head attached to his neck with loose strands of flesh alone.

Ember

I don't need cover now; the Void Sage is handling that all on his own. The curtains of void energy all around his fight with Lillith protect me as much as they protect him, but they *do* protect him. I can't hit him; I'm supposed to provide support from a distance, or keep him distracted at the very least, doing what little I can despite my weakness, harassing him from a distance and watching Lillith kill him. That was the plan, anyway.

Instead, I am forced to form and fire arrows uselessly into an empty void. With the magnification created by my light mana, I catch glimpses of the others, each flying through the air like volu, but the sage who ended my life is never visible for long enough to reliably aim and fire anything at him. Each time I see him appear between the falling night sky, I grow angrier. Memories run through my head like deer from a lion. Memories I'd been denied for decades by the very man who created them, just so I could serve as some kind of pawn he'd never have to think about again.

The simmering rage I have lived with for so long starts to boil.

The Void flies past a narrow gap, and I try to fire at him but only hit the moving night as it falls from the sky. I hiss in rage.

This rage has been directionless and without a source for too many years. And now that it has one, I can't even touch him. Again, I catch sight of him. Again, I fail to hit my target. My fathers' faces flash through my mind, their kind smiles, their gentle reprimands. A small home with warm breakfasts, then volu tearing them from me and throwing them into torment. Flying me away from my country and my parents to become his slave.

I can't contain the anger. I can't hit my target. I need him to hurt; I need him to die, or this rage will burn me from the inside out. I have to reach him and give him as much pain as I can for my parents. For my life. For my childhood of training with a trembling tail. I bare my fangs as I catch just a flash of the man who destroyed me, wrapping my next arrow in mana and pouring my fury into it. I have tried to grasp this endoaspect before, but without understanding my anger, I couldn't manifest it.

This time, I don't even have to try. It has a name and a face. It has blood, and I can draw it out. My own veins boil as I fill my mana with every ounce of resentment I can, and I feel the mana accept it. As I shroud my next arrow in the rage mana I've just created, it glows like gold. I don't have to look for my target this time. I don't need to wait for him to show himself, and I don't have to aim for a gap. I can feel him. I know where he is, and so does my rage mana. It comes from him, after all.

As I let loose my next arrow, I can't see the Void Sage at all, but I still fire directly at the center of his Nexus energy. Tearing through his defenses, justice rains down as my arrow rips his flesh.

Lillith

Still, he heals. Scraps of skin and muscle find each other and weave together, forming a bloodied but furious man. Finally, my body recovers from the shock, and I am able to dive toward him, sending my force mana through one of his void falls. It emerges nearly a mile below us, catching Riley. I can't control her as I have been, but I manage to slow and then throw her back toward us.

White mana grazes me as I dive through the air, tearing an ugly crescent wound into my side. I ignore the blood and visible bone as I keep flying toward my enemy. Oakley tries to shield himself with white void, but Riley is approaching from below, and she attacks him as a distraction while I catch her with force. At the same time, she cloaks me in her own mana, protecting me as I finally reach Oakley.

Wrapping my tail around his torso, I plunge my stinger into his side and fill him with venom. The shoulder he took an arrow in is still healing, so I dig the fingers of both hands into it. The steel claws of my right gauntlet meet their organic counterparts, and I fill him with venom from these as well, even as I start to pull. As he snarls at me, I do the same, sinking teeth and fangs directly into his face and sending directional sound directly into his ears, shattering his eardrums as my hands separate, slowly tearing him apart.

My hands grow greasy with blood and sinew as I rip the man into two separate pieces, using heat mana to literally cook him as I do. He is still screaming as my tail crushes his lower half. Throwing his upper half into the air, a new golden arrow . . . No, an entire *sword* finds him just as I follow him with lightning. *The fuck is Ember smoking right now? I could use a dose.*

The arrow's explosion blinds me for a moment, and I almost miss the stubbornly healing man fleeing into his void. I spit as I use heat to cauterize my side. "What's it going to take to kill this fucking guy?" I groan. I lift Riley up to my level, and she answers by vomiting. The moment of calm is giving her time to process the wild flying through the sky.

She looks up at me, eyes carrying a real response that never makes it to her lips. Our rest ends as black and white bullets begin to fly from random directions. I barely shove myself to the side in time to avoid one while another tears through my right wing. "Fuck, why is it always the right side," I complain as Riley frantically tries to block the oncoming attacks. She can surround us on all sides, but that will obscure our vision. She tries shrouding most of our bodies in it like she did while I was attacking him, but it's not enough. Oakley seems to have condensed both of his abilities into dense but small projectiles.

One rips through Riley's calf, diminished in strength but enough to leave a hole where her muscles have just been . . . deleted. Whatever these bullets hit simply stops existing. The one silver lining of this attack is they seem to take longer. He can only fire at us maybe once every two or three seconds, but we never know where they'll come from, and we can't see Oakley to attack the source.

I try to fly us both out of the way, but they are too fast. He must not have perfect control when aiming from inside the void, or maybe because he is still regenerating half his body. If he had perfect aim, we would be dead already. We barely avoid lethal hits repeatedly, one carving a new scar along my face as I nearly fail to move aside in time.

One shot at a time, we lose little chunks of ourselves, nicks, cuts, and holes appearing all over us. We have to dive into the void; we'll be on his turf, but if we can't see him, we can't fight him.

Just as I'm going to communicate this to Riley, one spears my chest, leaving a dime-sized hole in the already still organ. It won't kill me, but it sends me spinning, and I lose my grip on the force carrying Riley. We both go into an immediate free fall while I try to flap my wings; it helps a little, but there are multiple holes in them, and I can't catch the wind. It's an eternity before I get my bearings enough to catch myself with force, and it feels like being punched in the gut when I do. I freeze in the air, opening my eyes to find Oakley's void bullets surrounding me but equally frozen. I hear the flap of wings like a massive hummingbird, and Sara floats up in front of me with Riley in a princess carry.

"If I weren't in so much pain, this would look hilarious," I cough, taking in the sight of the tall, muscular woman in my girlfriend's arms. Sara rolls her eyes.

"Look at you, you're a mess," she complains, already attempting to heal me. Riley looks good as new, but my body, already at its divine magic limit, struggles to heal even with her help.

"Thanks, you look nice too," I reply. "Do you think you can affect that void shit over there?" She gives it a glance.

"Affect how?" she asks. I extend my force mana, catching her and letting her wings rest. She sighs and tries to gently drop Riley, who comically grips her more tightly.

"Limit the size inside, keep it small, and stop Raggedy Asshole from getting out," I suggest. She flexes her fingers, extending a couple of extra arms to gently separate herself from the gladiator wrapped around her neck.

"Definitely. What's the plan?" she asks. I start pushing as much light mana as I can into a group of unenchanted scales on my legs, then unceremoniously tear them out and grip them in one fist.

"I've got one more poison to try. A lot more dangerous, and not safe for anyone if I use it. At least not if their target isn't locked in their own separate reality, anyway," I reply. As I do, I wrap each individual scale in its own dense light barrier. "Are you ready?"

She looks confused but nods, then I fire the scales like bullets of my own, each entering Oakley's void from a different spot. Sara understands my intent and immediately does . . . something. I can't always tell what she is doing, but based on her focused expression and the lack of horrible radiation levels escaping the void, she is doing exactly what I asked.

The void tries to fight back, but Sara strangles it like a trapped snake. It can wriggle, but it will never escape. It grows more violent and unstable, almost taking on the quality of static, and then, finally, it begins to evaporate. After a few moments, only the upper half of a man is left, and Oakley falls through the sky with no power left to save him. As I approach ahead of the other two and wrap him in a dense light barrier, I'm mildly impressed by how much of his torso he managed to grow back before this point.

All three of us follow him on his collision course with the ruined earth below, landing one by one by his side. Riley pushes back her relief at being on solid ground; she has something more important to tend to. Oakley, stubborn as ever, is still alive, covered in boils and with bloody vomit running both down his shirt and directly out of his severed body. He is coughing, trying to move his one still complete hand and grasp at the shards of the strange sword still embedded in his chest.

I maintain the radiation barrier while letting visible light through, which is much more difficult than it sounds. But that's all right; the others can finish him off now. He glares at me, and I shake my head. "I may have been the woman you've been afraid of for so long, but I'm not the one you should have feared."

"No, she isn't," a new voice says. We all look up to see Ember finally approaching the group on foot; she must have been running since the void collapsed. She has an aura of pure gold just like the mana I'd seen on the arrows. Oakley tries to speak in response, but he lacks the complete equipment to do so. "This is for my fathers," she growls.

"And for mine," Sara whispers.

"And for Mom," Riley agrees.

I'm not sure which attack kills him: the axe or the arrow. It doesn't matter. Ember and Riley together finally end the man who ruined their families, while Sara finally gets justice for her time in the Radiant Woods; at least from one of her abusers. And me? Well, I'm just finishing the job I started with an old friend a long time ago. Once I'm finally certain he is dead, I fall back on my ass, wrapping my tail around myself to make room. Then I glance at Ember. "Nice upgrade; how'd you do it?" I ask. She looks down at herself.

"Rage mana," she answers simply, as if it should be the most obvious thing in the world. Well, that's new. An endoaspect, interesting. She must have been enchanting her arrows with it rather than using it directly.

"Where'd you get the sword?" I ask.

"Stole it from one of the other sages. I saw that it cuts through mana; figured it would have a stronger effect on the Void Sage. Had to enchant the hilt, since the blade already had that," she replies. She's unusually calm for someone currently cloaked in literal rage. I'm about to comment on this when I process what she said. They had mana-dispersal weapons. Shit, of course they did. They came to fight me.

I slowly climb to my feet, holding one fist to the slowly healing hole in my chest. "We need to regroup with everyone," I say. "The others may need help, and Alpha is still out there. We aren't done yet."

CHAPTER TWENTY-FIVE

Empathy

A few hours ago, I was in a fight to the death, outmatched, and sustaining what should have been lethal and irrecoverable injuries multiple times. I miss such simple times.

I'm currently lying on my side on a bedroll in the back of an open wagon, my suggestion to cut a large tail hole in the floor rudely rejected. Surrounding me is Sara, Ed, and . . . Charlotte. Leo is about a mile ahead of us with Ember and Riley. Impossibly close, and infinitely out of reach.

Apparently, Sara's connection to the hat shop is shaky right now. Even with the border down, the hole in my heart is seemingly reflected in the core of the shop. I'll need Sara to explain to me why that is at some point. Again. She's tried, but it is apparently hard to put into words. In any case, to solve this problem, Charlotte is using her mana to heal me where Sara's can't. And I'm grateful, I really am. But I can't look her in the eyes. I trusted Charlotte; even though I never knew her as well as Leo, I trusted her. And she killed Henry.

I understand why. I can't hate her like I hated Oakley, Baldwin, or Darian because she's not evil. She's not self-obsessed and cruel. She's not even pragmatic to the point of consuming her own intentions like Godfrey. She is, above all else, empathetic and compassionate. She lied to me, but I lied to and betrayed Godfrey because my goals were good and his were bad.

By all accounts, she isn't even as bad as Autumn, who betrayed me in the same way and to the same person, at least in intent, for years. She may have been a child when she did it, but she didn't tell me the truth as an adult until it was too late. And she did it for herself, for her parents. Neither acted with any malice, both doing what they had spent their lives learning and believing was the only right and safe thing to do.

But Charlotte . . . she didn't do it for herself, not entirely. Yes, like Autumn, she was looking out for her family, but she did it to save me and my family, my friends, knowing and accepting she would be hated for it, knowing she would never be free and that Sara and I would never be able to finish with her transition. Her betrayal, however much it hurt, was an act of sacrifice. I know this. It isn't an excuse for it. Pavement for the road to hell and all that.

But of the people I blame for Henry's death, she should not be the one I hate the most. I left him there. I promised Mom I wouldn't and I did, abandoning him before I knew he was safe. I taunted the man who killed him. It was my plan that got him killed. My failure.

And Autumn. She was right there; she watched him die. Some part of me has never accepted that she couldn't have stopped it, that there was nothing she could have done. She sold me out, then she slept in my family's home for years. She slept in my brother's bed and smiled and joked with me at my family's dinner table. She became part of that family, and all the while, she knew we were all in danger because of her actions, yet she said nothing. The dispersal circle that left Henry vulnerable was there because of Autumn's perpetual and violent silence.

I don't kill people that don't need to be killed. It's a line I've never crossed, whatever many may say. But when Autumn told me this, I very nearly pushed her from the top of that tower. I felt a brand-new arm twitch with a command I barely held back.

But Autumn lost Henry too. She loved Henry as much as I did, probably even more, so in Autumn, I saw myself. What she tore from me, she also tore from herself. My hate for her carried a need for company, and we've had time to heal together, to grow used to that shared blame, and to start to forgive. Start. And me? Well, I've been punishing myself since Henry died in any way I could think of, to the point it became selfish.

But Charlotte barely knew Henry, and this is the first time I've been anywhere near her since she helped Autumn and I kill my brother. She and I have had no time to heal, and she didn't lose Henry the same way I did. So I know. I know she is kind, and brave, and empathetic. I know she loves and is loved by people I care about, and that she has lost people the same way I have, which is exactly why she did what she did. I know she was trying to do the right thing, and that she understands the hurt I'm feeling.

And I don't fucking care.

I hate her.

She is healing me, taking the burden off Sarafyna, and helping get all of these people home. And I hate her. I just want her to go back to Leo, where I have an excuse to avoid her. I want her gone, and I never want to see her again.

I turn my head away from her and make eye contact with Ed, who looks the most at ease he has in a long, long time. He fought next to Charlotte and has been seeing her regularly for months now. They don't seem close, but he clearly doesn't hate her. Hell, he doesn't even hate me.

He should be dead, another brother sacrificed to one of my plans. Of course some sages would know how to at least make a flintlock; I hadn't even thought of it. Ed should be dead, and I should be on my way to hang my head before my mother again, telling her I killed another of her "real" children.

But Charlotte saved him. I've had a rocky relationship with Ed, but he went from an unpleasant child to a good man, and I do love him. And Charlotte saved him. She's gone through just as much change as I have since we killed Henry together. She has somehow become the embodiment of hope, when it was hopelessness that led to the mistake I hate her for. And I don't know how to feel, because I am so grateful, so unbelievably happy she was there for my brother when he needed it.

I can see it in Ed's eyes. He's been healed in more ways than one; he's come to terms with something he's been struggling with for so, so long. He has the chance to go back to Mariah and finally be happy, and Charlotte gave him that.

So how can I hate her?

I turn back to her as my last wound closes. My eyes meet hers, and I can see the ice they carry in the shiver that washes over her face. "I–I'm done," Charlotte says. I should thank her for saving me, twice now. For sparing my brother and making today possible. Instead, I sit up and stretch, adjusting my tail so I can sit on the roll with my legs crossed. My eyes meet hers again, and I fail to speak. "I'll . . . I'd better get back to Leo."

I just watch her as she collects herself and climbs awkwardly out of the wagon. My eyes linger on her for far too long, and she's fading into the distance by the time I come back to myself.

I've been doing moderately well the last few months. As soon as I stopped trying to suppress my grief in public, it stopped feeling so urgent to suppress it. I haven't done anything . . . intentionally stupid. My good humor has become more and more genuine with every passing day. But as I turn back to Ed and Sara's stares, I feel water starting to run down my cheeks.

"You're going to regret that later—if you don't already," Sara finally says. I tense up. She's right. I know she is. I open my mouth to agree, but the words are hot and sweet like sickness, and I choke them back down. So I focus on Ed. He's rubbing his hand against his throat. We haven't had the chance to catch up yet, as Sara has been the only one traveling back and forth. I grasp onto that in hopes of changing the subject.

I don't have to say anything. He sees the pleading in my watering eyes.

"So," he starts awkwardly. "You, uh . . . have a tail." I offer a half smile.

"And wings," I agree, wiping my eyes on my right sleeve. "What do you think? I look hot, right?" He wrinkles his nose at that, familiar enough with the slang by now.

"You still look like my snot-nosed little sister," he counters. "Never did understand what Sara liked about you." I actually grin at that, even with my eyes still red.

"It's my friendly charm, I think," I reply. He snorts but doesn't contest the claim. We are both quiet for a moment. Sara hasn't taken her evaluating eyes off me.

"I missed you, Lily," he says. I'm assaulted by a dozen memories of his sneering, then his guilt, and finally his eagerness to help. And now he misses me when I'm gone. It's stupid, but the water runs again. I missed him too, which wasn't always the case, and he nearly died before I got the chance to see him again. But he didn't, and he doesn't even have a scar. Because of Charlotte.

"I missed you too," I whisper.

"Of course you did; I'm your big brother." He grins. He really does seem more confident than he has in years.

"Aren't you my little brother, actually?"

He scoffs. "Hardly! I'm years older than you!"

"Are you though? I'm like, I don't know. Forty-six, I think? Fifty-three, in a way. I'm old enough to be your mother," I counter.

"By that logic, you're older than your own mother." He laughs.

"That's that and this is this; quit changing the subject. I'm obviously the big sister," I sniff.

"You're not the big anything at that height," he teases, and I roll my eyes. I'm going to quip back, but I catch a glimpse of Sara. She is still looking at me with eyes like weights around my neck. I was enjoying seeing my family again, even if it's only Ed. The distraction almost worked. But Sara isn't going to let me move on, because Charlotte is hurting, and I am letting her. My sheepish grin fades as the weight of the world settles on my shoulders again.

Ed catches this and sighs. The air is dense with silence for a few seconds, and when my brother speaks again, he isn't teasing me.

"I pushed him over and ran," he says. I raise an eyebrow, and he looks up at the sky. I invite him to continue by refusing to fill the silence, and I notice a slight tremor in his shoulders. "When they came for us, as kids. Henry was picking me up. He was only in danger because of his drunk and fucked-up older brother. Even so, he wanted to work with me so we'd both escape. I agreed to his plan, let him start the distraction, and then I pushed him over and escaped alone. And the worst part is . . . I think his plan would have worked. But I was a coward.

"I was a coward, and I used him so I could escape. The time he spent in captivity, the danger you were in, that scar on your eye. It's all because I was a coward." He pauses there, but his trembling lips carry a few more words. So I continue to wait. He takes a deep breath through his nose. "Today, I was willing to let myself die to save someone else. I was ready for a quick, unceremonious death, like the men in our family always get. It turned out all right in the end. A lot of my mistakes have, really. But . . ." He trails off, and Sara finally joins the conversation.

"But mistakes aren't better just because the consequences aren't as severe," she finishes. Ed nods in agreement, offering her a grateful glance. I don't know how to process what Ed is saying, but I understand Sara. "Annie, you've told me a lot about your time in that arena. So has Autumn. Even Ember. And you know what, Annie? Ed has a point."

"I know that. And I understand why Charlotte made the choice she did. But that doesn't mean I owe her my forgiveness," I challenge. Sara and Ed both nod.

"Of course you don't," Ed agrees. "You owe her neither forgiveness nor friendship. No more than Henry owed me his. But . . ." He trails off and looks toward Sara, who moves over next to me and sits down.

She is quick to pick up in his place. "We have all been through a lot of pain. I would be as good as dead without you, you know that. And I know how much you are hurting. I've heard every word you had to say about the painful ways you've grieved for your brother. I've heard everything Autumn had to say too, about how afraid she was every time you went into that arena and risked yourself, and how panicked she was. Your reasons aside, we were all counting on you. People's lives depended on you; people you brought into danger with the promise you would protect them. And every day, sometimes multiple times a day, you chose to risk not just yourself but all of them.

"Every time you walked into that arena and hurt yourself, you risked the twins' lives, not just your own. Because you were so broken down, so drowned in despair after you lost someone you loved. And I understand. Believe me, I would drink the sky and shatter the world to keep you with me. I hurt and isolated myself in the Radiant Woods for years longer than I needed to. I understand like I understand how to breathe. But what if your actions had gotten August killed? What if you brought too much attention to the people you brought into danger, and they died while you were trapped? That didn't happen, but you did risk it, and you didn't need to. You did put them in that position," she says.

Her words are sharp, but her tone is soft. They sting nonetheless, because she's right. The drunk drivers who haven't killed someone aren't better people than the drunk drivers who have. They've simply been luckier so far. And she's not saying the quiet part: that I did what I did for my own sake, and Charlotte did what she did for everyone. Charlotte, Autumn, and I all share responsibility for the lives lost that day, including Henry's. And we all did what we thought would save the most lives. But when I asked Autumn to come with me to danger then risked leaving her there alone . . . all for my self-destruction . . . that wasn't for anyone's sake.

Charlotte has lost everyone I have a dozen times over. Her very existence as who she is has been the truest public symbol of liberation Potestia has had since long before I got there. And she's lost so much, been left alone every single time. Over and over again she fought, and over and over again she was left with nothing but blood and empty seats at the table. She is exactly fucking like me. She was wrong, and she risked people for the wrong cause, but she is still exactly like me. And I still don't care. I just want to go back to joking with my brother.

"I can't just be her friend again," I whisper. "I know it's stupid. I am still a type of friend with Autumn, even if I can't stand her either. But that took work, and she lost Henry too. And I just don't have the time left to put in the same work with Charlotte."

"I'm not asking you to," Sara replies. "I'm not asking you to be her friend or talk to her or forgive her. What she did hurt you and a lot of other people. I'm angry at her too. As Ed said, you owe her none of these. I'm only saying any of this because I love you, and I know you. I can see the oncoming regret in your eyes. Because you both lost hope, but she still tried. She still tried, and you, who risked the same loss for someone else? You may not owe her forgiveness, but you owe her empathy. All I am suggesting is that you let yourself feel that." She runs her finger along my face, lingering on the piercings that still connect my grief to the people of two countries.

"I don't know what to do, Sara," I reply quietly. She shakes her head.

"I'm not asking you to do or say anything at all. I am saying I can feel what you want to feel, and I can see you suppressing it. And if we have learned anything at all, it's that you are at your most brilliant when you let yourself feel. And you are at your happiest when you wear your heart on your hat," she answers. The twisted expression puts a small smile back on my face.

"It's 'heart on your sleeve,'" I correct. She puts a finger to her bottom lip.

"I'm pretty sure you told me it was *hat*," she insists. I smile, then sigh. She is, as always, correct. I don't need to be Charlotte's friend; I likely never will be. But Leo needs her, and so do we, because her choice to live as a woman is the embodiment of the liberation I have dedicated two lives to fighting for. And because she is the woman who aspected hope.

I nod at Sarafyna, turning my head and putting one hand on her neck before I kiss her. It's a long kiss, and Ed is remarkably interested in his own fingers when I finally come up for breath. I look my girlfriend in the eyes and shake my head. Then, I leap from the stupid wagon and fly ahead, landing just out of Leo's range. I use light mana although I fly with my wings just so the shining and sound will let Charlotte know I'm here. We need to speak with their group anyway. Since my heart is healed and Sara's connection with the hat shop is back to full power, we can get everyone but Leo home the quick way.

I can feel the edge of Leo's influence as I stand outside it, an innate sense of dread coming over me at the thought of taking a single step forward. I will die if I spend even a breath inside, and I won't come back. My heart aches again at the thought that I will never see Leo again. I can't even use a whisper sphere to hear his voice. Charlotte will be the only real connection I have to my friend, and that alone is reason enough to speak with her.

She seems to understand my intent, or I hope she does. Either way, it's her and Riley who climb out of the still wagon ahead and walk to meet me. Riley was only there to protect Leo in case we were attacked, but she plans to come with Sara and me to pick up the twins. She's going to stay in the Republic and help them deal with the consequences of their missing mind-controlling warts. They may not have been the actual ones responsible for governance, but they were the knife at the throat of the citizens. Things are gonna get messy there. She wants to start right away, and she can let us know what we can do to help. Sara and I are going home for a few days while everything settles down, and Ember is coming with us.

Riley also seems to understand, holding back for a few moments and letting Charlotte approach me alone. As she gets closer, I see her literally trembling with nerves, like a desperate woman on her way to be fired. I still have to grit my teeth, but I let myself feel the empathy this inspires. Because I remember going to face my mother after I broke my promise to bring Henry back. I understand.

She tries to steady herself as she stops maybe two feet in front of me. She doesn't want to shake, and I can see her fighting it, but she does. I hate inspiring that response in anyone. I hate her. I understand her. I need her. I want her to feel okay again.

I consider apologizing; I know I should thank her. I wonder if we should just throw everything out in the open. None of those feel right, but I have to say something.

We stand facing each other for what feels like hours, feeling the stillness of my heart in a way that seems unique. Finally, I let out a breath I didn't know I was holding.

"We're both learning how to hope again," I finally say. "Can we do it together?"

CHAPTER TWENTY-SIX

Farewell Tour - Brothers

There are twelve towers now, apparently, and some interesting changes to the landscape I notice as we approach. I can see where defenses are still set up, just in case. Sara, Ed, the twins, and I lead a full army through multiple large gates, bypassing the walls set up almost like a maze. Arrows etched into the walls make the maze easy to navigate even without the gates, if a bit tedious. They don't keep anyone out, as walls typically do. It's an interesting solution to stop anyone here from getting hurt without killing our assailants.

Sara told me all about this setup before we got here, but it's strange to see, nonetheless. These currently aren't needed at all, since assaulting us with victims of the woods only serves to empower Sarafyna to fight back. Everyone sent to attack us has their minds and bodies back now after months of access to Leo, but Sara remains as strong as ever. Apparently, I am not the only heart powering the hat shop anymore.

I see volu flying around a few of the towers instead of wandering in the shop, indicating that they have found a new home. I do wonder how well that is going. A new species of person living in a new culture, and with a group they technically tried to kill only a few months ago. This community is built primarily by those who'd been rejected by society just for existing, and they all have that in common, but that doesn't make them immune to prejudice and fear. None of us are, really.

There are going to be more than a few issues to work through in the coming years, especially before it's safe for everyone to disperse back to their own communities. But I will have to trust everyone else to sort through these issues. My job is simple: I need to kill the malevolent god who wants us all dead and free his mother's corpse to leave this traumatic planet behind. Simple.

I'm not certain I'll be around to contribute much, in any case. I did accept that I want to survive, and asked Sarafyna to save me, which she promised she would. God, I love her. Even so, she has yet to present a certain plan for doing so, and while I trust her to put everything into it, just as I will, sometimes, there just isn't a way to get what you want. As things stand, the safe money is on a headstone and a six-foot pit.

I grimace at the thought but push it to the back of my mind. My new freedom to grieve openly has given me plenty of time to process what I have to face in the coming days, and I suspect I will be addressing it more as I speak to my family. I am back for now, but Alpha is out there, and he's going to make a move. We freed two countries from a huge number of their sages, but they were also one of his primary obstacles for . . . whatever his plans are. We have time to rest until we get a call from Riley, or Sara notices a change in the Radiant Woods. Maybe a few days.

Enough time to say goodbye. Just in case.

But Alpha is the reason these defenses are still up, which I understand, even if seeing such walls around a community I helped build makes me itch. They will fall the day Alpha does, and that's what matters.

I lean back and pull the hood of a borrowed cloak over my head as we finally emerge from the last gate. The first thing we see are the open fields in front of the various towers and a few hundred people waiting for us. These are mostly those who came from the Radiant Woods but didn't have the ability or desire to fight in the battle we've just won. Mostly, but not entirely. I see Gilbert and Dominic at the front of the group, and both of them turn to address the crowd briefly before they all start cheering uproariously.

I groan a bit before realizing I'm annoyed at something that isn't even happening. Even now, I can't escape how self-impressed I can be sometimes. In all fairness, I'm fairly famous around here; it's hard to kill gods and kings without a few people learning your name. It isn't insane to assume people are cheering for me and what I've just done, especially with my big brother leading the chants. But then I remember I have my face and wings covered, and my tail is hidden by the wagon walls.

They aren't cheering for me. At least, not me specifically. They are cheering for everyone's return: mine, Sara's, Leo's, Charlotte's, and every single person who fought next to her. They are cheering because their abusers are dead and their friends are alive, and that's a lot better than cheering for me. Only arrogance lets me think—even for a moment—that it could be anything else.

I smile softly as Ed looks around with wide eyes and water beading in the corners of his eyes. I offer a light, playful punch to his shoulder. He barely notices, and I understand. He has been spiraling in his own way since Henry's death; since long before that, really. And now, his ears are ringing with the chorus of a better world he helped fight for and win. It's no cure for what we've been through, but the joy of the liberated is a balm to the soul. He finally looks at me, his lip quivering.

"Do you think he can hear this?"

I shrug. "Maybe. I would have told you no, once upon a time, but there is nothing so special about me that I'm the only person with an afterlife. It's not impossible. But either way," I pause, making sure his eyes meet mine, "he would have admired you, and everything you've done." He looks at me for one more moment, his trembling chin growing more active before the built-up tears finally run down his cheeks.

Ed drinks it in, the cheering continuing after our wagon makes it to the first building and the rest of the group continues flooding through. I do attract more than a few looks as I jump down and people get a look at my tail, but they have started living with cat and bird people recently, so the threshold for astonishing things has risen a good bit. Dominic, Gilbert, and a woman I don't recognize jog over to meet us near the entrance, a wide smile revealing two rows of teeth.

"Gil! It's good to see you! How have you been?" I greet. Instead of answering, he wraps me in a bear hug, literally picking me up off the ground. "Hey! You're crushing my wings!" I complain, and Gil jolts, putting me down quickly. He looks like he is about to respond, but I interrupt him by putting my hands on his sides and lifting *him* up in turn, and with much greater ease. This actually attracts more looks than my tail does, seeing as he's maybe thirteen inches taller than me and considerably bulkier. Absurd comedy alone draws attention to the both of us.

"*Oomph*," he complains. "Okay, I get it, I get it. I was just happy to see you!" His voice sounds irritated but his expression betrays amusement. I do put him down as I smirk.

"See? It's startling, isn't it?" I joke. He rubs the back of his neck.

"I always forget about your insane strength." He groans, moving his hand from his neck to his abused rib cage. His eyes drift to my clawed hand and twitching tail as he does. He must have felt my wings as well when he was trying to crush them with his hug. "Damn, I thought Sara was exaggerating. You really did just . . . grow extra body parts, huh?"

I shrug. "I've been doing that for years; these ones are just bigger and harder to hide."

"Oh right, then this is totally normal; my mistake." He laughs. "Come on, you all must be hungry. Let's get inside and get a bite to eat." I nod, sharing a look with the others for confirmation.

"We're going to see our own parents; it's been too long," August answers. I offer him a meaningful and grateful look.

"All right, have a good time," I agree. "If you don't mind, I'd like to see you both again later, now that we are home and safe. Just to spend some time decompressing."

"Sure," Autumn agrees. "We'll let you know."

"I have my own reunions as well," Sara chimes in. "I know I've been coming back more regularly, but I still don't like to leave Dad and Pete worrying. I'll catch up with you later. It's good to see you, Gil."

"Yeah, all right. See you tonight," I agree. Sara offers me a quick peck before she eagerly runs off to meet up with her own family. That leaves me, Gil, Ed, Dom, and the unfamiliar—if admittedly extremely cute—woman. I stand there quietly while Gil fails to lead us into the building as he suggested. I give Gil and Dom an expectant look, and each of them offers me a curious one. My intent seems to dawn on the woman first, opening her mouth halfway.

"Oh, that's right. Dominic and I have just reunited ourselves, and he promised to take me out tonight! If you don't mind, we'll be excusing ourselves!" she speaks up, agreeing with my silent request.

"I don't rem—" Dom starts, but the woman tugs at his arm, interrupting him.

"Come along, my love. It's been a long day, and I'm famished!" she insists. I can't help but smile as the apocalyptically powerful mage is pulled away like a too easily distracted toddler.

"Ah, so those two are courting, huh? I wondered who she was," I muse. Gil's hands go to the back of his neck again.

"Uh, yeah. Sort of," he replies. "I thought Sara had noticed; did she not say anything?" I raise an eyebrow at him as I catch his eyes following the couple and his cheeks flushing. Then my own widen, and I snap my fingers.

"I fucking *knew* it!" I exclaim as a darker red floods his face.

"Come on, I'm hungry too," Gil says, gesturing for Ed and me to follow. We happily do, although Ed is still confused.

"What? I'm missing something . . ." he complains. I give my oldest brother a look, and he rolls his eyes.

"Go ahead; it's not a secret," he agrees. I grin and look at Ed as we walk.

"You know how Gil here has always had too much love to share with just one partner, right?"

Ed shrugs. "Sure, but he left all those women behind a long while back. Said they were more casual than Mariah and me. Why?"

"Well, he's got too much love to share with just one gender too," I answer. Gilbert fails to contest the claim, completely confirming my strong suspicions.

"Oh," Ed responds. He's quiet for a breath, then exclaims, "Oh! Why didn't you tell me that? You too? Really? And both of them?" I laugh while Gil chuckles.

"It's still new; we haven't put a label on it yet," Gil explains as we enter the cool tower and make our way past the indoor foliage and fruit trees growing through the middle of each walkway.

"Still, isn't that sort of a big deal?" Ed pushes.

"There are more ways to get laid, Edward, than are dreamt of in your philosophy," I quip. "It's not that surprising, is it? He's always had a little bit of that curious energy, especially after I started living with Sarafyna. Honestly, it's about time he—" I start, but a man loudly clearing his throat interrupts me.

"Excuse me," he whines. His eyes irritatingly flick between my torso and my tail as he crosses his arms and taps one foot.

"Uh, you're excused," I reply. "There is actually like, a shit ton of room to just walk past us. You know, if you didn't notice."

"Not this guy," Gilbert whines. I tilt my head, and the interloper rolls his eyes.

"I take it she has not been informed, then?" He snorts. I shrug.

"Depends on what you're talking about. I've been informed about a lot of things. A prohibitively expensive number of things, actually. You would not *believe* how many different insane jobs I had to take to keep up with student loans, but assuming you aren't talking about biology, release dates for Metroid games, or obscure *Zelda* trivia, yeah, probably not. What do you want, bud?" I respond. He lets out an exasperated and condescending sigh.

"For one, I'd like an explanation. What have you done to yourself? Scales? The tail of some kind of bug? How do you expect me to produce an heir when you look like that? No man wants to share a bed with a monster," he lectures.

"Ex-fucking-cuse me?" I gape. "Dude, who the fuck are you?"

"Your *fiancé*?" he answers as if it's the most obvious thing in the world. I look over at Gilbert.

"Why do men keep telling me I'm engaged to them? I know it's only happened twice, but that is a lot of times when I've never been proposed to," I complain.

"It's the Kingdom of Endings again." Gil sighs. "Apparently, you mentioned voting on a leader once, and they interpreted that as voting on the future king you would marry." My mouth opens halfway as my eyes narrow. I start to speak a few times but choke on indignation. I have to take a deep breath and rub my temples before I finally answer.

"All right. I once mentioned voting as a method of government. I did *not* say it was a method I liked, but even if it was, that's not how this works. That's not how any of this works!" I say, exasperation thicker with every word. "I swear to God, I will put a 'Right to Refuse Service' sign on my pussy if I have to."

"You are the queen, and you have a responsibility to your people!" the still unnamed "fiancé" insists. I just give him a blank, quiet stare. "If you don't marry, how are we supposed to have any government at all! I was chosen by your people, and I expect you to respect their decision!" Yet again, I simply stare at him. "And part of that will be returning your body to a presentable state and producing an heir!" he adds, uncomfortable with the silence. I take a step forward and put my hand on his forehead. "What do you think you're—Whoa, stop that!" he complains as I proceed to—very slowly—push him over.

He continues to shout at me as he loses his balance from leaning backward and falls to the ground, but I don't hear what he says as I gently bonk him on the head with my stinger and continue walking with my brothers.

"Can we go somewhere private before we eat?" I ask. "It's why I asked the rest of your . . . polycule? Throuple? It's why I asked your partners to leave. I wanted a minute to talk, if that's all right?" Gilbert looks at me with bafflement painted across his face.

"You didn't ask—" he starts.

"Yes, I did. I was just polite about it," I retort before he can finish.

"Interrupting people isn't polite," Ed notes.

"Suck it. You're my brothers; I don't have to be polite to you. So?" I dismiss, pressing for an answer to the real question.

"Yeah, sure. We can go to my room if you want. Why, is everything all right?" Gil asks.

"That's a complicated answer. I have a bit to catch you up on," I reply as Gil turns and starts leading us in a new direction.

Ed and Gil both watch me for a long time. I see Gil swallow hard and struggle to respond while Ed's eyes drift toward the scar on my left eye, as they often have over the years. The news that I am, in fact, already dead is hard to stomach, in all fairness. I am obviously walking and talking, growing, and for all intents and purposes, living. There is no easy way to explain the emotional weight that comes with living as a corpse to someone when I don't have any of the obvious problems one might expect with this issue. The knowledge that everything about me that looks *alive* is an expression of someone else's will . . . it may haunt me, but to them, it's a bit of a looks-like-a-duck-and-quacks-like-a-duck situation.

What they do understand, however, is what it means when we win. When Mirage is gone, and that will can't support me anymore. They understand that they might be losing their sister less than a year after they lost their brother.

The air is viscous with anxiety as soon as my explanation ends and they start processing that knowledge. Ed is the first to respond, and even he allows several dense minutes to roll over us before he does.

"Sara promised to save you?" he asks. I take a deep breath, then nod.

"She did. And she is certain she will," I agree.

"How?" Ed pushes. I can offer him nothing but silence, and he can see the answer written on my face. *I don't know, and neither does she.* "How can she promise that with no idea how to do it?"

"I trust her," Gil whispers. "She'll do it." He looks as certain as Sara does when she says the same. Confident enough it's almost easier to believe it's a certainty she'll succeed.

"So do I," I agree. "But trusting someone won't necessarily give them the power to do the impossible. I just want you to be prepared. Prepared for Sarafyna moving mountains and bending the world to her will, and still failing to keep me alive. I might not be coming back from this."

Ed's eyes lock on mine, and Gil shakes his head. "No. No, you're coming back. Sara has changed everything over and over. She'll change this too!" Gil insists. I look down at my mismatched hands.

"Maybe she will. If anyone can, it's her. I believe it's possible, at least. But I don't know how, which means if she does, I don't know what that will look like. I don't know if surviving means coming home. I just want a chance to say goodbye, just in case," I answer.

"No. No, we aren't going to act like—" Gilbert starts, but Ed reaches out and grabs his arm.

"Gilbert. . ." he whispers. My brothers look each other in the eyes, and Ed shakes his head. "We can hope and be ready at the same time. I never said goodbye to Henry. I never got to fully reconcile with him. I'm not giving up the chance to say goodbye, even if it turns out not to be a goodbye at all. It's rare to get the chance. Please, just . . . please." Gil looks back and forth between Ed and me, desperate and frantic, but we both make the same request with shipwrecked smiles.

"How? How do we just . . . enjoy the morning after what you just told us? Lily, I don't—I can't lose you too. I wouldn't be who I am without you. You're my little sister. I can't just . . . How?" Gil pleads. I shrug, standing and moving over to his table, absolutely covered with drawings.

"We'll start with food, a few jokes, and some stories? I still need to see Mom, and that's going to be . . . I just want to have a nice morning with my brothers. Can we do that, please?" I ask.

Gil shakes but nods so subtly I almost miss it. He struggles to respond verbally until I start looking through his art. He then turns bright red and suddenly finds it extremely easy to talk about something else as he scrambles to his feet and tries to stop me. He is too late, however, as despite the extremely interesting art of me, I home in on the salacious art behind it depicting himself, Dominic, and the new woman. It is the closest thing to a sex tape I'll ever find in such a medieval world, and even I blush a little looking at it.

"Wait, don't look through—" he starts before he makes it to his feet and sees the look on my face. "Oh, Collector's balls," he groans. I curl my lips in, trying to stifle a laugh before I put the art down and tuck it behind a few more safe-for-work pieces.

"What? What is it?" Ed asks curiously.

"Well, it's not a deer, at least. I'm glad you have evolved past whatever that was," I answer. Gilbert goes from horrified to confused.

"Lily, what the fuck are you talking about?" he asks.

I raise an eyebrow at him. "When we were kids, I knocked on the door. Interrupted . . . something. You tried to hide what you were looking at on your desk, remember? It was a deer, wasn't it?" I still remember this like it was yesterday, although we haven't spoken about it since. Way back when we were still looking for Henry. I kind of pushed it to the back of my mind, actually.

Gil goes back to horrified.

"Wait, seriously?" Ed asks. "He wasn't . . ." I nod in confirmation.

"That's not what happened! Have you really thought all this time that—" He stops, unable to finish his sentence. He has to take a deep breath. "There was something else under the deer, all right? Fuck. I should have just barred the door. Have you really thought—What the fuck, Lily?" I hold a straight face for a few minutes before I start laughing.

"No, I didn't really think that. But I have at least answered your question, haven't I?" I reply. He sighs and covers his face as Ed bursts into laughter.

"Fine," he says. "If you never mention deer to me again, we can just have a nice day," he agrees. I grin. The next few hours are gentle ones, filled with laughter only siblings understand and stories that aren't funny unless you have a clear memory of them. Stupid games and arm wrestles my brothers know they can't win. Gross food we all love, and shockingly cruel insults that bounce off their target like familiar jabs always do.

For one last time, I am just a girl with her brothers, and everything is okay.

CHAPTER TWENTY-SEVEN

Farewell Tour - Mom

Ray

R ay, are you all right?" Elric asks. I've stopped eating mid-bite. I'd heard the cheering, but such oddities are normal in the backward city, so I thought nothing of it. I pay little attention to rumors. I'm only here since I'm no longer welcome at my family's estate, not since I failed during the uprising. My name has been ruined, and I've been rejected. The only place where I can blend in, where almost none of my former peers exist to torment me for my failure, is here. For all its advancements, it lacks all the comforts of home, but it's the only place I can feel *mostly* safe anymore.

I always knew she lived here. I became more worried when we all had to move to the same settlement, but as the days turned to months, I thought she'd die before she ever came back.

Elric keeps trying to get my attention, but the sad little man is low on my list of priorities. Because, as we were leaning against the window, she came back. No one else seems surprised, meaning this must have been spreading around for days at least, but I try to spend as little time around the unwashed masses as I can. That was clearly a mistake.

Walking through the hall just across from the lesser-visited third-floor common area is the woman who hates me most in the world. That is, admittedly, a fairly high bar to clear, but this is the only woman who actually can, and *will*, kill me the moment she recognizes me. If I can even call her a woman anymore. I suppose I can. Even with her monstrous visage and her vile new tail, she still looks intoxicating.

But looking is all I can do because the moment she sees me, I'm dead. It's not just that she hates me more than almost anyone else does—it's that she must hate me more than she hates anyone else. There was a time when this wouldn't have worried me, but whether through trickery or strength, she has killed many of my peers. I don't care which it is. I just have to get out of here before she finds me.

It's a cruel joke of the Collector that the one place I can feel even moderately safe, at the cost of all the luxuries of my youth, is also where my oldest and most dangerous enemy lives. I have to leave before Lillith of Endings realizes I am here.

Lillith

Tempting as it was, I didn't drink anything while I was with my brothers. Because now, I need to see my mother. I need to know not just what name she is calling me out loud but what name I have in her mind. Am I Annie, or am I her Lily?

I take a deep breath as I inch toward her door. I haven't been back to my own room yet, and it's tempting to simply hide there instead. Hell, heading to her makes the wine more tempting rather than less. Or maybe a little green mist, even if no one makes it quite as well as Henry.

I'm distracting myself, and I need to do this. I just need to knock. *God.* She's going to take one look at me and feel even more alienated. The wings and tail, the scales, claws. I already didn't look like her daughter once she learned the truth. Now I look like no one she has ever seen.

I make it to the door and raise one fist but never make contact with the worn wood of my mother's door. Instead, a familiar and persistent meowing greets me from the other side. Suzume didn't used to react too much to visitors, but I have been gone for a long time. It's possible some of her habits have changed.

"Suzie, what's wrong? Who is—" Mom asks as she opens the door for the beautiful but whiny creature. Suzume trills as she excitedly dashes through the entrance and starts walking back and forth, rubbing herself against my legs. Mom freezes as she looks at me. She must have known

I was coming back soon, but considering where we left things, I suppose there wasn't enough emotional preparation she could have done. She scans me with frantic eyes as I awkwardly pick Suzume up and hold her to my chest. The immediate purring is comforting as I try to decide if I should speak first or wait for her.

It's almost funny when I think about it. Suzume is the sweetest cat in the world. I left her for months with no explanation and came back looking for all the world like the most terrifying predator she's ever seen, and yet she recognized me in a moment and is happier than I've ever seen her now that I've returned. My mother, on the other hand, is shocked into silence as she examines me.

We have been through a lot together—pain and joy—and we have loved each other the entire time. Until she learned the name Annie. Until I promised to bring Henry back safely and failed. My cat purrs against my collarbone as my mother examines me with horror.

"W—What happened to you?" She balks. I sigh internally as I force a heartbroken smile onto my face. So I'm still only *Annie* to her, then. No longer Lily, not in her heart.

My more monstrous appearance has been the first thing everyone has commented on, from my brothers to strangers in the halls. But when my friends and brothers saw it, they were mostly intrigued. Another oddity from the strangest woman they know. Sara understood what it meant and showed concern. After that, she'd actually expressed a certain level of attraction. But my mom? I know horror when I see it. She is horrified looking at me.

I fail to hold my traitorous tail still as nerves force it to twitch.

"I know," I rush to explain. "It looks worse than it is, really. But I did this for a good—"

"I can count your ribs! You're even thinner than when you were bedridden last year! And you're so pale! Are you sick? Haven't you been taking care of yourself?" she interrogates. I freeze, taken aback by the questioning and its surprising trajectory.

"My rib cage?" I question. "You're not worried about, well, the scales? Or the stinger?" I've been so prepared for rejection that concern hits me like a truck, and hard enough to send me to an entirely new world.

Mom finally makes eye contact, and dark circles struggle to hold weary eyes up. "Lily, you're my daughter, and you are obviously unwell. What do a few extra limbs matter when you're sick? Besides, they told me about all that. But no one warned me you would look so close to death!" she protests.

Most of her sentence washes past me like twigs in a river. My mind is caught entirely on *"Lily, you're my daughter."* Words I was certain she'd never say again. She'd called me Lily before I left, but I could hear the echo in the hollow name. But this time . . . This time, she says it like it's who I am.

"Oh no, Lily, are you okay?" she presses, this time not investigating my physical health. I'm crying, I realize as she looks at me with growing concern. *I'm fine. It's all right. I'm just tired. I don't know why I'm crying.* A dozen white lies queue up on my tongue, and each tastes like bile.

I shake my head. "No, I'm really not," I answer honestly. She doesn't ask any further questions, pulling me into the kind of hug only a mother can offer. My head rests against her chest, and Suzume purrs happily between us. "I'm scared, Mom."

My mom is scared too. She has been this entire time. Her rejection of me as her daughter was, at least partially, a defense mechanism against the exact future we are now facing. Sara has been suggesting I try and speak openly with my mother ever since her first visit back here, but I only ever processed the idea as another on a long list of anxieties.

Mom runs a brush through my hair as I sit quietly at the vanity in her bedroom. Suzume is curled happily in my lap, absolutely glued to me ever since I got here. Every moment that passes, my heart should be pounding in my chest, but it's not. And with its stubborn quiet comes the constant reminder of upcoming goodbyes.

Neither of us has much to say. If it weren't for Mirage, my mother might beg me to let someone else handle Alpha. She might tell me that I have fought enough, that I have won enough change, and that I have earned rest. I can hear these protests in every shallow breath, feel it in the deft way she navigates tangles in my hair without tugging, pulling, or hurting. I can see it in every gentle movement and every sidelong sigh. She wants to beg me to slow down, to stop fighting. But she won't.

"I'm proud of you, Lily," she whispers as she brushes, and she means it. She knows that I can't stop fighting; she knows I won't. And she knows it doesn't matter. Because I told her about Mirage. We have to let Mirage leave, and that will end me whether I fight or stay home. The only guaranteed safety for me is Alpha's death, followed by Mirage's continued imprisonment and abuse, and living because of the collar on someone else's neck would be far worse than death.

I don't need to explain this to my mother. Giving her all the details of the danger I am in was enough, and she understands because—however she may have struggled with the truth of my past—she knows me. She understands me. It's what made her so afraid in the first place.

And I understand. I do. Henry wasn't the only person to die that day. He wasn't even the only person whose death hurt me, and he certainly isn't the only one whose blood I feel between my toes with every step I take. But his is the death that hurts me the most. I can have all the empathy in the world, but the loss of someone I personally love will always have a sharper cut, so I understand the desire for distance. If she could believe her daughter had been dead for years, she could believe she wasn't at risk of losing me again. In a way, she was right, I suppose.

"Thanks, Mom," I respond quietly. There isn't much else to say. She went through most of this with Sara already, apparently. She's had more time to process it than my brothers have, and there is something in that. Because it's not just quiet resignation but understanding. My mother has accepted me as her daughter, despite the strange nature of our relationship and our similar mental and emotional ages. She has accepted an impossibility, in a way. It makes me want to do the same. So when I next speak, my voice is louder and steadier. "I asked her to save me," I say. The hairbrush pauses for a brief moment, then continues.

"Do you think she can?" she asks. Her voice is calm and steady, but it carries an indefinable quality, like hope hanging by a thread.

"No," I answer honestly, "but she does. And she is smarter than me in a lot of ways."

"That's true," my mother agrees easily. I smile, and I see the same on the corner of her mouth.

"You could have tried denying that, at least a little," I complain. Her soft smile grows by maybe a centimeter.

"I'm trying to accept things as they are, Lily. It's hard, but also easier in many ways." I narrow my eyes at her reflection. Her words are true and carry worlds of meaning, but bemusement dancing across her eyes reveals very intentional timing. It's good to see her smile, even a little. Even as she processes that we only have so many days left together.

"Do you think it's possible? Living every day as a goodbye while still believing it isn't going to be one?" I ask. She lets a long breath out of her nose.

"I don't know. I know it will hurt, but I also know it's worth a try. I'm glad to have you here, Lily, and . . ." She trails off, her gentle brushing pausing as she fights a tremor in her hand. "Try, please? Every day with you since you were seven has been a miracle. Every single day, the easy and the difficult. Please. Try to come home. And if you can't come home, then try and stay alive somewhere else. I just want you alive. I know it seems impossible, but that's what you do, isn't it? The impossible? Day after day, year after year?

"You came back to me. You drove Richard off. You saved Ed and Gil from being the men their father wanted them to be. You brought down the Tudors. You stopped a tyrant king. You picked a fight with the Collector himself. That's who you are, Lily. You're my impossible girl. So just one more time, please, try and do the impossible? Try and stay alive?" I take a heavy breath.

"Yeah, okay, Mom," I agree. "I'll try. It's just one more miracle, right? How hard could it be?" She only responds to that with a nod, like I just told her I'd go back to school after dropping out. She wipes a quiet tear on one sleeve and returns to brushing.

"Do you think . . . Do you think you could stay here tonight?" she pleads. I smile again.

"Yeah, Mom. I'd like that. I'd really, really like that."

CHAPTER TWENTY-EIGHT

Farewell Tour - Home

That's not fair; we agreed on no magic!" August complains as my javelin sails at least a hundred meters past his. I wear the most innocent face I can as I shrug.

"I didn't use magic—I'm innocent!" I insist. He glares at me.

"Magically enhanced strength is magic," he counters.

"I can't just put my Herculean muscles down and pick them up later, August! I can't help it if you forgot who the woman you were betting against was. Blame hubris for this loss, not me," I tease.

"It is, actually. If you had the decency to be a little taller, it would be easier to remember how strong you are. Your height is clearly an act of intentional deception," he complains. I shake my head in mock disappointment.

"Annie was too tall; Lily is too short and has too many gains. What does a girl have to do to make you dudes less sore about losing all the time?" I lament. August rolls his eyes and crosses his arms.

"Whatever. We just need to bet on something else," he suggests.

"What are you two even betting for?" Autumn interjects. "We don't even use money here."

"Strength and honor," I answer immediately.

"Pride," August adds.

"The love and admiration of women everywhere," I continue.

"An eternal spot in the legends of today," August finishes. Autumn looks back and forth between both of us, and a rare smile briefly creeps across her face.

"You're both ridiculous, you know that?" She chuckles before looking at her twin. "Why not just play cards if you want it to be fair? You know she made those javelins with her steel mana. She could have just made yours heavier."

"I would never cheat; I am a woman of honor!" I protest.

"She cheats at cards too," August grumbles. I mime a shot to the heart as he says this.

"How dare you! Math isn't cheating—it's just math! If you paid more attention in class, you could do the same!"

"No, I couldn't! You taught us that stupid game; how were we supposed to know there was a formula for it? Besides, I was talking about the other one? Where you clearly hid cards up your sleeve? Or does that not count either?" August accuses.

"Not if you can't prove it." I smirk before sticking my tongue out at him. Autumn rubs her temples, but I see the bemused smirk she tries to hide.

"Well, it doesn't matter now. Lily, your mom said to come get you. Your, uh . . . mushroom thing is ready."

I perk up immediately. "It's a portobello beet burger," I say, "and it's fucking outstanding. I'm glad; embarrassing August is tiring, as I'm sure you know. I could use something to eat."

"Oh, come on, quitting while you're ahead is poor sportsmanship," August complains while I laugh.

"If I don't, we'll be at this forever, won't we? Go on, find someone you can actually beat. Gil's gotta be around here somewhere," I poke.

August surely has something else to complain about, but I don't wait around to hear it; Mom is inside with food, after all. It's been a good day so far. Having made the rounds with my family over the past few days, we have had enough mourning for a future Sara has promised us won't come. While we wait for news from Riley, we've decided to celebrate the victories we've already had. My mom is cooking a massive dinner for all the friends and family who live here. She's not the only one either, since there are thousands of us who came back from winning their lives back. What started as a family dinner has somehow evolved into something of a massive festival.

Water and earth mages have created geysers and hot springs outside to keep people relaxed, cooks have set up stalls, and August and I aren't the only ones competing in pointless and stakeless games. Clarrise and Victor have set up their own oddities and amusements as well, like early vehicles. Not much use for travel yet, but very useful for entertainment as they drive people around the open fields in front of and between the various towers. It's the first time since . . . since losing Henry that my family has all gotten together just to enjoy ourselves.

"Excuse me," I say as a tall and somewhat rugged man steps in my way just before I enter the tower with the nearest public kitchen.

"What, not gonna say nothin'?" he asks. *Oh great. For such so-called unattractive body modifications, I sure do get hit on a lot.* "That just ain't right, Lil," he finishes. I squint as I examine the man. He does have a sort of familiar look to him, but in a way that could be anyone. Almost but not quite handsome in a himbo sort of way.

And then it falls into place.

"Tommy?" I ask. He grins. It *is* him. "Dude, what the fuck? It's been less than a year since I saw you; when did all this happen?" I am genuinely floored. I've seen him getting older over the years as I delivered supplies to the community he ended up in, but he still looked like a scrawny kid before I left for the Republic. I guess it was finally time for his growth spurt. It actually took longer than I expected, considering his rough age.

"You have a tail, Lil," he answers, and I pause.

"Yeah, all right, that's fair. Still, didn't you use to be shorter than me, at least for a little while?"

"Used to be a lotta things," he replies easily with a shrug. "Here I am though."

"Here you are," I agree with a grin. He's come a long way from the kid who helped me form the Mages of Penance. "You gonna be around for a while? My mom is waiting, but I want to catch up. Find out how everyone else is doing."

He nods. "Yep! I know Diana has been dyin' to see ya," he agrees. His sort of undefinable accent is far gentler than it once was, but it's still undeniably him.

"And I'd love to see her too. Hang around for a while; I'll be back in a bit," I respond.

Even as I leave the brief exchange, I have an extra perk in my step. He and I aren't exactly fast friends, but we went through a lot together as kids. Just seeing him doing so well makes it feel like everything has been worth it. Not that I have any doubt about that, but such a clear contrast from the starving and angry child I met all those years ago feels like a warm fire and s'mores on a summer night. A little reminder of the people whose lives are so much better than anything Potestia could ever offer. I have lost a lot, but together, we have gained so much.

I have even more energy as I enter the towers and finally find my mom, who is hovering over an almost boiling pot with a tantalizing smell. "Hey, Mom," I greet. "I hear tales and legends that my beautiful and kind mother has delicious food waiting for me; is this true, or is Autumn a filthy liar and a brigand?"

Mom sighs as I greet her. "It was true once," she replies with a faux sadness. "But the meal has since found a new, more punctual home." I put my hand to my chest and mime shock and offense. I then look around the room to see Ed—a half-eaten mushroom burger in his hand. He jumps and then rushes out of the room with all the innocence and grace of a child caught with his hand in the cookie jar. An extremely pregnant Mariah rolls her eyes and offers me an apologetic look.

"Betrayal and tomfoolery, that's what this is," I protest. "I came as soon as I heard it was ready!" Mom raises an eyebrow at me.

"Did you? Or did you have to leave August with a few more quips before you came?" she accuses, knowing I'd been making bets with the man for the last hour. I narrow my eyes at her and half open my mouth to protest, but the precision with which she nailed me down keeps the words caged. So I change course and put my palms together, bowing my head.

"My deepest apologies, dear mother. I have wronged you with my inattentiveness, and I shall regret my actions until the stars turn cold. Might I humbly request a replacement when the time to undertake such labor presents itself?" She furrows her brows and shakes her head despite the amused smile she wears.

"Of course I'll make you another one. Just don't go too far until it's done, all right?" she agrees.

"I will be at your back the entire time," I promise. "Just as soon as I have exacted my revenge on my traitorous brother." She laughs through her nose as she retrieves another mushroom from the pantry.

"Right, well. Exact your revenge quickly, then," she jokes. Then she pauses. "I thought you said space was cold, didn't you? So aren't the stars already cold?" I laugh at the honestly reasonable question.

"They are not, no. They are all suns, but like, super far away," I respond. She pauses and looks up at me, then shakes her head.

"They believed some strange things in your past life, didn't they?"

"Sure did," I agree. "We loved making deranged shit up back there. Ask me to tell you about the friendzone sometime."

"Lily, I have no idea what that means." She sighs.

"No one does, Mom. No one does." She returns her focus to cooking, having reached the threshold for my bullshit where everyone decides it's no longer worth pursuing. Which is, honestly, fair. In any case, I am left with nothing but broken mushroom-related promises and sympathetic glances from my brother's wife. While I wait, the least I can do is make Edward rue the day he betrayed me.

I stroll out of the kitchen and into the hall. Ed is nowhere to be seen, but I'm not worried. My mana may be loud and bright now, but I still have an old pair of enchanted glasses for a more subtle X-ray spell. I keep them on me most of the time, since they are very useful for tracking people down and making Sarafyna blush. Pulling them out of my bag, I slip them on, the world being replaced with bright colors which I struggle to parse for a moment.

There is, as I suspected, a man crouched around the corner and attempting to sneak away. He is practically hiding behind someone else, who is looking down at the crouching mushroom thief. I smirk. He certainly didn't get far. I begin to stroll easily toward the corner to confront the little shit when I catch a glimpse of another man approaching me. I pull my glasses off, worried he'll say something and give me away before I can startle Ed. It is, of course, August, likely hoping to redeem himself for his pitiful display with the javelins.

I hold a finger to my lips to prevent any traitorous greeting from revealing my pursuit. To August's credit, he recognizes both my intent and the importance of my quest, even if the details of my stolen dinner can't be easily shared with him. He nods and follows me as I turn the corner.

"Ha!" I shout. "Did you really fucking think you could escape my retribution? Today, you will pay the price for your treachery!" I have half a smile on as I shout, which quickly fades as I realize the man I'm yelling at . . . is not my brother. He looks vaguely familiar in the way a third cousin you met once at a funeral might.

He is still crouched behind another man, who looks at him with some mix of horror and confusion. "Uh, Ray, what exactly did you do to Lillith of Endings?" the taller man asks. I'm about to clarify my mistake when I catch the actual culprit out of the corner of my eye. Ed is grinning at me. I glare as he sticks his tongue out, takes another bite, and disappears around another corner.

"Little piece of shit," I grumble.

"Oh hey, I know you," August says, addressing the man I'd mistaken for my brother. "Ray doesn't sound right though, although it's close . . ." August trails off as he tries to identify the innocent man I've just threatened with retribution. I try to apologize and explain the silly exchange with my brother, but he throws himself to the ground before I can.

"Please!" he begs. "Forgive me! I was barely a man when we met! Barely more than a child! I've changed! I'm a better man now! I'm begging you; I will leave, I'll go back to Potestia! I swear!"

I stop short, an apology caught in a knot of pure confusion. Edward's sandwich-related treachery is forgotten as I squint my eyes and try to remember the man kowtowing before me. *Do I have a reason to be mad at this guy? He seems to think so.* For the desperation in his voice and body language you'd think he'd killed my cat in front of me or some shit. But if he'd done something worth this, I would surely, *surely* remember him.

The other man looks back and forth between his friend and me before deciding he doesn't want to be tangled up in whatever this is. I don't blame him; I don't much want to either. "Right," he says. "Well, Ray, I'll be outside. I think I saw someone cooking lamb earlier, so, uh . . . good luck." He awkwardly rushes off as I keep looking at the stranger at my feet.

"Ray . . . Ray . . ." August muses. Then he snaps his fingers. "That's right, you're Ralf, aren't you?" he asks. The man on the floor looks up at August with a face like flour.

"Y-yes," he acknowledges. "But I'm not the Ralf you knew! I left my noble house behind to come live here!" I put a finger to my lip in thought. A million faces flash through my head, but I just can't place this one.

"Ralf," I muse.

"I was just upset by the way you treated me when we met! I was childish, and they were only illusions! I was just trying to scare you! And the rumors about the duel were a mistake. I just . . . I just . . ." he stutters.

"That's right! I heard about that! People all over campus were talking about how you accepted a duel but were too afraid to show up! I forgot all about that after the thing with, well. Once you got famous, that rumor sounded silly to everyone," August explains. I raise an eyebrow. Had I heard a rumor about that? I suppose it's possible; there were a few rumors about me going around in school, but, well, that's just school, isn't it? If there aren't, it's because you're mostly unnoticed, and Godfrey wouldn't have allowed that.

This back-and-forth goes on for a while. Ralf apologizes for different slights, like claiming I was afraid of him, hitting on me, and insulting me when I spit at his feet, apparently. Harassing my empty room every night for years and following me around campus. Basically, a whole lot of childish shit. He'd been involved in fighting the uprising but had seemingly fled before actually contributing anything. All in all, he sounds like a prick who hasn't actually done anything to inspire violence, at least that I know of. No mention of slave ownership or anything.

I crouch down next to him, putting my clawed hand on his shoulder and making eye contact with him.

"Ralf," I say, looking to August for confirmation on the name. As August nods, Ralf feels like he is going to flee from his skin. "Man, I have to be totally honest with you here. I have no fucking idea who you are. I never slept in my room on campus, and I don't remember any specific time I was hit on. I have not been hunting you because I didn't know you were a person who exists. I was hunting a stolen sandwich, and that remains a higher priority than you. Sorry, buddy, I didn't mean to scare you. I just really thoroughly do not care about you or whether you thought I was hot but rude when we were teens. I don't know who you are, and if I remember after this, it's going to be because it's a funny story."

He stares at me. For the look he's giving me, it may have been kinder to actually kill him. Not knowing him seems to hurt his pride where pressing his forehead to the dirty ground didn't. I wave a hand in front of his face, but he doesn't respond. I suspect I just broke him. Shrugging, I rise to my feet.

"Well, that was fucking weird. What's up, Augs?" I finally ask.

"Honestly, I don't remember." August chuckles. "But I suddenly don't feel the need to salvage my pride from the last few losses. Turns out things could always be much worse."

"Yeah, someone could steal your dinner," I grumble. "Speaking of, I'd better get back before my traitorous mother feeds one of her other children instead of me again. You can go make bets against someone you can beat.

I just remembered I already have the love and admiration of women every-where, so I'm all set."

"Someone who plays fair, you mean?" August accuses. I shrug.

"Whatever makes you feel better." I laugh, then look down at the still crestfallen man at my feet. "People do make up the strangest version of events, don't they?"

"Oh, shut up," August scoffs. "That is that and this is this. We both know you cheated at cards at the very least!"

"So sad how all these men around me delude themselves." I sigh. August narrows his eyes at me as I casually slide one of my homemade cards out of my sleeve and offer it to him. "Here, a consolation prize. If you run into Ed, make sure to use it against him." I head back toward the kitchen and grin as I tune out his cursing. Shouldn't have played a game from my world and assumed I didn't know any tricks.

The rest of the day carries on much in the same fashion. I don't see Ralf again, although I suppose I didn't notice him during most of our other interactions either—if he is to be believed. When I return to the kitchen, my dinner has been stolen again, this time by my oldest brother and his entourage. Revenge goes by the wayside, however, as I eventually trade ancient knowledge with my mother in exchange for a guaranteed reserva-tion. That is, where I got my red earrings. Seeing as they go well with my eyes, a similar pair would look nice on her as well.

The knowledge does her little good. They were a gift from a guy on one of the island communities, given as thanks after I helped clear some grow-ing corruption in the emerging government. Luca, I think his name was. With no idea where this man is or if he'll be able to offer a second pair, she agrees to protect my next meal from my bandit band of brothers.

I finally eat, thank my mother, and continue to catch up with friends: Mages of Penance from Satusmor, revolutionaries from Visenar, and people from the different communities. I get to catch up with everyone, and it's good. There are volu and ailur wandering casually around, celebrating with friends they made next to Leo. In fact, I get to see everyone but him, and that hurts. But it's a good day anyway. I just have to figure my shit out with Charlotte, and we can at least pass letters back and forth. But that's for another time.

Today is about calm, about quiet, about rivers of tears already cried, and the warm soup on the other side. It is a day of rest as we wait for news about a battle we may not win.

After a while, I finally find Sara, sitting with her legs to the side under an acorn tree. As I approach, I raise an eyebrow. There are two piles of acorns on either side of her, and she is idly fidgeting with one. On closer inspection, I notice the ones in the larger pile each wear their cupule, while those in the smaller pile lack one. Fallen off, as they often do. I am confused for only a minute before it dawns on me, and a wide grin splits my face.

"Putting their hats back on, are you?" I ask. She pauses for a moment, acorn in hand, then blushes and pulls the wide brim of her hat over her face.

"Hey, Annie, having a good time?" she asks, completely ignoring the question but continuing in her task of rehatting the acorns. I sit down next to her and look up at the tree above us.

"Really good, actually," I reply. "I have needed a day like today for a really long time." She turns her head to me and smiles.

"I'm really glad. It's good to see you so happy." She grins. I smirk.

"You've definitely seen me happier than this," I joke. She rolls her eyes.

"That is an entirely different topic, and you know that," she rebukes. I grin nonetheless. I don't respond right away though. Instead, I just sit next to her and look at all the people around us. She's right. This is the happiest I've been in a long, long time.

"Do you still think you can do it?" I finally ask. The words claw at my throat on their way out, their poisonous taste clashing with the joy all around us. She doesn't wait a breath before answering, doesn't even ask what I mean. She knows. I asked her to save me, and she will never forget that.

"I know I can," she replies with a confidence even I have never felt.

"But . . . how, Sara? How can you save me? What did Mirage show you?" I ask. She pauses.

"I'm not sure how, exactly. It's hard to get a perfectly clear picture from Mirage. But—" She stops as both our whisper spheres go off at once. My cheerful demeanor melts like pissed-on snow as I nearly fumble mine pulling it out of my bag. When I activate it, the sounds are overwhelming. I think there are voices, but I can't make out what they are saying. A thousand sources of sound fight each other at once.

Riley's voice makes it through, but she only manages three words before the sphere cuts off.

"Help us, please."

CHAPTER TWENTY-NINE

Genocide

Archer

I grit my teeth while my heart pounds in my chest. I'm honestly not sure how my return to the abolitionists will go. I should be hailed as a hero; my plan has finally worked, in a way. I didn't expect Lillith to actually win, but I would have won either way. Had Lillith been killed, I could have inspired the people of both the Republic and the Council Lands to fight back. Some of them are already, but I could have organized them, directed them. Instead of random acts of resistance, I could have unified the country under our flag and fought strategically. I could have trapped the sages and ended them one by one.

In a way, however unexpected, Lillith winning is better. By playing them against each other, I've managed to eliminate all the major sages in the Republic, and most of the minor Council sages. The most powerful ones went dark just before the trap could be sprung, so they are still a threat. Either way, by luring Lillith out and faking a deal with the Void Sage, I am the one responsible for liberating one country and moving the other a few steps closer. I just need the rest of the abolitionists to acknowledge that.

Unfortunately, for all her talk of free will and not manipulating people, she has been using her connection to the sage relays to sow discord among my people. Many of them have begun to question me and each other, making organization difficult. Ever since Lillith started manipulating them to create division, I haven't known who to trust. Worse still, she was hardly strategic about eliminating the sages. The effects of their Nexus energy on the population are fading rapidly, leaving the average person confused and directionless.

I can give them the direction they need; I'm the only one who is willing to. I just need to free them from Lillith's influence and help lead them to something better. And I will. I still have allies left, or I did before the battle at the border. Before that sanctimonious and self-proclaimed *demon queen* decided to treat all our lives like plates spinning on a stick. I had people in place to help guide and respond to the chaos of this result, just in case, but they have either failed in their mission or in their loyalty. This country is a mess. Either way, they have not been answering their whisper spheres, and today, I find out why.

I take a deep breath before entering the safe house. It's a small one, known only to a few of us, the most trustworthy of the abolitionists, the most loyal. I chose this one over every other possible rendezvous point because it will provide the most immediate answer. If there is someone here, then I have at least a few allies left, and we can start the fight in earnest. If it is empty . . . then I have to start over from the beginning.

I open the unnaturally silent door and step into a tired room with water-stained wood floors. I set my jaw and sigh as I am greeted not by an ally but by a letter on a string hanging from the ceiling directly in front of the door, like if they'd left it on a table I'd be too dimwitted to find it. I tear it from the string and pull the letter from the unsealed envelope. My eyes grow weary at the first words I see as I unfold the traitorous paper.

Rochelle,

> *I remember such kindness, such passion. We all do. We all had such fury at a world that hated us, and we remember the first woman who ever hoped for something better.*
>
> *We remember you.*
>
> *But our memories were grand views through dirty windows. We thought the dirt came from us. Any doubts about what we could and couldn't see could be explained by the mud of our own minds.*

*But the window is clean now. Every memory we share
has been poisoned by the clarity of your control. You're not
strong enough, Archer. You're not strong enough to own us
without borrowing the sages' leash.*

*The fight starts today. It finally starts today because we
have finally left you behind.*

Goodbye, Archer. You are not welcome with us anymore.

It's over.

I let out a heavy breath. It's not as bad as it could have been. They are
still together, still ready to fight, which means they can still be given direction. I'll need to change my face again and find a new name to start over
as a new recruit in the fight, but it's not over. I still have allies; they'll just
believe I'm someone else again. My name will be remembered for its role in
ending the sages anyway, and perhaps, once we've won once and for all, I
can use an old name again. I'll decide when the time comes.

I take a few more steps inside. It won't be safe here. If they believe I am
like the sages, they can't be trusted to leave me alone, but the home may still
have some spare clothes or food at the very least.

Before I can find either, however, a voice speaks up.

"She told you about the hearts, I assume. In my Calm Stones," the Original
Sage says. I turn, my blood running cold as I see him sitting in the living
room, idly examining the leather of his chair. He sits facing the entrance in
such a way it should have been impossible to miss him. But of course, impos-
sibilities are the sages' specialty. "Did you ever wonder why that is?"

I swallow hard but keep my face in the shape of a stone. Pulling a chair
from the nearby table, I spin it around, sitting on it with the back in front
of me. It provides no safety whatsoever, but it does offer some comfort,
putting some kind of barrier between myself and the monster who wants
to consume me. I've heard the stories of the endless life inside his great
collection. I simply have to hope I don't have enough power to merit the
effort. He is waiting for me to answer, and fear forces the first guess I can
think of out of my throat like vomit. "Because they're alive?" I guess. The
Original snorts.

"Alive," he jeers. "I suppose they are, in a way. Everything connected
to Mirage is alive *because* she is alive. But not like you mean, no. In fact,
you might say their lack of sapience is why the heart is needed. You see, my

mother feels no connection to stone. She thrives on emotion, on life, on desire. She cannot be used to maintain a space with no life attached to it. Her power needs people: desperation and fear and love. The more the better, but she needs at least one. Without that, I simply can't keep her power tied to one of my little spaces. It would dissolve in an instant."

As he finishes this long-winded explanation, his eyes lock on mine. An invitation is extended through eye contact; an invitation like steel on flesh. He wants a response. My mind races. I've heard the rumors of the Original occasionally mentioning a mother. Some say she is dead, others say she is alive. But he is describing her like she is the Nexus itself.

"All right," I say. "So your . . . mother can only act through other people?"

"Not at all. She can do what she likes, of course. At least when she's not being manipulated and taken advantage of. But what power she has left me with—left us with—will not be maintained without a connection to someone. That's what you are, you know; all of you sages: her connections to the world. You offered her the deepest and thirstiest depths of your hearts, and she used that connection to reach this world." He begins picking at a hangnail, no longer looking at me. He seems almost bored. Yet, I can still feel the order, the demand for a response.

"So why an actual heart?" I ask. "That's not the same thing as a person." He pauses and grins.

"Isn't it, though?" he counters. "I'll admit my design might be a bit on the nose. Mirage may not picture a literal heart when she connects to a person, but she isn't making these connections alone. You see, her power can be enhanced with anyone, with any emotion from any person. But she already has a special connection to you sages, doesn't she? So I use sages as an anchor to create my Calm Stones. The Nexus as well, actually.

"It's simple, really. Mirage connects to you, and I use that connection. I build a world around it, designing entire realities around the hearts you use to steal my mother's power. You'll have to forgive my little joke of manifesting them in such a . . . poignant way. The heart is you, you see. Everything about you. Your love and your hate, your connection to my mother. All of this is what makes these Calm Stones possible."

I swallow hard again. My hands are shaking, but I force myself to remain composed. "Why just a heart, then? Why not trap the sage in the stone in their entirety?" I press. He sighs.

"The same reason I'm bothering to explain all this to you," he replies. "I can extract power from an unwilling heart. I can extract power from captives with little to no direct connection to Mirage. But, alas, my mother is something of a bleeding heart herself. It is always so much easier to manipulate and maintain Nexus energy when the sage I use agrees to help. It's almost like she fights it as hard as the heart itself does. In other news, I am here to make an offer."

My heart nearly stops then and there. "You want me to . . . volunteer to become a Calm Stone?" I ask. "To willingly help the enemy I have dedicated my life to stopping?" I am surprised enough by his audacity that I actually forget my fear for a moment. The Original shrugs.

"Consent through threats works a little, but Mirage still fights it. It's usually manageable, but unfortunately, you are weak. I'll need to be as efficient as possible with you, or the stone won't form. So yeah, I hope you'll agree to it. It's not a terrible deal. You will exist in two places at once, in a way, but you'll only really be conscious of one. You'll be free to do as you like," he offers.

"Free to do as I like while still under your control," I challenge. He shrugs again.

"I'll let you draw from my power. Just a little, but enough that you can regain your position with your little abolitionists. Enough to ensure you are respected. Remembered. Recorded in what history books are written about the fall of the sages. No need for a new name or to start over. Let your heart beat inside a Calm Stone, and you can have everything you want back."

He is lying. I know he is lying. There are a thousand holes in his offer, but even so, for just a moment, I weigh my options. *Perhaps that wouldn't be so bad.* The thought is brief but vibrant. *What if I don't have to lose anything?* The temptation is strong enough that, for only a brief moment, I think about agreeing.

That moment is all he needs. I feel ice climbing my heart and holding it in place while the Original grins at me; he could feel my intent to agree the moment I thought it. As I'm being connected to a massive, militant black stone forming outside the house, I consider fighting it.

I could make this harder for him. It was only a moment. Consent can be taken away, and if I do that, he will be forcing it. All the trouble he was trying to avoid with his offer can still be realized. But I don't, because it wasn't as brief a moment as I want to pretend. I want to take his offer. Even though I don't believe him, part of me does, and that part wants what he is offering. I worked so hard for this resistance, putting my all into it. It wasn't fair to take it away from me. My name belongs on the halls of history, and this is my best chance of making it there.

So I let the stone form. I offer my heart to it, and I dream of the power to create the future I've always wanted.

Riley

Heavy bags hang from my eyes as I enter the tavern. Returning to the Republic was the right choice. I thought I'd be fighting every day, rioting in the streets and protecting anyone who needed it from state mages. And though there is a little of that, it is a fraction of what I've been doing.

When Lillith started sharing her grief with the world, everything changed. When most of the Republic's sages died, everything changed again. It was a bit like pulling the curtains open to force a lazy child from bed. Scales firmly sewn over eyes all started to fall at once, and grief started returning to this country like a flood. Those who accepted their grief the first time it was offered have had months to prepare, and they are making a massive difference, adapting and setting up support systems for themselves and their friends.

It could be much, much worse. Had the entire country been handed their grief at once, I don't know what we would have done. Instead, people everywhere have been preparing loved ones for the return of grief. Things are better than they could have been, but that's a far cry from easy. The sages may have enjoyed authority without responsibility, but their control did serve some purpose, it would seem. A ruler has to work harder to control their subjects without mind control. Conversely, with mind control, the ruler may not put as much work in. And when that mind control is taken away, the house of cards begins to fall that much more easily.

The help I've been providing has been far less violent than I'd expected. It's largely involved finding homes and beds for people in my father's old estates. People come to me for help because they know I helped end the sages and because I have the means to help them. I'm no longer a slave of the arena nor a trophy of my father. My many siblings and I legally own all his property now, and even if we didn't, we have the trust of his staff.

Not all my siblings are people I would be overjoyed to see; not all of them would even survive meeting me. But as a side effect of my father punishing me so publicly, I am the most well-known, the most famously formidable, and the most obviously sympathetic. Returning was the right choice, even if I feel like a corpse.

"Welcome to the Missing Moose," the bartender greets as I shamble toward the nearest stool.

"Whatever's on tap," I request. The man behind the bar takes one look at me and declines to take offense at my terse response.

"Looks like you could use it," he agrees. He pulls a stein from under the counter and begins to fill it when the bell on the door goes off a second time. "Welcome to the Mi—" His greeting is cut short as he freezes in place. The beer begins to overflow, bringing him back to reality and prompting me to investigate who inspired such a response. As I turn, I freeze as well.

At first glance, the man who enters doesn't look threatening at all. In fact, quite the opposite. He looks squirrelly and slight—like I might kill him with a sneeze. He is nervous and twitchy, and I'd consider finding the poor man a blanket if I didn't recognize his face. There are only a few dozen people who are recognized by everyone, even citizens from another country. The Shadow Sage is one of them. One of the Council sages is walking into this tavern, and his eyes immediately find me. I summon mana as quickly as I can, but he holds terrified hands in the air.

"I-I'm not here to fight!" he pleads. I hesitate, my eyes flicking to the nervous bartender and back to the sage. "I want to save you!"

I furrow my brows. "Save me from whom?" I press.

"Can we talk about it in private?" he requests. I almost say yes. I want to get him away from the noncombatants in the room, but leaving them unprotected could be as dangerous as fighting him here. Perhaps more so. I don't know enough, and I doubt he came here alone, so I shake my head.

"Tell me what you came to tell me, or I show you how I managed to kill my father," I bluff. The Shadow Sage is a jumpy man and seems easily bullied, even if I may not be able to follow through on my threat. He glances around the room then holds one thumb to his mouth and nibbles on the nail. He whispers to himself as he does this.

"Is there room for all of them? Will anyone notice? Is it worth it?" he murmurs his thoughts for the world to hear before finally snapping his head back up and looking at me. "Fine," he agrees after a moment. "I'll take all of you, but we need to leave. Now!" I tilt my head.

"You'll need to do better than that. I'm not willingly going with a sage for no reason. Tell me what you want," I insist. He grips his head and pulls at his hair as he begins to pace a narrow diameter.

"She won't come. But she won't come either way. But we need her—anyone who can help, anyone brave enough to. We need her." He stops pacing and bites his lip before looking up at me again. "All right, I'll tell you. But after that, you need to come with me right away!" he insists.

"Depends on what you tell me," I reply. He groans and shakes his head, but he takes a deep breath.

"He is coming for you," he finally says. "The Original. He is coming to use you to empower his collector and himself. Your chimera or sage or demon, or whatever she is took so many of his captives, and he wants to use you to replace them, trapping you forever and using your desperation to strengthen his own connection to the Nexus. He'll be here any day now."

"Me? Because I helped kill the sages?" I ask. The Shadow Sage closes his eyes and takes a rapid but deep breath through his nose.

"Not you, specifically. All of you. He wants to replace the thousands he lost with millions. Every man, woman, and child in the Republic or the Council Lands. He plans to consume . . . all of you," he explains. My heart begins to struggle in my chest, beating like the wings of a caged bird. But I hold my composure.

"All of us? Everyone? Surely he's not powerful enough to do this, especially not without all the stones he has lost over the last few months," I protest. The Shadow shakes his head, looking over his shoulder as if he expects to find the Original waiting for him.

"Don't worry about how! Just know that it's going to happen. But the remaining Council sages and I . . . we have a plan. A shelter underground for a few thousand. People we can hide. It will be small, but we'll still have a society, human connection. Please, come with me. We can get you out before it happens!"

I cross my arms. My heart is beating faster. There is no lie in his voice; his fear is real. It isn't surprising to me that the sages, when outmatched, want to maintain any power they can, even if it means ruling over a hidden world. But the Original. This seems too far, even for him. Perhaps the Shadow has been lied to about the severity? Perhaps this is a trap, and they knew he'd believe it and sell me on the idea.

"Why me? You must know I don't love the sages. Of all people, why the one person in this country who has killed them? Why would you want me in your little society?" I press.

"*Because* you've killed sages. We need fighters. We need defenses. If we are going to survive, we need people who are capable of it. Does everyone want you there? No. But I do. I want to survive, and I don't care who I have to work with to do that. Please, just come with me. All of you come with me!" he pleads. A few people stand, frantically gathering their things. I can see they either believe him or simply can't say no when a sage gives an order.

"No," I respond easily. "If what you're saying is true, the fight is here, not hidden underground. I didn't kill sages by hiding and waiting for them. I killed them in the open air. So no, I won't go with you."

He grips his chest. "You either lose everything or save one small piece of the world! That's all I'm asking for. That's the only choice you—" He turns mid-sentence, his grip on his heart tightening as he does. A shadow looms over the entrance even though it's early in the morning. "No. No, it's too late. Shit. Shit, shit, shit."

The Shadow Sage melts into the darkness and disappears. I swallow and stand, still exhausted and still without a drink, but with that indefinable energy that panic always offers gripping my body. I take one step forward, and a volu Guardian of Stone bursts through the door. He tries to drive a spear through my shoulder, but I consume him with void mana before he can. Another three follow behind him, each targeting a patron of the tavern. I clench my fists. I've never been good at aiming my mana around other people. I can't risk just shooting it, and I don't have my axe.

I shroud my fists in mana instead, running toward the nearest guardian and driving void mana through his back. A man behind me screams as he is pulled out. I run to another volu, pulling a clean fist from a furiously bleeding spine. The viscera disappears when it hits my mana but leaves my clothing bloodied.

I go to the door in an attempt to catch the guardians in a funnel. I allow one to collide with my deadly mana as she tries to pull an ailur woman out with her. When another tries to fly in, I kick him as hard as I can, hitting him with another void fist once he collides with the doorframe. Again and again, I do this. No guardian will enter without meeting my void mana.

I have killed maybe fifteen by the time it happens. The riot spike activates, and my mana vanishes, but that's not enough to stop me. I step in the gore created by my previous opponents, catching the next guardian by the arm. I shove my other hand into his shoulder, forcing him into the wall, then wrap the first arm around the front of his neck, bending his spine backward as I force his body into the air and use the momentum of his fall to snap his neck.

I catch the next by her left wing, the force of her movement spinning her around me before I use my leverage to force her into the ground. I step on her back and grab her other wing, then with both hands, I pull and I tear. I can't tell when the screaming starts and stops anymore. I know one of the voices is hers, but many more come from outside, and one may even be mine. I don't know. I just fight, and injure, and kill.

But it can't last forever. There are too many of them. As I am breaking one arm over my knee, a spear finally catches me in the thigh, then another in the back just before a knife finds its way between two ribs. The man whose arm I've just broken rams his forehead into my nose, cracking it immediately. I take hit after hit, even as I pull the knife from my side and stab it into the nearest assailant. I can't hold them off, and I find myself being pulled from the tavern and into the air.

Dammit. Not this again. As three separate volu try to hold me still, I catch glimpses of the world around me. Half a dozen massive black stones hover around the city, each of them with bodies falling into them as volu guardians drag civilians into the sky and drop them. It nearly looks like a flock of birds from a distance. Hundreds of thousands of us all being corralled, all being abandoned. The city is burning. The whole country must be. It's the most horrific thing I've ever seen.

"You know he is going to do this to all of you too when he is done," I say. "He's not going to spare you." My captors don't respond, they just carry me. I struggle to free one arm. Lillith needs to know. She needs to know Alpha has made his move.

I try to pull out my whisper sphere, but my arms are being held in place. Until they aren't. The city below me turns to empty blackness as I am carried over a stone. Just as I touch my whisper sphere with the tips of my fingers, I am dropped. I hate falling. I'm falling, and I still can't grip the whisper sphere. As I try, it falls from my inner pocket, the blackness below approaching rapidly as I struggle to catch it. There are people all around me—other victims. This must be why I'm so far above the stone below. I take a breath, then stretch as far as I can. The sphere falls next to me, and my fingertips brush against it, then again and again.

As the long fall's length is cut in half, I realize I don't need to catch it—I just need to activate it. Lillith has to know what's happening, or everyone is fucked. Everyone. As my fingertips brush the sphere again, I knock it just a little further away from me in the air. But it's all right. I only need one mental command, and it lights up as I do. Lillith, as reliable as ever, answers immediately. I am nearly out of time, so I don't wait for her to greet me before I speak.

"Help us, please."

These are the only words I manage before I am swallowed by the Calm Stone.

CHAPTER THIRTY

Anarchy

Sarafyna

Mirage knew why I'd come to see her alone. She knew what I wanted to ask, and she touched my mind like settling dust. It's strange, how she can feel and understand the canyons of desperation in our hearts. So long as we are near her, she can connect to them. And if that desperation is offered to her, she can answer it.

"How can I save her?"

It was a simple question with no certain answer. She answered anyway. The images she offered are embroidered onto my mind like regalia. They aren't a promise, just an idea that relies on everything I have and more. An idea that may only exist in the mind of an ancient and abused god. A separation from everything I know, and a sacrifice of everything I have.

I'm going to do it.

I don't have the time to figure it out. I have far less room to breathe than I'd hoped. We don't know exactly what Alpha has done, but we know it's cut us off from the Republic, and we know it is making him strong. Unfathomably strong. So much so that we can't even afford to investigate directly. But based on how I got a similar advantage . . . the implications twist my stomach. I have to stay in the hat shop to hold it together, and the Radiant Woods are pressing in on it with the weight of an ocean.

We have to free Mirage now. We have to beat Alpha and let Mirage go, which means I have to figure it out *now*. Annie is going to stop him today. She is going to end all of this *today*, which means if I can't save her, I lose her. Today. It takes so much strength to fight against Alpha's ever-growing power. If I step out of the hat shop for even a second, he will crush it, and Annie's heart with it. But that's all right.

This is where I am the closest to Mirage. This is where I can see the images she offered me the most clearly. This is where I can risk everything I have to save Annie.

"Please, save me." The words echo through my soul like fresh paint. They brought so much color to my world. They were the most desperate—and the kindest—words I'd ever heard. "Please, save me." *I will, Annie.*

It feels like my bones are cracking under the pressure of Alpha's attacks. I hold him back. I keep everyone safe. And I hold that image close to my heart.

I will get everyone through this. Everyone.

Lillith

Above all else, I want to thank you, Lily.

You were my first friend, you know. The first stranger who ever made me feel welcome. I was safe around you. Not physically safe; I was that, but there is another kind of safety often taken for granted at places like that school: I was safe to exist. I always knew you would use the name I chose over the one I was shackled with. Above all else, I was safe to feel joy, to joke and to laugh. To know there was no contempt concealed by an amiable smile.

A lot happened after that night. I wish I'd spent longer with you. I do. I can't see you again now. This letter feels like such a weak reunion, but I am here, and so are you.

You were my first safe place; at least the first outside of my mother's arms. Joking with you was the first spark of joy I'd had in a long time. And now, I can offer that same safety and joy to so many others.

So thank you.

I guess, all this is just to say . . . I miss you. Thanks for being my friend.

Stay alive.

I finish the letter and look up at a nervous Charlotte. I sniff and look toward the tree line of the Radiant Woods. Leo is so close, but forever out of reach.

"This is gonna suck," I lament. Charlotte offers an awkward but sympathetic smile. I'm still having trouble acting normal around her. All that resentment doesn't just evaporate overnight. And—I realize now—I may have been letting her shoulder an unfair portion of the burden. She was gone, and Autumn wasn't, so I redirected the vitriol toward the perpetrator I couldn't reach, whom I half believed I'd never see again.

I don't have the luxury of dwelling on it, however, because whatever my feelings are toward her, she is too important to leave behind. We don't have the time for me to work through all of that. Whatever move Alpha is making, we have to stop him, and there is nothing I need more at my back than the hope Charlotte has come to personify.

I sigh. "He knows I miss him too, right?" I ask. "I was a stranger in this world, and he was one of the first people who reminded me of home. Bigots used to pretend that we didn't exist in the past; people like you and me. In every era, they wanted us to be a new invention by the young and confused. When I got here and everyone had already been disposed of or silenced . . . I felt so alone. But then I met Leo, and he made me feel safe too. I was comfortable around him, and that never stopped."

I look toward Leo. I can see him in the distance, talking to Ember. We just have the four of us: Leo, Ember, Charlotte, and me. The four of us against the evil god of this world. Everyone else has somewhere else to protect: My home is protected by Dominic. Visenar by Ed and Mariah. The twins are in the hat shop, taking care of Sarafyna. The four of us are all we have to stop Alpha.

Charlotte bites her lip.

"I had a friend once," she answers. "Amelia. I met her when I was only a child. She did that for me, showed me the world of color that existed outside of my parents' hateful minds. She was so kind, and I loved her so much. The kind of love only a child can feel. I understand how much they mean, the first person who tells you you aren't alone. Who tells you that you aren't insane or sick. It's like your first drink of water after a day in the sun."

I tilt my head. "So, is that a yes?" I ask. Charlotte grimaces.

"You know he knows," she replies. "The same way he knows the same about you. Because we all know that feeling. We all recognize our first friend as home; the first peer we don't need to wear a mask around. I'm sure you had others in another life, but Leo was your first here, and he understands that. That connection goes two ways." I don't reply, keeping my eyes locked on Leo in the distance. She's right. He knows.

"Will you tell him anyway?" I ask. She takes a deep breath and nods.

"Of course. I know what that separation is like too. The knowledge you'll never see them again . . ." She trails off and sighs again. "I'll tell him."

I feel guilty when she says this, because even now, I don't like Charlotte. Even now, I'm angry. Because, while she didn't lose Henry like I did, she does understand the same loss. I finally shift my gaze to meet the glass that lives in her hopeful eyes.

"I had a friend named Amelia too, once. Funny how that sort of coincidence happens even across worlds. I wonder why that is," I muse. Then I offer her the reality of a certain type of guilt we share. One I was reminded of as soon as she mentioned the name of her childhood friend. "I got her killed."

Amy came with me to kill Oakley of her own volition, but it was my plan that got her killed, nevertheless. Charlotte and I really aren't all that different, at the end of the day. It won't make me like her, not so long as Henry is dead, but perhaps it will let her like herself. Because it's just as she said: it helps to know you're not alone.

"Amelia," Charlotte whispers under her breath. Then her awkward smile returns as she closes her eyes, turning her face toward the sun. "Who knows? Maybe she has a second life of her own now somewhere out there. Maybe they both do." There is so much hope radiating from her. It doesn't feel like wishful thinking; it almost feels real. And fuck, maybe it is. I hope so.

Her words hang in the air for a long moment, but the Radiant Woods are calling. The world is screaming for an end to Alpha, and that's what we came here for. The brief moment to read Leo's letter was gentle and kind, but it must end.

"I have to go in now," I finally say. Charlotte nods solemnly.

"I am sorry," she says.

"I know," I respond. That's the extent of our goodbye. Even now, as we connect, we aren't friends. But that's okay, because we both have hope. She turns and walks gently back to Leo and Ember, leaving me alone in the barren land in front of the tree line. As I clench my fists and close my eyes, a thousand images flash through my head. Years of fighting and blood, but also years of kindness.

I take a step forward. Mom's amused smile drifts through my head like smoke. Every note of her laugh plays like a scale in my mind.

I take another step. This time, I see Gilbert and Edward. They are pushing and shoving each other, but their smiles betray a lack of hostility. The warmth of the memory brushes past me like a breeze as both look at me.

I take another step. Godfrey's kind but calculating eyes greet me. He's flipping through some cheesy romance novel and waiting for a pastry that will never come. This one feels like lake water on a winter morning. A memory full of kindness and regret.

Another step, and I see the twins. Trusting me in the woods. Relying on me in school. Helping me learn to grieve in the open.

Another step, and I'm with Leo, competing over how much pancake we can fit in our mouths at once. I see him scared in the dirt. I see him surrounded by a family of thousands, a joyful face decorated by laughter like a battle cry.

Another step, and I'm surrounded by the Mages of Penance. Another, and I'm with Riley and Ember. One more, and I freeze. Henry is sitting at a desk, smiling and laughing. I've interrupted his work, but he doesn't care at all; he's happy to talk with me for hours. The only person in this world who pays attention when I talk about biology. I choke back the memory and force myself to step again.

The last memory is Sarafyna. I'm in her arms, her head against mine and her hands running across my wings. I want to stop here and live in this memory, but the real Sara is out there fighting to hold the world together and doing everything she can to save me. So I step again.

Finally, the shape of a woman forms before me, and she is screaming. She has always been screaming, and I am determined to listen. I breathe in the heavy air and step through her. She is like shattered glass and too many memories. As soon as I pass through her, the screaming grows louder, and the earth aches under my step.

I am in the Radiant Woods for the final time.

"I know you can see me," I call. I don't bother shouting. He's heard every word I've ever spoken in this fucking hell. "Don't you think it's time we stopped playing games? Because I'll tell you what, man. I'm exhausted. I'm so fucking tired. I have met you so many times, again and again and again across two lifetimes, and I am just . . . weary. Don't you all ever get tired of this? Don't you ever wonder? Don't you ever think about just . . . letting the rest of us live our lives? Wouldn't it be easier for you to stop trying to own people? Doesn't it get tiring?"

There is no answer for a long time. I can still feel Mirage nearby. I can still hear her scream. I clench my fists. "Come on, you fucking coward! Let's just end this! I want to be done! Don't you want to be done? Show your goddamn face and fight me! You'll never get everything you want from the shadows! It is time to settle this shit so we can both just . . . rest," I taunt. Again, the only sound I hear is the constant screaming of Alpha's first victim. Mirage's voice rings through my head like tinnitus while her abuser hides.

"Where is your pet?" Alpha's voice finally rings out. He still hasn't shown himself, but at least he is fucking talking.

"Suzume? My mother's keeping an eye on her, I think. Why? Discovering a fondness for cats?" I quip. The trees around me groan as impossible flora rapidly grows toward me. As it approaches, I flare heat mana, turning it all to ash before it gets closer than twenty feet. No. I am not screwing around. If he wants to touch me, he'll need to fight in person.

"I thought you were done playing games?" Alpha responds. I shrug.

"That's all on you and your microdick, Alpha. I'm happy to get this started once you grow balls half the size of mine and show your pathetic face," I reply easily.

"Sarafyna. Where is Sarafyna?" he presses.

"Where the fuck do you think? Why are we wasting time on questions we know the answers to? Get the fuck out here so I can tear into you and check if you ever had any kind of spine at all!" I shout.

"You either have Sarafyna or you have nothing of value to me, child. Come back with your pointless taunts when it's not a waste of my time," he dismisses. I scoff.

"She is out of your reach, and she isn't showing up again unless my life is in danger. Which means you fight me, or you never see her again."

"Even if I take everyone from your home? If I consume them all? If they all find their way here? She won't come out even then?" he asks.

"She won't," I confirm. "I will fight for them; you know that. But my girlfriend fights for me. You can't use me to manipulate her anymore. Neither she nor Mirage will keep you away from me anymore. The answer is obvious: if you want her, the easiest thing to do is use all your power to put me in danger. That's your only shot."

"I am taking the hearts of everyone, Lillith of Endings. I am consuming the world—every soul in this world. I grow more powerful with every passing breath, and I will crush her sanctuary eventually. I will take it back, and then I will have her. All it will take is patience," he says.

I shake my head. "We'll stop you. Every soul you bring here? We'll find them, and we'll direct them to Sara. It may take years, maybe decades, but we will send them all from here to there, and you will be crushed eventually. Your best chance is to fight me now, because I am not patient. Because we will fight you now, at the height of your power, rather than force your people to suffer for that long. But if you choose the long route, we will win."

"You . . . four?" He chuckles. "You may have a negative mage, but do you really think that will be enough?"

"You're growing stronger by the second? With every soul you drag here? Well, guess what, asshole? So do we. You squeeze power from people like water from stones, but us? We are with them. We fight on their behalf with the emotion they offer us. We have grief and rage and hope and joy, and we all feel them together. Not us four—all of us. Every person you think you own is connected by those four things," I reply.

He sighs like a teacher addressing a stubborn student. "Endoaspects; one of many ways you people desecrate Manara's corpse. It's disgusting, but that's all it is. It won't save you. Are you children? You aren't in a storybook. The power of hope isn't going to stop anything."

"Of course not. It's not magical emotion that is going to kill you—it's what people do when they feel it. It's the connections they make, the trust. Each and every one of these inspires action and violence. Grief, rage, hope, and joy. Where I'm from, we call that anarchy, and it cuts the hearts out of tyrants. And you are afraid of it. I know you're afraid of it, because whatever you might want to say, you would be fighting me already if you weren't afraid.

"You've wanted me gone for years, haven't you? So Sara can realize her potential? I know you; Mirage showed me everything. You need Sara so you can force Mirage through her open wounds and can trap your mother in a form that's more comfortable to look at. You need me dead. Well, here I am. We both grow stronger with every move you make. Are you going to end this now, or are you going to let us win?"

"You disgust me," he spits. "Abusing her, manipulating her, using her and rejecting her in the same breath. You owe her a home—you all owe it to her after everything you've done. Fine. We end this now. Trigger whatever clever traps you've laid for me. It's time to give Mirage a voice. It's time to bring Manara back. It's finally time to eradicate all of you and free them from your control."

"No traps," I assure. "Just you and us."

I feel it when he arrives, flowing through the trees like they're water. He can use the woods like Sara does, appearing anywhere at any time. I feel Mirage at the same time, like she's holding my hand and sharing her pain. She warns me when Alpha makes his move, a surprisingly close-range attack. I don't know why he closed the distance, but it works for me.

Pain like a dozen blunt knives tries to tear all thought from my head as his fist tears into my chest and his hand wraps around my heart. Blood immediately trickles out of my grinning mouth. It's agonizing. It's hell. But I grin anyway, because Mirage is touching me, and my hands are on either side of Alpha's head.

I see horror all over his face like a rapidly forming rash. The rage and denial. The fury that shakes him the moment I break down his mental barriers and force him to hear his mother's screaming.

CHAPTER THIRTY-ONE

Her Own Way to Burn

Sarafyna

I stand in the room holding Annie's heart as the pressure grows. I feel like an insect under a boot, but I refuse to give an inch. Even as the world feels like it's going to crack around me, I just grip the podium displaying the strange heart, grit my teeth, and push back.

I can feel Alpha growing stronger with every passing moment. I can see . . . everything. Every exit from my hat shop and anything near any of them. I can feel the tension and the fear from all over the world. Or . . . Mirage can feel it, and she is sharing it with me. As much as I fight to hold this world together, she fights to free herself from Alpha's grip. I suppress a scream with closed lips as my world tries to collapse around me like a migraine, a guttural sound vibrating through my throat as I nearly buckle.

"What is it? How can we help?" Autumn asks.

Beads of sweat plaster hair to my face as my lips open and I manage to push a response out. "Tell—Tell everyone—" I stop, nearly collapsing to one knee as the pressure grows like sand in an hourglass. I let the images all around the world swim through my head. I can see it now: the stones in the sky, the guardians flying and running toward every single city and community en masse. This must be happening everywhere. It's no wonder he's getting stronger.

A few thousand supporters let me wrestle so much of the woods away from him, and now, he's gathering millions of victims to fight back. And I am his target. He is pressing down on me with everything he has, but he doesn't want me dead. He wants me for something else.

He won't get his way.

"Tell them—what I told you. It's—It's not safe out there. It's a risk. But—" I cough as something starts to literally crack, like the feeling of fractures forming in my spine but more . . . mental. "But this is their last chance to leave this place. It's—It's not safer here than it is out there. P—Please, explain it. Please."

Autumn puts a hand on my shoulder to ask if I'm sure, but I finally fail to maintain my posture and actually fall to a single knee. "Go!" I shout, and she jumps.

"A-all right," she agrees. I can feel more words at the back of her throat, but she gets the hint that it will only distract me and rushes out of the room. It really isn't any safer here; this whole place could collapse any second. I don't think even Alpha realizes how close he is to winning. If that happens, everyone will find themselves in the woods anyway, and even if it doesn't, they'll never see their homes or families again. They deserve a chance to choose what risk they want to take.

The cracks in my mind spread like a spiderweb, and I start coughing under the intense attack. My mind goes back to my father. He ran and ran and ran when I was taken, nearly running himself to death chasing the cart I was trapped in. I could hear him for hours, screaming, fighting to get me back. Even then, his body was weary and tired, but he pushed back past the impossibility and the exhaustion. He loved me, and he fought until his mind could no longer control his body. Even after that, he gave up his life, shouting in the face of powerful men and accepting enslavement for the chance to bring me home. He cared for that hat block even then.

And I am his daughter.

He's a simple, kind man. A common stableman. A man named Sam. And he was unbreakable for the sake of someone he loved. I am the daughter of a simple man named Sam, and I will break no more easily than he did. There is a woman I love out there. Alpha can rest the world on my shoulders and hammer it down, and I won't break. He can spit and flex and abuse, but I won't break. Even as I feel my mind crack, I glare at the empty space in front of me. He can feel it, and if he can feel it, he can fear it. I don't care if he's stronger than me right now. I don't care. Because he can break, and I cannot.

The pressure builds and builds until finally, his focus shifts. He is angry; he is scared. I'm not certain there is a difference for him. A moment later, I see it: the imprint of five fingers wrapping around the heart in front of me; they press in, and they burn. He is trying to kill Annie.

I spit to the side. "No," I whisper. "I refuse." Wrapping my own hand around it, my will wrestles his. Where he burns, I heal. Where he heals, I burn. He won't lay a finger on my girlfriend without paying for it. He may understand pain, he may know how to hurt Annie, but I understand him, and I make him pay the price for that pain.

Lillith

Mirage has been silent in Alpha's mind for so long. No matter how much pain he causes, she is silent to him. For millennia she has suffered, and for millennia he has held his hands over his ears and shut his eyes tight. His finger has pointed at anyone he could find and carried accusations of abuse and manipulation while he has tortured his mother with every word.

He can hear her now. His divine magic flows into me, and I recognize Markus's power over pain and agony. My chest cavity has shattered, and his fingernails cut into the still meat of my heart, but the pain is more than that: it is a state of being that vibrates through me like sound and tears through every cell like acid. But I don't scream. My eyes water and my mouth tastes like copper, but I don't move. I dig my claws into the side of Alpha's skull, and through my touch, allow Mirage to scream into his mind.

"Your mothers only ever had one abuser, you fucking creep! Only one person who could really hurt them ever lived. They were happy! They were happy and kind and curious! And now listen! Listen to the sound of a woman stuck in your control for eternity!"

Suddenly, all the pain in my body is blown out like a tired candle. At the same time, Alpha's grip loosens, and acid climbs his veins. He tries to tear his hand free—and my heart with it—but I catch his wrist. His bone cracks in my steel grip, but he regains his composure as my focus on his mother wavers. I don't wait to see what he does. Sara is helping me somehow; I can feel it, and I don't intend to waste it.

My left hand joins my right on his arm, squeezing and crushing with all the force I have. At the same time, my foot catches his chest and throws him miles through his own woods. I maintain my grip the entire time, and the tearing of flesh and bone rings through my ears as his body is separated from it.

In the brief moment of safety, I cough and struggle with the now limp limb. Just as I'm wondering how I'm going to liberate it from my chest cavity without further injury, it begins seizing and wriggling like a panicked fish. As my eyes widen in confused disgust, it seems to be sucked into my heart and just . . . absorbed. I grimace. *Well. That solves the problem, I guess. But also, what the fuck?* It was Sara. It was obviously Sara. I don't know how, but it must have been. Goddamn, though. Top-one contender for least pleasant experience of my life.

I can't dwell on it, however. Whatever I may have said to provoke Alpha, time is not on my side, and I have to press the advantage. As I throw myself through the woods with force mana, I feel a wave of peace wash over me, and I grow more and more certain I can win this and survive.

It's Charlotte. With Ember's help, she is watching the battle. This hope means she's stepped outside of Leo's influence and is using a relay staff to send her mana through the connection to my piercings. It's a risk, but so long as I handle Alpha, she should be safe.

With her hope comes healing, and the hole in my chest closes. Rigid scales rapidly grow over the self-stitching skin, and the stinging and aching fades away like it was never there. When I finally catch up to Alpha, I groan; I'm not the only one healing at an unnatural rate. The creep already has a fresh arm, and he is practically snarling at me.

"You are all so pathetic!" he screams. Divine magic and mana fill the air like humidity as his blood boils. "All of you are parasites!" The world around me turns to darkness in an instant. "All you've ever wanted to do is mold her into your image!" Nearly as quickly as the light disappeared, it breaks back in through one crack at a time. Almost like bullets opening paths for the sun. But it doesn't feel right. "To manipulate her! To make her think she had to give you everything—to *be* everything you wanted her to be." Every entrance the light comes through is like looking directly at the sun. It burns and blinds with even more violent urgency than the darkness had.

"Whatever made *you* feel good. Whatever made *you* happy." It is the sun. It's impossible, but the unmoving sun frozen at midday in these woods is beating down on me from every angle. "You never cared about her! None of you ever cared about her!" The darkness breaks, and the world breaks with it. I can no longer tell up from down; I'm not certain either concept even exists in this space anymore.

The Radiant Woods are wrapped around me like a kaleidoscope, impossible and mixing flora growing from the sky as easily as the soil. Between them, the sun burns my skin from beneath the ground with the same intensity as it does from above the clouds. "No more than you cared about clay to be molded into whatever shape you imagined for it! Listen to her! Listen to how she screams after so many years of your demands! After so long being pulled this way and that to satisfy the demands of people who see her as nothing more than a means to an end!"

My force mana hums around me in a frantic song whose notes move like a hummingbird. I try to scan my environment with my radar spell, but this is immediately blinded by radiation surrounding me from all directions at once. I immediately put up a light barrier to defend specifically against such waves, but I can already feel my body fighting the inevitable sickness.

"They were like *children*! Don't you understand that?" Alpha continues. "Ancient as they were, their minds were still so malleable. So easily taken in! And you . . . *insects*! You showed up and you rejected them! You lied to them and you consumed them! You're all the same! Sick! Wrong in the head! You took Mirage and Manara, and you fooled them! You changed them! You led them down dark paths and away from a happy eternity! And I won't rest until every single one of you has been exterminated!"

As he shouts this, I try to track him down, but I can't. I don't know where to attack, so I focus on defense. Force that could flatten mountains pushes away from me, creating a shield that could kill any living thing with pressure alone. It doesn't stop him at all once he starts attacking in earnest. The music of my mana is drowned out by the sound of a falling sky. A literally falling sky, with shards of the blue expanse shattering, splintering, and flying toward me.

They ignore the force barrier, and I summon a wide shield of steel in every direction as a final attempt to protect myself. Even this poses an obstacle to nothing but my sight. A thousand needles of pain and no substance I can identify tear through me and force my blood to pour down my entire body from more pin-sized puncture wounds than I can count in this lifetime. As a wave of mixing stomach acid and blood pours out of my open mouth and fouls the air with the stink of death, my mind races.

I knew he'd be powerful. I knew he was growing in strength every moment. But this is incredible. I barely have a chance to cast, and when I do, it does nothing to protect me. But it's all right. He is still screaming about our abuse, shouting about the ways the people of this world have perverted his parents. Even against all of this, however, I don't lose hope. I know I can win, and with that belief comes Charlotte's healing.

The bleeding stops, and the dizziness fades. Even my cancer starts to recede at an unprecedented rate. An eldritch mass of flesh and tree roots sprouts from all directions like blooming roses and descends on me like hell itself. Even then, I have hope. They scream through the air around me like banshees at an impossible speed and aim for my heart. Still, I hope. Until I don't. But when the hope evaporates, rage takes its place. Ember is helping now in Charlotte's place.

I snarl at the air as Ember's mana joins mine. Summoning two massive axes, I hold one in each hand, wrapping both in the strange mix of rage and grief mana. They whistle and shine through the air with the effects of my mana, and cut through the attack with the effects of Ember's. The mass literally bleeds as I cut through it, and I grimace at the implications. But my mana doesn't work against the will of the grieving, so there is either no sapience in the flesh, or it doesn't want there to be. Either way, I cut it to pieces and finally lay my eyes on Alpha again. He is flying away, and I suspect I know where.

Sarafyna

My dress is soaked with sweat. I am flushed all over, and my scars have begun to literally bleed. The pressure is ebbing and flowing, forcing me to adjust how hard I fight from moment to moment. At the same time, I have to protect Annie's heart and monitor the world around the hat shop. I also have to reach out and keep Annie close enough to Leo for Ember to magically watch the fight.

However Annie took Alpha's arm, it is helping. I pulled it from one heart to another in a moment of inspiration, and the divine magic it carried could have belonged to a dozen sages. I feel a stabbing in my chest as hundreds of microscopic holes open up on the fabric heart in front of me, and Annie's blood decorates my already filthy face and clothing. They close up a minute later, but I lost focus when Annie was hit. It was only for a breath, but that was enough to give Alpha the advantage.

The pressure doubles down, and I'm knocked to my hands and knees trying to hold it together. I need to hold on. I need to hold on like my father would.

People are still evacuating through the portals. People have been fleeing through the hat shop from our growing city and into an empty field a few days' travel from civilization. But that's going to end soon. I can see that. Because they finally got them: Dominic and Gilbert. Ed and Mariah. The Mages of Penance, and anyone else who stayed to fight.

One by one, they've all been caught by riot spikes and dropped into hell as grist for the Radiant Woods. There is no one left to protect those who can't fight, and they can't reach my shop anymore. A few more minutes, and it'll be complete. Every person Annie and I saved from slavery will have either returned to something worse or are now waiting somewhere to see if they will be caught as well. Those willing to stay with the shop no matter what are still inside, and the rest are huddled together in the middle of nowhere. I'd have put them farther away, but they need to make it home after this is all over, and the hat shop can't be relied on to take them there.

And then it happens. The last body falls into a stone, and a moment later, the stones expand and start collecting the volu who were feeding them before. It's time.

My skin pulls apart as if my muscles were growing too large for it. I can't spare any focus for controlling my body, so I just bite through the pain and push. I throw myself against the world, and both of us crack. My vision grows blurry, and I push. My body numbs, and I push. Red swirls into my eyes as blood bursts inside them while I push and push until I'm looking down at my own limp body and the world around me implodes into nothingness.

Lillith

I worry he's going to reach the others before I can stop him, but the rage recedes, and I can tell Ember has retreated into Leo's influence. This leaves me vulnerable as the world tries to collapse in on me again, and I brace myself for the oncoming pain, but before anything touches me, the woods immediately revert back to their normal state. It's so jarring I almost crash into the trees. Alpha is no longer going after the mages supporting me. He's no longer attacking me either. In fact, he somehow brings me directly to him as he lands on the ground the same way Sara moves me through the woods.

He sighs as if relieved. "Well now. I've been trying to do that for years; it's so much easier when there is no one left taking my mother from me. It barely takes effort, now that Mirage is all in one place again," he muses. He then looks at me and whispers a single word. "Stay."

That feeling like blood being drawn seizes my entire body. Grief mana flows through me from every single person he has trapped here, and I manage to barely hold off the control behind his command, but I have never felt mind control get so close to crushing it, and I am frozen in place anyway. Not by his command as he hopes, but by my own eyes.

He snaps his fingers, and every steel part of my body is torn from me before I even hear the sound. My nerves were wired into the fiber of those limbs, and sinew is pulled loose like hair from a drain. But I don't feel it. I don't feel anything because of the reality in front of us. The undeniable and impossible-to-process reality of failure.

Because lying, bleeding and motionless in the dirt, is hopelessness.

There is no light in the eyes of Sarafyna's corpse.

CHAPTER THIRTY-TWO

Alpha and the Omega

Alpha

I feel it all returning home. Finally. *Finally*, I am taking Mirage back; I am bringing Manara back. And with this world free from the parasites who tried to take advantage of them, we can be happy together again, like we were in the beginning. I can hardly process it. I fall to my knees and start laughing. The type of laugh pushed out by joyful tears.

I worked so hard, and I know it's hurt, but I'm back. We're back. And everything will finally be as it was when we were happy. I finish consuming the last of the sages. Once I got most of the citizens, I had little use for the Calm Stones anymore, and the sages were the real prize; they were the ones who actually carried parts of my mother, so the stones turned on their masters and consumed them. For the first time in thousands of years, all of Mirage is here in my collector's space.

I have a body for Mirage so we can actually speak. It's still brimming with her energy, and its former owner seems to have abandoned it. I'm not even sure how I managed that, but I can feel it from here: I have turned her into a corpse while maintaining her ability. It must have been tied to something one of the sages I've just absorbed could do, something even they didn't realize. It's the only reason the other girl still lives, but that's all right. It's over. Once Mirage can speak to me? Once she can actually hear me? She will understand, and we can work together to use that body too. Lillith is connected to every mage on the planet now, after all, which means that in the same way I am connected to all of Mirage, she is connected to all of Manara. I am going to bring them both back.

Ice slides through my ears as Lillith speaks. "You're wrong, you know." It isn't a question but a statement. I ignore her and go about my work. I need to pull Mirage together and put her in her new home. "You have spent so many years telling yourself that everyone else was abusing your parents. That they were hated and rejected and manipulated to be new people. Even now, you've convinced yourself that the family you loved was forcibly changed to their detriment, that Mirage and Manara were happiest when it was just the three of you, that their minds were poisoned and you just need to find the right way to communicate with them about that. But that's not what happened at all. She showed me what happened, you pathetic sack of shit. She showed me who you are."

I pause for a moment. She can't know about the beginning. She can't know about my time with my mothers—unless she is telling the truth. "You're perverse." I scowl. "Disgusting. She touched you. She blessed your mind with her own, and still, you twist everything she showed you. You ignore the facts for the fantasy world inside your head, and villainize the only person who ever loved them. Fucking perverse." I sniff and return to the task at hand. I can feel it, all of the energy that is so broken. It's coming back, and I'm gathering it in Mirage's new home. Lillith scoffs.

"You never loved them, and you know that," she accuses. I feel the anger bubbling inside me, but I breathe. Soon, Mirage will be back. She will be able to speak, and she will be able to hear. She and I will share her power. I will maintain six-tenths of it until she has adjusted, but we will be equals again. I will be weaker than I am now, but together, we will be too powerful to ever be challenged again. I will be the most powerful sage—the *only* sage. And I will have my family back. Lillith can spit her poison until I'm done and I've emptied her head out and filled it with Manara.

"You call them family but that's not what they have ever been to you. If they were, you would have been happy when they were happy. You would have grown when they grew. You would have loved when they found new things to love. But to you? They weren't family—they were things, objects. Abuse? Manipulation? Nah." She almost laughs.

I continue gathering Mirage inside Sarafyna. I will take her back.

"It was an undermining of *your* authority that bothered you. A subversion of *your* control over what you believed was *your* property. Mirage and Manara were growing, learning, and they were living the lives that called to them in the way they saw fit." I am almost there. Mirage is almost herself again. She is almost free, and her screaming can finally stop. Meanwhile, Lillith continues her drivel.

"Abuse doesn't make you angry. It practically defines you, and you ignore it every chance you get. You use it as a tool, structuring entire societies with abuse as a backbone. You have never given a single shit about that. That didn't make you angry, no. You're upset for a far more pathetic reason: You're angry about thieves, not abusers. That's what has always mattered to you. Where I kill for liberation, you kill for property. Everything you have done, every power structure you have built for millennia, has been about getting your property back and never losing it again.

"But that's not how it works, you absolute fucking loser! Mirage has a mind and a heart, and so did Manara. Do you think giving them ears to hear commands and wrists to chain will do anything? They'll still be people; they'll still have their own hearts and minds, and they'll still want the life they want. They are not your property, and no one letting them live the life they wanted was abusing or manipulating them. It was only ever taking something from *you*; something *you* felt you were owed. Something *you* believed you could give and take as you pleased but Mirage and Manara lacked the autonomy to do themselves. You're *pathetic*," she lectures.

I pause for only a moment. "You have an awful lot to say for someone who doesn't seem to care that her girlfriend is dead," I jab. "Talk about never actually loving someone." Lillith laughs, which irks me. But I still won. I'll survive a little irritation.

"You think Sarafyna is dead?" she jeers. I pause as I feel my collector dissolving. The negative mage is on his way. I almost chuckle. Is she trying to stall? I'll be done long before he gets here. "Let me guess, you don't even know how you killed her, right? You just assume it was your oh-so-great power? Yeah, nothing strangely convenient about that, right? And she just happened to fall out of the hat shop?"

"I crushed her fucking hat shop. It's gone. There is no shop—only me, my collector, and Mirage. She isn't in her hat shop anymore because it is gone!" I gloat.

"Then why am I alive, you incredible idiot? Why am I still here to mock you?" she challenges. I scoff.

"The body is still tied to Mirage and you. That's all it is. Cope however you like, but it's just the residual but fading effect of Mirage's power on the girl's body."

"Really?" she says. "That's strange, because that hat shop was centered around my heart, and you crushed it. Now, admittedly, I haven't practiced with the useless organ in a while, but you and I both know the connection between it and me was more than just physical. Do you really believe it could be destroyed and I would be fine?" The hairs on my arms rise at that question, but I dismiss it.

"Her corpse is right here, you child. And it's about to be Mirage again," I reply. And then, I finish. Gathering enough of Mirage, I flow her through the body's veins instead of blood, and the corpse coughs. I grin furiously. "Welcome back, Mother," I whisper.

Mirage convulses a few times as she acclimates to the new body, but after a moment, she seems to understand how her limbs work. Tears run down my face as she extends a shaky hand to me. She wants my help standing. She understands; I always knew she understood. She can see it now. Now that she has eyes and a mind to think with, she knows I only want to protect her.

I reach my hand out to help her, and she grasps it the moment I do.

I feel such joy. Joy like I haven't felt since Manara died. I feel like eating, singing, and dancing. Colors I've never seen before swirl around me. She is doing it—she is sharing her joy with me! Laughter demands to be free, and I try to let it loose . . . but it fails to come. I open eyes I didn't realize I had shut and realize the environment has changed.

We are back at the beginning, or near to it. Mirage is here as she was when we loved each other. Manara is here too. There are thousands of faces I can't tell apart. Everyone who was alive at the time is here, eating and sharing, telling stories and using my mothers' powers, and . . . Mirage and Manara love it. They drink it in. *No. This isn't how it happened.*

"Where am I?" I ask. "Why aren't I here? If you were sharing such joy, where was I?"

I feel a pang of regret, and I realize all these emotions are Mirage's. She is sharing with me like she hasn't been able to for hundreds of lifetimes. And then dread descends on me—dread and confusion—as a monster with hundreds of smiling teeth faces me. I feel trust and apprehension as the beast reaches out. He grabs at me, digging claws into me, and he tears. I have never felt pain. Mirage had never felt pain. This was the first time.

The monster doesn't look like he used to look. He lacks the kindness he used to share. Instead, he tears, and he rips, and he grins. Oh, does he grin. He shares joy, but it's a painful joy. It's satisfaction. It's smugness. It's vindication and victory. Manara tries to save me, begging the monster to stop, but he uses me like a weapon against her. He takes from me, and he chokes the life out of her with it. I don't understand.

I don't understand.

I don't understand.

And then it's not a monster—it never was. It's just a man, and he's even more ugly that way. Because he is me, and he is smiling. But I don't remember smiling; that was the worst day of my life, why was I—I . . . I recoil and pull my hand back. What had I just seen? I spin around to find Lillith and ask her how she poisoned this memory, but she is gone.

My heart beats like the drums sounding in the sky, a sound I didn't hear until my heart seemed to sync up with it—because it's the same. It's drumming to the beat of a heart. I look up and see Mirage there as I've never seen her. Sarafyna's body is gone, and Mirage is massive. She is made of mist, and she stands as tall as the dozens of towers Lillith hid her people in.

It's her heart that's beating. I can hear it; I can see it. A dark and furious mass. I lift myself into the sky to meet her, and her heart beats louder and louder. Inside the mist, it beats like lightning, like Mirage is a storm and her heart is electric. And I can see each individual beat, the colorful mass at the center of my mother's chest moving through the sky like wings. Beckoning me. Calling me in.

"That's not what happened!" I cry into the storm that is Mirage. She looks down at me with tired, angry eyes. I don't understand how they can weep and rage like that at the same time.

It's a lie. It's a lie. I have to prove it. I have to touch her heart and show her the truth. But as I approach . . . as I lock my eyes on the beating heart, I realize it doesn't just look like wings. It actually is. Lillith is there. Protected by my mother like I never have been. Raging inside her heart. Poisoning her. The woman has only one working limb, but the others seem to be . . . growing back.

That fucking hope mana. I will kill her for the way she's poisoned

Mirage, for the lies she's convinced my mother of. I'll—All thought stops as screaming fills my mind again, and with one flash of her lightning, Lillith disappears from my mother, and glowing red eyes glare at me from a pace away. Before I can wonder when she got so fast, I find myself flying through the air. The screaming only lasts a moment, and the air is again filled with the strange discordant music of Lillith's obnoxious mana. I taste blood and realize I need to heal myself.

Lillith is still in the air, following my flight path as Mirage watches us both. I try to twist the world around her again, but Mirage's eyes catch me and offer sorrow and judgment. I kept most of the power, just in case, but such a large spell is apparently beyond me when Mirage is fighting it. Before I can try something else, the cymbals of Lillith's lightning ring out, and I feel electricity coursing through my body.

A scream consumes my thoughts, and by the time it fades, Lillith has closed the distance. Her one remaining arm swings at me, scaled knuckles digging into my side and snapping something before I find myself careening toward the forest floor. It happened again: while she was in contact with me, I could hear my mother's screaming.

She connects me to Mirage—her touch, her mana. Whenever she makes contact in any way, I can hear the screaming. It's infuriating; she's taunting me. *Look what I've done to her. Look how I've ruined her. Look how I took her from you and taught her to hate you.* I want Lillith dead. I want to grind her into the dirt, and I will. She has gotten a few half-decent shots in, sure, but even with such control over Manara's power, all she can give me is pain. And I can give her more.

As I collide with the dirt below, I dig my fingers into the earth and send what I can from both Manara and Mirage into the deciduous trees around me. They grow and contort like tentacles, waving through the air with more weight and force than any tree could possibly maintain. Even as this attack tries to end her, I can feel that strange and furious mana being fed to her through her piercings. I should have ripped those out with her arm. She creates another axe in a flash and tears through the trees like so much paper.

I'm not done with her, however. Colossal cliffs rise from the ground and careen toward each other on either side of the furious mage in the sky. Far too thick to cut through with an axe. Lillith doesn't even try. Instead, as if to infuriate me more, Mirage steps forward and catches one slab of stone in each hand. She doesn't even look like her body is physical, and still, she holds them apart. As I try to force them together with all my strength, my traitorous mother keeps them just wide enough for Lillith to travel through them. With enough time and effort, I will win, but I am tired of being patient.

Instead of crushing her, I shift tactics, using the narrow path I've created to guide the broken woman. I flood the gap with blue fire like a wave, using the more mundane heat-based attack to disguise my real goal. Lillith doesn't slow down. I can feel the rage mana mixing with her grief mana and trying to cut through the flames. She protects herself with heat mana as well, but my fire is far too hot for that. While she is distracted, I snap my fingers again, trying to tear her piercings from her face and stomach.

My mother throws her will against mine once more and tries to block me, but she is already putting her all into stopping me from crushing Lillith, and this is a far more specific attack. The powers of the Steel Sage are new, but they are mine now nonetheless. I manage to grip every piercing I can find in my mind and pull, feeling the satisfaction of tearing as I do: a bar from her belly button, three earrings from each ear, one from her nose, and another from her lip. The enchanted piercings fly through the fire and toward me as Lillith burns.

If I can get my hands on them . . . Well, the transfer of power goes both ways, and I can kill her little helpers. Maybe they'll even run to the negative mage and I can kill her too. Not that it matters either way. With none of her piercings, she won't have their support. No healing. No cutting through Mirage or Manara's power. But I will still heal.

Just before I manage to catch the earrings, a world-shattering sound rings out all around me and literally drives me to the ground. All other sound stops; all sound except, of course, my mother's screaming. As I look up, Lillith is emerging from the fire, chasing two of her own lightning bolts, which strike me one after the other. Each one sounds like music until they hit, and once they do, the instruments are replaced with screaming. Every fucking hit carries a scream. I can take the pain—I'm already healing—but the screaming . . . She'll pay for forcing that into my head.

When I finally see her, she is a nightmare to behold. The fire burned too hot, and she was inside for too long. One red eye glows with fury and grief; the other runs down the visible skull on the left side of her head. It blends and mixes with melted flesh and muscle, all of it dripping from exposed bone and a half-loose jawbone. It's already healing. *Why is it already healing?*

I run through all my interactions with the woman—everything I watched her do from a distance—and the answer comes to me: that nonsense gesture she made to the Void Sage, when she stuck her tongue out at him—that had a piercing too. I roll my eyes. I have no idea if that's the only artifact she has left. I missed one once, and this tactic isn't worth wasting time on. I will simply beat her to death faster than she can heal.

I send wind out in every direction to buy a few seconds as she closes in on me, then sink into the shadows using one of my many new abilities and wait for her to land. She pulses heat in every direction, but I am safe here while I create a mass of sage flesh with a thousand teeth. She doesn't entirely land, of course; she doesn't have a leg to stand on. She does slow for a brief moment when she is near the ground, however, and I use that moment to strike, emerging and feeling the teeth sink into her flesh before I pull.

She fails to scream as I tear her final limb from her body. At least, of her original four. I fade into the shadows again, emerging on the opposite side of her. Over and over again, I hit her with whatever I can: steel and fire and molten earth; shards of reality and plasma. I hit and shave away at her while she tries to catch me, but I always fade into the shadows. I am killing her faster than she is healing. It's almost done now.

That is, until she screams and light mana sings from her like a choir, scrubbing the area around her of shadows. This creates more behind the nearby foliage, but it's not close enough to maintain my current tactic. It's all or nothing here.

I open up the earth beneath her, creating a titanic worm of stone which erupts and swallows her whole. I spit, ready to finish her off, when Mirage's massive foot descends on me. I send my own power to hold her off, which is easy enough. I'm still the stronger of us. Except, as I am fighting my mother's attack off, blades of steel sing like violins as they tear through the worm's stone stomach.

A healing Lillith emerges, an unsettling eye replaced in a skull socket that hasn't regrown its skin or scales. She is surrounded by hundreds of blades she controls with precise and rapid force mana. I try to exert my own control over the steel, but the power is new, and she is too fast.

A blade cuts into my side, and I hear my mother screaming. Another, and another, and another slice through me like so much meat. I can't focus with all the screaming. As I try to hold off the onslaught, I become vaguely aware that Mirage is literally picking us up.

Steel and screaming. Lightning and screaming. Blood and screaming. I heal as fast as I am injured, and I have to use the Gladiator Sage's control over pain to numb myself and maintain any focus at all. Even then, Mirage's voice won't allow me to think.

I heal a burst eye as a blade flies into it, and I've already lost an arm. As the arm heals, my jaw breaks, and as my jaw heals, blades cut into my spine and neck. Lillith grows faster and faster, radiating rage and hope. Still healing. Still connected to her pawns. Mirage throws us, and I can't respond as to why.

The. Screaming. Won't. Stop.

"Shut up! Shut up, shut up, *shut up!*" I shout at the top of my lungs. But it doesn't. Mirage won't stop screaming, and Lillith won't allow me to stop hearing it. I scream myself, hoping to counteract it, but it only resonates through my skull. I'll go mad. If this keeps up, I'll go mad. Time seems to slow around me. I can't feel the words; I can't think of a spell. My muscles are seizing with electricity as soon as they heal. Sound explodes in my ears, and Mirage fucking screams. My heart beats faster and faster despite the slowing of the world. I look up at my assailant and shudder.

Her face is back, and it parades contempt. Red eyes glare down a newly healed nose, and my heart feels a jolt of energy I don't recognize. As the sun is blocked out by this woman's contempt and my skin grows clammy, all I can do is think through the screaming and try to find a name for it. I realize I have felt it before, but it tasted different. Less urgent. Her face gets closer, and the emotion grows. I feel fangs sink into my neck, and the emotion freezes me, slows my mind. The insectile tail wraps around me, then the stinger sinks into my side. Fleshy masses I think must be slowly growing arms wrap themselves around me.

The screaming doesn't stop. It feels like it will never stop. That unfamiliar feeling shortens my breaths, and my heart feels like it's being stabbed. Her onslaught has slowed, but her grip is impossibly strong. I can't get away. I don't understand the point of this attack until I hear the laughter. Lillith's fangs leave my neck, and she throws her head back in unbridled laughter. Her face is split with a grin like I've never seen. Her girlfriend is dead. She can't permanently hurt me, and she is overflowing with joy. It makes no sense. It feels like an endoaspect is affecting her, but she isn't receiving anything through the relays.

And then it clicks: we are falling. She has me in some kind of disgusting bear hug, and she is getting joy mana directly from a mage. *No. No, no, no, no. No!* We are falling toward the negative mage. "You'll die too!" I scream. "If you do this, you will be nothing more than a corpse!" This only sends another wave of furious laughter through the woman.

"The end, you sad little boy." She cackles. I struggle, trying to reach for Mirage's power, but my mother pulls it back. I can't fight it with this fucking screaming in my head! We fall and fall, and my heart beats faster. Sweat beads form all over my body, and I struggle to complete each breath as a new one trips over it.

I feel the moment we pass into the negative mage's sphere of influence. I look down at him, and he looks up at us. Lillith's arms go limp, but her tail is frozen around me. Not that it matters anyway. I can already feel it coming—the reality recoil. My denial of death for so long. All the force I've used. There is no surviving this.

It's not fair. I almost had my mother back; almost had my home back! As I spin in the air, I catch a glimpse of Mirage. She still looks like she's made of storm clouds, but somehow, her expression could not be any clearer.

Relief.

As for me, I finally remember the name of the emotion that has dug its claws into my heart. I start sobbing as the words drift through my finally clear head. *Fear.* So this is fear.

CHAPTER THIRTY-THREE

A Better World

Edward

We all saw the fight in the sky. I don't know if Mirage showed it to us, or if Alpha brought us all closer so he could draw more power from us, but whatever the reason, all of us saw it, having ended up in the same place. Mirage was hard to miss, even in a screwed-up place like the Radiant Woods.

We were all terrified, each of us torn from our homes sometime between hours to moments earlier, our bodies and minds already starting to change. If you ask any given person what the worst day of their life was, the battle of Mirage will likely be the first thing they say.

For me, it was different. I knew Lily would win—that's what Lily does. Against lords, kings, or gods. Lily beats them. As a kid, I hated her for it. As a man, I love her for it. Watching her on flashes in the sky wasn't terrifying because of what her loss meant; I didn't even consider that possibility for a moment. No. Watching that battle hurt because, win or lose, my sister was supposed to die at the end. My own body was being taken from me, manipulated, changed, but I knew I'd change back when Lillith won.

But I was terrified I'd never be able to thank her for it. When she and Alpha fell from the sky like a falling star, I knew it was over. It wasn't immediate; it took a few heavy moments. But the giant woman made of mist began to cry, wearing relief like a crown, and all of us felt it: Her regret. Her gratitude. Her sorrow. We felt her grieve for a sister she'd never see again. That emotion nearly knocked me off my feet.

Altogether, there was no mystery to what she was doing. She'd been part of this world since long before any of us were born, and whether we knew her or not, she was saying goodbye.

I wanted to beg her to stay because it was her presence that offered Lily life, but I knew it would be selfish, and I knew Lily would die before she kept anyone chained to their trauma for her sake. This world had hurt Mirage; she may have loved it once, but it held nothing but pain for her anymore.

As the mist started to blow away like the wind, the woman in the sky was scattered to the stars like dust. A moment later, the Radiant Woods began to dissolve with her—all of it: the endless forest, the frozen sun. It left like a scab falling from a wound.

All around me, people appeared, fellow victims Lillith had just saved. Again. Many of them hugged each other. Strangers and friends. I began to look around frantically until a hand rested on my shoulder. I spun around to find Mariah wearing an uncomfortable grimace, her other hand resting on her pregnant belly. I panicked for a moment, but she quickly reassured me everything was fine. The grimace was for my sake.

With her permission, I ran. I ran and ran until I reached the spot where Lillith had fallen. Leo, Charlotte, and Ember all gathered around one spot. They were on their knees, their bodies obscuring what they were looking at. But I knew. I knew, and I pushed my way through them.

I was terrified. My mind was frozen in fear of what I might find, and when I looked down—

"Ed! Ed, you drifted off again!" Mariah reprimands. I jerk awake and look frantically around the cozy cabin room. My heart is beating in my chest, and sweat is beading on my brow. I have to smack the sides of my face to bring myself back to the present. I haven't had that dream in years. It's a little foreboding having it now.

"Sorry, love. It's just been a long week," I apologize. She rolls her eyes at me.

"Yes, what an exhausting vacation we've been having," she teases. I laugh, growing more comfortable in the present moment as the dream fades.

"All these people have left me with a lot of dishes to do! And you know how exhausting Gil's family can be," I whine.

"Well, next year ask someone else to organize the trip, you ridiculous man. In the meantime, we have work to do. We've got more guests in today, right? What's the final head count for dinner?" she presses. She sits down next to me and pulls out her planner.

I hold out my fingers to count. "Well, so far we have Gil, Dom, Ry, Frey, and . . . shit, what's the new girl's name?" I ask. Mariah shrugs.

"I don't really know her that well yet, sorry. But it doesn't matter for the moment, we're just looking for a count," she replies. Fair enough, I suppose.

"Right. So that's five for Gil. Then we got Victor and Clarrise, so seven. Riley just got in today as well. Charlotte and Leo, of course. Then you and I make twelve," I answer, folding the second finger on my right hand down. Mariah gives me an unamused look.

"Aren't you forgetting a couple of important attendees, Ed, dear?"

I snap my fingers. "Right, sorry. Lily and Sara, so fourteen." She shakes her head.

"I can't believe you forgot to include them. You should be ashamed," she pokes. I rub the back of my neck sheepishly.

"I didn't, I just . . ." I trail off as an excuse fails to present itself. New tactic. "Where are they, anyway?" Mariah narrows her eyes.

"Ed, I swear, you live half your life with your head in the clouds. They are catching up with Leo right now," she replies. I give her my goofiest grin and dissolve her playful ridicule into a blush.

"Right, well, maybe I'll go join them. It's safer in Leo's room—no snarky wives there," I quip.

"Hush, you," Mariah orders. "You mind sending Lily my way when you do?"

"Sure, I'll let her know," I agree. I lean over and give her a peck before I stand. "Be back in a few!"

I emerge from my cabin and breathe in the forest air, glancing around the campsite, an old community that hasn't been used since the attacks. The biggest cabin is obviously Gil's. His relationships demand more space than most of us. I have to walk around that to reach the main site, where I quickly spot my targets.

"Hey, Charlotte," I greet as I meet the woman tying her hair up and clearly heading for the same destination. "You look like you have something of a mission; no one was hurt, were they?" Charlotte remains one of the greatest doctors in the world now, especially since divine magic is gone. Mana is all we have left.

"Lily just scraped her knee, nothing too serious. You know how she tends to throw herself into things without thinking," Charlotte explains. She has a soft smile that nearly never leaves her face anymore. We're lucky she and Leo were nearby for this little gathering. The two have been traveling for years, helping anyone whose body doesn't fit them. It's not as quick a process as it once was for Leo, but with Charlotte's hope mana and some old notes of Lillith's, they are doing a lot of good.

"Yeah." I chuckle. "You absolutely don't have to tell me that." The two of us arrive together to greet Leo, Lillith, and Sarafyna. Leo has both of my daughters in his lap as he sits in front of an unlit firepit. I recognize the tone in his voice and realize he's at the tail end of their favorite story: the exaggerated and dramatized legend of the "Otherworldly Anarchist," whatever that means. It sounds like a collection of words Lillith always liked, but it carries little meaning to me—or many other people, for that matter. Most of the world still thinks of Lillith as a demon queen who participated in a near world-ending war, so calling our version a legend may be a bit of a stretch.

"But why does that bully Lyle keep making fun of my name?" Lily complains. "He says everyone hated Auntie Lillith." Leo lets out his familiar, crystal-clear laugh. No matter how quiet and subdued it is, it always rings through the air like winter bells.

"Well, because sometimes kids are mean," he answers. "And you know what? Bullies never liked your aunt. They didn't even like hearing about her talking to other bullies. And she wouldn't have it any other way."

As Lily is distracted, Charlotte inches closer to her. However painless Charlotte's healing is, it still scares both of my daughters to see it. Thankfully, Leo captures my daughter's attention in a clearly practiced way while Charlotte barely touches her with hope mana. As expected, the young girl doesn't notice as the ugly red mark on her knee fades completely.

"Well, I think he's a jerk head. Everyone should be nice about her! I like my name! So does Sara! Right, Sara?" Lily asks, looking across Leo's lap at her shy little sister. Sara blushes and fails to form words with all these people around but nods furiously.

"Lillith never really wanted to be remembered as above reproach," I cut in. Lily and Sara's eyes light up as both immediately hop down from Leo's lap and run to me.

"Dad!" Lily calls as she clings around one leg. Then her excitement is replaced with curiosity with the speed only a ten-year-old could manage. "What's a repoach?" she asks.

Charlotte chuckles and leans down to speak to Lily at her level. "Your dad just means she doesn't mind if people don't always remember her for only nice things," she explains.

"That's stupid." Lily pouts.

"See?" I ask. "She wouldn't even mind you calling her stupid." Her pout only grows more urgent as I turn her words around. Before she complains, however, her little sister finally speaks.

"Daddy, I have a question," she whispers.

"Go for it, sweetheart," I invite. She grabs the bottom of her shirt and pulls nervously.

"Um . . . why do you always talk about Auntie like she's gone, but Miss Charlotte doesn't?" I freeze. Unlike her big sister with all her strong will and tunnel vision, Sara is remarkably perceptive. I share a glance with Leo and then Charlotte. None of us are exactly sure how to answer.

We all saw the same thing, after Alpha's death. We are all revisiting the memory of looking down at Lily after the fight, remembering the torrent of emotion that fell on us as we tried to process what we were looking at. But we all interpret it a little differently: Charlotte with hope, Leo with joy, and me with just a touch of melancholy. I don't know how to respond to my daughter. I'm not even sure what I think myself.

Nevertheless, I take a deep breath and open my mouth to respond.

Gilbert

I rest my head on Dom's shoulder while Ryanna wraps one arm around my waist. Frey and Eileen have already left for lunch, but the rest of us want a moment of quiet. We haven't had many of these over the last decade. It's a different world than the one we grew up in, and everyone has had to put in extra effort to find a way forward. These yearly reunions have gone a long way in keeping all of us sane.

We watch the woods through the window and sigh. I had the dream again last night, of the Battle of Mirage. It always makes me nervous when I have that dream, like something is going to change again.

"Are you all right?" Dom asks. "You feel . . . tense." I think about the question for a moment. Ryanna runs her hand along my back in a comforting way, and I sigh.

"I just always think about the past when we meet up with the family," I admit.

"Do you want to talk about it?" Ryanna offers. I nod.

"Yes, but . . . I think I want to talk to Ed—if that's all right?" I ask.

"Of course," Ry and Dom agree in tandem.

"You don't see him that often anymore; maybe it's on his mind too?" Dom suggests. Tension I didn't realize I had relaxes at the idea. If anyone understands, it'll be him. I let out a breath, then look up and share a long kiss with Dom. I then turn and look down, meeting Ry's lips with mine next. It's a gentle, tender moment—but I am too anxious to live in it for long.

"Go," Ry encourages. "We'll be here when you get back." I smile at both of them, then nod.

"I'll be back in a bit, I promise." With that, I finally free myself from the other two and leave them to enjoy the open window together.

Ed seems to be everywhere, according to everyone I find. Charlotte and Leo send me back to Ed's cabin, where Mariah and the girls direct me to Charlotte and Leo. It takes an unreasonable amount of back and forth to track him down, and when I do, it's after I've given up already. He is sitting in my cabin, on my bed. Dom and Ry are nowhere to be seen.

We make eye contact, and both of us chuckle. Clearly, we had the same thought. I sit down next to him and sigh. Neither of us speaks for a long moment.

Ed breaks the silence first with a simple question.

"Do you think she'd like it? Everything everyone has built?"

"Oh, absolutely not." I laugh. "You know Lil. She would always want a better world than the one she was in. The only way she could ever let herself rest would be if no improvement could be made."

Ed chuckles again. "I know. And we haven't exactly put together a society like the one she always said she wanted. I guess I meant . . . do you think she'd say we are failing?"

I lean back on my hands and examine the wood ceiling. I think of everything we have been a part of building. How we have worked to put so many countries and cultures back together in the wake of their oppressors' deaths. Even after a decade, we still have so much left to do, and we damn well know most of the cultures rebuilding themselves aren't following the horizontal structure Lily idealized.

"No. I really don't think she would. Yeah, she'd want everything to be better. She'd probably still have someone to beef with—she always did. But she was never out to direct us only toward her own design. Lily . . . Lily was only ever after one thing. She just wanted people's future to be one they chose. She wanted this world to move forward, and she wanted to crush the mountain standing in its way. And whether everyone is building the society she would have preferred, we are moving forward. Maybe someday it will be exactly what she wanted; maybe not. But either way, we are moving forward. Either way, we have the choice to do so. Either way, we have empathy and we care about what we are doing," I answer. It's funny. I'd had the same question until the moment I answered it.

Ed seems to relax, recognizing the truth in the words at the same time I do. He curls and uncurls his fingers a few times, then asks another question. "What do you think happened to her?"

I grimace this time but put my hand on my brother's back. "You said you saw her body, Ed. You're the one who said it was unmistakable. So I guess I'd have to ask you that. Do you think she could be anything but dead?" Ed tenses again, and his fingers curl into a tighter fist.

"I did. But it just . . . it never felt real. I thought it was shock, then denial, then a thousand other things. But even now, it still doesn't seem right. Like her death is the answer to a riddle, but not the one that was asked. And then there's . . ." He trails off, but I finish for him.

"Mom," I whisper. He nods.

"And the twins, and Sarafyna and her family. So many people disappeared that day. People who'd been in the hat shop. I just . . . I don't know. It feels like there is something more to it," he says. I rub the back of my head in thought.

"Well," I begin, but the rest of my answer fails to follow. Because I can't tell him he's wrong. I feel exactly the same way. Our lives are so much better than they once were. And there's also the rumors that Sara and the twins knew the hat shop would disappear before the end of the fight, that they asked people to evacuate despite the attacks outside. Ed is right.

The pieces just don't line up. So I change course as the reality of my heart finally settles on me.

Maybe it's Sara's certainty before the fight, maybe it's being so close to Charlotte's hope mana, but at this moment, I decide what I'm going to believe for the rest of my life.

"I think they're alive," I admit.

Leo

My joy hasn't faded once since that day. It hurt, seeing Lily's body. She died because she approached me, but she approached me knowing she would die. I still remember the look on her face before the recoil hit: she was satisfied. Her time in this world had an impact, and people's lives were better for it. So even then, I felt joy on her behalf. Joy for a woman who lived exactly the life she was desperate to live. I like to imagine it's not unlike mine. For all the pain and fear of my childhood, I arrived at a life of unadulterated joy.

My body and mind are in harmony, and every day I help more people feel the same. I don't have access to the same abilities I did before; I can't approach a person and give them their body back. But I can still give them joy, and Mom can help with the rest. Her hope mana makes up for Mirage's absence; healing has more forms than just closing wounds, after all. With Lily's notes, Mom's hope, and my joy, the strict boundaries the world's former rulers invented have started to melt.

We get to see so many new worlds, so many societies built in such different ways. We travel across the world, offering what we can do to everyone there, and leaving as much knowledge as we can behind. And in our wake, we leave thousands of communities where we are safe. Not everywhere; the world won't bend to accept us unilaterally just like that. Change and loss of control is so terrifying for so many people.

But we take steps forward every day, and more people reach out to us for help with each passing month. Some places welcome us with open arms, and others leave us with only small communities. But everywhere we go, *someone* is happy to see us, and *someone* is left with a little more joy and hope than they had before.

We also travel because everyone who was ever left in the Radiant Woods has their life back now. Some died before Alpha died and Mirage left, but millions didn't, which means somewhere out there, Amelia may be alive. Mom's childhood friend. She may be alive, and she may need our help. This is why Ember travels with us as well, providing us protection, her fiery rage mana giving her an advantage over most.

She travels with us to find her parents, men who may be alive out there somewhere. She is as unpleasant as ever, but she loves us in her own way. She can't live in that anger, not on her own, and the joy and hope we offer keeps her safe in a different way than she helps Mom protect our group. She didn't come today, of course. The rest of our caravan still needs protection, and she doesn't feel the sentimentality we do.

"Are you ready, Leo? Dinner is just about done!" Mom calls. I take a deep breath as I pull a shirt over my head, looking up at the ceiling and somehow feeling the sky above it. We are here to remember Lily. To stay in contact, at least partially for her sake. Because she is gone, and I saw her body—but I also saw the knowing smirk that still danced across it. I don't know where she is, but I know she is happy, and I know she is alive.

"Yeah, Mom," I respond. "I'm ready."

CHAPTER THIRTY-FOUR

Lillith of the End

Lillith

I wake up to a soft purring, practically having to peel my eyes open from all the accumulated gunk around them. Suzume trills the moment I do, crawling farther up my chest and happily licking my fingers as I try to rub my face.

"Hey, girl, good to see you!" I greet. A long black curl falls over my right eye as I push myself up in bed. I blow it out of my face before my mind catches up with the inconsistency. That being, I *don't have* curly hair. At least not in this life. I did once, but I was also a brunette.

I struggle with the thought while settling my back against an unfamiliar headboard. Everything feels a bit off, now that I think of it. Familiar and foreign at the same time. As my mind clears from what must have been at least twelve hours of sleep, I notice the first real inconsistency aside from the fact that I haven't slept more than three hours in one night for years.

I stare at my right arm, holding it up in front of my face. "Whose arm is this?" I ask to an empty room. Suzume answers the question by happily pressing her head into my hand in a bid for pets. I comply readily enough, even as I stare at the arm.

It is very much human and organic, and it is very much mine. The complexion is tanner than it should be, at least until it reaches my shoulder, at which point, a jagged line marks a sudden change to a slightly paler skin tone. As I follow the lines of my body with my eyes and the fog starts to clear, a thousand other oddities present themselves. The most obvious thing I notice is that I don't have any scales at all. This feels wrong somehow, but the moment I think it, a few sprout like flower buds, growing onto patches of exposed skin. Exposed and untattooed skin, I might add. Another thing to be remedied as quickly as possible. I shake my head in confusion but move on.

My proportions are all wrong as well. Or rather, they are completely correct. All this to say, I seem to be as pasty white as I was as Lillith, but with a more similar build to the one I had as Annie. It's just like my hair. It's like I have the body of one life and the color palette of the other, except on my right arm and, I suspect, the fully human feet and leg under the blanket. For these, my proportions and complexion seem to both belong to Annie.

I continue my examination. My piercings are all gone. My hair is, in fact, as curly as it ever was on Earth. I am also lying on my back, which means I have left my kemonomimi days behind me. Or . . . maybe I have. I curiously eye the scales popping up in little patches on my skin.

I try to send mana into my body to examine it more thoroughly, but I seem to lack mana altogether. I furrow my brow as I continue examining myself. No fangs. No claws. I'm starting to wonder if I got my dumbass *isekai'd* again, but Suzume's purring calls that theory into question. Although the last thing I remember was plummeting to my death—again—there really is only one explanation: She did it. I asked Sarafyna to save me, she promised she would, and . . .

I jump at the realization and quickly press my two left fingers to my neck. It takes me a moment to find it, and once I do, it speeds up. A heartbeat. Not only did I not die—I am somehow actually alive.

My eyes start to water as I'm overcome with emotion, but scientist that I am, I don't let the tears running down my cheeks stop me from examining the scales. I didn't have these as Annie, so they shouldn't be there.

As soon as I think this, they start to dissolve, leaving smooth skin in their wake. *Huh.* There is no biological knowledge involved in this one. No effort at all, really. *I should have claws*, I think, and as I do, my fingers narrow to points while venom builds at the tips in little buds of liquid. *I don't have claws*, I think, and a few moments later, I don't. Perhaps my kemonomimi days aren't behind me after all. *I wonder if this is what it's like to be Sara.*

I finally climb out of bed despite my little sousaphone's protests feeling . . . amazing. I haven't felt so good since the cancer first showed up. The room is cozy, quaint. Hardly royal accommodations; more what you might find above a shop in a New England town. There is no dresser, so there is little solution to my current nudity, which doesn't bother me much at the moment, truth be told. Suzie is my only witness, after all.

There are two doors, and I guess which leads to a hallway and which to a washroom based on their position, my feet meeting warm wood floors as I walk through the empty room. My guess is correct, and I enter a comfortable bathroom a moment later. I'm pleased to find a mirror—and surprised to find what looks like a fully functional shower. Surprised and even more pleased.

I lean against the counter, but I don't have to examine myself for long. I know at a glance that my theory was right: my face looks exactly like it did on Earth. My hair has the same curls, and my build is far less boyish than I had in Potestia, but the colors all match my body when I was Lillith. I am somewhere in between the two versions of myself. *Thank Christ. I'm finally tall again.*

"Hey there, Annie," a voice says, and I nearly jump out of my skin. Which would be a shame, considering how shiny and new it is. Turning with little care for my current state, I break down into sobs the minute I see Sarafyna standing in the doorway smiling at me.

"You scared me!" I rebuke as I run toward her and wrap her in a hug. It feels a little strange—since I've gained about half a foot and am now taller than her. I have to duck past the brim of her sun hat to look her in the eyes.

"Sorry, I didn't mean to start—" I cut her off as my lips lock with hers and my fists grip her dress in tight bundles. She doesn't argue with the direction I've taken the conversation, wrapping her arms around my waist in return and dissolving into me. This lasts for several tense seconds before she giggles and gently pushes me off. "Slow down, slow down!" she protests after clearly enjoying the reunion for more than a few seconds.

"I saw your fucking corpse, you bitch!" I complain while she huffs.

"Yes, well, I can only imagine what that must have been like," she responds. I pout, but can't think of an effective riposte. That is . . . fair, all things considered. I went around showing her my corpse like it was some kind of new and popular hobby. Like planking, but with X's for eyes.

"Fine, fine. Even so, I wouldn't mind some kind of explanation!" I reply. She looks down at me.

"I built you an entirely new body and you still have demands?" she teases.

"Oh, you built this, did you? Is that why my—" I start while Sara rolls her eyes.

"Your mind chose your new appearance, not mine! This is how you think of yourself on some level. You can change it back if you want; it's very malleable," she interrupts. I'd figured all of this out already, truth be told. My body is very obviously one I've owned before. Still, the slight pink in her cheeks makes the prod worth it.

"Fine, fine. But seriously, I've had a rough day. I'd really like it if you could help me put two and two together."

She nods. "Sure. Let's get you dressed, and I'll show you."

"What, you don't like my current outfit?" I joke. She smirks at me.

"I think it might make a few other people blush a bit if you don't choose a more substantial one," she replies dryly, gesturing to the clothes she brought where Suzume is already sleeping on at the corner of the bed. Fair enough, I suppose.

She has chosen fairly comfortable clothes, at least; one elastic waistband away from pajamas, really. I scratch Suzume's ear and shoo her off before unfolding the outfit, sneezing at all the cat hair invading my brand-new sinuses, but I slip the simple shirt and soft pants on anyway. She offers me a pair of moccasins as well, allowing for maximum comfort.

God, I love her. She knew exactly what I'd want when I woke up, to the degree that, despite everything, I'm not panicking at all. I'm pretty sure we've just . . . won. And I can't wait to help build something better.

"Come on, let me show you around."

I dutifully follow her out the door, immediately recognizing the scenery when we leave the room. The hat shop. The supposedly crushed hat shop. My heart flutters as I see all the different hats hanging on walls and displayed on shelves. I actually grab one—a bucket hat to match the comfortable clothes—and put it on, which inspires a silent smile from Sara. So far, nothing is particularly strange. I have questions, yes, but I imagine once we get outside, they'll be resolved quickly.

This is—of course—evidence that a woman can kill one god and free another while still being a bit of an idiot. I only have more questions after we round a few corners and, instead of passing through one of the portal exits Sara had set up before, we simply find ourselves outside. Sand from the beach actually runs into the hat shop a little, as if they were each part of the other.

There are jungle trees a few miles back from the beach, and a truly strange mix of buildings in between. Everything from cabins to huts, mid-century Earth houses, and the sort of building I wouldn't expect to see outside of the SyFy channel. None of these are what really surprise me, however. It's the sky that takes my breath away. Because I recognize this place. I know exactly where we are, but I don't understand it.

"Is this . . ." I trail off. Sara nods.

"Yes," she answers. "It's exactly what Mirage showed you before." Color swims through my vision as I watch ribbons fly through the empty space above like rain, dancing and crying and searching for new homes. Homes I can also see. Worlds like suns and stars. If I focus on any particular star in the sky, I can almost understand it, know if it's populated by humans or volu or ailur. Interestingly, these seem to be the only three I can find easily. If I focus on a ribbon, I can feel the soul of its owner, the life it's lost, and the life it's going to. And us? We exist in none of them.

"I don't understand," I whisper. She nods.

"I know. It was the only thing I could think of. I wanted to just go with Mirage, but her home had no place for us, and with her gone, our old world didn't either. In fact, there was nowhere. I asked for Mirage's help, but there was nowhere we could exist. Nowhere but inside the hat shop, and the hat shop couldn't exist on any world without Mirage. I couldn't save a corpse, and I couldn't create a new body for either of us that wouldn't be rejected by any world it was on. At least, not unless Mirage was also there—and still offering her power to me. But she couldn't leave without all of herself. She needed what she had given me, or she would forever be stuck wherever I was, at least a little bit," Sara explains.

"Is that why you . . ." I trail off, leaving the question unasked. She understands anyway and nods.

"Yes. I was tied to her too strongly; I'd consumed too many people who were tied to her. She couldn't just leave me. And honestly, I was sick of living in a body partially made up by the men who hated me. I had to leave it behind. For her. But hey, you needed a living one anyway, so I figured we could both use a fresh start. I left my old, aching skin behind for her, and

I carried my hat shop out here, outside of reality, where our bodies could exist without offending the world they were a part of," she answers. I take a deep breath.

"So this . . . all of this, it's part of the hat shop?" I ask. She nods.

"Not exactly a hat shop anymore. Except for my favorite bits. It's sort of . . . an island. A refuge for people who have nowhere else they can exist; outside of every world. A lot of people wanted more than hats to look at, for some reason that is, frankly, beyond me." She laughs. I examine the strange buildings scattered around the beach.

"Is that what all this is about?" I ask.

"Yep. Pretty much anything we can observe in any world we find can be created here. People have gotten a bit creative with housing solutions," she replies. I rub the back of my neck despite a complete lack of pain. Just out of force of habit.

"That explains the modern shower, I suppose," I muse.

"I thought you'd like that." She smiles.

"So wait, there are other people here?" I ask, finally catching up to the conversation in my mind.

"Oh yes. Lots of people felt the same way about the world we came from as Mirage did. That it had nothing for them but memories of pain. I let them choose if they wanted to come with us or risk staying there. Others, of course, had other motivations. Sometimes, ribbons even land here, and we get new friends or kids," she replies. She pauses as we reach the edge of the beach, which simply empties out into nothingness. She sits down and kicks her legs over the side. It seems a bit bold, but I trust her and accept the invitation her eyes give me, sitting down and doing the same thing right beside her.

"You talk like everyone has been living here for years," I say. She laughs.

"Oh, we have," she replies with a chuckle. "I showed up in my body right away. Everyone else still had their original. We've got a full-on society going here; one you'd be proud of. I either had more trouble pulling your ribbon into this body because I wasn't steering it myself and I couldn't control how quickly you took to the new body . . . or because I chose to spend the rest of my life with the most stubborn woman in any world, and you were just being obstinate. Either way, you've been in that bed for a few years now."

I get a shiver at that revelation, feeling the unspoken words. The brilliant and overflowing relief and exuberance that I am finally awake, that we are together again. She doesn't have to say it. It lives in her eyes like a reflection. It sings in her voice like a flute. Just by waking up and ending a yearslong wait, I have given Sarafyna a gift I'll never match again. And knowing that my presence alone is what is inspiring this feeling in her . . . it sends butterflies through my stomach like I'm still a schoolgirl. But something sticks out to me.

"The rest of your life?" I ask. "We aren't all like, immortal now or something?" Sara shakes her head.

"Would you even want to be?" she asks. I think about it for a moment and shrug.

"I guess you're right. I'm not the immortal-being type, really," I agree. "Why didn't you tell me all of this before?"

Sara closes her eyes and smiles. "I barely understood it at first, and I was sort of figuring it out as I went," she admits.

"Well. Thanks for knowing not to make me immortal," I joke.

"I couldn't have managed it anyway. We may exist outside of reality, but I still made us human. We'll grow old and age just like anyone else, although we may be able to extend that for a bit. I'm not certain," she explains. I watch the colorful ribbons flying through the air. All the people, leaving their old lives and looking for new ones.

"Henry?" I whisper, a slight pleading tone in my voice. She sighs and shakes her head.

"Sorry," she replies. "He'd found a new home already by the time we got here. In a way; time seems a bit strange here. In any case, he's started a new life elsewhere. That's why Joan came with us—it was the only place she could see you, Henry, Gilbert, and Ed all at the same time, watching from here." The word *sorry* tempered a rush of hope and anticipation her explanation had stoked in me, and the familiar aching has already started to settle in as I accept the loss of my brother again. But as she mentions my mom, I perk up again.

"Mom is here?" I ask. Sara nods.

"The twins too," she says. "All three of them have been visiting you regularly since we got here." I smile at that, even as the realities it implies sink in. My brothers. Leo. Everyone else I love. I can watch them, yes, but I can never speak to them again. They'll never know I'm still alive. Or . . .

"I know we can't go back," I whisper. "But . . . can we help them? At all?" I ask.

"There is . . . one thing we can do. It's difficult, but it can affect the worlds around us," she hesitantly agrees. I perk up immediately as she continues to explain. "But it won't be very direct." She looks at the ribbons and reaches out to them. Her hand runs along one as it flows by.

Oh. She doesn't need to explain it. I can see it as soon as it's suggested to me.

"We can pick where they land, huh?" I ask. She nods.

"And let them keep their memories too, but . . . well, I think it's kinder not to," she affirms. I can understand that. Still. In a way, we can at least reunite a few people. It isn't much, but . . . "It's better that way. For you," she says. And she's right. For me and, honestly, for Mom. Because I am finally somewhere where I can rest, where I can live my life with Sarafyna, where all the blood stays behind my back and I have no more to wade through.

I thought I'd feel empty if that day ever came. Directionless. But I don't. Maybe if I'd been alone, but . . . I'm not. I reach my hand out and wrap my fingers around Sara's. Resting my head on her shoulder, I watch the worlds like stars, the ribbons of people's souls drifting to them like the dust in sunbeams.

"I love you, Sarafyna."

"I love you too, Annie."

I am a woman who needs to burn, but I don't have to burn like a furious and consuming fire anymore. I don't have to burn like the trees before the river. I will always miss it. I will always miss my siblings, my friends—on more worlds than one. In a way, finally having a moment of calm I know won't end, that grief feels more real than it ever has before. But with Sarafyna's hand in mine . . . with her pillow resting on my bed and her remaining years dancing with mine . . . the two of us can burn like stars together, brilliant and bright, shining light on the lives of the ones we love but can never touch. Always together. Furiously in love.

Together, we can burn like joy without the rage until we fade out into the quiet of the night, hands still clasped together.

As I look out into eternity with the woman I love, I feel a gentle, soft, and all-encompassing warmth. Like nothing will ever be wrong again.

About the Author

Dreamer's Riot is the author of the Otherworldly Anarchist series as well as a computer scientist and indie video game developer. Based on his experiences in the US Air Force and later as a student, his stories aim to tackle themes of power and autonomy.